STEPHEN HAGGARD was born in 1911, the son of a
consular official. He went to school at Haileybury, where
he formed a close attachment to one of the masters,
Wilfred Blunt. At nineteen he lived for a period in
Munich, where Blunt joined him for some time, later
taking him to Venice and introducing him to people such
as Roger Fry and Lowes Dickinson. An extraordinarily
attractive man—though not, to Blunt's sorrow, homosex-
ually inclined—Haggard was an immediate success, both
socially and, after a spell at RADA, on the stage. Shaw
praised his acting, and by 1938, when he was twenty-
seven, he was an established performer. His last and most
famous role was as the Fool to Sir John Gielgud's *Lear*,
in the Granville Barker production at the Old Vic in the
early months of the war.

He now turned to a literary career, planning a three-
volume autobiographical novel, and writing poetry, some
of which was published, an unpublished short novel, and
a collection of letters to his sons which was brought out
posthumously as *I'll Go to Bed at Noon*. *Nya* was the only
prose work published in his lifetime.

During the war he joined the Army and became an
officer in Intelligence; he died by gunshot, almost certainly at his own hand, in a train from Jerusalem to Cairo
in 1943.

FRANK KERMODE was formerly King Edward VII Pro-
fessor of English Literature at the University of Cambridge. His publications include *The Oxford Anthology of
English Literature* (co-edited with John Hollander) and
History and Value, a study of literature of the Thirties and
the reasons for literary neglect, which discusses *Nya*.

NYA

Stephen Haggard

INTRODUCED BY
FRANK KERMODE

OXFORD UNIVERSITY PRESS
1988

Oxford University Press, Walton Street, Oxford OX2 6DP

Oxford New York Toronto
Delhi Bombay Calcutta Madras Karachi
Petaling Jaya Singapore Hong Kong Tokyo
Nairobi Dar es Salaam Cape Town
Melbourne Auckland

and associated companies in
Beirut Berlin Ibadan Nicosia

Oxford is a trade mark of Oxford University Press

Published in the United States
by Oxford University Press, New York

Introduction © Frank Kermode 1988

First published 1938 by Faber and Faber Limited
First issued with Frank Kermode's introduction,
as an Oxford University Press paperback 1988

British Library Cataloguing in Publication Data

Haggard, Stephen

Nya.—(Oxford paperbacks)
I. Title
823'.912[F]   PR 6015.A19
ISBN 0-19-282135-0

Library of Congress Cataloging in Publication Data

Haggard, Stephen, 1911–1943.
NYA.
Reprint. Originally published: London:
Faber and Faber, 1938.
I. Title.
PR6015.A19N9 1988   823.'912   87-31348
ISBN 0-19-282135-0 (pbk.)

Printed in Great Britain by
The Guernsey Press Co. Ltd.
Guernsey, Channel Islands

INTRODUCTION

FRANK KERMODE

NYA was the first and only published novel of the actor Stephen Haggard. The son of a consular official, Haggard went to school at Haileybury, where he formed a close attachment to one of the masters, Wilfrid Blunt, the brother of Anthony. This friendship, which continued after school, is described in a chapter devoted to Haggard in Blunt's autobiography, *Married to a Single Life* (1983). Christopher Hassall's biography of Haggard (*The Timeless Quest*, 1948), to which Blunt contributed much information, maintains that Nya's experiences at school were adapted from the author's at Haileybury; the sympathetic schoolmistress in the novel is based on Blunt.

When he was nineteen Haggard lived for a period in Munich. According to Blunt, who spent some time with him there, it was now that Haggard discovered for the first time 'the most elementary facts of life'. He had his first sexual experience with a prostitute during the *Fasching*. To Blunt's lasting sorrow Haggard lacked any homosexual bent; but he continued to admire the older man, who took him to Venice and there introduced him to Roger Fry and Lowes Dickinson. With Fry he discussed Tintoretto, with Dickinson Wagner, and Blunt remarks that although he knew very little about Wagner and even less about Tintoretto, he was an immediate success. Though obviously not an immodest young man, Haggard must have got quite used to being an immediate success.

In Munich, having rather remarkably won an acting competition and played a leading role at the Schauspielhaus, he had firmly decided on a stage career. On his return to England he therefore went not to university but to RADA. Although his teachers there unkindly described him as 'unsusceptible to technique', his success as an actor was, characteristically, immediate. Shaw praised his performance as Marchbanks in *Candida* (with Ann Harding and later Diana Wynyard); he also played the lead in dramas about Chatterton and Gaudier-Brzeska and in a play of his own called *Weep for the Spring*. Quite extraordinarily attractive, he was already type-cast as the romantic young artist.

By 1938, when he was twenty-seven, he was an established performer, and quite well off; but he now began to think of a different future, and of literary rather than theatrical success. His last and most famous stage performance was as the Fool to Sir John Gielgud's Lear in Granville Barker's Old Vic production during the early months of the war. Not everybody liked his interpretation, but it made a considerable stir. James Agate said he gave the role a beautiful silliness; the word has a Bloomsbury resonance, connoting a sort of personal and secular sanctity advocated, and occasionally practised, at Cambridge and in Bloomsbury. It also has homosexual overtones, doubtless intended by Agate but inappropriate, of course, to Haggard.

The last words he ever spoke on the stage were those of the Fool: 'I'll go to bed at noon', and he used them as the title of a book consisting of a series of letters to his sons, who had been evacuated with his wife to the United States. Like many of his contemporaries, and not without reason, Haggard feared that he might die

2

young, and wished to leave, primarily for the benefit of his children, some account of his life and beliefs. *I'll Go to Bed at Noon* was published posthumously, and with considerable success, in 1944. It is not a distinguished book, though the autobiographical material has interest for readers of *Nya*. Haggard speaks of a childhood spent, by reason of his father's profession, without a real home; of his adolescent fear of women; and of a first love affair in Germany.

He joined the Army and became an officer in Intelligence. But war service, which ended his theatrical career, did not stifle his literary ambitions. He wrote an unpublished short novel, *The Magnolia Tree*, apparently about a love affair interrupted by the German invasion of the Low Countries in May 1940; and he began an autobiographical novel, meant to be extremely long, which he called *The Wave and the Moon*. He also wrote poems, some of which were published. He died by gunshot, and almost certainly by his own hand, on a train from Jerusalem to Cairo, in 1943. He was in his thirty-second year.

Nya, his only book of any substance, was published in 1938 by Faber and Faber. It has been out of print and forgotten for the best part of half a century, and its present revival is due entirely to a series of accidents. Having read it long ago, I occasionally had a vague memory of it as a book that had moved me in my youth; and eventually, at a time when I was pondering the whole question of literary survival, it occurred to me to read it again; for here was an example of a book which apparently survived in one man's memory only. I found a copy in a bookseller's catalogue, and, in my sixties, reread the book that I had apparently found more affecting than the large number of books I read

3

in wartime and soon forgot. The decision of the Oxford University Press to republish it is further testimony to the peculiar chances that can determine literary survival; what I said about the book in a lecture at Oxford (now printed in *History and Value*, OUP, 1988) induced Kim Scott Walwyn of the Press to read it. I had cautiously hedged my remarks with a series of what used to be called limiting judgements, but she was interested; and so the book has been given a second life.

It tells the story of a love affair between Simon, a man in his middle twenties, and Nya, a thirteen-year-old girl. This is a subject that might on the face of it have seemed dangerous, more so in 1938 even than now, but nobody seems to have accused the novel of impropriety. One reviewer did say that it was 'a theme before which even an experienced novelist might quail', but in the event he found the book 'fine and sensitive'. Looking at it again, one can understand why the official and unofficial censors held their hands. *Nya* is a love story, and in its way a passionate one, but a good deal of its poignancy arises from its chastity. It describes a revolt against established sexual convention which, without actually failing, still leaves the walls of culture unbreached by the forces of nature.

Nya herself combines the appeal of the noble savage with that of the child, a doubly pastoral effect. Brought up in Nyasaland to live naturally, she finds herself back in England, excluded from a society 'organized entirely in favour of grown-up people'. The uncle and aunt with whom she lives are more or less completely dominated by the middle-class manners of the period. Simon, the young man Nya loves, is of the same class, and might in time turn out to be much the same sort of person as the father he for a time replaces, or the

4

guardian uncle, hiding behind his *Times* and his pipe smoke. In his youth, however, he has at least two temporary advantages—virginity and an exciting yacht. The first he preserves as honourably as he does Nya's; the second is his means of escape from the world of office work and temptation.

Haggard at one time thought of rewriting the end of the novel in a more cynical vein, but was wisely dissuaded from doing so; he would undoubtedly have ruined it. In its present form it offers the satisfactions of pastoral—preserving the purity of the lovers, allowing us to think of their eventual union—while reinforcing the ethical imperative which keeps them separate, thus endorsing, with some reluctance, the values of bourgeois society it at first appeared to be challenging.

Nya's aunt is determined to give the girl 'an English training', and this is something hard for a child of nature to bear; but despite her clumsiness and rigidity—she is very much the type of middle-aged woman whom Haggard early learned to dread—the aunt is honest, and in any case there is no bitter conflict; Nya and Simon will wait, chastely, before presumably becoming in their turn a middle-class couple.

Yet the story must have seemed in some ways pretty unusual to those who read it in 1938, and it will perhaps seem even more so to their successors fifty years later. A girl crossing the threshold from latency to adolescence is as difficult a subject for a young male writer as for a young male lover. Nya is convincingly female, though with a certain boyishness; her *not* being a woman is clearly an important part of her attractiveness. There is doubtless something in Hassall's opinion that Haggard used himself as model for both Nya and Simon. In any case, the modest success of the book

5

probably owed something to the fact that the 'risky' story had the innocence as well as the charm of the author.

There were other reassuring features. The love scenes were not so bizarre as to be remote from the experience of most readers; and the milieu in which they were set was also rendered with comfortable familiarity. For example, Poole Harbour, in and near which most of the action occurs, is described in considerable detail (Haggard unavailingly asked the publishers to reproduce the Admiralty chart of the harbour on the dust-jacket). Indeed, it is in the harbour scenes that one is most conscious of the genuineness of Haggard's talent; his use of Brownsea Island as an image of death is impressive, and so is the dream in which Nya, flying over Poole Harbour (according to Freud dreams of flying signify 'a longing to be capable of sexual performance') makes her course conform to the marked channels and avoids the shoals, as if she were not flying but sedately sailing. Her flight, so regulated, takes her to Simon's yacht, but the person she finds on board is her father. This is a brilliant encapsulation of the main themes of the book. It is also an allegory of Haggard's own performance, since he, too, confines his imaginative flight within established channels.

The years since 1938 have seen great changes not only in sexual ethics and practice, but also in the manners of the respectable middle class, and in the notion of 'an English training'. Nya has some but not all the qualities of a 'nymphet', the word revived by Nabokov to describe pre-pubescent charmers on the model of his own Lolita; part victim, part seducer, Lolita is associated with a very different culture, and observed by a lover to whom the idea of 'an English training'

6

would have seemed comic in itself. *Lolita*, questionable in 1955, has long been respectable; we may not have quite lost a sense of alarm and disgust at the sexual appropriation of very young girls, but we certainly have surrendered some of the old capacity for indignation at sexual aberrancies. *Nya* is likely to seem even milder than it did in 1938. Conscious of apparent progress, we may accordingly underestimate the force of Haggard's imagination and undervalue the measure of boldness with which he represents a powerful but socially repressed sexuality.

It is often said of Nabokov's book that it is not pornographic; its effects proceed in good measure from devices of allusion, of joking and coding, which are themselves, in part at any rate, ways of not speaking out; of course they have another purpose, and are meant to provide access to an 'aesthetic bliss' which mirrors and is mirrored by the sexual bliss of the subject. If we value deviousness of means, virtuosity, artifice of surface, Haggard isn't entitled to be mentioned in the same breath as Nabokov. It can never have occurred to him to write a book in which the violation of civilized norms of behaviour could be at the same time an assault on conventional notions of both nature and art. Yet within his limits he has his own boldness and his own finesse.

Nya is not without its naïveté, its limits of understanding and technique, even on occasion its clumsiness; it was, after all, a first novel by a man who undoubtedly hoped to write many more and many better books. The theme of the third and last section of his big unwritten novel was provisionally entitled 'If Love be Pain', which may in itself sound a bit novelettish; but his intention seems to have been to

7

produce, in this final section, a synthesis of the first and second parts. In them natural instinct is suppressed by 'intellect', whereupon 'everything goes wrong'. The third part would celebrate 'the return to instinct'. How this was to be done, whether indeed he could have done it, we can't know. But it does sound rather as if *Nya* ends as it were with the second part, and that Haggard may have felt that the submission of the lovers and their instincts—to their own decency, as well as to external forces—was not the end of the story.

However that may be, it is impossible to regret that he ended the story as and where he did. Admittedly there is no impropriety, no violation, only the shadow of a possibility of such a thing. And admittedly the tactics of the forces of decency, and the structures of feeling that lie behind middle-class resistance to the lovers, will strike us as archaic. But Haggard wanted to reconcile passion with respect for normal conduct; and as long as the passion is made to seem authentic, the period character of the machinery of repression doesn't matter. Because it succeeds in this respect, *Nya* must be allowed more merit than mere period charm. It presents the ancient argument between nature and custom in a new light—new, certainly, in Haggard's day, and still interesting in ours. For although the terms of the discussion have altered, the old argument still goes on.

PART I: IMPACT

I

By the time Nya was nearly thirteen, the day when she ought to have been sent back to school in England was, of course, long overdue. The subject had been intermittently discussed between her parents and herself for nearly a year but as soon as any decision was about to be reached all three of them shied away from it like startled horses and none was ever made.

"After all," her mother said, "she's still young. I don't believe in sending children to school too soon. Not boarding-school at any rate. Children should learn to do things with their hands and feet before they start overtaxing their brains."

"That's what we've always agreed," her father would rejoin, pipe in mouth, "but I'm not so sure that we're right. Out here one loses touch with things at home. And after all England is the place that matters. We attach too much importance to hands and feet, because up to a point we use them in self-defence, but at home they balance these things up better. After all, they play a deuced lot of games at school—even at girls' schools."

"Well, I think we should wait until John has to go too. Then they can go together. Perhaps by then we can all go, some one may have remembered that your leave is seven months overdue already."

"And will be a lot more overdue before I get it. But that's not the point. The point is——"

"Am I to go to school in England or am I not?" Nya interposed, accentuating the words with a spoon on the table. She knew the course of this conversation backwards. So did they all. Certain sentences recurred again and again and were like landmarks to show that no progress was ever made.

"That *is* the point." Her father smiled at her and removed his pipe.

The fact was that nobody wanted Nya to go back to England—least of all Nya herself. They were all too fond of each other: her departure would have left an unthinkable gap in their lives. John, who was three years younger than Nya, was as passionately opposed to the scheme as any of them, although full of plans for what he would do when he was allowed to go to school himself. He adored his sister: any one who could ride and jump as she could, who was called "Nyalugwe"— little leopard—by the natives, who could tell him where birds built their nests, what were the animals whose spoors they sometimes saw when they rode over the plantations, and even what some of the stars were called, was an altogether superior being, and worthy of nothing less than adoration.

So Nya stayed on through the dry, cold days and nights of winter, until spring brought back the myriads of wild flowers, every one of which she loved and knew by name. And as the summer came, just at Christmas time, fate settled the difficult question by carrying off her mother and her small brother after a virulent attack of blackwater fever.

She had to go back to England then. Her father insisted. He had been up country dispensing an unofficial form of justice to a settlement of Zulus who kept their squabbles—however trivial—against his quarterly visit, so great an esteem did they have for his methods of arbitration. They fared badly this time: for he left them the moment he heard the news of his wife's and boy's illness and came back as fast as his legs, his canoe, and the old Ford car could carry him. Nya too, they said was ill: but nobody could tell what was the matter with her.

"It's pretty obvious," thought her father grimly; and raged at the slow rate of travel to which the country compelled him.

When he reached home his wife and son were dead, and Nya was beginning to recover from her unknown malady which was vanishing as unaccountably as it had come. Never had father and daughter felt so closely bound together now that they had not only love but also grief in common. Nevertheless, life had to go on—especially Nya's life, thought her father. From every point of view the sooner she was taken from this Godforsaken place and safely tucked away in England, the better. He made arrangements for her departure, though not without consulting her, for that would have been a breach of friendship. He was very firm in his intention, Nya had never known him be so firm at home. She expostulated, cried, shut herself up in her room so that he had to break the door down to get in, and refused to eat in order to show him how monstrous she thought his decision was. How could he ask her to go away from him, the one person she had left in the world, now of all moments? She would never see him again. At one fell blow she would have lost her father, her mother and her brother. What would there be left to live for? She would rather kill herself, she told him, crying, crying, all the time crying, with her arms round his neck.

The poor man nearly broke under the strain. He managed to take a few days' local leave, during which he never moved out of his house, but even then there was so much to be dealt with, enquiries, filling in of papers, registrations and other formalities, quite apart from the terrible strain of the funeral, and the difficulties attendant upon the burial of those two coffins, so poignantly different in size, so tragically similar in the treasures they contained.

Eventually he realized that he must ask for Nya's departure as a favour to himself, that he must convince her that her life, though it might mean little to her, was precious to him, and was, indeed, the only thing he had left. In England no possible harm could befall her, but out here. . . . His shrug of the shoulders, and the grey despair in his face convinced her better than pleading. She calmed down and talked to him more reasonably.

"But, Daddy, you can't be all on your own like this. I'm sensible. I could be useful. Somebody's got to look after the house." She spoke seriously, as one grown-up to another. He couldn't help smiling. "It won't be the first time I've kept house for myself," he said.

"No, but still—oh, Daddy!"

Then she clung to him and cried again, but less hysterically now, and soon she cried herself into a more peaceful state of mind. She lay wide-eyed in his arms, playing with the lapels of his coat. Now that the strain of fighting her was over he relaxed too, and his eyes filled with tears which dropped, one by one, on to his cheeks and trickled down to his moustache. In a little while Nya noticed them, and, sitting up, put her arms round his neck again. But this time they were strong little arms full of a tender energy, arms which no longer clung but which tried to soothe, to encourage and support him. And because he had never had any more shyness before his little girl than she before him, he broke down utterly for a few minutes.

"Poor Daddy," she whispered, "poor darling Daddy, don't cry. Poor Daddy. Don't cry, darling Daddy."

There were more tears from Nya when the day came for her to leave him, but she was able to joke about them now.

"I feel like the day when you took me to Umballa to have my tonsils out," she said.

"Don't worry," he answered, "*that* need never happen again. You've had everything out that we could think of—except teeth. For some reason you don't seem to have had toothache much."

"No, *I* was lucky, wasn't I?"

He noticed the slight emphasis on the "I", and instantly they were both near to breaking down. He knew, and she realized he knew, that she was thinking of John, who had suffered agonies with toothache until he was nine years old.

He saw her on to the boat at Beira and loaded her with books and sweets and presents—even clothes, which she liked most. She had a pair of "Oxford" brogues, and a new panama hat; but the crowning joy was a coat and skirt of grey flannel, which would have made most girls of thirteen look wrongly dressed, but which Nya wore with a self-confidence that many an older girl might have envied. They had seen the costume in a shopwindow in Beira and a couple of hours' work by the tailor, added to much exhortation on Nya's part, had sufficed to convert it into a garment that she could wear. It aroused much critical comment from Mrs. Chalmers—an acquaintance of her father's from up-country with whom Nya was to travel home. But Nya was unperturbed. Daddy had helped to choose it for her, and this made it altogether perfect.

A week had to go by, and with it the ever-changing scenery and the gradual acquaintanceship with the variety of people on board the ship, before the ache in her heart began appreciably to diminish. After this she felt it only at night: by day time the brown-eyed, re-served little girl became increasingly friendly and gay. Her travelling companion, a kind but stupid woman, was both pleased that Nya should at last be relaxing a little and shocked that she should apparently so soon have forgotten the tragic deaths of her mother and little brother. She would have made inexhaustible capital out of such an event in her own life, and she had not the perspicacity to see that Nya welcomed the distractions of life on board ship with the gratitude and fervour of a child who is trying not to think of nightmares. They were such a splendid drug, those distractions—except during the darkest hours of the night.

By the end of the voyage Nya was far better able to look after herself than her fellow-passenger, who began to fuss about her charge a week before the boat (an obstinate and unhurried one) was due in at Southampton.

"What if your aunt doesn't meet the boat?" she asked anxiously. "I shall have to take you to Bournemouth myself, and I don't know what my boys will say if I waste a whole precious day before seeing them."

Nya was privately incensed that the woman could be such a fool as to torment herself with imaginary terrors when there were quite enough real ones to be dealt with. "Who says my aunt won't be there?" she asked herself scornfully. But she said nothing aloud. She had discovered the inadvisability of becoming too intimate with any one—especially this woman. The first night out from Beira she had cried in her bunk till she thought her heart would break. When Mrs. Chalmers came into the cabin to go to bed, Nya had allowed herself to be comforted and cuddled for a few minutes; it was such a relief to hold on to someone, someone soft and kind like Mummy had been. But Mrs. Chalmers, instead of accepting Nya's confidence as one would the timid advances of a wild animal, was stupid enough to regard it as a compliment to herself and urged Nya to "tell her all about it".

"Auntie May will understand," she said. But, like a tortoise whose shell has been jarred, Nya withdrew at once. After that the two were friendly strangers—nothing more: nor did Nya ever cry again, except up on the boat-deck, inside one of the lifeboats where nobody could see her. People seemed to take unfair advantage of one's confidence if one showed them one's real feelings.

One of the officers who had heard her story from the talkative "Auntie May" ran into her up there one day. She liked him. He used to chase her down the deck whenever he met her—except when the boards had been swabbed and were too slippery to run on. Then the chase was restricted to a "slow walk" which was in many ways more terrifying. He could take so much longer strides than she; he would gain on her slowly but remorselessly, as pursuers do in nightmares. In the end she usually broke into a run; but then, of course, the victory was his, since this was not allowed by their rules.

"Hello, hello, hello," he exclaimed, as she bumped

into him round a corner. "What have you been up to? Don't you know this is Wednesday and you are not allowed on this deck?"

"Why not?"

"Because the Captain's holding an important Free Masons' meeting," was the glib retort, "and nobody's allowed to be present."

"What's a Free Mason?"

"A man who builds houses for nothing."

"Are there any in this ship?"

"Hundreds. All the stokers, and the stewards, and the officers, and even some of the passengers. Your Auntie May's one."

"She's not my aunt. And anyway, you said they were all men."

"Not all. Mrs. Chalmers is one of the exceptions."

"I believe you're making it all up."

"And I believe you've been crying."

"Not at all. Piece of smoke got into my eye."

"A *piece* of smoke? Shall I help you to get it out?"

"I got it out by myself," she retorted with dignity; then, realizing he saw through her pretext, she turned the joke against herself and added, "out of both of them."

He laughed.

"Bothersome thing smoke."

"Yes, isn't it? I think I had better go down."

"Are you in a hurry?"

"Not particularly. Are you?"

"Not particularly."

"Haven't you got to go and set the course or something?"

"No: they did that at the office in Beira, before we started."

"Do we keep the same one all the time?"

"Except round the corners."

"Who steers round the corners?"

"The Captain. It's his privilege."

"Lucky man!"

"Yes, isn't he?"

There was a pause. She looked at him and laughed. "You do talk nonsense, don't you? I like you for it."

"Thank you. But I can be serious too. I'd like to know why you've been crying."

"It's rather a long story I'm afraid."

"I've got oodles of time."

"Oodles?" she asked, not understanding.

"Ages," he explained.

"Oh!" She stopped, evidently trying to make up her mind to something. "Also it's rather a dull story."

"Not to me."

So she told him the whole tale—quite dispassionately, as if she were speaking of another person. She told him what life had been like in Nyasaland, what Mummy and Daddy and John and she used to do and say at all hours of the day. And she told him about leaving Daddy behind.

"You see, there isn't anybody else except him now, is there? I don't see why I should have to go to England and leave him all alone. Anything might happen to him."

"Less likely than something happening to you out there."

"I know. That's Daddy's point of view. But he doesn't seem to think of mine."

"Perhaps he does—more than you realize. When does he get leave?"

"In about five months."

"Come. That's not so bad."

"I suppose not. But it seems an awful long time to me. You know——" she began again, with renewed interest; "I've got to go to school in England. What on earth do you suppose that will be like?"

"That depends. There are schools and schools. I expect you'll find it difficult at first."

"I hardly *know* anything—except what I've read about."

"That won't matter so much."

"What will matter?"

He had to lift up the peak of his cap and scratch his head, before he could decide how to answer. "You're more natural than the girls you'll meet at school. You probably won't understand the way their minds work at all, and they certainly won't understand yours!"

"I shouldn't think there was much to understand in mine."

"On the contrary, there's a great deal. Oh well——" He got up. "I'm not good at talking. Who are you going to live with, by the way?"

"My aunt and uncle—my real aunt and uncle."

"What are they like?"

"I don't know. I've never met them. He's Daddy's brother. I hope he's like Daddy."

"So do I—for your sake. Well, I must be getting along, good-bye."

"Good-bye."

The officer seemed to grow suddenly shy of her after this; for even though she met him once or twice he always said he was busy. It was annoying because there were lots of things she wanted to ask him about English girls' schools and how she ought to behave in one.

"Perhaps he really is busy," she allowed, without much conviction, "all the same, it's annoying."

20

Three days later the boat docked at Southampton without her having had a chance to put him a single question.

To Mrs. Chalmer's huge relief Nya's aunt met the boat. The arrangement, as had been agreed by letter from Beira, was that Nya should stay with Mrs. Chalmers in her cabin until her aunt came to fetch her. The meeting in the tiny cabin somewhat enhanced everybody's embarrassment—especially Nya's—where the bustle and freedom of the quayside would have tended to dissipate it. However, "Auntie May" kept Aunt Ethel in conversation most of the time with full information as to every one of Nya's actions since the ship had left Beira. Of the episode on the first night out, fortunately, she did not say a word, as much because she felt it had been a blunder on her part as in order to spare Nya's feelings. Nya sat quietly on the lower bunk, with her eyes cast down.

Aunt Ethel was a tall, freckled woman, with bright blue eyes and a tight mouth. She was simply and practically dressed and looked energetic and determined, but kind. Nya didn't make advances, and Aunt Ethel had more sense than to expect her to; but she was reserved herself, so their relations were constrained at first. Aunt Ethel soon wearied of Mrs. Chalmer's recitation and cut her firmly but politely short with the remark that they had a train to catch to Bournemouth and that they had still to find their way to the Central Station, quite apart from the business of sorting out Nya's luggage and getting it through the Customs.

Mrs. Chalmers said she quite understood, and after an unsentimental farewell, due entirely to Aunt Ethel's brisk manner (for which Nya was profoundly grateful to her), she set about her own preparations.

Aunt Ethel had no difficulty with the Customs and they were soon in the train that was to take them to Bournemouth. When they arrived at Bournemouth Central Uncle Nick was waiting for them in the car. He was sunburned, though, of course, not so brown as Daddy, but he looked enough like him to win Nya's heart and to give her a strange pang of longing. Uncle Nick said very little. Nya thought he was probably concentrating on the traffic, of which there seemed to be a terrifying amount.

When they arrived at "The Rising", in the village of Sandbanks, Aunt Ethel said:

"This will all seem strange to you at first. We will, too, I expect. So I want you just to do what you like to begin with. Afterwards I'll tell you all about what we've arranged. Lunch is ready, now, as soon as you've washed your hands. After that we're both going out to play tennis. You can come too if you like, but I'm sure you'd be happier if you stayed here and found your way about. It's only a few minutes' walk to the harbour, which is very pretty—any one will tell you the way. Be careful of the traffic, though, if you go into the main road. We shan't be back until about six. You can ask Emily for some tea at half-past four."

To all of which Nya could only answer, in some bewilderment, "Thank you, Aunt Ethel."

2

There were still three weeks before the term began at St. Monica's. Aunt Ethel, who, with her household and poultry to look after, her tennis and bridge to play, and her women's club to organize, was a busy woman, spent some ten days of this time in fitting Nya out for school. Luckily almost everything she needed could be bought in Bournemouth and, for what was not to be found, it was possible, as Nya was still young, to make a substitute do.

"Later on, when you're older," said Aunt Ethel, "I expect we shall have to go to London for some of your things."

Later on! In Nya's imagination the word conjured up an endless vista of shopping expeditions at which clothes and shoes would be bought for her which were ugly, heavy, drab in colour and, so her aunt said, hard-wearing and eminently practical. Already her coat and skirt had been taken away from her and reserved for best, "though it looks a little strange on you, I must say", said Aunt Ethel. However, Nya insisted on wearing it on Sundays or whenever anybody of importance came to "The Rising". It made her look older than she was, and gave her confidence. In its place Aunt Ethel had procured her a gym tunic and blouse, and a blazer to wear over them—not, of course, a St. Monica's blazer.

"It would never do for you to wear it until you've been at least one term at school."

Like her tunic her blazer was dark blue—a colour that she hated—though she made only a feeble remonstrance when Aunt Ethel chose it.

"It will be very useful, dear; and you can wear it at home in the holidays to save your school one."

The rest of the holidays Nya spent in exploring the district; there was plenty to see and plenty to do, and people were, on the whole, not unfriendly to a small girl alone, especially to one who showed such interest in everything. She made friends with some boys who played cricket in a road near "The Rising" and they sometimes took her on their expeditions, but she didn't tell her aunt this; she had a vague apprehension that Aunt Ethel might not approve. They used to give her chocolate, and she accepted it reluctantly. She would rather have bought it for herself. She had a little money, which her father had given her, but to tell the truth she didn't know its value.

Their favourite expedition was to Poole Harbour, where they watched the ships of every kind that were anchored there, and played on the shore near the yacht yards. They invented a whole host of characters with which to people the deserted Brownsea Island.

"*Somebody's* got to live in all those houses," said one of the boys, "you can see they're all empty, even from here. I think there's a kind of pirate lives there, see, and he won't let any one else come on the island, see, 'cept his minions who steal and smuggle for him. And he's eaten all the people who live in those houses and now his minions live there, see?"

"Eaten? Go on. Pirates don't eat people nowadays," said the eldest.

"Aren't any pirates, any way," said the third boy.

"Yes, there jolly well are—just 'cos you don't hear about them all the time, you think there aren't any. But he's a deep one, this one is"—and so on.

To all of this Nya listened with pleasure and a kind of good-humoured contempt. She was sensible of the honour which the boys conferred on her in asking·her —a girl—to join their band, but she felt a great deal older and wiser than they, although she never let them sense this.

But the greatest joy, and one that gave her as much pleasure as them, was to stand on the jetty where the boats left for Poole and Shell Bay and to watch the bustle and traffic of the harbour. In January there was, of course, not much tourist traffic but every form of ship went out of the harbour mouth or forged slowly in against the current when the tide was ebbing: pleasure-yachts, pinnaces, sailing-dinghies, tramps, and coal-barges.

One day the boys attempted to organize an expedition to Shell Bay to walk along an unfamiliar stretch of beach.

"We might find all sorts of things there like we did last summer, and if there's time we can go over the other way to Studland," they said. "Let's have a collection and see how much money we've got."

But the boys between them could only raise fivepence halfpenny and the fare was threepence per person. Two other boys, who sometimes joined their expeditions, had no money at all. Neither had Nya.

25

"Oh well, it's no good then," said the boy and started to whistle, kicking his feet along the planks of the jetty.

Then Nya remembered her money at home.

"I've got two pounds," she said, "will that do?"

"Two pounds! Golly."

"Yes. My father gave it to me." She waited to see what they would say to her offer. She was not quite certain how much two pounds was, but she felt it must be enough.

"Gosh. We could hire a motor-boat for that."

"Shall we?"

"Yes," came the answer from four lusty young voices.

"No you don't." The leader's voice came in with determination. "Nya wants her money. She's going to school next week and she'll need it. Never know what it mightn't come in handy for. Books and clothes and tuck. Greedy little blighters, girls are. Except for you, of course, Nya. I think she's jolly generous."

"So do I."

"So do I."

"So do I."

The oldest boy turned to Nya, like a general at a conference. "How much can you spare, Nya?"

"As much as we need. How much is that?"

"That's what I say. As much as we need, no more, and no less."

"What's it come to?" asked one of the smaller boys.

"Let's see. Five people at threepence return, that's fifteen pence, one-and-three, and the grasshopper here, he's a half, that's one-and-fourpence halfpenny."

"I'm not a half," indignantly affirmed the grasshopper, who was undersized.

"You shut up. You're not worth more anyway."

"I'm not a half. I tried it on yesterday when I only had twopence, but they wouldn't let me."

"Oh well, I suppose you'll have to have a ticket then." He turned to Nya. "One-and-sixpence—say two shillings in case of accidents."

Nya had already started down the jetty.

"I shan't be long," she said, "five minutes."

The fascination of exploring unknown beaches and sandbanks made them lose all sense of time and, when Nya at last realized that it must be late, the sun had set and it was beginning to get dark. They caught the next boat back; but even so she arrived an hour and a half late for tea, and two hours after her aunt expected her.

"Nya, you're a very naughty girl. I particularly asked you to be in at half-past three so that we could try on your underclothes before tea. They're only on approval and have to go back by this evening's post. What have you been doing?"

"I'm awfully sorry, Aunt. You see I didn't know what the time was and I forgot to ask."

"But it's dark. You must have realized that it was getting late."

"Yes I did, of course, but we were so far away. It took some time to get back."

"We? Who's we?"

"Some boys I went with."

"Where did you go?"

"To Shell Bay."

"Across the harbour?" From the way Aunt Ethel said this she evidently thought it a criminal offence.

"Yes. We went in a boat."

"Who paid for it?"

"I did."

27

"You did. Oh well, at least it will teach you not to throw your money away like that."

"But it wasn't thrown away, Aunt. I enjoyed it. We all did. I am sorry I am late."

"Oh well, come and try your things on now. If we hurry we'll just catch the six o'clock post with them."

Aunt Ethel couldn't prevent her mind from dwelling on Nya's escapade, though she had no desire to bully the child. Ten minutes later she said:

"Tell me, who were those boys?"

"They're three boys I know. We go down to the harbour together sometimes. And there are two others, friends of theirs."

"Are they nice boys?"

"I like them."

"Yes, but——" she was at a loss how to put the matter delicately. "Are they street boys?"

"Well, I met them in a street."

"I was afraid so. I can't say how upset I am, Nya, that you should treat me like this. I've tried to find boys and girls of your own age—nice ones, I mean—for you to play with and you've had nothing to do with them."

"But I've never been rude to any of them, Aunt Ethel."

"No, that's the trouble. You've suffered them in silence. It shows quite plainly that you are not interested in them. I honestly believe that you *prefer* these horrid little street boys."

"I do. But they're not horrid, Aunt. They talk differently from you and me——"

"I knew it!"

"But they're awfully kind and they've got lots of good ideas. We have great fun together."

"I can quite imagine it," Aunt Ethel rejoined acidly.

"But in future—or rather for the rest of your holidays—I forbid you to have anything more to do with them, do you hear? By next holidays I hope you will have the good sense, and the good *taste* to have forgotten them."

"Oh, Aunt, you don't want me not to see them any more? How can I do that? We are such friends."

"I only want you not to see them again before you go to school. We can let the rest take care of itself. I've no doubt that by next holidays they will have found other *boon companions*." She shuddered slightly as she spoke, rather as if her lips had formed words she found it distasteful to utter.

"But I'm to meet them again to-morrow!"

"You are not to go out at all to-morrow."

"But why?"

"So that you cannot meet them. You can play in the garden to-morrow."

"Does Uncle Nick think that about them too?"

"I haven't told him about them yet."

"Well, I will."

"Not until I have seen him."

This seemed final, and, although Nya harboured no suspicions as to the integrity and honour of any single person, least of all of her own aunt, she couldn't help wondering what sort of a version Uncle Nick would hear. When she did consult him he was no help to her. He had turned out to be the greatest disappointment of all in this topsy-turvy, uncomprehending England. Most of the day, when he wasn't playing bridge or tennis, he was out fishing, or perhaps he would play a round of golf. He seemed to know people in Bournemouth and Poole, and even as far afield as Swanage and Dorchester. On rare occasions he would stay at home and tinker with the car. It was then that Nya would approach him

29

and go to any lengths to get him to talk. It ought to have been easier than at meals, when Aunt Ethel seemed to think she was the only one to whom Nya's questions were addressed, even though they were often prefaced by a "Please Uncle Nick". But even in the garage he never gave her encouraging answers, and after a time she gave up trying. He noticed this, and was slightly, inexplicably hurt. He was keener than she could have guessed to have her admiration, or at least a certain measure of her confidence; and when she ceased to make overtures his last chance seemed to have gone, for he was too tongue-tied to put the matter right.

In the case of the "street boys", she attached a certain importance to his opinion, if he had cared to give it. It would have been something with which to counter-balance Aunt Ethel's outrageous and purely arbitrary view of the matter.

On occasions such as these there was always one re-source, thank heaven! A resource that was admittedly of no great practical or immediate value, but still, a resource of unflinching faithfulness and truth. "If only Daddy weren't so far away and letters didn't take so long to get there." She had not even heard from him in answer to her letters since she had left Beira. But it gave her great relief to write to him. She poured out her feelings upon pages and pages of paper—they resembled love letters in their passionate intensity. Indeed they were love letters: the love she felt for him was the strongest emotion she had yet experienced, and also the most soothing, and she abandoned herself to it without inhibition.

They made him both happy and apprehensive, those letters. It was strangely satisfying to him to feel that he had such utter confidence and love from the child, but

he feared the pain which her fierce feeling might ultimately cause her.

"Now more than ever is the time when her mother
should have been alive to help her. How futilely mis-
managed this life is."

The business of the "street boys", naturally, loomed
very large in the letter she wrote him that night, though
when his answer came she had put the matter out of her
mind, especially since, in whispered colloquy through
the garden fence into the road behind, she had thoroughly thrashed out the matter with the boys before she
left. The advice he gave her, beside confirming her own
suspicions of Aunt Ethel's disease (a new one, as far as
she knew, called snobbery by her father and "stuck-
upness" by the boys), stood her in good stead for her
dealings with her schoolfellows. He had reckoned that
she would be at school when she received his letter and
he painted a fairly accurate picture to himself as he
wrote it of the state of mind she would be in: so he
confined himself to telling her all he could remember of
the way to treat little boys or little girls in the mass, and
of the attitude of mind with which their strange notions
of humour, kindness and morality could best be com-
bated.

3

Nya was not sorry to leave "The Rising" for St. Monica's. Her stay in it had meant so little to her, hardly more than staying in an hotel. The change from the leisurely life of Sandbanks to the hurried, scrambling existence of St. Monica's was exciting enough to make the first week pass quite pleasantly. It was after this that reaction set in. As soon as they had acquired confidence and settled down some of her schoolfellows began to be tiresomely attentive to her. They seemed to want to know everything about her. They teased her for her name, asking "what it meant"; they invented a silly game in which they rubbed her neck and arms to see if her tan came off. They hid her clothes and books, "just to see", as they explained to a mistress who happened to find out, "what she would do". But this soon stopped when they found that she had a temper when she was roused, and was not in the least afraid of hitting them if they annoyed her.

The mistress, who had the deepest contempt for little girls and, indeed, for all her sex, hailed Nya as a potential example of the "New Woman". She had never seen a girl who grasped things so uncompromisingly, who gave as good as she got, both of kindness and cruelty, who had such fearless eyes. The first time Nya came up before her she had the impression of speaking to an equal: and this was strange for by all appearances she should have felt the opposite. Nya's arithmetic, grammar and French were non-existent, while she had scarcely heard of Latin, and scripture was for her nothing but a confused jumble of fascinating stories; with the result that, after a short examination, she was relegated to a form whose average age was not quite twelve.

"I find this very surprising," said the headmistress. "What did they teach you out there?"

"Well, we lived miles up-country. It was difficult to learn anything really. Daddy taught me some history, and Mummy taught me music and needlework and cooking."

The headmistress smiled.

"I'm afraid you won't find those of much use to you here. Let's hope your history is sound."

But even her history was not very good, or if it was there seemed no way of bringing out the child's knowledge. She knew very few of the Kings of England. Palmerston and Wellington were names she recognized; about Hannibal, Jinghiz Khan, Charlemagne, Magellan, Purcell, and Goethe she seemed to know a little, and strangest of all, about Jeremy Bentham, Keats, and Bernard Shaw, a good deal. Her knowledge of contemporary politics was confined to the dictators and Paderewski.

The headmistress shook her head at this. She could see, of course, what the subordinate mistress had seen: namely, that Nya was a girl of no ordinary stamp, and that quite possibly she would one day achieve distinction. But for the moment that was beside the point. All that mattered was to fit her into the school. She had to

33

be got through the curriculum and enabled to matriculate. After that—well, at least the responsibility would belong to somebody else.

The girls had an excellent handle by which to grasp Nya now. In their eyes there was a certain amount of disgrace attached to being in a form whose average age was a year less than your own. They made this plain to Nya—so plain that, although she knew perfectly well that it had involved no disgraceful action on her part, she began to believe that after all there was a disgrace somewhere. She couldn't be quite certain what it was. Perhaps it was a disgrace to have been born and brought up in Nyasaland, to have learned to ride and play the piano, instead of to add and to construe and to translate. Perhaps, after all, it was a disgrace to be in any slightest way different from the three hundred girls of St. Monica's.

Her prowess with her hands and feet was of little use to her. Although she was naturally quick and soon picked up the knack of a game, she had never seen either a net-ball or a hockey stick before, and certainly didn't excel in handling them. There was no swimming, it being mid-winter. There was riding, and Nya immediately put her name down for it; but so few girls rode that she gained little kudos from her fine horsemanship, and the animals were so bad that she derived no pleasure from it. When she found that continuous "riding lessons"—as they were called—would involve the purchase of a habit, and necessitate further shopping with Aunt Ethel on half-holidays, she abandoned the project altogether.

At last letters began to arrive from her father. They were a delirious joy, but they had to be read in the lavatory for there was no other spot in the whole build-

34

ing where privacy might be obtained. These letters, private and personal and hallowed as they were for her, constituted a kind of spiritual food which, thanks to her father's perspicacity in such matter, arrived just often enough to sustain her starved young soul and to keep her reserve of fortitude from being entirely exhausted. Daddy seemed to know in advance exactly what would be most troubling to her spirit; he sensed the loneliness she would feel in the midst of all those gregarious hooligans, where, physically speaking, to be alone was an impossibility. Some parts of his letters puzzled her; in his anxiety to forestall all possible pain he sometimes outstripped even her imagination, so that whole sentences held no meaning for her at all. But she realized that this was simply because she had not yet reached the stage at which that particular piece of advice would come in useful; so she kept his letters very carefully, hidden beneath the piles of underclothes she had tried on that fateful day when Aunt Ethel had been so angry. Nobody else wrote to her except sometimes Aunt Ethel who enquired on a frigid piece of octavo how she was getting on, adding, not unkindly, that she must be sure and say if she wanted anything.

"After all, even if I didn't think you ought to have it, there would be no harm in our talking it over, would there?"

This everlasting desire to "talk things over" was another idiosyncrasy which everybody seemed to possess except herself. She couldn't understand it. Either it was right to do a thing, in her mind, or else it was wrong. Therefore, you either decided whether you would do it, and reckoned what the consequences would be, or else you dropped the idea like a red-hot brick. She would never have dreamed of asking Aunt Ethel for anything unless she had really needed it; in which case, what was the point in "talking things over"?

Luckily Aunt Ethel was neither a possessive nor a sentimental woman, so she took no offence from Nya's polite but uncommunicative letters.

"The poor mite is going to have a terrible time settling down to English life," she said to Nicholas. "I always thought it was a mistake to bring the child up out there. Not that she has been brought up, of course. Miss Little-wood tells me her lack of knowledge is appalling. I always said the child should have been sent back here years ago."

"Tom and Mabel had their own method of bringing her up. That's why they didn't let her come sooner."

"We shall see if it has worked."

But, as she judged its success or failure by the standards of Miss Littlewood and a hundred thousand other headmistresses and mothers all over England to whom Tom and Mabel had never given a thought when they evolved their method, this was hardly a fair test for it.

"I don't expect it will work, now that Mabel's dead," Nicholas added, unexpectedly, a few minutes later. . . .

"For which very reason she had better accustom herself to an English training as soon as possible."

"I suppose you're right. Poor little brat!"

The weeks wore on. If she had not been so continuously occupied Nya might have lost heart and given up the struggle. After all it would have been easy enough to get away from the school, though of course it would have been no use going back to Aunt Ethel's; and, but for her, Nya knew not a single soul in England. She was not afraid of the prospect of knocking about by herself; twelve years in Nyasaland had taught her self-reliance and determination. She supposed that life in England on one's own would be quite easy; one could always get a job as a maid in an hotel or somewhere. All the same, that didn't lead anywhere. And then there was Daddy to be considered. He might think that wasn't playing fair; although she was sure he would agree that a great many people at St. Monica's, too, were not playing fair by her. Anything more unjust and absurd than the decrees which governed her life she couldn't imagine.

So she never seriously considered the prospect of escape; partly because it was easy of attainment and was therefore always at hand for a last resource.

Towards half term too she received some encouragement. She had made such progress with her lessons that she began to outstrip all but the most brilliant members of her class. And at half term Miss Littlewood (who, of all people at St. Monica's, was perhaps the only one who might have appreciated her father and mother's educational system), broke every precedent and tradition of the school, and promoted her to the next class, where she stumbled and floundered along in some bewilderment until the end of the term. This promotion involved an entire reorganization of the two classes, and caused no little turmoil. But Miss Littlewood's kindness and perspicacity had their reward in the child's flashing glance of pride and gratitude when she was told.

"You're not really up to it yet," said Miss Littlewood, in the study where the winter-jasmine came in at the always open window. "You won't understand a word of anything at first. But you'll like it, I think."

She went out, walking on air. But she told no one—no one except Daddy, to whom a special letter was, somehow or other, scribbled and posted that very night.

Her new form-mistress it was who, at the beginning

37

of the term, had seen that Nya had more in her than the other mistresses could find. She treated her considerately now—so much so that the other girls in the form, trained by long practice to detect undercurrents, hinted at favouritism. But in spite of the embarrassment which this caused Nya (the mistress of course was not aware of it), she was never actually molested; and, from her remote corner at the back of the form-room she looked peaceably and not too distrustfully at the tiny world she lived in, and began to grow almost reconciled to it.

She might even have begun to feel happy, presently, for she was not so herded and driven as she had been in the lower form; but fate again chose an unlucky moment in which to play her one of its tricks. She had been feeling unwell for some days, and could not in the least imagine what was the matter with her. Living in Africa had reconciled her to the thought of disease, both in herself and other people, and the swift deaths of her mother and John had brought home to her the importance of immediate action. But it was a strange illness that was affecting her now. At times it seemed to affect her mind, and at times her body. She thought more than ever of her father, and the longing to see him and to fling her arms round his neck became at times quite unbearable. Then, too, there was a grasping, wrenching pain in her stomach, a kind of pain she had never felt before. She was sure it was not plain tummy-ache; but just to make sure she asked matron for a dose.

"Feeling queer," asked the matron, who thought she knew the signs.

Nya didn't trust her enough to take her into her confidence.

"Not exactly, Matron."

38

"I see. Well, let me know if there's anything I can do. It's my job, you know; and, by the way, nobody else ever hears things from me."

"All right, Matron. Thank you."

When she undressed Nya searched her body for signs of pimples or spots, or any possible symptom of one of those many inconvenient diseases like chicken-pox and scarlet fever that she knew she would one day have to catch. There was no sign of anything. She came to the conclusion that she must be sickening for 'flu. The regular Easter-term epidemic was due, the girls said. She hoped she wouldn't be the first to catch it. No doubt they would hold it up against her if she were.

The next evening, after a peculiarly agonizing bout of pain, something happened; something terrible and overwhelming, something that had never happened to her before, that drew her attention to a part of her body of which she had scarcely been aware up to now. She rushed for the only place where she could be private, and there, with horror, contemplated herself. She was terrified. She did not know what to do. Had she cut herself? Or had she caught some strange, some frightful disease, about which she had scarcely heard and certainly never thought? But how could she have caught it? Where did it come from? And why should *she*, of all people, have been so attacked? What had she done? A thousand nightmarish spectres stampeded through her mind, each one leering more fiendishly than the last. She was too numbed with terror even to cry. With trembling fingers she arranged her clothes and, blindly, made for the matron's room; not with any clear intention, for her one thought—if she had been capable of thought at that moment—would have been to keep this dreadful secret to herself. Obviously she was an outcast, a leper, a criminal almost, who was not fit to consort with human beings.

Fortunately, however, her instinct took command over her reason and remembered Matron's words of the day before. And, a few seconds later, there stumbled into Matron's spotless parlour a white-faced, shuddering girl, lips pale, and throat parched with terror.

"Matron. I—I——"

"What is it?"

"I don't know. Something awful."

Matron understood at once. She picked Nya up and laid her on the couch, just as she fainted.

When she came to, she was in bed, in a clean, white bed, and that terrible pain had nearly gone. Matron was standing nearby, and so was her form-mistress, Miss Bowden-Smith. Before she opened her eyes she became aware of two kind voices, speaking from far away.

"What is it, Lucy?"

"The usual thing."

"Oh. Poor child! She passed me in the passage without even seeing me. She looked as if she was fleeing from devils."

"She was. Oh God, why can't women prepare their children for it? Do they forget so easily how terrifying it is?"

"She hasn't got a mother."

"Perhaps that accounts for it then."

Nya opened her eyes.

"It's all right," Matron said, "you'd better stay there for a bit. You'll soon feel all right."

"What happened?"

"You fainted, that's all."

"Oh yes, I remember; but I wasn't in bed."

"No," said Miss Bowden-Smith, "we put you there—I should stay there if I were you," she added as Nya tried to raise herself.

"I suppose I've been an awful nuisance. Oh, but it did hurt! What was it? Is it all right now? Have I got some dreadful disease?" she asked, hysteria mounting with each question.

"Disease. What nonsense," said Matron. "It happens to every girl your age. Now you stay there and forget about it. Try and go to sleep."

Nya fell back luxuriously. She had complete confidence in Matron now, and Miss Bowden-Smith was nicer even than in the classroom.

"Oh well, I suppose you ought to know," she murmured. "You're sure it's all right?"

"Perfectly."

"Thank heaven! I *was* frightened though." She smiled ruefully, but her eyes were closed in blessed relief.

"It was a shock I expect," Miss Bowden-Smith said. "It's bound to be if one knows nothing about it."

"Oh well—Mummy did tell me of course. But I was so terrified I forgot. Besides, I didn't expect it would be quite like that."

"We none of us do. That makes it all the harder to be forewarned, doesn't it?"

"Yes. That's what Mummy said." She sighed and turned her face to the pillow, and a few minutes later fell asleep.

Now, for the first time, something had happened to her of which she could say nothing to her father. It seemed mean, as she wrote her next letter, to have to skip all the terrible worry and fright she had had; she had always told him even the smallest detail about herself. But this it was out of the question to repeat, and that

41

was that. "How unreasonable it is," she thought. "I wonder why things are so badly arranged. It's stupid, being so shy. I only want to tell him how frightened I was, not knowing what had happened to me. But if I did he mightn't understand. Oh, I wish I could tell him."

Nevertheless she didn't seriously consider writing to him about it, even in vague and circumlocutory form. So a whole chapter of her life was sealed and shut away, never to be read by him. From this moment, though he did not suspect it for some time, she became a different person, and their relationship began imperceptibly to alter.

She soon overcame her distaste for thinking about what had lately happened, and it gradually took its place among the numerous apparently necessary but certainly unjust and unpleasant conditions under which, it seemed, she would have to live her life from now onwards. She made greater friends than ever with Miss Bowden-Smith, who one day took the trouble to explain to her a great many things which she had not even suspected and which she only partially understood. And Matron gave her much sound and practical advice which, in the circumstances, was extremely welcome.

By the end of the term she was happy enough to regard the approaching holidays as a break—even if a pleasant one—in what promised to become an interesting routine of work and friendship. When the maid finally announced the arrival of Uncle Nick and Aunt Ethel in the car, she said good-bye with real regret to Miss Bowden-Smith, the Matron and Miss Littlewood, and turned and waved an affectionate farewell to the hideous block of buildings.

4

It was the beginning of April, and Daddy was due back at the end of May. That was still two months away, but she now began to feel that the time was getting nearer. Sometimes she found herself wondering whether he would still be the same as when he shouted good-bye to her from the quayside at Beira; she had changed a lot herself, she knew. Not that she could really imagine Daddy changing whatever happened to her or to the world. He at least would remain the same. Still, the world was an unreliable place, as her first term at school had proved.

It would be fun to talk to the "street boys" again; they were honest, straightforward people. If they thought you had done a rotten thing, they told you so straight out, without moralizing about it; whereas Aunt Ethel, like some of the mistresses at school, made a kind of lesson out of every one of your misdeeds.

On the first day of the holidays, however, Aunt Ethel said:

"I had meant to say nothing to you about those little boys you used to play with last holidays. I hoped you would have forgotten about them. But I think I should be failing in my duty to you not to drop you a word of warning. Forewarned is forearmed you know," she said, with a smile which was not nearly so encouraging to Nya as she meant it to be.

The boys had come to the garden fence that morning to find out whether Nya was back. She had agreed to meet them later on by the jetty; but Aunt Ethel seemed to be going to spoil this plan. However, Nya had learned from her schoolfellows that it was sometimes possible to disobey orders so she simply said, "Yes, Aunt," and determined to make no alteration in her plans. As long as Aunt Ethel didn't find out, she wouldn't be hurt by it, and it could certainly do nobody else any harm.

Nya began to forgive her schoolfellows a great deal. She understood now why they acted as they did. Apparently, if one was to live in England, which seemed to be a country organized entirely in favour of grown-up people, one had to pretend to conform to their laws, while seizing upon any pleasure that one could get when their backs were turned. This led to all forms of deceit which, if not moral, were at least excusable as a means to an essential end. If, furthermore, one could persuade these grown-up people that one was keeping their law, when one was breaking it, that was better still, for punishment was much less likely to follow. It was punishment that Nya hated most—not the physical but the mental effect of it. Why should it be necessary to punish people? Until she went to school nobody had ever punished her except when, as a tiny unreasonable child, punishment was the only form of corrective which she understood.

That, at least, was how the matter struck her when she was first punished at St. Monica's. Later on she came to admit that certain things were worth doing in spite of the punishment they brought with them. In that case one simply had to reckon with it. It was rather like Aunt Ethel's method of "talking things over". It meant you never took any decision except in cold blood; which seemed horrid and calculating to Nya, but there it was.

"I don't like having to do things that Mummy and Daddy would think dishonest, though," she would say to herself, "I wish it all fitted in better with what they used to tell me. I don't think they can know what it's like to live in England—especially at school."

The boys wanted to know how she had liked school.

"It's a jolly fine place," the eldest asserted, "at least mine is. Did you get into any teams?"

Nya said no, she had not got into any teams.

"Oh well, it's a bit early really. Very few people get into a team their first term." He said this proudly. It was a feat he had accomplished himself, as his youngest brother, who hero-worshipped him, quickly explained to Nya.

Nya complimented the young hero rather formally, and, to prevent further questioning said: "What are we going to do?"

"Well—it's really only us four to-day. The other two haven't broken up yet. I like it best that way, really, don't you, Nya?" He put his arm round her waist.

"Yes," she said, taken by surprise. "I do."

"You choose, what shall we do?"

There was only one thing Nya wanted to do, since she was already committed to this escapade—to go as far afield as possible and to make the most of it.

"Let's go to Shell Bay. D'you remember what fun it was last time?"

"What about your aunt?"

"Never mind about her."

"Is she still as stuffy as last hols?"

"No, not really," Nya answered, vaguely. "Let's go."

"All right," said the boy, "and I'll pay this time. My uncle gave me ten bob this morning. Jolly useful having an uncle to stay for the hols. I bet you wish your aunt was like that?"

His remarks about Aunt Ethel jarred on Nya's sense of propriety. After all, whatever one might think of one's own aunt, one didn't without being asked venture an opinion about somebody else's. It had disconcerted her, too, when the boy put his arm round her. It was a perfectly friendly gesture, which last holidays would have betokened his respect, but now, all at once, she felt it to be familiar. As soon as she politely could, she moved away from him. She felt suddenly much older than he, than all of them. To her surprise she discovered she wasn't very keen on going to Shell Bay with them after all.

However she couldn't get out of it now, so there was nothing to be done except to go. Perhaps she was being "stuck up", which was an unforgivable crime. That put her in the same class as Aunt Ethel immediately.

They decided to go by car ferry, a terrific extravagance since the fare was twice as much, but the eldest boy assured her that the additional excitement was worth more than double. Since he was paying for it, she didn't feel that the decision rested with her. In fact, she found she cared very little how they went, or whether they went at all.

"Come on, then," he said, "we'll just catch it. They're letting the cars on now."

She turned abruptly to follow the others, and knocked into a young man with a pipe in his mouth. For the fraction of a second she thought it was Daddy; he had the same blue-grey eyes, and he held his pipe like that, too, in his teeth. Then she saw that he was much younger than Daddy. She saw, too, his pipe fall out from between his teeth and crash on to the planks of the jetty. By that time, partly to steady himself and partly for fear he had hurt her, the young man had his arms round her shoulders.

"Now, now, now, young woman. You're in a tremendous hurry."

He didn't seem upset about his pipe, for he only stooped to pick it up when Nya had found her feet again.

"Oh! I'm frightfully sorry. Oh! I've broken your pipe."

"Never mind," he said, as he stood up again, "it was a very old one."

"But still—men like their oldest ones best—don't they? I'm awfully sorry."

The young man smiled. He was deeply tanned, more by the weather than by the sun: this and the blue jersey he wore gave him particular charm in her eyes.

"You know a lot about human nature for one so young."

"Well, you see – Daddy does," she explained.

"Ah, I see."

"I'm awfully sorry about the pipe."

"It doesn't matter at all."

There was a crowd moving along the jetty; one of the passenger boats had just tied up at the steps, and people were hurrying either to or from it, all round them. They were much in the way. Nya knew she ought to go or she would miss the ferry. She could hear frantic shouts from the other jetty. Probably that was the boys calling her. Still, it was awfully hard luck on the man having his

47

pipe broken. She was really very sorry. She wished there was something she could do. He watched her hesitating. His smile was replaced by a puzzled, serious glance. She looked at him, confidently, hoping he would say something, tell her to go and get him another pipe, tell her once again that he wasn't angry, tell her even to go and catch up the boys—it didn't matter what, so long as he said something. The silence was making her feel shy, but she was unable to go before he gave her permission. Uncomfortably, unaccountably, she felt a strange magnetism in his eyes which held her there. Then he looked away and the spell was gone.

"Ha—hadn't you better go and join your friends? They seem to be shouting for you." He jerked his head in the direction of the shouting.

And indeed the whistles and clanking of the ferry as it moved off scarcely drowned the frantic shrieking of the boys who watched it drawing slowly out of reach. They had missed it; and it was Nya's fault.

"Yes! perhaps I'd better," she whispered, and the young man strode off towards the end of the pier without a backward glance. He descended the steps and got into a tiny rowing boat. She followed him automatically and looked over the railing, his strange magnetism still on her.

His little boat spun round upon the water until it was facing in the right direction; then he began to row away from her.

The boys came up. The eldest was frankly furious, and red in the face with anger and the exertion of running.

"You silly fool, what d'you want to go and make us miss the ferry for? What were you doing? We were shouting like hell all the time. Don't you want to come?"

48

"Yes—of course." Her eyes strayed back to the figure in the rowing boat which was rapidly drawing away. At that first glance he had seemed so like Daddy. And even afterwards his eyes had twinkled just as Daddy's did. An overwhelming homesickness attacked her, a longing to see Daddy again. It was so long since she had seen him, it felt like a hundred years. And it was weeks and weeks before she could hope to see him again. She wanted to cry, but the boys were all round her like angry wasps to remind her to preserve her self-control.

"Well then—what's the matter?"

"Nothing."

"Nothing? Were you just doing it for a joke? 'Cos I think that's a rotten sort of joke."

"Yes, it would have been. A rotten sort of joke."

She knew she was talking nonsense, that she was not answering the question she had been put. But her mind refused to function properly; it was revolving other things than expeditions to Shell Bay and diplomatic explanations of her conduct. There was no explanation. She had knocked into him, and he had reminded her of Daddy, that was all. Oh yes, and she had broken his pipe.

But, after waiting for a few seconds for her to speak, the boy grew impatient again.

"What's the big idea then?"

"I don't know."

"You must know."

"Oh—don't bully," she flashed.

His anger subsided in a moment.

"I didn't mean to bully," he said, contritely. "I only wanted to know."

"Well, I shan't tell you. And what's more I'm not coming to Shell Bay with you. I'm going home."

"Why?" all three voices expostulated.

"Because I—I don't want to. I don't feel like it. Let's go another day."

There was an ominous silence in the group on the busy jetty. The smallest boy was the first to break it.

"Spoil sport."

"I don't care if I am."

His brother silenced him at once. "Shut up. You mind your own business. This has got nothing to do with you."

Nya had turned away and her eyes again sought the retreating dinghy. The boy put his hand on her arm. Again she felt a curious resentment when he did this; no, it was more than that. It made her feel uncomfortable and, somehow, ashamed. But she realized she was behaving very stupidly towards the boys, so she allowed herself to be questioned and finally cajoled into setting out with them as they had intended.

The ferry worked continuously, so they didn't need to waste much time. But the expedition was not a success. Nya's spirits had sunk very low. She was almost in tears on the outward journey, and the boys, as a result, found her such dull company that they left her out of their conversation. She didn't mind. Towards the end of the morning her spirits revived somewhat, but then a slight drizzle began, and as none of them had raincoats, they got wet and cheerless.

When Nya arrived back for lunch Aunt Ethel flapped and fussed because she had got wet; but fortunately it never occurred to her to ask Nya whether she had been playing with the "street boys". In Aunt Ethel's opinion her warning had been couched in the terms of a command. Nya closed her eyes to this. She set her conscience at rest by arguing to herself that there had been no

explicit command in what Aunt Ethel had said that
morning, only a lot of beating about the bush. In any
case it was unimportant now. She realized that she
didn't want to go on playing with the boys any longer.

"In fact," she decided savagely, "I never want to see
them again."

5

"The Rising", when the curtains were drawn and dinner cleared away that evening, seemed a dreary place. It was doubly dreary now, because Aunt Ethel had inaugurated a series of Bible lessons for Nya's benefit ever since she had discovered, from a well-meaning but ill-advised question of Nya's, that the child had never said her prayers and had only the haziest inkling of what the church service was about. She blamed Tom and Mabel, of course, for bringing up their daughter "like one of those little heathens out there".

"I really shall have to do something about it. She knows nothing at all about religion except some of the more obvious Bible stories," she said to Nicholas.

"She'll learn all that at school," was Nicholas's unfavourable response.

"Yes, but I mean, she doesn't even say her prayers—and they won't teach her that at school."

"She's bound to learn them—nobody could help learning them if they had to say them twice a day year in and year out. Then, if she wants to say them on her own, she will."

"You're as bad as Tom and Mabel. I believe you

sympathize with their educational methods in your heart of hearts."

"I wouldn't go so far as to say that."

"Suppose the child died—I mean she might, mightn't she—chicken-pox or whooping cough or something. What do you suppose would happen to her soul?"

"Nothing that you could avert by teaching her a few prayers."

"Nicholas, you're incorrigible. Someone must help the poor child, and I think it's my duty to do so."

"Have it your own way."

Uncle Nick was never present at these Bible classes. He would slip away to his smoking-room when Aunt Ethel began significantly clearing her throat; and Nya was left, as she felt, at her aunt's mercy. She didn't particularly mind learning "Christianity", as she privately termed it; some of the stories and characters in the Old Testament were very interesting, and there was a fascination about parts of the Gospels, though she didn't understand them very well. She didn't think they could be of real importance—not to know by heart at any rate—since Mummy and Daddy had never said much about them, though she recognized bits here and there—bits that Mummy or Daddy had made familiar, in another form.

What she did detest, however, was Aunt Ethel's version of it all and her manner of conducting her Bible classes. Aunt Ethel was a fresh-air fiend, and wanted Nya to be out of doors as long as it was light; so she relegated the classes to the evening, which made it much worse, for you felt you had it hanging over you all day long. Occasionally on blissful evenings, Aunt Ethel would depart, reluctantly, Nya believed, to whist or bridge. Then the lesson was held over until the next day; or she was given "homework", a short psalm to be learnt. Nya was good at memorizing and found this no trouble. In fact it was the only part she liked; the language was so beautiful, it reminded her of when Daddy used to read poetry to her.

In Aunt Ethel's view of Christianity the outward and visible sign mattered more than the inward and spiritual grace, it seemed, for she attached great importance to teaching Nya prayers, though she cared very little how Nya said them.

"Well, dear," said Aunt Ethel, after the lesson was over and they had prayed together, kneeling on the sitting-room floor. "Are you glad to be home again?"

"Home?" thought Nya blankly. "Was this her home, this house where she was a stranger and had always to be on her best behaviour? Could one feel at home in a place like this?"

It was some seconds before she answered. She sat down on the hearth, as close as she could to the fire.

"It's nice to be in a warm room, after those huge, cold classrooms," she said at last.

The mending was brought out and they began to darn, Nya her own stockings and underclothes from school, Aunt Ethel a pair of Uncle Nick's socks.

"Were you happy at school?"

Again there was a pause before Nya answered. This place might not be home but the mere mention of school made her realize how much cosier and kinder it was here. There were no hordes of girls chattering all day long, giggling and teasing each other; no mistresses (or at least only one mistress), with eternal commands that must be unquestioningly obeyed—above all there were no bells ringing every three-quarters of an hour. And, best thought of all, there was no need to get up

54

to-morrow morning until half-past eight! They had broken up at six o'clock that morning, and Nya was tired.

"Oh yes, it was all right."

"I expect you found it a little strange at first."

"Yes, I did rather."

"Did you make any nice friends?"

"Yes, one. There was an awfully nice mistress—she was my form-mistress after half term."

"A mistress?" Aunt Ethel was a little shocked. Her tone implied her conviction that friendship with a mistress was undesirable, if not indeed impossible.

"Yes, Miss Bowden-Smith she was called."

"But I meant, didn't you make friends with any other little girls? There must have been a great many to choose from—of your own age, too."

"Oh no," said Nya. And her tone implied that friendship with one's schoolmates was impossible, even if it were desirable.

They talked listlessly for a few more minutes until Aunt Ethel sent her to bed. "God bless you," said Aunt Ethel, as she kissed her.

And Nya, thinking of her comfortable bed in the little room upstairs (there would be a hot-water bottle in it she knew), of the yellow eiderdown and the cretonne curtains, was suddenly overcome. The heavenly peacefulness of it! The privacy! Oh God, at last, a little privacy again.

She put her arm round Aunt Ethel's neck and kissed her warmly for the first time.

Aunt Ethel sat for a few moments after she had gone, staring into the fire. Then she wiped away a small tear that had rolled down her cheek and lay trembling on her nostril, and went to join Nicholas in his smoking-room.

6

Nya slept well that night, without a dream, and Emily had to shake her vigorously before she could wake her.

"I've brought you some tea, Miss, as a special treat. And there's some bread and butter. Now you drink it up and go to sleep again. I'll bring you your hot water in twenty minutes' time."

"Thank you, Emily. How lovely."

It was a pity not to have had any dream at all. Looking back she couldn't remember a single one. What a waste! Because they would almost certainly have been nice ones; perhaps she might even have had a flying dream again. Well—at any rate, it was a relief not to have dreamt the sort of dream she always had at school. The loneliness of those dreams, the high-ceilinged, endless rooms, the corridors which never, never turned in the right direction, and down which she raced frantically in order to get somewhere—she didn't know where—in time for something—she didn't know what; the clanging of the bell which grew louder and louder, pursuing her down those slippery, draughty mazes, the cold green light that was over everything. It was impossible to escape from them—these ever-recurring dreams—because when you woke up you found they had more or less come true.

After breakfast she went out. The boys were being taken by their father on an excursion to Southampton, to see the ships, which was rather a relief because it meant that she was saved the necessity of making an excuse to avoid them. She didn't envy them. It was much more fun to wander about on one's own. After being at school for three months one was badly in need of being alone. It would be so easy to get out of practice, and that would be a bad thing, because of course, except for seeing Daddy occasionally, she was always going to be alone, all her life.

Instinct, or some even deeper urge, drew her to the jetty. With the boys out of the way the jetty was hers. Shell Bay was hers. The whole of Poole Harbour was hers. She stood for some time looking at Brownsea Island, and wondering what it would be like to land on, if only one was allowed to. Of course all that stuff about ogres and pirates that they made up last holidays was great fun, but it wasn't really necessary to make such things up. There were plenty of real ogres and pirates in the world. Probably there was some perfectly good reason for all those houses standing empty. Perhaps they were damp, or full of rats. Or perhaps the water on the island was not good for drinking.

There was a seaman standing next to her with whom she had a nodding acquaintance. He was an employee of the boat service to Shell Bay. She had often watched him clipping tickets and shepherding people from one boat into another. Sometimes he drove one of the launches himself, when his place at the barrier would be taken by another man. He would be sure to know about Brownsea Island, she thought. So she asked him.

"Who lives on that island?" he repeated. "Why that's Brownsea Island. Nobody lives there. At least no one except the owner and one or two farmers' people."

"Who are all the houses for then?"

"For the people that used to work on the farms in the good old days. There used to be five farms on that island, employing about a hundred and twenty people. Very good farms they were too."

"But why don't they work on them now?"

The man smiled and caught the eye of his mate, who was standing by.

"You mustn't ask me that, Miss. You must ask the owner."

Well; that was unsatisfactory. But the man's soft West Country voice and his kind manner gained her confidence, and she was prepared to question him till doomsday. There must be something behind all this. Nobody would allow their farms to go to wrack and ruin, and their houses to stand empty, without a reason.

"Wasn't it you who bumped into Mr. Byrne yesterday, and bust his pipe?"

"Yes. Wasn't it awful of me?"

"I thought it was you, though there was a bit of a crowd at the time."

"He wasn't very angry, was he?" she asked.

"Angry? Not he. He's a nice fellow, he is. Known him off and on for five years now."

"Do you really know him?"

"Yes, he's got a yacht here in the harbour. He lives in her some of the time."

"Does he?"

Nya's eyes were large with wonder. That anybody should actually know the man who looked so like Daddy and have spoken to him, not once, but many, many times, was an excitement in itself.

"What's he like?"

"He's a very nice gentleman. Quiet-like, never talks unless he has to."

"He talked to me!"

"Did he now?"

The seamen turned to each other. They had already joked about her encounter with Mr. Byrne.

"He doesn't often talk to ladies at all. I reckon you were lucky, Miss."

"Why not?"

This must have been a huge joke, for the two men laughed out loud.

"He took a lady on board once, to go out sailing—a pretty young lady she was too—but he brought her back in an hour. She was as sick as a whale."

"How rotten for him. I wish I could go out with him."

"You'd better ask him then. He looked as if he liked you yesterday!"

Again they roared with laughter.

"But you'd better buy him another pipe. He's lost without his pipe."

"That he is. Except in a gale. He's got no time for it then. We always know there's going to be a lot of wind if he sails out past here without his pipe in his mouth."

Once more they laughed. Nya couldn't be certain that they weren't making fun of her. She determined to go away and think it out. But the first seaman, seeing the perplexity of her expression, repented at last and did his best to atone.

"That's his yacht, over there, that yawl."

"Which one?"

"D'you see that white patch on the island, where the cliff's fallen down—just below the trees?"

"Yes."

"Well, to the left of that's a big schooner, isn't there?"

"Yes, I see her."

"Ay. She's big enough. She's been at anchor there for two years now, she's practically a landmark. Well, to the left of her's a small black ketch——"

"Yes."

"And to the left again is the *Puffin*. That's Mr. Byrne's boat."

"She looks nice."

"Ay. He keeps her well enough. Fine yachtsman, too."

"Is he?"

"One of the best, hereabouts. He's been to Scotland, Norway, Holland, Gibraltar—don't know where he hasn't been on her."

"Gibraltar!"

"Ay. Single-handed, too. Always alone, he is."

Nya walked thoughtfully along the jetty towards home.

"Gibraltar! And Norway!" They were hundreds of miles from Poole. Not as far as Beira of course. But still —fancy going there all alone on such a tiny yacht!

"I wish I could go with him. But I suppose he wouldn't want me. That man said he didn't like girls. In any case he wouldn't like any one as young as me, I expect. Oh well. . . ."

7

Aunt Ethel was specially kind to-day. She wanted to know, but not inquisitively, what Nya had been doing all morning. Nya said she had been watching the shipping from the jetty. She asked Aunt Ethel about Brownsea Island, but Aunt Ethel had to refer her to Uncle Nick for information.

"You ask him, dear, he's been there once."

"Have you?"

Uncle Nick soared in Nya's estimation. To have set foot on Brownsea Island was nearly as impressive an achievement as to have sailed alone to Gibraltar.

"Yes, I went there one afternoon, about twelve years ago. It belonged to somebody else then. A nice friendly chap he was. I met him playing bridge and he asked me over."

"What's it like?"

"It was very different in those days. There were quite a lot of people, labourers and so forth, on it then. I believe there are only three or four now."

"It looks mysterious from the jetty."

"Yes. It is mysterious. Especially after the big fire there two years ago."

"What fire?"

"They say somebody set fire to the trees to spite the owner. I don't know whether it's true or not. You can see where it's burnt, on the other side, from Poole."

"What a rotten thing to do."

"Yes. I suppose it was. Some people say they were justified, but nobody knows much about it."

"How could anybody be justified in setting fire to an island?"

"Oh, just getting their own back, you know."

"I don't understand how any one could think that! What good would it do them?"

"You may well ask."

"I'm glad to hear you say such a Christian thing, dear," Aunt Ethel said.

"I didn't mean it to be Christian, Aunt."

Aunt Ethel was taken aback. "Then your good nature was getting the better of you."

Nya didn't understand Aunt Ethel's last remark. She was out of her depth. There were moments when Aunt Ethel made you feel like that, clumsy and stupid, almost as if she had deliberately led you into a trap. On these occasions she would glance at Uncle Nick with a strange gleam in her eye, but he never glanced back, so he was evidently not in the secret. Nya was grateful for that, at least; if both Uncle Nick and Aunt Ethel had taken sides against her it would simply have been like school again, where every one took sides. You were either somebody's friend or somebody's enemy. You were never allowed to be a looker-on. More often than not you changed from one side to the other, according as your friend became popular or unpopular with the other girls.

After lunch she went down to the shore again. There

would be yachts on the water, and watching ships fascinated her more at the moment than anything else. Besides, there was always a chance of seeing the *Puffin* come down the harbour to go out to sea.

When she arrived on the jetty the seaman hailed her.

"There he is, Miss. He's gone out to her. Now's your chance!"

And sure enough, the *Puffin*'s sails were already hoisted and she was beginning to swing round over her anchor. Nya knew that the man was only teasing her; but as she stared out towards the yacht she felt again that strange magnetism that Mr. Byrne had exercised upon her yesterday. It was tinged with a feeling of homesickness, like her dreams about Daddy.

"Oh I wish," she thought, "I wish, I wish, I wish."

But she wasn't quite certain what she wished, or at least her mind scarcely formulated her desire. She leaned on the railing, chin in hand, watching the distant yacht. The *Puffin*'s anchor was aboard by now, and she was beginning to drift with the tide. Slowly her mainsail went up, and she gathered way.

Nya lost all consciousness of her surroundings. She was not on the jetty any longer. Her thoughts, her longings, her imagination, her very self were all aboard the yacht. She found herself inventing a scene in which she and Mr. Byrne took part. She had stowed herself away aboard the yacht, somehow or other; perhaps she had swum out to it through the icy water and arrived, exhausted and blue with cold, at the *Puffin* as she rode at anchor just off Brownsea Island. There she had scrambled aboard, found an old blue jersey and a pair of shorts, and lain down on the floor with a blanket round her to keep warm. There Mr. Byrne had found her when he came out in his dinghy. He hadn't been surprised to see her—at least not very surprised, not enough to make him angry. On the contrary, he had been very kind; and they had sat down together and "talked the matter over."

"Well, now you're here," he had said, "there's nothing for it but for you to stay. I'm off to Gibraltar this afternoon and I can't possibly stop and put you ashore again."

The scene had all the delightful inconsequence of a dream, but it was better than a dream because you could control the course of the action. A dream, even if you'd got quite good at dreaming, was apt to take charge and do the most extraordinary things to you. Sometimes it was fun, but more often than not it was rather frightening.

There was nothing frightening about Mr. Byrne. He didn't say much on the way to Gibraltar, except to count the stores and to find that they had enough to get to France with.

"Things are much cheaper in France," he explained, "especially tinned asparagus. We'll wait and buy food over there."

Then he relapsed into silence again, while he sat at the tiller with his eyes on the sails. Nya washed up, and cleaned the ship.

"Perhaps", she thought, "he's thinking of that pretty lady who was sick. I wonder if he still likes her. I must be careful not to be sick, or he'll probably put me ashore."

She came to herself with a start to see the *Puffin* sailing swiftly down with the current. She hadn't once taken her eyes off her; but during the last few minutes she had been watching, not this phantom ship, which she would never know, perhaps never see again, but another, far more real *Puffin*, a boat she knew quite well, and loved, and could even sail all by herself. It was a shock to find that there were two of them, hopelessly different and unreconcilable. And yet! She could see Mr. Byrne quite plainly now. He was not more than sixty yards away. He sat at the tiller with his eyes on the sail, just as she had imagined him.

"There he goes," said the seaman, just behind her; and she turned with a start. "He won't come back till Monday morning now."

"But", she was about to say, "you can't get to Gibraltar and back by Monday morning." She caught herself up in time and said nothing. Fascinated, she watched the *Puffin* sliding past the jetty to the open sea. Mr. Byrne was smoking his pipe ("he must have bought a new one!"), so evidently he didn't expect there to be a storm. She saw him feel in his pockets, slowly at first and then more hurriedly; he even left the tiller for a fraction of a second to peer into the cabin. When he returned he was still unsatisfied, for he cast his eyes about the cockpit and felt in his pockets again. Then he glanced at the shore once or twice. Nya wondered if he saw her. She wanted to wave to him, but she hadn't courage to make so definite a gesture. He glanced back once again, then the ebbing tide carried him beyond the car ferry and he vanished from her view.

Well, that was that. There wasn't much more to be done that afternoon. She didn't feel inclined to talk to any one or to go anywhere in particular. After wandering about the shore for a quarter of an hour she decided to go home. It was a long time till Monday morning, but, somehow or other, it had to be filled up. She never questioned the fact that Mr. Byrne would be back on Monday morning, nor was she surprised or ashamed to be so certain that until then life wouldn't be worth living again. On the contrary, it was perfectly natural for her to think so. Unknown to himself Mr. Byrne had won her heart in their short conversation on the jetty the day before. It wasn't only that he looked like Daddy —that was chiefly an impression for which her own imagination was responsible. Nor that he had been kind and hadn't minded his pipe being broken. She couldn't have explained *why* it was, even if she had thought an explanation was necessary. There had been something in his eyes when he had looked at her that was both a command and a petition.

"Are you lonely?" he had seemed to say. "Are you puzzled and untrustful of life? I can give you confidence."

She didn't formulate it so clearly to herself. It wasn't till many years later that she realized what had been in his mind when she spoke to him on the jetty. But her instinct was at work; one term of school in England hadn't been enough to destroy it or to weaken its power in matters that concerned her deeply. Now once again, as on that terrible occasion last term, it took triumphant command over her reason.

She spent another ten minutes throwing stones along the sand, and picking up shells; then she turned homewards. As she reached the top of a sandhill she glanced back at the bay once more to see how far *Puffin* had gone: to her surprise the yacht was nowhere to be seen. That was very strange because there was only one direction in which it could have gone, namely southwards along the channel leading to the open sea. For an instant Nya harboured an agonizing thought that *Puffin* had come to grief and sunk like a stone; absurd as it was, there seemed to be no other explanation. She felt again that curious pang of loneliness. What would she do if

Mr. Byrne were drowned? She felt she had known him for a long, long time, and that they were the greatest of friends. Yet something told her that it was absurd to think that he could have been drowned, or that *Puffin* was anywhere except buoyantly riding upon the water. She searched in the other direction now, towards the jetty, and sure enough she saw *Puffin*, heeling over to the wind, splashing her way back against the ebb.

So Mr. Byrne hadn't gone out at all! He must have put about again soon after she had lost sight of him. She watched him for a few moments, wondering why he was returning so soon. Had he never meant to go beyond the harbour mouth? Or had he forgotten something and was returning to fetch it? Unconsciously she began to retrace her steps towards the jetty.

By the time she reached it he was nearly abreast of it and was beginning to shorten sail. It seemed as if he intended to come alongside. She had never seen a yacht tie up to the jetty, but she supposed it was possible. To him all things were possible in her imagination. She watched; and again came that uncomfortable longing.

Puffin was moving slowly, just holding her own against the current. The seamen were astonished to see her return so soon. One of them hailed Mr. Byrne as he drifted towards the jetty.

"Anything wrong, sir?"

"No. No tobacco, that's all."

"What are you going to do, sir?"

"I want to tie up alongside."

"I wouldn't do that, sir."

"I can't drop anchor here. I shan't be long."

"All right, sir. You know best."

There was respect in the man's voice, though it was evidently a highly irregular proceeding which he was

67

abetting. And indeed it wasn't easy to bring an eight-ton yawl alongside in that state of tide and weather. It was managed, however, by dint of a terrific expenditure of force on the part of the two men, who alternately hauled on the rope Mr. Byrne had thrown them, and pushed at the *Puffin's* bows to prevent her from bumping. Nya watched it all from above. She could see Mr. Byrne quite plainly. He cast his eyes, as it seemed, all over his ship at once, but never in her direction.

"Thanks," he said when the *Puffin* had been made fast to a pier stanchion. "I must have lost my pouch overboard or something. Can't go a whole week-end without tobacco."

"No, that you can't, sir. You'll have a job to get out though, sir. It's a bit near to the ferry. Better wait till the tide turns. With this wind it won't be too hard against you at first."

They gathered in the flapping jib while he climbed up the ladder. Nya was standing at the top of it, and, now that she watched him coming up towards her, hand over hand, she was suddenly frightened. She wanted to run away, but something rooted her to the spot. There was a pain in the pit of her stomach. Or perhaps it wasn't a pain. Anyhow, she waited until his face appeared over the edge of the boards. It was red beneath its tan with the exertion of bringing the yacht alongside. He didn't look in the least like Daddy now. She was glad of that. It somehow lessened the spell he cast over her. He didn't notice her but, casting a last glance at his yacht, he strode along the jetty to the tobacconist's kiosk.

Now was the time to run away. She could slip past him as he was buying his tobacco, and then she could take good care never to run into him again. It was too painful, this silly, imaginary hold she allowed him to have over her. It was the sort of thing she despised, like the "crushes" in which the girls at school indulged. Now was the moment to end it.

But she was still there when he came back. She felt like Andromeda, tied to the railings, waiting for the sea-monster to devour her. Every step he took along the planks towards her reverberated through her own body. She was not between him and the steps, and he might again have passed her by without noticing her. But as he drew abreast of her, something caught his eyes and forced him to look at her.

"Hello," he said, and his breezy voice told Nya that he felt nothing of the turmoil inside her. "It's you again."

By a superhuman effort she discarded all her shyness. She wiped out of her mind everything she knew about him. All the things she had said to him in imagination, all the things they had done together—all except what had occurred between them yesterday on this very spot.

"Yes, it's me."

"I lost my tobacco pouch. Stupid of me, wasn't it?"

"You've got a new pipe. Is it as nice as the old one?"

"Far nicer. The old one was getting a bit insanitary."

She laughed. There was a slight pause.

"I'm just off, for the week-end," he said.

"I know. I watched you going out. Then, when you didn't go along the channel I thought you'd got drowned. But you'd only turned back."

"Were you sorry?"

"What about?"

"When you thought I'd been drowned?"

"Oh—that. Yes. I thought it would be a pity."

"Oh you did, did you? Well, it was nice of you to give me a thought."

"Not at all."

Again a short pause, while he began to look at her with fresh eyes. This was an unusual child. The frankness, the hot fervour of her glance, attracted him. She couldn't be very old, sixteen perhaps, at the most. Some eight years younger than himself. But she didn't look like other girls of her age. She was better grown—tidier, somehow—a more definite personality. What would she be like to talk to? Probably she would be tongue-tied, and he himself was no expert maker of conversation. No, perhaps after all, it was not worth wasting a week-end's sailing for the sake of a little conversation.

"Well," he said, "I mustn't keep the men hanging on to my boat. They're upset enough as it is, at my landing here. Good-bye."

"Good-bye."

"See you on Monday perhaps."

"I don't expect so."

The denial was so round that it arrested him as he turned to go. "Why not?"

"I don't expect I'll be here."

"Oh. That's a pity. Well—some other time perhaps."

"Yes."

He climbed down the ladder. At the bottom he repented of his brusqueness and shouted to her:

"Want a bit of fun?"

"What kind of fun?"

"Watch me crash full tilt into the car ferry when I cast off."

"All right. Mind you do."

He started his engine and was well out in mid-stream by the time he came abreast of the ferry. He remembered the little girl on the jetty just well enough to turn and wave to her. She waved back, a little forlornly as he thought, then he hoisted sail and made for the open sea.

8

She spent the rest of Saturday in a state of joy because
Mr. Byrne had recognized her and spoken to her again.
That night she had a flying dream. It was the first she
had had since she came back to England. Flying dreams
gave her greater pleasure than any others. In them she
became a superior being who could float through windows and up staircases and fly quite long distances
across country. She usually flew across the jungle near
Daddy's estate, because as a child she had been terrified
of snakes and wild animals in the undergrowth, and
therefore the only safe thing to do was to fly over it.
Now she was flying over Poole harbour, at least it was
a kind of glorified improvement upon the harbour.
There were all the same lines of buoys, and shoal-
markings, and the extraordinary thing was that, even
in the air, you had to keep above the channels. If ever
you got over a shoal you couldn't fly any more, and
would probably drown. It wasn't very difficult because,
from the air, you could see the shoals quite plainly, even
at high tide. In fact, spread out below you the harbour
looked just as it did on Uncle Nick's chart, except that
it was in brighter colours.

She was not alone as she flew. Presently Mummy joined her, and she brought John with her. They came from the direction of Brownsea Island, and Nya suddenly realized that of course *that* was why all those houses were empty, or appeared to be empty. They were for Mummy and John and lots of other people who had died of blackwater fever. Daddy wasn't with them, but Mummy suggested that they should go and find him.

So they flew down the pool to the jetty at Sandbanks and out past the harbour-mouth along the channel to the open sea. There they found the *Puffin* at anchor, and standing in the cockpit waving to them was Daddy. It was just daylight, and in a second the sun came up and sparkled on the water.

To have to wake up from such a dream was a bad enough beginning to the day. And the rest of Sunday was inexpressibly tedious. They went to church in the morning, and none of the hymns were good ones. The sermon had a promising text, but it was neither interesting enough to hold her attention nor dull enough to allow her thoughts entire freedom, so she came away with the unsatisfactory feeling of having accomplished nothing at all—neither the moral feat of listening to the sermon, nor the imaginative one of inventing a story to while it away. Then came lunch and, as often happened on Sunday, tea seemed to follow very soon after. That left only a few more hours till bedtime, and brought Monday morning near at last. She intended to go down to the quay in the morning and watch for the return of the *Puffin*. The seaman had told her that Mr. Byrne usually came ashore quite early—about seven-thirty.

If only she didn't oversleep!

She woke up at five and fearing to get up lest she

should wake the household, stayed in bed until six, although she nearly fell asleep again. At six she began to dress. When she was ready she sat on the bed reading a book until nearly seven. Then she stole out of the house. It struck the hour just before she reached the jetty.

The weather was the same as yesterday: cold and inclined to drizzle. She searched the harbour anxiously for signs of the *Puffin* and saw her at anchor where she had lain on Saturday.

She tried to see whether there was any sign of life in the cockpit, but *Puffin* was too far away. It was worth waiting for a little, just to see if Mr. Byrne came ashore. No doubt he worked in Poole or Bournemouth during the week, and would probably have to be at his office by nine-thirty.

Sure enough, ten minutes later, a dinghy put off from *Puffin* and began to row towards the mainland. She could hardly believe her eyes; she had almost given up the hope of seeing him again. She leaned on the rail, despite the cold wind, and watched him drawing nearer. He had his back to her and didn't see her until he had dragged his dinghy up on to the sand and made it fast to the pier. While he was doing this he was barely six feet below her. She could have put her foot on his head.

He didn't come up on to the jetty but started to walk along the beach. Again she was acutely disappointed. She had wanted to meet him as before, almost by accident. Now she was faced with the alternative of letting him go without talking to him or of calling to him. She didn't want to do anything too definite for fear he should think her a nuisance. Yet it needed more experience and self-control than she possessed to allow him to disappear without a word.

"Mr. Byrne."

The wind blew her words away, and he didn't hear them. She called louder:

"Mr. Byrne."

He stopped uncertainly and looked about him. Could any one have called his name at this hour of the morning? The beach looked deserted.

She started to run towards him. All barriers were down now that she had made the fateful gesture. Let him think her a nuisance, it didn't matter. She cared for nothing, now, but to talk to him, to make him stop and look at her.

"Why, good gracious me!" he said coming to meet her. "It's you again."

"Yes. I know. Please don't be annoyed. You aren't are you?"

"Of course not. What is there to be annoyed about?"

"Oh, a good deal really. I expect you think I'm an awful nuisance. But I won't be. Not again. I only wanted to say hullo."

Her gabbled excuses amused and touched him. He smiled and answered politely:

"That was nice of you. But you shouldn't have come down at this hour of the morning. It's so cold, too. Whatever time did you get up?"

"About the same time as you I expect."

"Oh, I'm used to it."

There was silence, while they looked at each other. He was at a loss for words, though he felt no resentment against the odd child before him; rather a kind of affection. There was something in her eyes that spoke to him, something she wished to say. He had no inkling of what it was but he was now fairly certain that something was troubling her. If only he were not so damned tongue-tied himself! Nya tried hard to read his thoughts, but she had too little knowledge of him to know what he might be thinking. His eyes were kind, but she could read no actual encouragement in them. All at once she felt frightened at what she had done. What had been her object in pursuing him like this and making him stop and talk to her? What had she to say to him?

She didn't know. She only knew she didn't want him to go, she wanted to stay with him, she wanted him to be kind to her, even if she had nothing to say.

"Please say you aren't angry with me."

"But, my dear child, that's absurd, of course I'm not angry."

He came closer.

"Look here. Is there something wrong? Can I do anything?"

Then occurred something which made Nya blush for shame until a year or two later, at the mere recollection of it. Suddenly, without any reason at all, she burst into tears.

Mr. Byrne was distressed. For a few seconds he was at a loss what to do. Then he put his arms round her and tried to comfort her. He had never done such a thing before, but it seemed quite easy. This heart-broken little child made it the most natural action of his life.

She sobbed uncontrolledly at first while he wondered what to say to her. He decided that silence was better sympathy than words, and said nothing. Soon she quietened down and began to hunt for a pocket handkerchief. He got out his own large one, and, entirely forgetting his inhibitions, turned her face towards him and began to wipe the tears away. Then she took the handkerchief herself.

"I'm—awfully—sorry. I honestly—didn't mean—to

cry. I don't know why I did." She tried to laugh. "You must think me an awful idiot."

"We're all idiots sometimes. Now, don't you be unhappy any more."

"I'm not unhappy really. I'm really awfully happy."

"Nobody would think it to look at you."

"I suppose not." She laughed.

"That's better. That was quite a genuine laugh. Now, we'll go and have a cup of coffee at the hotel and then you'll be all right again. Will you?"

"Yes."

She thrust the handkerchief back at him and, without raising her eyes, allowed herself to be led towards the hotel. Mr. Byrne didn't say anything on the way there, and she was quite glad because that gave her a chance to pull herself together. Really it was most embarrassing to break down suddenly, without expecting to, like that. She was ashamed. However, she was walking beside Mr. Byrne and, for the moment, that was all that mattered.

She had herself in hand by the time they reached the hotel. The place was deserted but it was open. A polite request from Mr. Byrne set a man scurrying to order coffee for them.

Mr. Byrne took her into a corner of the empty diningroom. Only two or three tables were laid, the rest were still either bare or scattered anyhow about the room as the cleaners had left them.

"Feeling better now?" he asked.

"Yes. I'm sorry I was so silly."

"It's all right. But I have a kind of feeling that something's the matter, isn't it? Now I come to think of it I thought the same on Saturday."

"There's nothing really the matter only——"

She hesitated, digging holes in the tablecloth with a fork.

"Come on. Won't you tell me?" His voice was encouraging but she dared not meet his eye.

"Well, I don't know that I can explain, really. It's rather a long story——"

"I've got twenty minutes before my bus goes," he said, with a glance at the clock.

"It began when I bumped into you on the jetty. You looked so like my father, you do now in a way," she looked shyly at him, and immediately lowered her gaze. "Especially when you've got a pipe in your mouth. And —well I love Daddy more than anybody, and I think that started it."

Mr. Byrne was still mystified as to how a chance encounter should have led to this morning's tears. His voice betrayed this, as he asked bluntly:

"Started what?"

This was a puzzle. "I don't quite know," she said ruefully. "My wanting to see you, I suppose."

"To see me?"

His astonishment was genuine. At last a light began to dawn on him as he understood some of the implications of her remark.

"Yes. I've thought about you since I first met you, and about your being like Daddy. I miss him so much. I haven't lived in England long and I find it a very odd place."

The words came tumbling out. What a relief it was at last to have someone one could talk to without reserve! Writing letters to Daddy was all very well, but that wasn't the same as talking, actually talking, to a person who sat opposite you and replied to what you said.

The coffee arrived and he poured it out. It was warm and delicious. Nya hadn't had coffee for breakfast since she left the ship at Southampton.

78

"Won't you tell me the whole story," he said, "beginning at the beginning?"

So she did. She told him everything from the first thing she could remember—rather hurriedly because she knew he had to go—but managing to leave very little out. When she reached the episode on the jetty she said: "So you see, that's why I was so glad to see you. I never realized you might not be so glad to see me." And she hid her shyness in her coffee cup.

"Well, well, well," he said, and the twinkle came back into his blue-grey eyes, "what are we going to do about it?"

She put down her cup with a clatter and gazed at him, wide-eyed.

"Oh, you don't have to do anything about it, honestly you don't. It's quite all right. Only, thanks for letting me tell you."

"That's all right. I enjoyed hearing about it."

"And thanks awfully for the coffee. I do love coffee—don't you? I wish Aunt Ethel had it for breakfast."

"Why don't you suggest it?"

"I don't think she would approve. She thinks I've never had coffee."

"Does she? She must be a little old-fashioned."

"Oh, she's quite nice really. It's just the way her mind works."

"And yours works the other way, does it?"

"Well—in regard to coffee anyway."

He got up and called for his bill. "Look here," he began, then realized that although she had told him her brother's name and her aunt's name and her uncle's name, and the name of one of the mistresses at her school she had quite forgotten to mention her own.

"By the way, you never told me your name?"

79

"Didn't I? I expect that's because I'm so used to it. It's Nya."

"Nya?"

"Yes. It's because I was born in Nyasaland. It means 'little Leopard'. That's what the natives used to call me. I think it's a good name, don't you?"

"Yes I do. A very good name."

"What's yours?"

"Simon."

"I like that. Simon called Peter," she quoted. "I was reading about him on Saturday with Aunt Ethel."

"I'm only called Simon. But you can call me Peter if you'd rather."

He picked up his kitbag and they walked towards the entrance of the hotel.

"My bus goes in two minutes," he said. "If you hurry *you'll* probably get back in time for breakfast."

"Yes, easily," she said. "It's only ten minutes' walk from here. I wonder what tea tastes like after coffee."

"Pretty horrible I should think. . . . I'd try plain milk if I were you."

His tacit realization that she would have to drink something unless she wanted Aunt Ethel to ask questions delighted her. He was evidently a companion after her own heart, to whom one didn't have to explain everything. He understood already.

"Thanks," she said, "I think I will."

The bus drew up and Mr. Byrne got on to the step.

"Would you like to go for a sail on Wednesday afternoon?" said that surprising man.

"Yes. Oh yes, rather," Nya stammered, her face glowing.

He smiled. The bus gathered way.

"All right. Meet you on the jetty at half-past two."

9

Wednesday was only two days away—a measurable distance. Not so much as the six or seven weeks she still had to wait until Daddy came home. Daddy? It was something of a shock to her to realize that she had hardly thought about him at all in the last few days. She hadn't written for over a week. There had been so much to do at school, examinations, packing, breaking up. And since Friday her thoughts had been occupied with Mr. Byrne. It seemed as if she had known him far longer than three days—not as long as she had known Daddy, of course—nothing like as long. But still, a good long time. Simon, he was called. Simon! What an odd name. Simon called Peter. It was rather a nice name, though she hadn't liked it much when she first came across it in the Bible.

She really must write to Daddy. He would be wondering what had become of her. Outside it was cold, and the morning's drizzle had evidently come to stay. It was no use going out. Now was the time.

"I haven't really got used to school yet, every one tries to make you feel young and stupid. Not on purpose, of course; I don't think they mean to. But it isn't so much fun *learning* as it used to be. You feel you only want to

81

learn as much as you have to, instead of being interested in everything and wanting to find out all about it."

That topic exhausted, she laid down her pen for a moment, and instantly Simon came into her mind. Should she tell Daddy about him? She pondered, and scribbled on the blotting-paper and at one time took a new sheet, determined to tell him the whole story. After an abortive attempt she gave up trying. Nothing she could think of to say would meet the case. She could have recounted the episode of the pipe, of course, and even of the cup of coffee, but that wouldn't have been telling the true story of Simon. The true story was a far more intimate affair, most of which had happened in her own imagination. For the second time in her life, she encountered a secret that she didn't wish to share even with her father. So she just wrote that she had met a man on the jetty "who looked exactly like you—pipe and all".

She passed some of the time on Tuesday by walking down to the jetty and gazing at *Puffin*, as she lay off Brownsea Island. She romanced to her heart's content without fearing the awakening that always had to follow her daydreams. She was going sailing with Simon to-morrow, so what did it matter if she did wake? As she stared at the yacht in the distance she was well content. The world was an exciting place and not every one in it resented her existence, as she had at first suspected. She remembered her dream about the island; the explanation she had found for the deserted houses was absurd now, in the light of day. Still there had been a kind of comfort in the dream, though Daddy and Simon had got a bit mixed up in one another. But perhaps they were, after all, connected in some way. They were the only two people in the world she loved.

10

On Wednesday morning the sky was overcast, but the clouds were high, and there was a fresh breeze. The seaman to whom Nya anxiously confided her doubts about the weather was consoling.

"Be fine by lunch-time, Miss, I shouldn't be surprised. Good sailing weather."

It was what she had been praying for for the last forty-eight hours.

Punctually at half-past two he arrived. "I hope I'm not late," he said. "It's always a bit of a job getting away from the office. But here I am."

They got into his dinghy, which he had left tied up to the jetty. He began to row out into the harbour.

"I say," Nya said, hesitatingly, "I'm awfully sorry about my clothes."

"What's wrong with them?"

"Well—they look rather stupid, don't you think? I hate gym dresses. But Aunt Ethel won't let me wear my good clothes."

"Quite right too. You'll probably get soaking wet."

"I'm all prepared for that."

They said no more until they reached *Puffin*. They

were both a little shy. Mr. Byrne was wondering what had possessed him to make such a gesture to a girl. It was true she was quite young still—not even full grown. But she was a female; and at the age at which females held least attraction and most embarrassment for him.

They were both relieved when they reached the yacht, where there was a good deal to be done in the way of getting up the anchor and hoisting sails. Conversation was restricted to commands and requests. Nya instinctively. complied with both, and Mr. Byrne did not seem embarrassed at ordering her about.

"I'm afraid I know nothing about yachts," she said. "But I'm quite intelligent, really."

He smiled. "You'll soon learn."

He had no scorn for her ignorance; he didn't even mind her having her gym dress on.

"I think I'll start the engine until we get out of the harbour. Tide and wind are both against us."

He spent some moments tinkering with the machine, while Nya watched avidly until eventually it fired. Then he got up the anchor, and made her lend a hand to guide the chain through the navel-pipe as it came in. He started the engine again and took the tiller, and the yacht began to move. As they slid past the buoys and began to leave Brownsea Island astern, Nya felt that there could be no more delightful sensation in the world. As they neared the jetty, however, and she saw a crowd of people standing on it, she became acutely self-conscious of her appearance. "Gosh!" she thought panic-stricken, "what if Aunt Ethel or Uncle Nick happen to be standing there, and see me going out with Simon? They'll probably send a launch after us to take me back."

"Please," she said anxiously, "could I go into the cabin just until we pass Sandbanks?"

"Of course," he chuckled. "Why, have you got a guilty conscience?"

"I have rather," she answered from inside. "They can't see me here, can they?"

"No. Even I can't see you in there."

"Tell me when we're out of sight of the jetty."

When she came up again his eyes were twinkling.

"What crime have you committed?" he asked.

"No crime, really. I just thought you mightn't like them to see me in your boat."

"Why on earth not?"

"Well—in my gym dress and then———"

She stopped, realizing suddenly that she was about to presume upon the information the seamen had given her about him. "He doesn't often talk to ladies at all." That meant he would probably rather not be seen with her. She could hardly tell him, however, that she knew why. She hesitated, and was silent.

"And then?" he queried.

"Oh—nothing."

"You're a strange person, aren't you? I don't think I've ever met any one quite like you before."

"I'm sorry. It's because I was born in Africa and I've only just come to England. Aunt Ethel says so, all the time. But I will improve, honestly."

"Nonsense. Don't you dare. You're much nicer like that."

This was astounding. That anybody should think she didn't need improvement was more than gratifying. It was almost unbelievable, so continually did she have her faults brought home to her. But then she might have expected this of Simon. He was better than the invention of a dream. He was perfect.

"I'm glad, if you really think so. It's no good trying

to be different if you aren't going to make a success of
it. Here I have to try and be different and I know I'm
a hopeless failure."

"I'd give up trying if I were you. There's not much
to be said for being just like everybody else."

He left the engine running while they hoisted sail.

It was a most unseamanlike business, hoisting sail
with Nya. It was just as well, perhaps, that the sea was
calm enough to allow the yacht to steer herself. For he
had to name every part of the sails and halyards, and to
explain their purpose to Nya. Nothing escaped her
notice; cringles, belaying pins, parrels, his marlin-spike,
all came under her inquisitive eye.

"Hi, steady on," he said at last, "you can't learn it all
at once you know. Hang on to this halyard and don't
talk so much."

She grinned at him and obeyed, while he hoisted the
mainsail bit by bit. When all the sails were set, he let
Nya handle the jib sheets which made her blissfully
happy.

Out at sea, some two miles from the shore the wind
began to freshen, and *Puffin* scudded along, shouldering
the water from her lee side. All formality was dropped
now between her captain and his passenger as she
heeled over to leeward, came up, went about, her sails
flapping for an instant, and then made off on the other
tack.

"What d'you think of it?" he asked after a long interval of silence.

"It's splendid," she shouted back, and then laughed
and spluttered as the flying cap of a wave slapped into
her face.

"I told you you'd get wet."

She nodded. There was no need of words, and in any

case she didn't know what to say. Her heart was suddenly full.

He made short tacks and went about as often as possible in order to give Nya something to do.

"Is that the Isle of Wight?" asked Nya, pointing ahead to a yellow cliff that was just visible in the distance.

"Yes. The Needles. Ever been there?"

Nya shook her head.

"Here," said Simon, "you come and take a turn at the tiller while I light my pipe."

This was a new and exciting sensation. It wasn't any good simply keeping the tiller straight, for the yacht soon came up into the wind if you did. This happened several times before Nya realized that steering a yacht was not like, say, steering a car must be.

"Watch the luff of the mainsail," he said, "the forward edge of it, that is. As soon as it begins to flap you'll know you're sailing too near the wind."

He made her hold the mainsheet then, to feel the wind in the sail. But she found it almost too much for her.

It gave him pleasure teaching this child how to sail. He hadn't been out with a passenger for nearly a year now. It was disgustingly unsocial of him, of course, but if the only two people he enjoyed cruising with both insisted on burying themselves in India because they thought the Government needed them out there, it couldn't be helped. It had really been very mean of them both to go off into the blue like that. Since their departure he had felt little inclination for human society, least of all aboard his yacht.

He watched Nya now. Strange to say he didn't resent her presence on board *Puffin*. Quite the contrary. The last female who had boarded her had seemed, with her

87

perfume and her lipstick and finally her seasickness, to pollute the ship, but this shy little girl, with her brown eyes and her frank expression seemed to belong here. She was like a dolphin, or something with a puzzled face that had come up out of the sea.

Nya soon began to show an instinctive judgment of the wind in the sails. Simon made her beat to windward for a short stretch, all by herself.

"I'll do what you tell me," he said. "You're captain for a bit."

But she was not so expert or so confident of herself as the occasion demanded. The wind was freshening all the time. He wondered whether it would be wiser to turn back.

"When have you got to be back?"

"About six o'clock. I asked Aunt Ethel to let me off tea."

"It's getting a bit choppy, perhaps I'd better take you back."

"Oh, don't make me go back." There was passionate appeal in her voice.

"All right. I only thought you might be feeling green."

"Lord no. I'm feeling grand."

She fascinated him. On the surface she was the same as any other girl of her age. She looked the same; she had the same sort of interests and longings as other girls, presumably her home life was the same. She thought the same. And yet, did she? Was he not, rather, attributing to her the same thoughts as he knew most girls possessed, simply because he didn't know anything about her? How could he appreciate the workings of her mind? How could he know what her secret longings and desires were? Till now, her conversation had been unusual, if only in its directness and lack of artificiality. What she knew to be a fact, she stated; and when she was in ignorance she said so. He would have liked to talk to her for hours. She seemed to have an instinctive, if misguided, appreciation of the motives behind people's actions; at her age, as far as he could remember, he had taken people's actions for granted and never questioned their motives. And the poor child had evidently had a difficult time in the last few months. For this reason he was neither angry nor amused by her naïve breakdown on the quayside on Monday morning. Because he resembled her father, whom she loved, he had been singled out to be the recipient of her confidence. It pleased and touched him that this should be so.

"I think we'll make for home, now," he said, his eyes on the horizon. "If it's your first time out there's no point in overdoing it."

"Oh what a shame!"

"There's still a long way to go."

"Yes, but it's in the wrong direction."

"Don't you want to go back at all?"

"No. I like being with you."

He was silent. She searched his face, fearing she had offended him, but when he caught her eye he smiled, and a load was lifted from her heart.

He put the yacht about, and they sped home with the wind behind them.

"Come and take another turn," he said. "You'll find this a lot easier."

They didn't talk much on the way home, except about the things they could see. Christchurch Head, and "Old Harry" and his wife, and Studland, and a paddle-steamer churning along towards Bournemouth.

"Horrid place," said Nya, with her eyes on the clusters of houses by the seaside.

"Yes, isn't it?" he agreed. "That's where I live!"

"And where I go to school."

After a moment she added: "I wish I wasn't so young."

"Why?"

"I'd like to be finished with school, and with always obeying people older than oneself."

"I have to do that too."

"Not in the same way. You can always tell them to go to hell if they annoy you."

"Why don't you try that one day?"

"I wonder what would happen if I did."

"I recommend it. They can't do much to you. Whereas I can be sacked, or put in prison for that sort of thing."

She laughed.

"Oh well. I suppose there's some advantage in being under age then, after all."

"A great deal of advantage."

I I

The tide was against them when they reached the harbour mouth. Nya stood by ready to be allowed to help, but she soon realized that she was in danger of getting in the way. Simon could do it all so much more easily himself. He lowered the sails, then the anchor, and the yacht came to rest riding unsteadily on the short swell. Nya almost overbalanced once, but saved herself by clutching on to the forestay. Simon looked up from the counter and grunted:

"It's the wind blowing against the tide. That always makes it a bit choppy."

When they had made all snug Nya supposed she would be taken home, though it was still only five o'clock. But to her delight Simon said: "Let's make a cup of tea; there's no milk, but you can have tinned if you like."

"I like it better without milk."

She could have drunk salt water and said she liked it.

"So do I," said Simon, "and I'll tell you something. Do you know how tea tastes best of all?"

"How?"

"Cold. You make it in the ordinary way and then let

91

it get cold. It's quite as good as beer. And if you get one of these high-falutin china teas, you can make quite an exciting drink."

"I've never tried that."

"I'll make it for you one day," he said, kneeling over the primus.

Her heart leapt. Was it possible that he meant it, that he would let her see him again, that this was not the last time she was to come aboard the *Puffin*?

No, she decided after some reflection, that was too much to hope. Besides, she had never expected that. She had taken it for granted that this afternoon's sailing was the highest point of happiness that could be reached. What could there be after that? She hadn't envisaged a sequel to such a climax. Now that her pleasure was nearly over she became aware that she would have to go on living as before. She stared, a little dismayed, into a future as unhappy as her life had been before she met Mr. Byrne. For, of course, he must have been joking just now. Or else he was being polite. Grown-up people soon got tired of being kind to girls of her age. It was only natural. They walked and thought on a lofty, god-like plane to which she couldn't aspire. So she said nothing in reply though she watched him all the more avidly as he prepared the tea, in case this should be her last glimpse of him.

Finally he stood up.

"It's a little devil, as a rule, that primus, but it seems to be behaving well to-day. I expect that's because you're here."

"I usually have the opposite effect on things," she said wistfully.

He felt again that curious mixture of command and petition in her glance. It was as if she were putting out a hand towards him, groping for something, for his help perhaps, or his sympathy, or merely for companionship. She was probably lonely; her whole manner made one think so. And kids of her age who were lonely lived the most extraordinary lives in their imaginations, created experiences that were real and graphic to them and that often had as much effect on them as the actual thing. He felt drawn to her by her youth and inexperience. To his surprise he was not frightened of her, nor embarrassed in her presence any longer. Even when he looked her in the eyes, though they seemed at times to glow with a passionate intensity, he could see nothing in them that was not good and pure, that was not wholly beautiful.

"Why do you always run yourself down?" he asked gently.

"I'm sorry. It's self-pitying, isn't it?"

"Not if you really feel that way, and aren't putting it on."

"I expect it's a bit of both."

"The way to live in this world is to crack yourself up. People believe you if you tell them you're no end of a person!"

"It's better still if you don't need to tell them anything."

"Well, perhaps it is," he agreed with a wry smile. "There are no flies on you, I can see. There's marmalade, but no butter I'm afraid."

"I don't mind. It's awfully nice of you to give me tea at all. To think that I might have been listening to Aunt Ethel talking tennis, instead of to you——"

"Talking rot, eh?"

"I wasn't going to say that."

"Well, I expect you'd have been right if you had."

He stretched himself across the floor of the cockpit, leaning against the lockers. She sat on the counter above him.

"I usually find I talk rubbish, when I'm keenest to talk sense," he said.

"Now you're running yourself down!"

"So I am."

There was a pause while they ate. Then he looked up at her and laughed.

"We might come to an agreement never to be humble in each other's presence," he suggested.

"If there is any 'again'," she said.

"Wouldn't you like there to be?"

"Yes, very much. If I don't annoy you?"

He sat up. "Now look here," he began, "what is all this?"

But she stopped him. To her own great surprise she actually had the courage to stop him. She dropped her biscuit on the counter of his beloved yacht and put her hand over his mouth, to stop the words she was afraid to hear. It was only for an instant; but his lip felt the touch of her palm, and the caress of her fingers as she drew away her hand again.

"Sh——" she said, "I'm sorry. I won't say it again. Only you see——" she turned to retrieve her biscuit, but her mind was not on that, for she only pushed it about the deck with her finger instead of picking it up. "You see, it seems so odd to me that you shouldn't be annoyed at the way I've bothered you. I'm so young compared with you; so you mustn't be angry if I am humble even though you tell me not to be. I can't help feeling humble. But I'm awfully happy, so I don't care." She picked the biscuit up and took a hurried bite.

He gazed at her with increasing wonder. She avoided

94

his eyes, looked across the harbour, pretending she was interested in something or other in the distance. He could gaze his fill unrebuked. He was so near to her that he could hear her breathing. She had a strong, handsome little face. About her there was none of the unprepossessing lack of character which at her age she might have shown. Her features were like her body, delicate, but firm.

"More tea?" he said at last.

"Yes please. It's jolly good, isn't it?"

They finished tea, and washed up without further conversation except about the business in hand.

"Now it's for you not to be angry with me. I'm going to take you back to your aunt."

She sighed, and gazed out across the harbour. Dusk was falling, and one or two lights had begun to twinkle. The Brownsea beacon flashed its yellow eye intermittently.

"Oh well, if you must," she said. "It *has* been lovely. Thank you ever so much."

On their way back in the dinghy they ran aground on a shingle bank. Simon swore, to Nya's delight. Then he asked her pardon.

"It's all right," she said. "I wish I could swear like that. Sometimes you need to be able to. When you bark your shins for instance. That hurts like the devil, doesn't it?"

When he had pushed off again, he said: "I know that shoal as well as I know my own name. Fancy bumping into it like that!"

"I wasn't looking. I ought to have shouted directions to you."

"No, no. I was just vague."

"What were you thinking about?"

95

"Well, to be frank, you."

"What were you thinking about me?"

"How much I like talking to you."

"I like talking to you, too."

"Will you come out with me again?"

"Yes, please."

"That's grand, then. When? Next Saturday?"

"I'll have to try and fix Aunt Ethel again."

"I'll fix her if you like."

But Nya answered like a flash, "Oh no."

It was a very emphatic refusal!

"Just as you like."

After a few minutes' silence between them, Nya grew constrained. "You see," she explained, and there were tears in her eyes though she was not aware of them, "you're the one person here who's—who's not like the others. Not like Aunt Ethel and Uncle Nick and their friends, and their friends' children with whom I'm always being made to *play*." She underlined the word savagely. "Going out with you in your yacht is like escaping back to Nyasaland—to the time when—before —before Mummy and John died and we were all together and everything was fun. I wouldn't like Aunt Ethel to know, though, or somehow I'd feel that she was butting in. Do you understand what I mean?"

"I understand. Not only that but a lot of things now."

By the time they reached the jetty it was getting dark. They walked to the bus stop, where Nya turned and made as if to say good-bye to him.

"Shan't I take you?" he asked.

"I'd rather not. Good-bye," she murmured, paused an instant and was gone.

As a rule a walk along a dimly lighted street, especially in such a place as Sandbanks, where occasional footpaths or clumps of trees might well shelter a lurking figure, held no little terror for her. Such a walk was like the unending itinerary of a dream, beset as a dream was with dangers of every kind, although, unlike in a dream, it was possible to take to one's heels and run towards a patch of light if one's fears got the better of one's common sense. To-night, however, there was a contentment in her mind that lulled her fears to sleep, and she walked slowly, at each step savouring a new recollection, reluctant to reach home. If only she could remember everything that had happened to her that afternoon, everything she had seen or felt, every word that Simon had said to her, if she could only heap it all up in her memory and lock the key upon it before she got home, neither Aunt Ethel nor the atmosphere of "The Rising" would any longer have the power to defile her precious store. But although she went carefully through the events of the afternoon in her mind, one recollection leading to another, her thoughts ran in circles round the momentous fact that Simon had asked her to go out again on Saturday, and returned to it over and over again as bees to delectable flowers.

"Your aunt's not back yet, Miss. Dinner'll be late to-night," said Emily as Nya closed the front door.

"What's for dinner, Emily?" was Nya's audible reply, though in herself she gave thanks for Aunt Ethel's absence.

"Chops, Miss, with carrots and potatoes. And after that there's angels-on-horseback."

"Hooray. I'm hungry."

"You'd best go and get washed and tidied, Miss. You look all blown about."

"Yes, I think I will."

12

She decided to have a bath. There was something a little wicked and grown-up about having a bath before dinner. "Auntie May" had always done so on board ship. It was evidently what you did when you led a really gay life with cocktails and smoking and dancing. Besides, Aunt Ethel always hurried you up when you were too long in your bath. It would be nice, for a change, to be able to lounge in it for a little.

She undressed with great deliberation, dropping each garment on the floor as she took it off. This was something of a pleasure, since both here and at school she was constantly told to fold her things up. Now, as if in defiance of the rules, she held her clothes out at arm's-length, contemplated them for a moment and, lazily opening her fingers, let them drop.

She had been standing in the middle of the room for some minutes as naked as a babe before she remembered that Aunt Ethel would soon be back. There would be no time to lounge in her bath. She shivered, for the room was cold. If there were a fire everything would be perfect. But the fire was only lighted on special occasions, or when you had a cold and were in bed, Aunt Ethel said.

The first two nights of Nya's stay at "The Rising" had been special occasions; so had the night before she went to school. But there had been no fire to greet her on her arrival after the term was over.

She crossed the room to fetch her dressing-gown and, on the way, caught sight of herself in the dressing-table mirror. It was tilted slightly downwards, so that she could see herself from her neck down to her ankles. Her head and feet were cut off. She giggled at the silly appearance she presented in the mirror—like a figure in "Heads, Bodies and Legs". How odd you looked when you were naked. Your body seemed wrong, somehow, shapeless. The strangest thing of all was that your body changed as you grew older. That had been an embarrassing discovery at first, but she was used to it now, and found it rather exciting. You never knew what mightn't happen next. She had never seen a grown-up woman naked; "Auntie May" had been fearfully shy when she came to bed, and always undressed behind a dressing-gown. But she supposed that they were much the same as herself. The girls at school seemed to suppose this. Some of them, more experienced than the rest, hinted that you changed an awful lot when you got older, especially when you got married. But from the way they hedged when you asked them questions, it was evident that they didn't know very much. Probably they were making it all up. She didn't see how they could know, anyway, until they had been married themselves. Mummy had said that when you were married you *felt* things differently. It was part of being in love. You only got married if you loved your husband; and if you really loved him everything came right of itself and you didn't have to worry about it. When Mummy spoke about it, it sounded exciting. Exciting enough to make you want to

99

know more. But when the girls talked about getting married they made it seem perfectly frightful. Of course Mummy was the one to believe. Still, it was frightening.

She filled the bath and got into it. Her thoughts, which a few minutes before had been straying rapturously along carefree paths, were now suddenly fettered to an uncomfortable theme. And, somehow or other, this theme was bound up with the events of the afternoon.

"If only Mummy were here I could ask her what was bothering me. She'd know all right. She always guessed straight away."

She had long been reconciled to the fact that she would never see Mummy again, but she still couldn't realize that she was dead—that she existed nowhere, nowhere at all, or at least nowhere within the reach of human beings. Daddy said he was quite sure that Mummy was alive and happy somewhere, or else it wouldn't be possible to think about her and to love her, as he said he still did all the time. She understood what he meant; she thought about Mummy and John sometimes, too, but not very often. She was too puzzled by death to be able to think of them in its terms. She saw them thoroughly alive and active as they had been at home. And that, she supposed, was mistaken. You couldn't be both alive and dead. Not unless death was quite different from what you were always told. Perhaps it was! If people invented horrible lies about marriage and babies they probably invented them about death— in order to frighten you! Most people who were afraid of things seemed to want you to be afraid too. Daddy said he wasn't afraid of death. Perhaps he knew all the lies that people told and saw through them.

"If you live as well as you can, and always remember

that you will die one day, you will find when you come to it that death isn't frightening, but natural. You'll find you'll long for it, just as you long to be able to go to sleep when you've been lying awake too long."

Something like that Daddy had said. It was probably the same as getting married and having babies. Most people longed for them, even if they said they were afraid of them.

The slam of the front door interrupted her thoughts. She got out of the bath, had dried herself swiftly and was back in her room before Aunt Ethel even came upstairs to take her hat off. By the time Aunt Ethel called her she was half dressed.

"Just coming," she answered. But two minutes later Aunt Ethel came into her room without knocking.

"Well, dear, what sort of a day have you had?"

Forgetting herself for a moment, Nya put the whole of her youthful gusto into her answer.

"Simply lovely, Aunt Ethel."

"That's nice. What have you been doing?"

A short pause of dismay. This question was not so easy to answer.

"Well, to begin with I've been having a bath."

"You don't mean to begin with, dear, to end with if you like. So you're wearing your costume again, you funny child!"

Nya was allowed to change for dinner if she wanted to. As often as she dared, she put on her grey flannel coat and skirt that Daddy had bought in Beira. It was more than ever her favourite garment.

"Yes, Aunt, you don't mind, do you?" She turned round and seized both Aunt Ethel's hands in her own. "Dear, dear Aunt Ethel, you don't mind do you?"

Aunt Ethel had had a bad afternoon's bridge and was

feeling in need of sympathy, which Nicholas, on their way back in the car, had not been disposed to offer. Nya's affectionate manner warmed her and she reacted to it instantly.

"Of course I don't mind, you silly child. If you want to put it on you can. Do you hate your other clothes so much?"

"Yes, Aunt Ethel."

"Well, we must see what can be done about them. Perhaps we could get you a simple frock to wear in the evenings. I don't like you to wear your school things at home if it can be helped—except your gym dress of course. That's so nice for playing in, isn't it?"

"But, Aunt Ethel, you talk as if I were the baby. I don't want to play any more."

"Don't you? Then you will tell me what you've been doing this afternoon for example. Did you stay at home?"

"No, I went out."

"Well then. You were playing about on the seashore, I can quite imagine it. You would have ruined your nice clothes if you had had them on."

Nya was brushing her hair at the dressing-table. Aunt Ethel came over to her, and playfully patted her on the shoulder.

"Aren't I right?"

There was no alternative but to agree. "Yes, Aunt. But you will get me a pretty frock, won't you? A blue one—light blue, not dark blue, with puffy sleeves."

"You've got brown eyes. Don't you think brown would be nicer. Or even dark green. With a skin your colour you could wear green I am sure."

"Do you think I could?"

"Oh yes."

"Still—I don't think I like green. Brown perhaps."

She turned round. "Could we go and choose one to-morrow? Then I could wear it on Saturday."

As soon as she had spoken she realized her mistake. Aunt Ethel, noticed an unusual eagerness in the way she spoke.

"Why Saturday, particularly?" she asked.

"Oh—only that, on Saturdays, everybody seems to put on something special here. It's more like Sunday than Saturday, isn't it?"

"Perhaps. But I think you should keep it for a Sunday. It's a pity Easter's over. It's always nice to wear something new on Easter Sunday."

"And will you really get it for me?"

"Well—we'll see."

But there was a smile on Aunt Ethel's face. It was a sign that Nya thought she knew. She flung her arms round her aunt and kissed her.

Aunt Ethel was pleased and touched, and privately resolved to choose the dress the next day. But for the moment she wanted relaxation and she proposed that after dinner they should take Uncle Nick to the cinema.

"We'll make him take us, you mean," Nya corrected, frivolously. Life was beginning to get easier. Here she was even going to a cinema—her first since Beira.

She was not allowed into Aunt Ethel's room; so she hung about the landing while Aunt Ethel tidied herself. Then they went down to dinner arm in arm.

Uncle Nick approved of the cinema plan. Marlene Dietrich was showing at a picture-house in Bourne-mouth: he suggested that they should take the car and drive there. Aunt Ethel demurred at first, but she had never seen Marlene Dietrich and was secretly keen to find out whether she had as much wicked glamour as people made out. Nya listened to their conversation without speaking. Going to the cinema at all was delightful enough; she didn't care what they were going to see. Aunt Ethel's chief doubt was on Nya's account.

"Do you think it's all right for the child?" she asked Nicholas.

"Of course it's all right. Nya's a woman of the world, aren't you, Nya? There's nothing children don't know about life nowadays. Not like when you were a girl."

"No, but still——" Aunt Ethel countered feebly, thinking of that embodiment of sophisticated wickedness about whom the film revolved.

"If there's anything your Aunt Ethel doesn't approve of, Nya, you'll have to pretend you don't understand it. And I vote we celebrate our razzle by having a bottle of cider. What do you think, Nya?"

Cider? Cider was like a fire in one's bedroom: it only appeared on extra-special occasions. Things *were* looking up!

Uncle Nick was in good form all the evening. Towards the end of dinner Aunt Ethel told him he had drunk too much beer. He retorted by saying she had had too much cider. And Nya, whose head was pleasantly light after two glasses of it, giggled, which made Aunt Ethel blush.

As it turned out Aunt Ethel's fears for Nya's morals were unfounded, for the film proved to be perfectly harmless as long as it was outspoken; and when it was not the meaning of the innuendo escaped Nya. There was one uncomfortable moment which raised Aunt Ethel's apprehensions. Nya, feeling how anxious Aunt Ethel was, began to be embarrassed on her account, until Uncle Nick made a joke about the situation which raised a laugh from both of them and put them at their ease again.

On the way home Uncle Nick told Nya about his first

attempts to earn a living, before he finally drifted into the army. It seemed he had tried everything from being a clerk in a railway station to driving an old gentleman's pony-trap. The last had been the most fun, he said; especially when something in the breeching of the harness broke and the shafts of the trap rose into the air and deposited the old gentleman in the road.

"Did he sack you, Uncle Nick?"

"I'm afraid he did. Most unreasonable, because it wasn't my fault. I was rather glad really. I had been looking for another job for some time."

She dreamt that night that she was with Uncle Nick in a yacht that sailed along roads and never went near the sea at all. She wasn't quite sure how many other people were on board the yacht, which was much larger than *Puffin*; several people kept appearing and disappearing. One was a man who carried a bottle of beer about with him, and offered to let people drink out of it. As far as she could remember in the morning nobody took advantage of his offer. Eventually he was thrown overboard, but when he landed (in the roadway), he turned into an old gentleman with a red nose, who sat back and shouted at them. They soon left him behind. "That was my employer," Uncle Nick said.

Uncle Nick was steering, and the yacht had a wheel instead of a tiller. It also had gears. She wondered what Simon would say when he saw it; for of course the yacht belonged to him. But at that moment he looked out of the cabin door, with a marmalady biscuit in his hands, and said, "When you see the edge of the sail beginning to flap you must put her in reverse." Uncle Nick laughed at this, and she remembered feeling furious with him for doing so.

The sail didn't flap however, for in a few seconds it

disappeared and gave place to a bath towel, with a striped pattern on it. Between the stripes was written:

> *Blow the fire*
> *Of Desire.*

Desire had a capital "D". She thought this funny at first until she realized that what she saw was the clue to a cross-word puzzle with which she had been helping Uncle Nick, and that it was something to do with films. As soon as she understood this she ran to tell Uncle Nick but on the way downstairs she woke up.

13

Aunt Ethel was as good as her word and the dress was bought next morning. It was the only shopping expedition with Aunt Ethel that Nya had enjoyed. To her surprise Aunt Ethel took almost as much pleasure in choosing the dress as she did herself. They had to go to four shops before they found it; and when they did find it it was totally unlike what either of them had imagined. Instead of being light blue or brown or even green, it was dark yellow. And it was not made of silk, as Nya had privately imagined, but of wool. And, of course, it had not got puffy sleeves but quite plain ones, which came right down to her wrists. Nya tried it on, terrified lest it shouldn't fit, and she would be compelled to have another one. But it did fit, there was hardly any alteration required—not more, anyway, than Aunt Ethel could manage at home, she said.

"I'll help you, Aunt Ethel, shall I? I can sew, you know. Please, please let me have it. Can I?"

"Just a moment, dear. We must ask how much it is."

But Aunt Ethel already knew how much the dress cost, it was the same price as all the others near it. To Nya's delight Aunt Ethel didn't think this was too much and the dress was bought.

"Now this one you really must keep for best, dear. It's got to last you a long, long time."

"Yes, Aunt. I'll be careful of it, I promise."

And privately she resolved at all costs to wear it on Saturday. After all, if Saturday wasn't "Best", what was?

The rest of Thursday passed, and even Friday. Saturday morning Nya spent wondering whether she would have to betray her secret to Aunt Ethel or whether she could manage to keep it a little longer. It all depended on what Aunt Ethel's plans were, and they were seldom made in advance. Usually the telephone rang at about eleven o'clock, and Aunt Ethel and Uncle Nick were asked to make up a four at either tennis or bridge. If nothing happened by twelve o'clock it meant that Uncle Nick would be at home anyway, though Aunt Ethel usually went out in the afternoon.

This morning the telephone was exceptionally silent. It did ring once—but it was only Emily's young man arranging to meet her that evening.

Aunt Ethel passed through the hall.

"You shouldn't be hanging about indoors on a morning like this, dear. Why don't you go down to the beach? There'll probably be several of your friends there."

But Nya had to keep an ear trained on the telephone; so she spent the next half-hour dodging Aunt Ethel round the house. Eventually, at twelve o'clock, it rang. Aunt Ethel answered it.

"Hello. All right, thank you. How are you? Oh my dear. I'm sorry. When did he go in? You never told me!"

Then followed, evidently, a long tale of woe from the other end of the wire, for Nya, listening from the upstairs landing, could catch nothing but occasional sympathetic noises from Aunt Ethel. Suddenly Aunt Ethel's manner changed; she adopted a defensive attitude. Nya knew it well.

"Well, I'm not sure. I believe Nicholas needs the car. He's going out golfing or somewhere—— Well I suppose he could. I'll ask him. Yes, I know it's terribly inconvenient to get to without a car. I remember finding that when Nicholas had to have his adenoids out. Very well, I'll ask him."

She laid down the receiver and went across the hall. But she made no effort to find Uncle Nick, who was always in his smoking-room reading *The Times* at this hour of the morning. Instead she opened the baize door to the kitchen, and said:

"Emily. We'll have lunch as soon as you can get it ready. I shall be going out this afternoon. Ask Maggie if she can manage it by one o'clock."

Emily's reply must have been in the affirmative for Aunt Ethel said, "That's good," and shut the door. She returned to the telephone:

"Are you there? Yes, it's all right. He says he can get a lift from his partner and I can have the car. I shall enjoy it. It's a pretty drive. All right, at two o'clock then."

She hung up the receiver.

"Two o'clock!" That was splendid, thought Nya. She hadn't to be at the jetty until half-past two. By that time Aunt Ethel would be well out of the way. She had no idea what Aunt Ethel was doing this afternoon but she was evidently going somewhere fairly far afield in the car. This certainty was worth all the gold in the world. Even the slightly dishonourable means by which it had been obtained were justified. After all, if Aunt Ethel could tell a lie about asking Uncle Nick for the car in such a trivial matter, Nya's momentous appointment warranted at least as great a privilege. And anyway, listening to somebody talking on the telephone wasn't so bad as telling a lie.

Everything happened as Nya could have wished—even to Uncle Nick's saying he had to see a man about a dog in Bournemouth, and would Aunt Ethel give him a lift as far as she was going. That would save him ten minutes in the bus. Aunt Ethel said:

"I'm taking Mrs. Hollis out to see her husband. He's in that sanatorium near Kinson, where you were."

"Terrible place, cold as the north pole. Can't think why I ever went there," commented Uncle Nick.

"You got well very quickly, Nicholas."

"You bet I did. Anything to get away from it."

Aunt Ethel turned to Nya: "Dinner's at eight to-night. I've got a committee meeting. I'll order tea for you at half-past four."

"Please don't bother, Aunt. I don't think I'll have any tea."

Aunt Ethel surprised and pleased, reminded her: "Dinner's late you know, and we're having an early lunch."

"Yes, but I don't honestly want any tea."

"Very well then."

She said grace, and they left the table. Ten minutes later she and Uncle Nick were out of the house.

Nya flew upstairs to her wardrobe, where, all ready to be taken out, was her new yellow dress. Frantic with excitement she laid it on the bed; then almost tore off her gym tunic, her black stockings, her blouse. With trembling fingers she picked up the new dress and slipped it over her head. As she shook it out round her knees, and wriggled her hips to make it slide down properly she panted with delight and eagerness. Hastily she did up the fasteners, put on some nice stockings, and her best shoes. She spent five whole minutes on her hair and her general appearance—probably the longest time she had ever spent before a mirror—and at last she was ready. Hatless, she ran downstairs and out into the road.

14

This time Simon was there before her.

"I'm awfully sorry," she panted, "have you been waiting long? I couldn't get away before. I'm terribly sorry."

"I thought perhaps you'd changed your mind," he said, to tease her.

"You didn't, did you?" She was quite upset. "Oh, you couldn't have thought that. I'd have gone through hell to get here."

"I hope you didn't have to," he said, with a serious face.

"No, I was lucky. Aunt Ethel went out at the last minute. I'm sorry you had to wait."

"It's all right," he said, smiling at last. "It's still only twenty-five past. Shall we go?"

"Yes."

She took his hand. It was the shy, trustful gesture of a small child, and it moved him. It was impossible to be conventional with her; she hadn't the faintest idea what convention was. That was a unique quality in her, one that attracted him most of all. At the same time it made things more difficult, both on account of the construction other people might put upon their friendship and also because it made intimacy more difficult to avoid, especially as he found he only half desired to avoid it. He knew that she was in love with him; but no, "in love" was not the right expression. It was probably something more akin to hero-worship that she felt for him. At any rate, for the time being he was her god, and the only thing to do was to accept with a good grace his exalted status in her eyes. The question was whether he would harm her by doing so, or whether it would hurt her more if he refused to. He felt as if she had entrusted herself to his care at a crossing and it was up to him to see her safely to the other side. What happened afterwards it was for her to decide. Probably her judgment would have matured by then. Perhaps there might even come a time when they would meet on equal terms.

But in the meantime it was difficult to know quite how to behave towards her. He knew now that she was about thirteen years old. Most girls of thirteen were gawky, inarticulate children. Nya was a child, too; she had the virtues of a child, simplicity and trust, but scarcely any of the faults of one. Some of her unique qualities must be due to character. He believed that, child though she was, she had left the stage of gawky inarticulacy far behind, if indeed she had ever passed through it, and was in some ways as grown-up as himself. She had a clear vision and an uncompromising judgment. He guessed, too, that nearly all her opinions were spontaneous; she was not the kind of child that trots out phrases it has heard on its elders' lips.

He looked down at the girl walking so eagerly beside him. Neither had spoken a word, but they were on the best of terms. She squeezed his hand. He smiled.

As they got into the dinghy he told her to be careful of her dress.

"The boat's full of water," he said, "perhaps you could bail her out as we go along."

Nya tried, but she did it so messily that it seemed as if her dress would be ruined.

"I say, do be careful," he said anxiously. "It's such a nice dress. Is it new?"

She nodded.

"Do you like it?"

"Very much. Is it your best?"

"We only bought it on Thursday."

"I ought really to scold you for putting it on to-day. One should always wear one's oldest clothes for sailing."

"I wanted you to see me in it. I chose it, you know. All by myself."

"You've got excellent taste."

"I haven't really, but I just had a hunch about this one."

"That's what good taste is—having hunches about the right things."

"Aunt Ethel said I was only to wear it for best occasions, but if she finds out I shall tell her this *is* a best occasion."

He wondered whether "Aunt Ethel" suspected his existence, but a moment's reflection convinced him that Nya couldn't have said a word about him. He hoped the aunt wouldn't make trouble if she found out. It would probably make Nya unhappy. He realized that this, above all things, was what he wished to avoid.

"What will happen if she does find out about the dress?"

"God knows. I've behaved quite well so far, so I've no experience to go by."

"Anything unpleasant?"

"Oh no. I don't expect so. I don't know if she could do anything really horrid. She's too Christian."

"Too Christian?"

"Yes. You know what I mean. Like other people's aunts in books."

"I see what you mean. What sort of books do you read?"

"All sorts. I like Kipling—but not just the Jungle Books," she added hastily. "And Katherine Mansfield and Thackeray and Jane Austen. Have you read any of them?"

"Some of each of them, I think. I like Kipling, too. He writes all sorts of things. Have you read *The Ship that Found Herself*?"

"Yes, rather! And have you read *The Brushwood Boy* and *The Bull that Thought*?"

This was fascinating conversation! Her eyes were bright, and she leaned forward eagerly. The bailing-tin fell out of her hand, and sank half-way in the remains of the bilge-water.

"Yes. I have."

"And then there's a story in one of his books about some children and a blind lady. I think it's called *They* —or perhaps that's another one——"

"No, that's right."

"D'you know it? I never quite understand it. Sometimes I have to read a thing several times—like in *Kim* for instance—to understand everything that's meant. It's as if Kipling made each sentence mean as much as two or three."

"Yes. He's a marvellous writer."

Puffin was as they left her three days ago, except that she had evidently been popular with the seagulls as a roosting place, for their marks were everywhere.

"Good sign," Simon grunted. "Seagulls only like really nice ships."

He disappeared into the cabin, while Nya made fast the dinghy at his request. She was proud to be allowed to carry out even so simple an operation. In a moment Simon's head emerged through the fo'c'sle, followed by the rest of him carrying a wooden bucket on the end of a rope. With this he sluiced the decks while Nya went round after him with the mop, until there were no traces of seagull left.

"That's the worst of leaving her so far from other ships and people," he commented.

"Let's leave a scarecrow on her when we go," Nya suggested. "We could dress up a cushion in one of your blue jerseys, with the mop for a head, and two fenders for legs."

He laughed. "Yes. It's not at all a bad idea."

He prepared to hoist sail. Nya understood better this time what he was doing, and managed to be of use. He noticed this and said: "I see you're an old hand already. But I'm worried about your dress. Look here. I'd much rather you put on something over it. I've got quite a light oilskin in the cabin."

"Oh no, it doesn't matter," she said. But he could sense the doubt in her mind.

"I'd put it on," he said. "Safer."

"All right."

"You know where it is? Over the clothes on the fo'c'sle bunk. Here you can go down this way." He pointed to the fo'c'sle hatch.

Just as she reached it he added: "Wait a bit, though. It would be better still if you took your dress right off, wouldn't it?"

He said it in a matter-of-fact voice, not realizing at

116

first what she might think. She looked up at him quite naturally, and said with a grin:

"My underclothes aren't very expensive, you know."

He laughed at that; but then he began to blush. Fortunately Nya had disappeared into the fo'c'sle and didn't notice. She reappeared in a few seconds and said: "Having inspected the garment in question, I have come to the conclusion that I shouldn't be decent in it without my dress. Still"—she examined her dress where it had come into contact with the salty hatch, and added wistfully—"it would be better to take it off. What could I put on?"

"Oh that's easy," he said. "Pull all the clothes off the bunk and pick out what you want—sweaters, trousers— there's even a pair of shorts I think. And I know there's one jersey that's far too small for me."

"Right."

She dived below again. In a few moments a muffled voice said: "I've got some grand things. Can I put them on?"

"Of course. Go into the cabin. More room in there."

"All right. I'll shut the door."

There was no trace of embarrassment or even formality in her manner. He felt at ease again.

She emerged presently, dressed in a blue jersey and a pair of shorts.

"The shorts were too big round the waist, so I tied a handkerchief round. You must have had a huge tummy at one time."

He grunted. "You look like that scarecrow you were talking about. I think I'll leave you on board in future to keep away the seagulls."

She put her tongue out at him and continued excitedly:

"Look, this jersey's just like the one you've got on. You won't be ashamed now if they see me on your yacht, will you? They'll think I'm the cabin boy."

He let her chatter on, passing her ropes and corners of sails to hold, until all sails were bent and they were ready to take up the anchor. Then they made for the mouth of the harbour.

They were the greatest of friends. It was almost as if they were old friends meeting for the first time for many years, longing to tell and to know all, and completely uninterested in the world around them. As soon as they were clear of the buoys Simon set the yacht to run before the wind. He took the mainsheet and gave Nya the tiller, and for nearly half an hour they discovered their minds to each other. Nya talked more than he; but even he, taciturn as he was by nature, found his tongue loosened by her naïveté. She revealed so much to him, she made him feel it would be churlish not to be as frank with her.

But she could, of course, only show interest or curiosity in these things that she knew already, or half suspected; of the more complicated processes of the mind, of the flow of emotion in a grown man's thoughts, she knew nothing. But what she lacked was merely experience; not wit, nor intelligence, nor instinct, nor the desire to understand. It seemed that it could not be long before her keen mind had unravelled the most complicated of his inhibitions. One or two she touched on now; and when he winced and sought to draw away from her, she sensed it at once and she changed her touch so quickly that she appeared never to have touched him at all. And when she did this he not only loved her for her perspicacity, but he felt his inhibitions dwindle and dissolve in her omnivorous understanding.

He would have been puzzled by the paradoxical qualities she possessed if he had not realized that she was, to a remarkable degree, a creature of instinct. She loved, understood, and foreknew entirely with her instinct; and her brain was responsible solely for her fears, her ignorance, and her misconceptions. That was as it should be; those fears could be so easily removed in course of time. No doubt many of them would vanish as her instinct learned gradually to work for her intellect instead of against it.

"I often wonder whether some of the girls at school have parents like Aunt Ethel and Uncle Nick," she remarked. "They don't seem to be allowed to do anything exciting in the holidays—or even to go anywhere alone. As if they were babies. We were always allowed to go where we liked in Nyasaland; and England must be a much safer place."

"In a way, yes," he said after pulling at his pipe. "But England is an over-populated place. It's like a huge town. And people in towns aren't quite like people who live in the wilds. They're never up against things in the same way, and that brings out their worst characteristics and sends their best ones to sleep. So you get them doing mean, cruel things that people from your part of the world would probably never think of."

"I see. But if one *doesn't* do mean, cruel things oneself, surely other people will stop doing them in time."

"Did you find that with the girls at your school?" he asked drily.

"No, that's just it. They didn't understand. They wouldn't leave me alone, sometimes, though I was quite happy by myself, and I wanted to leave them alone."

He smoked for some time in silence before he replied. He could well understand the jealousy which Nya would have inspired in her schoolfellows, and their longing to pierce through her aloofness, to drag her down to their own level of familiarity.

"I expect they disliked you a bit," he said, "because you didn't feel the way they did; you weren't impressed by the things that impressed them. Perhaps you weren't properly enthusiastic about the right things and the right people."

He smiled, but she wore a puzzled frown on her forehead which would not be dispelled.

They had both forgotten that they were sailing. Even Simon found his watch on the mainsheet was mechanical, and his occasional adjustment of the tiller when Nya allowed the yacht to run too much by the lee was more the preoccupied action of a man plunged in thought than the rebuke of an instructor. He brought the yacht nearer to the wind now, and she sailed apparently more swiftly, heeling over towards the wave-tops.

Nya awoke to the pressure on the tiller and was soon as absorbed in sailing as she had been in conversation. He noticed that her control of the yacht had improved since last time. For some reason it increased his respect for her to know that she might one day make a good yachtswoman.

It seemed a pity ever to stop talking to her, or watching her; his next opportunity might be snatched from him so easily. She was still a child, and several people, in one way or another, had control of her life. He was not one of them. If he had been, he would have made sure that she never felt his control, that she always remained the wild, free thing she seemed at this moment, with her face wrinkled against the blowing spray, and all her young muscles braced against the helm. In spite of himself he longed for some control over her life, some power to influence her decisions or, best of all, her impulses. But that needed an intimacy with her which he was hardly likely to achieve in one or two odd days of sailing. In so short a time he could scarcely even make a strong enough impression for her to remember him by, when subsequent events should crowd the memory out of her mind. Of course, as long as they both wished it, his relations with Nya need not cease. The bond between them was strong, considering how quickly and apparently casually it had been formed.

Ironically enough he was due to go away for a holiday this very evening. He was to sail *Puffin* round the coast to Essex, where he had arranged to go cruising with a friend. This meant being away for three weeks; it probably meant not seeing Nya for a much longer time, since she would have gone back to school by the time he returned. Would their friendship survive the separation?

His eyes had been fixed on the horizon, as if they had sought out the farthest possible point from Nya upon which to focus; but now they turned to meet her gaze. She was looking up at him with a mixture of enquiry and shyness.

"What's the matter?" she asked. "Are you wondering about something?"

"As a matter of fact I was. How did you know?"

"You looked sad."

"I think I was rather."

"Why?"

"If I said it was something to do with you?"

"With me?" Her eyes grew large with astonishment. "Am I making you sad? What have I done?"

"No, no. You've done nothing—except to be your attractive self."

"Oh, don't tease." There was more than a hint of wistfulness behind her laugh. "I know I'm not attractive. Every one tells me I look awful. Perhaps I shall improve, though, when I grow up."

"You *are* attractive," he said seriously. "The people who tell you you're awful are wrong. They don't know a good thing when they see it. I do; and that's why I'm sad."

He spoke in an even voice, without emotion, stating a fact as it appeared to him. Was he teasing her, as his words seemed to show? Or was he genuinely upset?

"I believe you're teasing me," she said. "But never mind about me. Why are you sad?"

There was no need to beat about the bush. Already it seemed to be tacitly agreed between them that only direct questions were allowed, and that for your direct question you were entitled to a direct answer.

"Because I've got to go away," he said.

"When?"

"I'd thought of starting to-night. The tide and wind are with me."

"Are you going in *Puffin*?"

"Yes."

"For how long?"

"About three weeks. That's as long as I get for my holiday."

Her eyelids flickered an instant, and she turned away her head. She forgot all about the tiller. Simon had to lean over surreptitiously and take it from her.

After a few moments she spoke, but still without looking round.

"I go back to school in three weeks," she said.

"I know," he replied. "I'm sorry."

"You'd thought of that?"

She turned to him now, and he saw that tears had welled into her eyes.

"I realized I shouldn't see you again until next summer," he explained.

He searched her face to try and read her thoughts, but, though her lip trembled once, he could not fathom the emotion which had caused it. Now, however, she seemed to make an effort to control herself, and in a level voice she said:

"I don't know if I shall be here next holidays. Daddy's coming home in May."

"Yes," he said, "you told me. I expect you'll be glad to see him."

"Yes, I shall. It's fun being with Daddy. He makes everything seem like a joke; you enjoy it at the time and then forget about it and go on to the next joke. It seems like years since I saw him, but it's only about five months."

She spoke fast, with scarcely a pause; her voice sounded forced, he thought. Was she trying to change the subject?

"I hope you'll be here in the summer. I want to see you very much."

"Oh, you're teasing again."

"No. I'm serious."

"I don't believe you any more."

"It's true all the same."

How could he be so cruel? His steady answers to her replies were like a brick wall that you couldn't get through, however hard you bashed it. She was hedged in by something that she couldn't fight against, something that made everything which a moment before had seemed gay and happy into a horrible nightmare. What *was* it that was hurting so much? Why did she want to cry? She wasn't going to cry of course. It would never do to cry in front of Simon. Not again. To-night, when she was alone, she would be able to cry, but not now. She must keep her tears back whatever happened. After all what was there to cry about? Simply that Simon had said he was going away? She had always known he would have to go away one day. Or else she would have to, and that came to the same thing. When you met somebody accidentally you parted from them just as accidentally. She had been out sailing with him twice—that was more than she had hoped for. A week ago she hadn't even known he existed. So why was she making such a fuss now? It was very silly of her. There was nothing hurting after all. That was imagination. And all the fun they had had together wasn't a nightmare. It was just fun. Now it was over; and that was that.

She forced herself to smile and looked at him.

"I hope you have a good holiday," she said. "How far are you going?"

He could feel the constraint in her voice.

"To Essex."

She flashed a smile at him. "Not to Gibraltar this time?"

"What do you know about Gibraltar?"

"I only know you went there once. Some men on the quay told me. All alone too, they said."

"That's not true. I went with my two friends. They're in India now."

"Those sailors said you were always alone."

"Since they left, yes."

"Do you want to be alone? Is that why you're going?"

"Oh, my dear," he said, "of course not. Did you think I wanted to get away from you?"

"I didn't know."

"Oh, but what an absurd thing to suppose."

He wedged one arm round the tiller and cleated the mainsheet. The yacht would have to look after herself for a moment or two.

"Come here. And look at me. Did you really think that?"

She nodded.

"You silly child. You're running yourself down again and we agreed we wouldn't do that, do you remember?"

"Yes."

"Well then. Don't you know by now that I like being with you. It's true we haven't known each other long, but there's been no need for that. We don't have to talk and talk and try each other out and be suspicious of each other like so many people are before we can be friends. You *must* feel that I like you better than anybody, and that I'm happy with you, don't you? You're such a sensitive person. I'm sure you must be able to feel that!"

He took her by her elbows and turned her towards him. She looked up at him, full of confidence, and there was a melting happiness in her eyes.

"I didn't dare to think you liked me," she said. "I thought perhaps you were being kind because you were sorry for me or something. And when you lent me this jersey and the shorts, I thought it amused you because I was a silly little girl. And, well, it did save my dress, so I was quite glad. And I have been happy sailing with you, honestly I have. I suppose it was stupid of me to be upset when you said you were going away."

There was a moment's silence while they looked at each other; then he drew her to him and held her against his breast. She put her head on his arm and stroked it

125

with her cheek. For a moment she stood quite still, then with another sigh, she disengaged her arm, and put it round his neck. How the yacht kept her course Simon didn't know. He had forgotten about *Puffin*. He saw and thought of nothing but Nya and the strange happiness that was welling up inside him. No one had ever put their arms round his neck before. How soft and small they were, her arms.

Shyly he caressed her hair with his lips, but he was afraid to kiss her, afraid almost to hold her too tightly lest she should take fright. Like a bird, or a squirrel or some timorous wild creature she looked, with the red glint of the sun in her hair; he gazed at her, his eyes not focusing, not seeing properly, careless of everything but that he held her in his arms. He sighed.

"Oh, Nya. Oh, little Nya."

And she lay still, leaning against him trustfully, perfectly happy now. There was an uncomfortable feeling somewhere in her body, at least not uncomfortable, really; in a way it was a delightful sensation, but disturbing. She wanted to be close to Simon. That was why she put her arm round his neck. That gave her a pleasant sensation too. She could feel his cheek with her wrist. She wanted to forget everything except the sun and the wind and the sea, and to stay for ever and ever close to Simon like this.

The yacht came up into the wind and lost way—and the canvas flogged and rattled now that the wind no longer filled it. He let *Puffin* drift. Everything—even his beloved ship—had ceased to exist. There was only Nya now: in his eyes, in his heart and filling all his consciousness.

She stirred and looked up at him. She was solemn and wide-eyed.

"What are you thinking about?" he asked. "Those wrinkles on your forehead, what are they for?"

"Are there wrinkles?"

He nodded. "Deep ones."

She sighed and rubbed her head against his shoulder. "I don't know!"

He could tell that she wasn't really thinking of what she said. Her mind was on something else.

"Don't you know?"

"No!"

He smiled again. What a momentous exchange of words! What did they amount to? Nothing. Because, of course, there was nothing to say, he realized. And again they were silent, until she said:

"We're not sailing any more."

But he was gazing at her fixedly, and his fingers touched the curls on the back of her neck. He didn't seem to have heard her. After a few moments she spoke again.

"Simon."

It was the first time she had ever used his name when addressing him, although he had been Simon in her thoughts ever since the morning in the hotel. She had been shy of letting the word pass her lips, but now all diffidence was gone.

"Simon, why are you going away?"

He answered deliberately, as if he were himself searching for the reason.

"Partly because I had arranged to, before I met you, and I didn't want to let a friend of mine down. He's been counting on it for some time. He saved up his last holiday you know—so that he could come away for three weeks, instead of taking ten days at a time. And then, I thought perhaps it would be better for you not to see me for a bit."

"Why?"

"Well. Perhaps it would be better for both of us. We haven't known each other long—ours is a strange friendship, isn't it? I thought perhaps if I went away and you didn't see me for some time you would be able to forget me if you wanted to."

She stood up now.

"Why should I want to?"

"Well—not *want* to. But perhaps you ought to?"

"But why? I don't understand. Do you want to forget me?"

"No. At first I thought I ought to, too."

"I don't understand that either."

He laughed, and putting his arm round her waist drew her towards him again. She leaned against his knee.

"You wouldn't," he said. "You're too good and too guileless to understand that."

"What's guileless?"

"The opposite of shrewd and calculating."

"Oh."

"You see," he began, hesitating in his choice of words, "the world—people, your aunt for instance—would think it was wrong for us to be too close friends. They would say that you were too young, or that I was wicked, or something of the sort. But you can't be too young to be friends with somebody. And I'm not too wicked to be friends with you. So I should like our friendship to continue."

"So would I."

But all the same, it will never be really easy. People will try to prevent us from being together—even like this, in the old *Puffin*."

"Why should they?"

"I'm not quite sure. Probably because most of them think the worst of other people. Anyhow they *would* try to prevent us, you can be certain of that. Even your father, probably. Unless he's a quite exceptional man, he would never hear of us being together for long."

"Daddy'd like you, I know."

"He might. But there again, there's something that you probably haven't thought of. It's a kind of jealousy. After all you're his only daughter—his only child now. He might feel I was taking you away from him."

They were silent. She pondered what he had just said, absent-mindedly running her fingers along the cable-stitching of his jersey.

"Well," he said, at last. "Now I've told you why I am going away. It's easier for me of course. But you live with your aunt, and that makes it hard for you. You don't want to make the situation at home too difficult for yourself. Of course I can go and see your aunt if you like——"

"Oh no, don't. You wouldn't like her," she interposed quickly.

"How do you know? We might get on very well. I'm sure she's not as bad as you make out."

"No, she's all right. But I'd rather keep you separate."

"Very well, then."

The flapping of the sails obtruded itself on his consciousness at last and he brought the yacht away from the wind.

"We'd better be making for home," he said.

"Yes. So as not to upset *Aunt Ethel*."

She made a grimace.

"Aunt Ethel defeats us at every turn."

She came and sat beside him. If she was to lose him so soon she felt she must keep as close to him as possible while he was still there. She was sad that he had to go; but she was more certain now that she would see him again. It was only the prospect of living out the dreary interval that filled her with misery. It was just like parting from Daddy all over again. Oh well—it was simply another of those necessary and unpleasant injustices of life. She was getting used to them by now. Everything that began well seemed to turn sour before you finished with it.

He was watching her narrowly. "Unhappy?"

"No," she said, listlessly. "If you say you've got to go, then you've got to and that's that. Oh, but I shall miss you."

"And I you."

"Will you? Can I write to you?"

Her eyes grew bright again. The pain of the moment was already half dulled by anticipation of the future.

"I'd love it if you did," he said. "I'll be calling for letters at one or two places. I'll give you the addresses."

"I'll write every day till I go back to school. Then I shall only be able to write once a week, I expect."

"When do you go back?"

"On the first of May. It's a Tuesday."

"Not till then? By Jove! And I get back, I hope, on the Sunday before."

"Shan't I see you at all before I go back?"

He looked at her.

"Nya dear, it's hard for me to say. I want to do what's best for you. But you're so very young. You may, you probably will, change your mind so often in the next few years. You may change it about me."

"Oh no, I won't."

"You never know. It may be something over which you have no control. You won't be able to help yourself.

You'll be growing up, and one changes all the time when one's growing. You've got to reckon with that."

"I couldn't change it, no, no, I'm sure I never would."

"I hope not, Nya. I should be wretched if you did. You see, I'm thinking of myself too; if I build all my hopes upon your not changing your mind and then you do change it, I shall feel that the bottom has been knocked out of everything. So I want to go away and think about it quietly by myself for a bit, if only to be quite sure that it's a wise thing for us to be friends for always. Because that's what I'd like to happen above everything."

She clung to him, and buried her face in his shoulder.

"Oh, Simon, dear darling Simon. I want to be with you. Don't send me away."

"Listen, little girl, do one thing for me! Will you?"

"Yes."

"It's this. Let me go on my holiday, because I told my friend I'd go with him. And while I'm away think about all we've said. Don't even write to me unless you want to. And when I come back, we'll meet once more, by hook or by crook, before you go back to school. Shall we? Then everything will have straightened itself out in my muddled head and it'll be plain sailing."

She laughed through the tears that had so nearly come, and looked at him.

"All right. But you will write to me once, just once, won't you?"

"Yes, Nya, I will."

For most of the way back to the harbour Nya sat with her head in his lap. When they turned the yacht into the wind she took over the jib-sheets automatically, but whenever possible she kept her eyes fixed on him. His impending departure didn't seem so dreadful any longer.

She and Simon were engaged upon a kind of adventure, and if he had to go away alone for a time it was only to keep his vigil like one of the knights of old. He would return, strengthened in mind and courage, and they would resume the adventure together.

15

A contrary wind made progress slow along the channel, so they started the engine. He was anxious to lay in some stores that evening before starting, and it was late.

"She's ready provisioned for practically any emergency," he said, "except for things like butter and milk. But there are still some things I've got to get. I can get those best up in Poole, so if you don't mind I'll drop you at Sandbanks as we pass and then go on up the harbour."

She nodded, too miserable now even to reply.

"Don't be angry with me for going away. It's breaking my heart."

She had scarcely said a word on the way back, and he had soon given up trying to make her talk. He didn't feel like talking himself. How absurd to be so upset by this parting when he had only known her for a week.

"You will come back, won't you? Say you will."

"Yes, Nya, I will."

She took his hand and pressed it to her cheek. She was not at all embarrassed with him now, and almost all her inhibitions with regard to physical contact were gone. It was wonderful to him to hold her hand, to feel its lithe young fingers grasp his own. There was a strength in them which appealed to him. They seemed to be expressive of herself. They were delicate and tender and firm. It was disturbing, too, to feel her body against him; young though it was, it was almost mature in its power to arouse his passion. It beat so vigorously with passion itself, even though that passion was still mute and incoherent. He thought of her with tenderness and a kind of whimsical affection rather than with passion; but he was no longer afraid to let his feelings for her control his actions. As long as he kept her confidence in him, as long as he subordinated his feelings to her peace of mind, no harm could possibly come to her through him. He was in love with her—he might as well admit it.

"Is it wrong of me to want to be with you?" she said. "You must tell me if it is. I shan't mind. You know all about it and I trust you."

"Of course it's not wrong, Nya."

"But you think people will try to keep me away from you, even Daddy you said."

He could feel the anxious decision behind her question. Smiling, he shook her by the shoulder.

"Still doubting me?" he said.

She hung her head.

"No," she said in a small voice. "Not really. I only think it's strange that you should like me."

"It isn't strange. It's natural. It's the best and most natural thing I've ever done."

"Do you really think it's natural?"

"Well—perhaps not as other people see it. To me it is. It's a question of instinct. One ought to be ruled by one's instinct in all difficult and important questions."

"Yes, I think so too. At least, I *did*. But at school it

134

always came out wrong. I don't know why. And now I'm afraid to trust my feeling any more."

"Poor little Nya. Have they ruined your confidence in yourself?"

"Well, about some things. Not about you. Only it's all so difficult because if I trust to my feelings about you they make me want to hold you tight so that you can't go away. And I expect that's wrong."

"No, Nya. That's right. You must hold tight to the certainty that you and I are friends. As long as you trust me and believe that, I'm not afraid that anybody will spoil our friendship."

16

There was not much to be stowed away for Simon was sailing again at nine o'clock that night. Nya still had to change. It was an excuse for staying on board a moment longer and she welcomed it.

"I tremble to think what your Aunt Ethel would say if she saw you in those clothes."

"That's just what I was thinking."

She dived into the cabin, and he sat and waited for her. He heard a muffled thud from inside, and a yell.

"Ow," said Nya's voice in evident pain. "Bother that beam. I hit my head on it."

"Oh, you'll do that lots of times yet before you get the knack of avoiding it," he announced cheerfully. "You wait till you have to eat and sleep and practically live in the cabin, *and* in a heavy sea when you get thrown about all the time. You can get a head the size of a pumpkin in a couple of hours."

"When will that be?" she shouted, still in agony.

Three days ago—even yesterday—that question might have nonplussed him. But so much had happened during this short afternoon to change his attitude that he found himself now actually answering it with pleasure.

"Very soon, let's hope."

"It would be worth having a head like a pumpkin."

In a few moments she emerged, clad again in her yellow dress. She looked sweet, he thought, demure, and lovable. The dress certainly became her. It made her seem a little older—seventeen perhaps. Her hair was dishevelled by the wind, and her face was flushed with the exertion of dressing in the cramped cabin.

"I put your sweater and shorts back on the fo'c'sle bunk."

"Thank you."

She stood beside him, smiling. He looked at her for a long time, his eyes taking in every feature, every part of her until she grew embarrassed.

"Do I look awful?" she asked.

"You look lovely," he said. "Much nicer than in my shorts. They don't fit you quite so well as your dress."

"I got the dress specially for you."

He took her by both hands. "It's a lovely dress," he said. "In fact, you're altogether a lovely little girl."

"I wish I were."

"You are! You mustn't be ashamed to admit it. It's not a crime."

"Not if you say so."

They were silent for nearly a minute.

"Well," he said at last. "I'm afraid we ought to go."

"Yes. I suppose so."

"May I say good-bye to you now," he said, "instead of over there, where there'll be lots of people."

She looked at him, her eyes grown wide with sorrow. A moment she hesitated, then flung herself on to her knees beside him and buried her face in his arms.

"Oh Simon, dear beloved Simon," she said, "I do love you." And each of these words that she had never

137

used before, except in her inmost thoughts, was like a prayer, fervent and adoring.

He clasped her to him. The pain of listening to her was more than he could bear. He closed his eyes. For an instant nothing existed for him, nothing, no sight, no sense but that of hearing, no feeling but that rapturous pain in his heart.

She began to sob. He could do nothing to comfort her. It seemed that even his powers of thought and movement were bewitched. For the moment her pain made less impression on him than his own. But yet her weeping persisted, and by slow degrees, as if waking from a dream, he became aware of it. Was she not calling to him again as she had called once before, asking him for his love with her sobs? But she had it, his love! It was hers utterly, not one particle of it stinted. Didn't she understand that it was hers, that he was hers already? What did their ages matter, or the fact that they had only known each other for a week, or even that he was going away from her for a while? Surely she knew that in their love was neither age, nor time, nor space, nor separation.

But no! How could she know this? He had not known it himself an hour ago. He awoke from his trance now and lifted her up. She hid her face and would not meet his gaze. He turned her head towards him. Her eyes were swollen in her pale cheeks, but he saw only the lustrous beauty of their glance.

"Little Nya," he whispered, "dearest little girl. I'm not going away from you, but from my own cowardice. I wanted to make up my mind. I also wanted you to make up yours. I don't believe now, that either of us needs to do that any more. But I must abide by my original intention for the sake of my friend. Only, you must understand, that even if I go a thousand miles away, I'm still here with you. I'm still your Simon. I shall be unchanged till I come back. You must promise me to remember that or else I'll be afraid to go away."

Her sobs grew quieter and she wiped away her tears with the palm of her hand.

"Yes," she said, "I'll remember."

"Look here." He got up, and still holding her with one hand, opened the cabin door with the other, and rummaged in the table drawer, and pulled out a pencil and some paper.

"I'll give you my addresses, and you must give me yours. And will you write to me and tell me that you've not forgotten?"

She nodded.

When they were ready to go he untied the dinghy painter and gave her his hand to help her into the boat. She held it for a second. He drew her to him and hugged her, trying to make it a friendly, encouraging gesture and no more.

"All right now?"

"Yes."

"And you won't forget me?"

"Never."

"As soon as I'm back I'll let you know, and we can see each other once more before you go back to school. Say in about three weeks' time."

"I hope they pass quickly."

"So do I."

There was nothing more to say, and they were silent until they reached the jetty. But Nya occasionally looked up at him, and when he caught her eye he smiled. She smiled too. Her mind was at peace.

On the landing-stage under the jetty, where nobody

could see them, she rested her head against his breast for a second. Then she looked up at him.

"Good-bye, Simon. Come back soon."

She kissed him on the cheek, waited an instant, then climbed the steps and went. At the turning she looked back and waved. He waved in answer. Then she disappeared.

END OF PART I

PART II: RECOIL

17

When she turned in at the gate of "The Rising" her heart sank, for the car was in the drive. Aunt Ethel was back. That meant almost certain discovery. She wondered whether it would be wiser to try and go in the back way, letting Emily into her confidence, or to risk getting through the front hall unseen. She decided on the front door. If there was to be a row it was better to have a straightforward one. She must brazen things out and not admit that she was guilty. And to enter by the kitchen, a thing she never did, was as good as a confession of guilt.

She opened the front door cautiously. Aunt Ethel's gloves and hat were on the bench inside; that meant she was somewhere about, for as a rule she took them straight up to her room. Nya peered into the hall as she shut the front door. There was no one there.

There remained only the stairs to be negotiated. She was up them in a flash and had reached the door of her room and was all but safe, when she saw that the door of the bathroom was open and Aunt Ethel was in there washing her hands. Before she could slip into her room Aunt Ethel looked up.

"Hullo, dear."

"Hullo, Aunt Ethel," Nya stood rooted to the spot. To go away abruptly just as Aunt Ethel spoke would raise her suspicion at once. It was very dark in the passage, the only light came from the bathroom. It was just possible that Aunt Ethel wouldn't notice the dress. Not that Nya had much hope that it would escape her. This was a matter of luck, and luck was a queer thing that had lately played her some scurvy tricks.

Her fears were justified for, Aunt Ethel said: "Come and tell me what you've been doing." Nya was speechless. It would be fatal to go into the bathroom into the full light. With an effort she blurted out:

"Just a second, Aunt, I've got to——" and darted into her room. There would be just time to change, perhaps, before Aunt Ethel came in, as she would be bound to do.

In point of fact Aunt Ethel was not in the least suspicious. She smiled tolerantly to herself, thinking what a jack-in-the-box Nya was—she was never anywhere for more than an instant, if you saw her upstairs one moment it would be safest to expect to find her in the garden the next. She thought she would finish drying her hands in the child's room. It would be a good chance to talk to her. Nya was very difficult to talk to, always reserved, even a bit abrupt. Perhaps in her own room she would feel more confident.

Fortunately for Nya Aunt Ethel stopped for a moment to tighten up the hot tap, which was leaking.

"I must tell Nicholas to see to it," she thought. Then she put out the light and went into Nya's room. Nya was just getting into her gym dress. She had thrust the yellow frock into the cupboard. She would hang it up properly later on, she thought, when Aunt Ethel was out of the way.

"Changing already, dear. Dinner's not till eight, you know, and it's only just after six."

In a flash it occurred to Nya that she was supposed to have been in her gym dress all day, and that therefore she should be getting out of it now instead of into it. She began to take it off again.

"I know, Aunt, but I thought it would be nicer to change now, and then I could read till dinner-time."

"I see. What are you going to put on? The Mandevilles are coming in after dinner to play bridge. You must look as nice as you can."

An awful sense of impending disaster sent Nya's heart cold. What complications might not the visit of the Mandevilles bring about? At that moment she hated the Mandevilles with all her heart.

"Why?" she asked.

How strange the child was!

"Why? Because one ought to look nice when people come in for the evening."

"Are *you* going to change?" Nya asked brusquely.

"Of course, dear."

"Oh. Well, could I please wear my white dress? It's quite nice."

"I thought you didn't like it much?"

"Oh yes—I do."

Aunt Ethel was puzzled and a little hurt by Nya's attitude. She had prepared a pleasant surprise for Nya in her mind; also she had hoped to find the child a little more forthcoming, for she was full of benignity herself. She always presupposed her own moods in other people. Now that she was disposed to be kind and even playful it irritated her to find Nya unresponsive. Not having children of her own had rusted the mechanism of her affections, which worked by fits and starts, sometimes too fast and sometimes not at all; and at the moment it was working at full speed.

"I thought perhaps you'd like to wear your yellow dress, your new one," she suggested quietly.

To her astonishment this met with no response from Nya. "I think I'd better wear the white one. The yellow one's not so suitable for the evening really, is it?"

"That's true," said Aunt Ethel perplexedly, "but I don't think that matters much. You look very nice in it."

"I'd rather wear the white one, Aunt Ethel."

"Why, good gracious, what a funny child you are. I thought you were longing to wear your new dress. In fact you asked me when we bought it on Thursday if you could wear it to-day. Why don't you bring it out and look at it once more. I'm sure you'll change your mind if you do so."

This cat and mouse game was getting on Nya's nerves.

"No, I'd rather not, Aunt Ethel."

"Very well."

Hurt and bewildered Aunt Ethel turned to go, but at the door she stopped.

"Nya."

"Yes, Aunt Ethel."

"You're behaving very strangely, you know. A girl of your age ought to know better. You ought to realize that you must do what I tell you even if you don't agree with it. I should have thought the mere fact that I am your aunt, and in charge of you, would have been enough to ensure your obedience. Of course, I don't like to command you, but——"

She paused, waiting for some sign from Nya. But Nya was both tired and nervous by now, and Aunt Ethel's lofty manner only made her angry. Since this afternoon she was no longer afraid of what Aunt Ethel could do to her. At that moment she was feeling more forlorn than ever in her life before; but at least she no longer felt like a small girl, and she resented very much being treated like one. Something had happened to her out there on the sea with Simon. It seemed as if she had grown up in the course of a single afternoon.

"Please don't bully me, Aunt Ethel."

There was a long silence. Aunt Ethel's chin went up and her back stiffened. Her face grew pale beneath her freckles, there was a parched dryness in her throat. For a moment she could think of nothing to say. Nya sat down on her bed, with her back to Aunt Ethel, waiting for the storm to break. She was still trembling from the effort to control herself, and its sudden failure. She wasn't sorry she had flashed out at Aunt Ethel like that; she was glad. Whatever was the result of this particular lapse Nya hoped it would establish more satisfactory relations between them for the future. She didn't mind hating anybody, even her own aunt. If you hated someone you knew where you were with them. It was more satisfactory, at any rate, than keeping up the appearance of friendliness when you disliked them in your heart. She found she did dislike Aunt Ethel. She had disliked her for some time, ever since she had told her not to play with the "street boys". Aunt Ethel had been right, as it turned out, they were not very nice boys, really. But that was no credit to Aunt Ethel since she had never met them. And it didn't make Nya dislike her less. There was a kind of pleasure in disliking your aunt. People always tried to pretend that you should love all your relations. Aunt Ethel evidently thought so too. They were wrong. A great many things proved that they were wrong—books, and the experiences of girls at school, and the case of Aunt Ethel herself.

The power of speech returned to Aunt Ethel. In a hard voice she said: "Nya."

There was no answer, no sign from the half-dressed figure on the bed. The very set of the child's back was obstinate and insulting. Aunt Ethel spoke again.

"Will you listen to me?"

Nya took a deep breath.

"Yes, Aunt Ethel."

"You're a very wicked little girl, and rude and inconsiderate and ungrateful as well. You ought to be whipped for speaking to me like that. I've noticed your strange manner these holidays and it's hurt me more than I can say. I don't know whether it's the effect St. Monica's is having on you. I should hardly think so. I shall write to Miss Littlewood and ask her. She's a very estimable woman and will, I am sure, understand how it worries me that you're not like other little girls of your own age. If I weren't reluctant to accuse you of it I should say you suffered from one of the wickedest sins of all that a child like you can commit—the sin of pride and of setting yourself up above your elders. Fortunately that can be corrected. Miss Littlewood will know how to set about it. And in the meantime I shall do the best I can to help her."

She paused for a moment to observe the effect she was having. Nya never moved from her position. To all appearances she hadn't heard a word Aunt Ethel had been saying.

But Nya had heard. With growing bitterness she listened while Aunt Ethel revealed the workings of her mind. Not only of hers, but of Miss Littlewood's also. It appeared that the two women were in league against her in an attempt to cure her of the "wickedest sin she could commit". And Nya, who foresaw, firstly, three

148

weeks of quarrelling with Aunt Ethel without even the solace of seeing Simon, and after that a term at school fighting Miss Littlewood's corrective discipline, was ready to burst into tears; it was only Aunt Ethel's unrelenting attitude that saved her. As long as there was a fight to be fought tears were out of place. But she felt a sick longing to run out of the room and down to the harbour to try and catch Simon before he left.

"I think, too," Aunt Ethel continued remorselessly, "that I shall take away that pretty dress from you since you are so reluctant to wear it. I shall keep it until you learn to be a little more respectful. Where is it?"

This was the end of everything. Aunt Ethel would find the dress in a crumpled heap in the cupboard, there would be questions and the whole story about Simon would have to be told.

"Oh God, please God, couldn't the house be struck by lightning so that Aunt Ethel doesn't find out about Simon!"

She got up from the bed. Her limbs would scarcely move and her heart was as heavy as lead. She went to the cupboard and took out the dress, just as it was, crumpled, anyhow.

"Bring it to me," said Aunt Ethel who had not moved from the door.

Without a word Nya handed it to her. She made no attempt to straighten its folds or to disguise the way in which she had thrown it down a few minutes before.

"So that's the way you treat your beautiful new dress? You throw it into the cupboard anyhow, without bothering whether it gets crumpled or not." She smoothed it out and began to fold it up. Nya watched listlessly. It was the last glimpse of her favourite dress—Simon's dress she called it now—that she would have for a very long time. Oh well—what did it matter since Simon himself had gone away?

"And what's this?" Aunt Ethel's eagle eye detected a stain on the skirt. "There's a mark here. That can't have been there when we tried it on. I do believe it's dirt." She looked up sharply. "Have you been wearing this dress?"

"Yes. I had it on all this afternoon."

"Ah." There was triumph in that grim nodding of her head. "Now I understand. Where have you been in it? What have you been doing?"

But Aunt Ethel asked in vain. Nothing but torture would have extracted the truth from Nya, not even the pleasure there would have been in horrifying Aunt Ethel still further.

"I just went out."

"Well, I shan't waste time now on finding out how you soiled your dress," she said. "I've got a committee meeting at half-past six. It's quite enough that you put it on without my consent. You will go to bed now as a punishment. Without supper."

She went out and, as she was about to shut the door behind her, she turned once more. "I shall have to tell your father about this, of course. It really is most dishonest of you. I don't think even he will deny that."

The door shut with a click and Nya was alone.

18

So Daddy was to be dragged into the league too! Aunt Ethel hadn't the slightest understanding of the real situation, she would be bound to explain it in terms of the way it affected her; and poor Daddy thousands of miles away wouldn't know what to think, and would probably end up by believing her. Unless, of course, Nya wrote to him herself. But there was very little she could say—in a way Aunt Ethel's attitude was perfectly justified. She had disobeyed orders, but it wasn't possible to explain why without mentioning Simon, and that she wanted to avoid.

Perhaps it was unreasonable of her not to tell them about Simon, but her instinct in this matter was peculiarly strong. She loved him, and when she was with him she felt the world was a perfect place and she had a right to her share of it; when she was away from him, with these other people, she wasn't at all certain that this was so. If, then, Aunt Ethel and possibly even Daddy, as Simon believed, would think it was wrong for her to be with him, to tell them about him now would involve her in a sort of confession, and that would lead ultimately to "repentance" and a condescending forgiveness from

Aunt Ethel. All would then be peaceful again at "The Rising"; but she would never be able to face Simon again, even if she were allowed to see him, which was hardly likely. That was the worst of being so young. You got sat on at school and harassed at home, and when you met somebody like Simon who was unique and wonderful, all sorts of difficulties were put in your way to make it hard for you to see him. It would be easy enough if you were willing to accept other people's standards; he could come and see her at "The Rising", and Aunt Ethel would occasionally allow her to go out sailing with him. But that would be no fun. It would be like having even your pleasure doled out to you on a plate. After a few days Simon would get sick of it, because he would see that she was exactly like any other little girl.

Nya undressed and got into bed. It was hard to have to go without supper after an afternoon's sailing and no tea, but she supposed it could be done. After all, mountain climbers and sailors and travellers in deserts often went without food for days. The very thought of food made her feel hungry; she must read some absorbing book to keep her thoughts occupied. She decided to re-read *Kim* for the third time. That was exciting and full of fascinating people.

She made several starts, but found her mind wandering off to the events of the afternoon. She recalled it as firmly as she could, and at last became engrossed in the book. After all it was no use thinking: there was nothing she could do. Simon had gone, Aunt Ethel was angry, her dress had been taken away and she had been sent to bed, without supper, too. That was that.

She heard Aunt Ethel come back from her meeting and put the car away, and come up to her room. Then

Uncle Nick came up. She could hear their voices across the passage; the door of Aunt Ethel's room was open. They were changing for dinner; Uncle Nick wandered along the passage from his room to the bathroom and back. When he passed Aunt Ethel's door, which was almost opposite Nya's, he would throw in a remark, or else answer one of Aunt Ethel's. Often quite a long time elapsed between her questions and his answers. Aunt Ethel didn't say very much but he was evidently in a talkative mood.

"Awful bore, old Mandeville, isn't he? Pretty wife, though. Damned good bridge player, too."

"Who?" asked Aunt Ethel. "He or his wife?"

Four or five minutes later came the reply: "Both I think. Don't you? He's not so good at contract of course. They say women make the best contract players. Wonder why. Because it's a sly, low-down game, I expect."

"Most people seem to think the men are better at it."

"Ah, I expect the women think that."

"Perhaps."

Presently Uncle Nick stopped outside Nya's door. He must have been putting on his braces, for she heard them flick on the panel of the door as he threw them over his shoulders. This had happened before. She supposed Uncle Nick preferred this part of the passage for putting on his braces. Perhaps the noise he made on the door reminded him of the occupant of the room for he asked:

"Where's the brown-faced brat?"

It was what he called her when he was feeling jovial; Nya felt a little pang of pleasure. Uncle Nick was kindly disposed towards her at any rate. Not that she imagined his mood would be of any practical value; he was too much under Aunt Ethel's thumb to remonstrate effectually with her. Still, it was comforting.

Aunt Ethel evidently answered his question by gesture, for there was no audible reply, but a moment later Nya heard the click of a door and guessed that he was being told the story of her sins. She thought she heard him expostulate once, but after that the voices were silent.

She took up her book again. Presently the gong rang. She looked at her watch. It had been Mummy's watch. Daddy had given it to her before they left for Beira. It was her most precious possession. She only wore it on special occasions; the rest of the time it spent in the top drawer in her chest of drawers. It was eight o'clock. She heard Aunt Ethel come out of her room and go down to dinner. Two minutes later she heard from the hall:

"Nicholas, are you ready?"

"Just coming," said Uncle Nick from his dressing-room. "You start in."

There was a stealthy knock on the door. She jumped, and the book fell out of her hands. The knock was repeated quickly.

"Come in," she said, with surprise.

Uncle Nick came into the room on tiptoe. She looked up at him uncertain whether to smile or pout. He put his fingers to his lips.

"Sh!" he whispered. Then he came and sat on her bed. He had his dinner jacket on. It made him look rather like Daddy again. "You bad girl," he said. "What have you been doing?"

He spoke in a friendly way, without a trace of reproach. She answered with a touch of bravado.

"I've been a damned young nuisance, Uncle."

He grinned.

"So I gather. And there's no supper for you to-night, eh?"

"No."

"Hungry?"

"Terribly."

He fished in his pockets and brought out two apples, and a biscuit.

"Rations for the troops," he said. "An army marches on its stomach, you know. It's bad policy to starve 'em, even in jug. Two apples from my bedside; one biscuit from your Aunt Ethel's. I didn't like to take more in case she noticed."

"Oh, Uncle, you're a brick."

"Will they do?"

"They're lovely. Thank you ever so much."

"Well—I must go down. So long. I wouldn't do it again, though, whatever it is you did do."

"I won't. I promise."

He smiled, nodded at her and stole out again, well pleased. He would bet his favourite old shoes she wouldn't do it again; and that would prove that Tom and Mabel's method was right after all. Interesting that. One day he would write a book about how to bring up children.

Whistling nonchalantly he entered the dining-room. Emily was serving the soup. She stopped uncertainly at Nya's place and looked at her mistress.

"Miss Nya won't be coming down to dinner," Aunt Ethel said. "I've sent her to bed. She's to have no supper. Nothing at all, Emily, you understand?" She fixed Emily with her eye.

"Yes, madam."

Uncle Nick ran his finger round the inside of his collar and then adjusted his black tie. He was trying not to smile.

The Mandevilles arrived at a quarter to nine. Nya

heard their car, and a moment later the loud voice of
Mr. Mandeville as Emily showed them into the drawing-
room. There was a murmur of voices for a few minutes,
then a hush fell over the house as they settled down to
bridge. Nya was half-way through *Kim* by now. She
wondered whether to read on to her favourite part
where Kim meets the woman from Shamlegh, high up
in the snows of the Himalayas, or to put the book away
and go to sleep. She counted the pages, and, reckoning
that it would take her nearly an hour to read so far,
decided to go to sleep. She put out the light and lay
down.

She was tired enough; but there was so much to think
about. She had lived a whole lifetime since this morning.
She was no longer even the same person as she had been
when she got up. She had to try and catch up with herself, so to speak. She had to re-live every moment of the
day before she felt that it truly belonged to her. Then
there was Simon. She tried not to think about him
because she knew her self-control might break down if
she did. And just at the moment there was an awful lot
that demanded self-control. She had to think, for instance, what she would say to Aunt Ethel in the morning
about her dress. Should she tell her the truth, or part of
the truth, rather? Or should she invent a lie and brazen
it out? Instinctively she decided on the latter. All that
was left to her now was Simon. She wasn't going to risk
Aunt Ethel finding out about him too. That would be
dreadful. Aunt Ethel would stop her seeing him and her
last hope would be gone. Whereas at the moment she
could still look forward to seeing him once again before
the term started.

Well, what *was* she going to say to Aunt Ethel? It
would be better to have a definite lie to tell, since one

had to be told; people saw through vague excuses too easily. She could always say she had been out with the "street boys" again, although she hadn't seen them for some days. They had come to the garden fence to arrange an expedition as usual, the day after their trip to Southampton, and Nya had made an excuse to get out of accompanying them. She was going to Bournemouth with her aunt to shop, she said. That was the day when Simon had given her coffee in the hotel. She wasn't feeling at all like going with the boys. She only wanted to think of Simon.

The next day they came again, and again she made an excuse. She said she wasn't feeling well. The boys refused to accept this. They were already suspicious of her because of her behaviour on the Shell Bay expedition; and an excuse like hers carried no weight.

"Yah, feeling ill!"

"You look perfectly all right!"

This made her angry.

"I don't care if I do. I don't want to come and that's that."

They departed after that, hurling abuse at her.

"Stuck-up, that's what she is."

"Got all grand after a term at St. Monica's!" And she hadn't seen them since.

Perhaps she *was* stuck-up. Perhaps after all they were justified in classing her with Aunt Ethel. It was worrying because when she told Daddy about the boys in the first place, he said one should choose one's own friends and not listen to other people. And now she couldn't help admitting that Aunt Ethel had been right. How complicated life was becoming. Even friendship and loyalty didn't seem to be straightforward any longer. All because she had met Simon.

"Oh, it's no use." She turned over restlessly. "I keep on coming back to Simon. I think I'd better read for a bit longer. It might send me to sleep."

She longed to let her mind dwell upon him and upon the scene in *Puffin* this afternoon. After all there had been some pleasure in it too, it had not been all unhappiness. He had put his arms round her and she had lain quite close to him. She had heard his heart beating. How funny to find that one really could hear people's hearts beating! She had thought that was one of the things they put in books that wasn't really true, but that "represented" something: Daddy said they were called clichés. He had read her bits of Bernard Shaw, because he said Bernard Shaw never used clichés. She wondered if Bernard Shaw had ever heard anybody's heart beating as she had heard Simon's.

Simon had stroked the back of her neck. It had made her shiver and grow warm all at once. It was a strange and pleasant feeling, though at times she thought there was a kind of pain mixed up in it.

How far had Simon got by now? He was going to Essex, he said. That must be a long way to go by sea. She wondered if he had passed the Isle of Wight yet. He would be out there all alone in the dark. How did one sail in the dark? With a compass, but it was difficult to guess quite how. He would have the stars to guide him. Instinctively she looked out of the window to make certain; to her relief the stars were there. She could see one or two above the fir-trees. By leaning out of bed and putting one hand on the floor she thought she could make out Cassiopeia's Chair, but you couldn't be certain without going to the window and looking out. Anyhow the friendly stars were looking after Simon.

"Please God make him arrive safely and make me see him again."

Aunt Ethel said there was a God, but she made him seem a very odd person. She got him all mixed up with Jesus Christ, who Daddy said was quite different. He was a wonderful man, but still, not quite like God. Nya often meant to ask Daddy what the real facts were. Daddy would be coming home soon. That was a good thing. She wanted to see him again so much. Perhaps he would understand about Simon. Yes, she was sure he would.

She began to fall asleep. Suddenly she thought she heard a knock. She listened. Yes, there it was again, and a voice outside her door said in a whisper:

"Miss Nya, are you awake?"

"Yes." She answered. "Is that you, Emily?"

Emily came into the room, leaving the door ajar.

"Wait. I'll switch on the light," said Nya.

"No, better not, Miss. Your aunt might see it from the drawing-room. I brought you some sandwiches. I thought perhaps you might be hungry seeing as how you'd had no supper nor no tea neither."

"Oh, Emily, you're a saint."

"Here they are, Miss."

She thrust a plate towards Nya in the dark. "I'd better take back the plate though. Maggie might miss it in the morning. Sorry I'm so late, Miss, I 'ad to wait till she'd gone."

"You darling." Nya spoke with her mouth full.

"They're only potted meat. I didn't dare take the chicken that was left over from dinner. But p'raps you'll 'ave it cold to-morrow, so you won't have missed it. I 'ope they're all right, Miss."

"They're scrumptious."

"Now I'd better go up to bed. Hope you'll sleep all right, Miss."

Emily groped her way to the door. "Good night, Miss."

"Good night, Emily. Thank you very much."

Nya turned on the light. Five sandwiches! Emily was a brick. Emily and Uncle! She had two friends in the house at any rate. That was a most encouraging thought.

She decided to read while she ate and then put the light out. But long after the last sandwich had been savoured crumb by crumb and finally swallowed her light was still on. It was still on when Aunt Ethel and Uncle Nick went to bed. They saw the light under the door, as they came up the stairs. They had never known her to be awake at this hour. Wavering between remorse and displeasure Aunt Ethel went into the room and Uncle Nick followed close behind. Nya had fallen asleep. Her face was in shadow, but the lamp lit up her tousled hair. She was breathing regularly; her uncle wondered if there was a smile playing about her lips, or if it was simply a trick of the light. She had evidently been reading when she fell asleep. An open book lay on her breast, rising and falling as she breathed. He leaned over to see what it was. It was *Kim*. Gently he picked it up and looked at it. It was open at a picture of the "Woman of Shamlegh". He closed it and laid it on the table.

"She looks rather sweet," he whispered. "I wish she were my kid."

"You'd find her a handful."

"Oh yes. She's got plenty of guts."

"You'd spoil her, I can see."

" 'Fraid I should."

"I wish I hadn't had to punish her. But I don't think I shall need to do it again."

"I'm sure you won't."

She would have liked to fondle Nya's curls, but she was afraid of waking her. Instead she made a clumsy attempt to pat the eiderdown near Nya's hand. Nicholas understood and smiled.

"Don't you worry, old girl," he said. "She needs to get used to us, that's all."

His wife leaned her head on his shoulder for a moment. Then they turned out the light and tiptoed out of the room.

19

Somewhere off the Isle of Wight *Puffin* scudded over the blue-black waters. Above her shone the same stars that were even now looking down at Nya as she slept. Simon waved them a greeting with his pipe-stem. They were friendly things. It was comforting to see them twinkling up there, keeping a watch on his course. They never changed and yet they seemed to sympathize with all one's moods. The weather was perfect for night sailing—clear, with a steady following wind and not too rough a sea. There was nothing to do but to sit at the helm and keep *Puffin* steady on her course. She needed little attention. She seemed to feel her own way through the inky waters and bounded along as if she were enjoying the passage. He mused, pulling contentedly at his pipe.

"I wonder if Nya's asleep yet. She must be by now, with her head on her arm, perhaps, and her curls all over the pillow. I wonder what her room is like, and whether she can see the stars from her bed."

"Give her my love, stars!" he said aloud.

If only she were with him aboard *Puffin*, speeding along in the starlight. She would love this. It would be pleasant to introduce her to the joy of sailing on a fine night.

There were many other things he would like to be the first to show her. Would he ever have the chance, or would her aunt or her father, or some third person, another man perhaps, come between them? Most of all he feared her extreme youth, and the likelihood there was that she would change towards him. It was no use worrying at present. He had only known her a week. She couldn't learn her own mind in so short a time, however sensible she was. It was his duty to hold back now, to give her a chance to recover her balance, and to change her mind about him if she wished. He had done right to go away.

A faint grey light began to steal along the horizon ahead of him—the first streak of dawn! He watched it eagerly. There was no sight so grand, no mystery so wonderful to him as dawn at sea. Instinctively he compared the flushes on the cheek of night to the tender pink which had blushed in Nya's cheeks as she stammered her apology for calling to him that morning on the beach; and to the dawn of love in her young heart.

20

Was it light yet? No, not properly, though there was a faint greyness perceptible beyond the pine-trees. Several hours were to be got through. She would have to try to sleep again. She had been dreaming. What about? The dream had quite escaped her. And yet one or two impressions remained. She strove to hold them fast and by means of them to bring back the other pictures of her dream, as a fisherman hauls in his line, hand over hand. It was about Simon! Yes, that was it. He had been sailing away from her down a long blue tunnel, with a grey light at the end. Or was the light the dawn that could be faintly seen outside? Perhaps it was getting mixed up with her dream. Yet Simon had been in it, of that she was positive, and he had been sailing towards the light. She could see him there below her at *Puffin*'s helm.

Below? Oh yes, of course, she had been flying. She remembered it all now. Emily had come and woken her and had said that somebody wanted her down on the jetty. She had flown straight there, taking off from the window ledge, but on her way she had found she wasn't going to the jetty at all. Somebody just behind her was guiding her flight, and soon they came to the sea. It was deep and blue, and now, of a sudden, the light dimmed and it was night and there were stars above.

It was then that she saw *Puffin* with Simon at the tiller. She called to him, but he didn't hear her, and sailed straight on, away from her, down the tunnel, till, just as he reached the light he disappeared and she awoke.

Was she awake? She sat up to make sure. Yes, there was no doubt about it. And yet she had a strange feeling that Simon was here, quite close to her in the room. It was absurd, of course; yet she couldn't throw off the impression. This was something she couldn't understand. A moment ago she felt certain Simon was quite near—she almost called out to him involuntarily; and now she realized she was alone. It couldn't have been a dream, not the last part of it, that came and went in a flash.

It was an "experience"—that was it! An uncanny experience, like when one sees a ghost. She seized on this idea, and the more she thought about it the more certain she was that there had been some strange, inexplicable connection, for one fleeting second, between herself in her bed at "The Rising", and Simon out at sea.

"It's a phenomenon," she decided sleepily. "That's what Daddy would have called it."

And, resolving that it was something worth remembering all her life, she forgot it and fell asleep.

21

Next morning Aunt Ethel repented of her anger. She had been up half the night talking to Nicholas and he had told her many things that he had never had the courage to say before. She had never known him so outspoken. All his experience of life, his treatment at other people's hands almost since his boyhood, had come out last night in his odd telegraphic manner of talking. He had forced her to take count of things which, until then, she had scarcely suspected and never admitted to herself.

It was bitter to learn that, at her age, she had so little real knowledge of human nature. And she had prided herself on having so much!

She couldn't remember how their talk had started. Something to do with Nya, she supposed. Nicholas must have felt very strongly to become so talkative all in a moment. He was evidently very fond of the child. She was fond of Nya, too; too fond sometimes, she feared, when she caught herself gazing at Nya as she ran about the garden, with her bare, long legs, and firm, young figure. It was really a very pretty figure, almost fully developed already. That was the effect of life in Africa, she supposed. She hoped the child wouldn't feel any ill effects as a result of it. She wondered whether Mabel had told her daughter all the things she ought to know about herself. It was impossible to find out; Mabel had died so suddenly, when Nya was still so young. She supposed it was her duty now to tell Nya. But her soul shrank from the horrible and embarrassing intimacy which this would create between them, an intimacy which she knew Nya would dislike as much as she. "At least we've sent the child to school. She'll find out there, from girls of her own age. I'm sure that's much the best way."

With this thought she quieted her conscience. It appeared that she had treated the child wrongly last night. Nicholas had made that clear to her. She loved him as well as she was able, in her inhibited way, and she believed the truth of what he said. It was up to her to make amends to Nya.

So she came in now, as Nya was getting up, with the yellow dress over her arm.

"Good morning, dear," she said.

"Good morning, Aunt Ethel."

"Did you sleep well?"

"Yes thanks."

There was a pause while both of them wondered what to do. In which quarter did the wind lie? Aunt Ethel had the dress over her arm. Could she possibly be going to return it?

"I think perhaps I was a little hasty last night," Aunt Ethel began. "After all, we did buy your dress so that you should wear it, didn't we?" She smiled feebly. "I was only a little hurt that you should have put it on without my permission."

Nya heaved a sigh of relief. She could tell from the

tentative manner in which Aunt Ethel spoke that she wasn't angry any more. This was obviously the moment at which to apologize without too much loss of dignity.

"I'm awfully sorry, Aunt Ethel."

"Well—we'll say no more about it. I've brought you back your dress——"

"Oh thank you, Aunt Ethel."

"And you can put it on if you would like to. We'll get Emily to clean that stain off with benzine after breakfast."

So that week began auspiciously, and Nya's relations with her aunt and uncle were gayer and easier than they had ever been. It was like living all the time in the mood in which they had gone to the cinema four or five nights ago. She didn't know what the cause of the sudden change was; but she didn't bother her head over the cause for very long. It was enough that life was pleasant. It helped to make Simon's absence a little easier to bear.

On Friday, however, the atmosphere changed again, and this was ironical because the reason was a happy one. A postcard with a view of "Yachts on the Orwell" arrived from Simon. It didn't say much—just, "How are you? We are at anchor just about here. Pushing off again to-morrow. Yours, Simon." It seemed a little brusque. There was no date, even, except the postmark; nothing that could be taken for deliberate, thoughtful writing. He had evidently scribbled it in a post-office and sent it off. Well—anyhow it was something. It made her heart leap with joy merely to see his writing. He had a nice bold hand and big spaces between his letters. She read it again and again before she began her porridge, while Aunt Ethel watched her. Uncle Nick was not down yet. He was seldom punctual for breakfast.

Ethel had seen the postcard immediately she came in

from letting out her hens. She didn't read it, but she looked at the picture. Very pretty it was. "Yachts on the Orwell". She wasn't quite certain where the Orwell was —somewhere on the East Coast, she thought. Who could be sending the child a postcard from there? Nya never got letters from any one, except when the mailboats arrived, from her father. Absurdly long letters they were, much too long to write to a girl of thirteen. What could there be to say? She racked her brains to think of someone, a relation perhaps of whose existence she was unaware, who lived near the Orwell. But she knew of nobody, and she was beginning to be really puzzled when suddenly the obvious explanation occurred to her. It was a girl from St. Monica's; of course that was it! How stupid not to think of it before! She longed to turn the card over—Emily had carefully put the picture side upwards when she dealt out the letters—in order to see the handwriting. But this would have offended against her personal canon of honesty. She decided to ask Nya.

"Your porridge will get cold, dear," she pointed out, as Nya gazed at the card.

"Oh yes," Nya came to herself with a start and took up her spoon.

"Has one of your little friends at school sent you a greeting?" Aunt Ethel asked.

She chose her words unhappily, for they jarred on Nya's sense of dignity and made her obstinate.

"No," she said carelessly. "It's from a man I know."

A man! That complicated matters considerably.

"A man? Ah, I expect he's someone you met in Africa, or on the ship coming home?"

Nya realized the opportunity she was being given of

avoiding an honest explanation, but there was something in Aunt Ethel's tone that irritated her and gave her a certain pleasure in speaking the truth.

"No," she said. "I met him here. He's got a yacht down in the harbour."

She regretted it the moment she had spoken.

"You met him here?"

In spite of herself Aunt Ethel's tone was shocked. Here was something she knew nothing whatever about. Nya suddenly felt frightened. Had she betrayed her precious secret, merely to gratify a momentary impulse, when she might so easily have kept it? It would have needed nothing but a lie—scarcely even that, for Aunt Ethel herself suggested a way out. Well, there was nothing to be done now but to go through with it. She believed firmly in Simon, absent though he was. His very absence made it easier for her; she had no fear now that Aunt Ethel would insist on seeing him. If she made too big a hash of things Simon would come to the rescue. And it would be rather a relief to tell Aunt Ethel the truth for a change. She plunged boldly in:

"Yes. He took me out sailing."

"When?"

"Oh, last Saturday."

"Last Saturday? So that was why you put your new dress on?" Her voice was hard, as it had been during Saturday's row. Gone were her kindness and tolerance of the last five days.

"Yes."

There was silence. Nya tried to eat her porridge but it made her gorge rise. She pushed the plate away. Aunt Ethel noticed. A base desire to bully, of which in her saner moments she would have been ashamed, took hold of her.

"You must finish your porridge if you want anything else to eat," she said.

"I'm not hungry, thank you, Aunt."

"Very well."

The door opened and Uncle Nick came breezily in.

"Morning. Lovely morning. Spring in the air," he said.

It was deep winter in Nya's heart. An ominous silence greeted Uncle Nick's remarks, though at first he didn't realize its significance. When he offered Nya some grilled sausage and she refused it, he began to be suspicious.

"No sausage. Must be something wrong."

He looked at his wife, but she avoided his gaze. He understood at once that all was not well. For an instant he hesitated, uncertain how to act. Then he made up his mind to affect ignorance. He turned to Nya again: "Sure?"

"Yes thanks, Uncle Nick."

She was very hungry and sausage was an extra-special joy at breakfast. But she couldn't be sure what Aunt Ethel was thinking; it was difficult to know how far you could go with her. In a ghastly attempt at jocularity Uncle Nick misquoted:

"What? No Sausage? So he died. And she very imprudently married the barber."

The effect of this on Nya was to relieve some of the tension. She giggled, half-involuntarily. It was a relief that Uncle Nick hadn't taken sides against her, though he probably would if Aunt Ethel dragged him into the quarrel. And yet, he might not! After all he had brought her those apples, the other night. That showed he didn't entirely agree with Aunt Ethel. Perhaps he would understand about Simon. It was worth trying, anyhow.

"I think I will have some after all, please, Uncle."

Out of the corner of her eye she watched Aunt Ethel. What would she do? Would there come a furious command? The porridge wasn't finished yet.

Aunt Ethel looked up from the letter she had been trying unsuccessfully to read. Her eyes were blazing, but Nya resolutely avoided them. Aunt Ethel said nothing. She took a kind of pleasure in keeping control over herself at such a moment. Later on, she would say all she had to say to Nya. She bit her lips and returned to her letter.

Nicholas put two sausages on to a plate, and took them to Nya himself.

"Ha ha! I thought you wouldn't be able to resist 'em. Maggie knows just how to do a sausage brown without splitting it. *There* you are!" He deposited the plate in front of her with a flourish. As he did so he caught sight of the postcard.

"Hullo!" he said. "Who's been sending you picture postcards? A young man, I'll bet."

"Yes." Nya smiled confidently up at him.

"I knew it! It always begins with picture postcards."

"What does?" asked Nya, intrigued. But she kept a watch on Aunt Ethel and wondered what she could be thinking. The letter in Aunt Ethel's hand quivered a little. Then it was put down suddenly, and Aunt Ethel took up her knife and fork again. Uncle Nick continued:

"I knew it. I knew it. There's spring in the air."

"I don't see what that's got to do with my postcard."

"Never mind. You will one day."

The tension had relaxed now; Nya felt like joking herself. Aunt Ethel evidently didn't intend to interfere, for the time being.

"Oh yes," said Nya scornfully, "when I'm older, I suppose."

"Not so very much older," Uncle Nick replied.

Under pretence of reading another letter Aunt Ethel was making a superhuman effort to control her temper. Her first intention had been to call Nya into the drawing-room after breakfast in order to find out exactly who this young man was who had sent her a postcard. Whatever the result of her enquiries, she intended to give Nya a good talking to. It was a pleasure she had promised herself; and her fraying nerves and the repression she exercised over her natural instincts demanded it. Yet somewhere, mixed up in the blind anger that was slowly rising in her was a small voice—Nicholas's voice—that had spoken so disturbingly on Saturday night. "I think you're a bit intolerant, old girl."

Well, he should see now that he had misjudged her. She was quite able to be tolerant if the situation required it. She would be tolerant now. She would forbear to do her obvious duty, which was to have it all out with Nya in the drawing-room. She would allow him to judge for himself whether the superficial results of a friendly discussion in such matters were of any significance. She would have it out with Nya now, while Nicholas was there.

She laid down her letter.

"Who is this young man, dear?" she asked in a honeyed voice.

Nya looked up, startled. She had steeled herself for a discussion later on, but not here, not in front of Uncle Nick.

"I don't know *who* he is, Aunt. He's just somebody I met."

"Well, how did you meet him then?"

"I bumped into him and broke his pipe."

Uncle Nick laughed.

"And that made you friends for life, eh?"

"Sort of," Nya admitted.

But Aunt Ethel couldn't look at the matter so frivo-lously as her husband did.

"What kind of a young man is he?" she asked; and her tone of voice betrayed a slight irritation, although she strove to make her question casual. Nicholas began to fear that the matter would be too narrowly discussed. After all Nya was a level-headed kid. She could hardly take harm from a casual acquaintance such as this, whatever the young man was like.

"I expect he's a nice young fellow or Nya wouldn't have much to do with him," he observed sententiously.

"That's all very well, Nicholas. You credit the child with as much knowledge of human nature as yourself. But she can hardly understand all the implications of this friendship."

"Bosh," was Uncle Nicholas's private comment, though he only smiled in a tolerant way.

"How often have you been out with him, Nya?"

Nya's bravado was by now beginning to wear thin. Her instinct warned her that, however exhilarating it might be to fight Aunt Ethel, it was a battle she was ultimately bound to lose. Aunt Ethel had too much power over her for the moment; one day things might change, or she might alter them herself by walking out of the house and never coming back. But for the time being she was at Aunt Ethel's mercy.

"Only once," she answered boldly.

"Then there can't have been much damage done yet." Aunt Ethel nodded, mollified for the moment. Her smugness amazed and angered Nya.

174

"What kind of damage do you mean?" she asked hotly. "How could Simon harm anybody? He's the kindest man I've ever met. He doesn't treat me like you do, as if I were a baby."

Her outburst disconcerted even Uncle Nick.

"Nya! That's not the way to speak to your aunt."

"I'm sorry, Uncle Nick. But I can't help saying things like that *sometimes*. You can't go on and on bottling up your feelings just because you've got to be polite. Daddy and Mummy always used to let me say what I felt, so there wasn't any need to be rude. But here I can't, and so it all froths up inside me. . . . Oh well, nobody understands, so what does it matter."

Uncle Nick understood only too well though his loyalty to his wife kept him from saying so.

"You'll find as you grow older", he observed, not unkindly now, "that it becomes less and less possible to speak what's in your mind. It simply isn't done among grown-up people. It would lead to too much embarrassment."

"But if every one always told the truth?"

"Life would be impossible. No, Nya, that's not the way."

She was silent after this. She had been rebuked but she didn't feel in the least quelled. Only it did seem rather futile to argue when you knew people weren't going to see your point of view.

"You have to realize, dear," Aunt Ethel remarked acidly, "that in some ways you still are a baby. At any rate you are too young to know quite all there is to be known about life, and especially people. And so you must trust in the judgment of your uncle and myself. After all, you're in our charge, you know. Your father asked us to look after you when your mother died, and

175

even if we don't quite take the place of your father and mother in your eyes, you must try and remember that you owe us a little consideration."

There was not quite a sniff at the end of her sentence; but she had worked herself up into a state that bordered upon tears. Nothing can disconcert a child so much as tears from a grown-up person, as she knew, and the weapon was too temptingly near at hand for her to refrain from using it. Nya sensed the tears in Aunt Ethel's voice and, disconcerted and slightly penitent, hastily apologized:

"I didn't mean to be inconsiderate, Aunt Ethel. I was only defending myself."

"If you trusted us a little more," Aunt Ethel rejoined, "you wouldn't feel you had to defend yourself against us."

There seemed to be no answer to this remark, so Nya said nothing. When the silence had become too painful to bear, Aunt Ethel broke it by adding:

"And you're not to go out with this young man again without asking my permission first. Is that clear?"

"Yes, Aunt Ethel."

22

From that day her relations with Aunt Ethel were politely formal and they continued so until she went back to school. Nya's direct logic was beyond the comprehension of Aunt Ethel's tortuous mind, so the latter made no further overtures of friendship. Even if she had, they would have been received with suspicion and some hostility by Nya who had neither the tact nor the experience requisite for dealing with them.

Uncle Nick, too, she treated with caution. Although he did his best to dissociate himself from his wife she could never quite relax in his presence; she was reminded that every tie, every inclination, bound him to Aunt Ethel and not herself. She was appallingly lonely during these last two weeks before Simon returned. As often as she dared she wrote to him, but the letters had to be written and posted in the early morning before anyone got up. She still had a little money left from last holidays, so she didn't need to ask Aunt Ethel for stamps.

The letters contained all her anguish and loneliness. The first one he received filled him with pain and longing. He had never had a love-letter before. Now at last he learned the exaltation that requited love can bring.

It didn't matter that Nya was young and inexperienced. Love was not a matter of experience, but of confidence and intimacy. Her trust in him was as profound as his adoration of her. What she felt she wrote, and he believed. She laid siege to his inmost reserve, and forced him to admit her into the most secret places of his heart; for his barriers were all down now that he was away from her. Though she didn't know it, it was with the simple passion of her first letters to him that she finally won his love. She asked so little and was prepared to give so much; and even her asking was so lacking in motive and presumption that it made him long to give.

"I've been sad since you went. Perhaps you'll be annoyed with me if I tell you. But I want to tell you all I think of; it's such a relief to write to you, whatever it may be like to read. I think I love you very much. I didn't know before what it was like to love someone, although I used to think I loved Daddy. But now Daddy seems to have faded into the background. Isn't it awful? Poor Daddy, I hope he won't ever find out what I've said. I'm sure he would be hurt. I'm all he's got, and he used to be all I had until I met you. When he tried to send me home from Africa I cried and was angry, because I loved him and I didn't want to lose him. Now I feel I have lost him, without being able to help it. Oh, Simon, why is it all so sad at the same time as it's being wonderful and sweet? Nothing has ever happened to me like this. It's like being in a lovely sleepy state of happiness, and not wanting to wake up even though part of you is lying on cobbles and is most uncomfortable. Dear, dear Simon, please come back soon and take away the cobbles and tell me I need never wake up again. But perhaps I oughtn't ever to ask you to do anything for me. Then what you did would be all the more wonderful and unexpected. I think it's only because I'm writing (all alone in my nightdress, sitting on my bed, no one has got up yet), that I have the courage to say what I think. If you were here yourself I should be too shy and stand in front of you as dumb as a donkey (until it begins to bray!). Dear Simon, I love you. Please may I write it just once more? Writing it does give me so much happiness; my fingers tingle and even the pen won't go straight as you can see. But if you don't like me saying it—if it makes you feel anything you'd rather not feel, if you hate me, or despise me or even only just laugh at me for saying it—then please let me know and I won't say it again. And if, now you're away, you've changed your mind about me and think that, after all, I am just a silly little girl, please tell me, and don't come back any more. Then I shan't get in your way and you needn't ever see me again, or know how my heart will be breaking."

There was a choke in his throat as he folded up the letter. Oh the sweetness, the childlike, adorable faith and modesty of it! Tears almost came into his eyes as he thought of her, despondent and alone, sitting in her nightdress on the edge of her bed and writing to him. Here was a strange, unusual love indeed; not a bit as he had imagined love would be. He could envisage no love more beautiful and mysterious than this love for Nya that was gradually taking possession of him. It was an adventure undertaken in innocence, with only one's instinct for guide. There were many forms of love, each, no doubt, delightful. Why should one necessarily start at what so many people thought was the end? There were so many wonderful and tender steps towards this end. Why should one wish to leap hurriedly across them? Was there not love that waited for many years to

be fulfilled—unspoken sometimes, yes, and even unsus-
pected? And there was love, too, that never was fulfilled. His love might well be like that. Nya was so
young; she might so easily change in a year or two; he
must be prepared for that. But in the meantime she
loved him as deeply as she could, and he felt for her all
the passion which he dared permit himself. He must be
patient, and above all gentle, and never, never importunate.

He nearly telegraphed to comfort her, and he was in
two minds as to whether to return at once. But he decided against both these things when he realized that it
was the presence of her aunt and not his absence that
was the real cause of the trouble. A telegram would
almost certainly attract her aunt's attention, and after
the episode of the postcard, which Nya had described to
him, this could only make matters worse. He had no
alternative but to continue to send her an occasional
picture postcard with as friendly a message as he dared.
It galled him to have to fail her when she obviously
needed his encouragement, but by appearing to write
under great difficulty and in tearing haste he managed
to convince her that his curtness was enforced upon him
and not voluntary. And he dwelt upon the fact of his
impending return as much as seemed politic. He only
called for letters three times, so that half his holiday was
passed before he even heard from her; and by the time
she had grown really wretched he was ready to return.

Nya's aunt and uncle, to do them justice, tried every
way they could of regaining her confidence; and Aunt
Ethel organized a series of picnic expeditions to neigh-
bouring beauty spots to try and make her happy. She
loved the downs and the rocky caves along the coast to
which they went; she even took kindly to one or two

girls of her own age whom they invited. But when Aunt Ethel suggested renewing the acquaintances she made, she met with no enthusiasm from Nya.

"Really the child is behaving extremely oddly," she remarked despairingly one day to Nicholas. "It seems impossible to interest her in anything. She does nothing but read and moon about the harbour-side. And she is very naughty to be so aloof with other children."

"I don't know what the matter is at all," Nicholas admitted. "I expect the only person who'll find out is Tom. Thank God he's coming back soon."

"She'll be at school when he comes. I hope he doesn't put off coming for too long. I quite understand that he wants to be here during Nya's holidays, but that would mean another three months before she saw him."

"Why don't you write and tell him? Damn it all, he's earned his furlough all right. Surely they could let him stay on till her summer holidays are over."

"I think I will."

She wrote the same night.

23

At last, at last, just as she had almost given up hope, for the school reopened in three days' time—she heard from Simon again. This was the most welcome message of them all. It said simply that he would be on the jetty on Sunday morning at seven-thirty. And to-day was Saturday. She kissed the postcard and then clasped it to her breast. Then she read and re-read it again and hid it in her knickers. Nobody was down to breakfast yet, so she was unobserved. She had lately made a habit of coming down early to see what the post had brought. Sometimes she stayed in the dining-room and was already at breakfast when Aunt Ethel arrived; but more often she went out in the garden, or back to her room, when Aunt Ethel was in the chicken-run, in order to come down again later. Aunt Ethel was quite taken in by this simple manœuvre as Nya knew, because she had once jokingly referred to the fact that "the young man" hadn't written again. Even the afternoon post didn't seem to bring anything for Nya—at least there was never anything for her among the letters on the hall table. No doubt the strange young man had decided to leave Nya alone. Perhaps, she had been a little too harsh with the child.

Nya heaved a deep sigh in which were mixed contentment, terror, and relief. Her terror was lest the moment for which she had waited so long would be cruelly snatched from her. A thousand things might happen to forestall it. Now that it was actually upon her she wavered and lost faith. What if he didn't come? What if his yacht capsized and he were drowned? What if he changed his mind? What if the postcard had been merely a sop to comfort her and he had never intended to fulfil his promise? What if Aunt Ethel found out? What if there were an earthquake to-night and she herself was killed? Simon might possibly be sorry, but his sorrow could be as nothing to her anguish at the thought. Yet she didn't think fate could be so cruel. She had waited so long for Simon to come back, and so much misery had worn out the time. It wasn't much to ask, was it, just to see him again?

The pleasure and relief soon drowned her fears. Simon had chosen the best possible time of day. He must have guessed from her letters how hard it was for her to escape from Aunt Ethel nowadays. Oh, he was altogether a perfect man. She felt a passing pang that her letters had been so full of misery, they must have depressed him.

And to-morrow she would see him—to-morrow at seven-thirty. It was her last chance for so many weeks.

She spent the next day in a frenzy of excitement. Nothing that Aunt Ethel said could have depressed her; even a request to help in the weeding of the path—which, as a rule, was a minor form of punishment—Nya gladly complied with. In the afternoon Aunt Ethel said she was going to tea with some friends who lived nearly ten miles away near Swanage. They had a lovely house, she said, and two children—the girl was just about Nya's age, the boy a little older. She thought it would be nice for Nya to get to know them; they might ask her over there during the summer.

"They have a lake in their garden, where you can swim and boat with the children," she tempted.

Nya was quite willing to go anywhere and do anything with Aunt Ethel to-day. Not with any thought of an invitation to the swimming-pool for the summer, but simply from sheer good spirits. Aunt Ethel seemed to have forgotten that Daddy was coming home—did she think she would waste her precious holiday with Daddy swimming with two strange children? Besides, there was Simon. Although she could scarcely see so far ahead, next holidays meant seeing Simon again. She wondered how this would fit in with Daddy being here, but the thought caused her no uneasiness. She would introduce Simon to Daddy and see how they got on. Most probably they would like each other and if they didn't, she could decide again. It was no good bothering about it now.

So, after an early lunch, she set off with Aunt Ethel in the car. It was a fine, windy day, with round white clouds in a blue sky. Nya blessed the wind for blowing Simon back to her. He couldn't be far away. Perhaps he was even now sailing in at the harbour mouth.

However there was no sign of *Puffin* in the harbour as they drove along the waterside. She joked and chattered to Aunt Ethel in the car. She talked nonsense like a child of six, and invented songs about the people they passed on the road. Even Aunt Ethel's rigid features relaxed, and once or twice she laughed out loud.

"You silly child," she said, "what nonsense you're

talking. You'll have us into the ditch in a minute.'

> "*You'll have us into the ditch in a minute*
> *And then we'll both be pretty well in it,*
> *And I shall say, 'Well, I didn't begin it.'*"

A weight fell from Aunt Ethel's mind as she listened to Nya's idiotic talk. At last the child had recovered her gay spirits; for a fortnight now she had been glum and often sulky. It had really been very difficult to deal with her at all justly. There was no use in frightening the child, or in creating more friction between them by being continually sharp with her. And yet a sharp word of command had been the only thing that roused her from her lethargy. She had expected a scene this morning when she suggested that Nya should accompany her to the van der Hemm's, and the enthusiasm with which Nya had accepted the idea had astonished her. Even Nicholas conveyed his surprise by a broad wink. She wished he wouldn't always wink at her like that; it was so vulgar.

Nya liked the look of the van der Hemm's house as they drove up to it. You went along low downs, in and out between the shoulders of the hills, and then you saw a white gate at the top of one of the humps. Then a drive led beneath some trees downwards to the house itself. It was a little frightening, though, when the door was opened by a butler, who took their coats and then announced them both by name. However, Mrs. van der Hemm was nice. She was simply enormous and dressed in purple, with a huge string of yellow beads, and several rings. She greeted Nya as if she had specially invited her and was very glad to see her.

"How nice of you to come too," she said. "Jessica will be pleased. She's been longing to get to know you. She says all the children near here are more or less babies and don't talk a word of sense between them."

She smiled at Nya with the utmost charm, and then turned to entertain Aunt Ethel. They talked for a few minutes, gossiping about mutual acquaintances, while Nya wandered round the room looking at its treasures. It was a beautiful room, with three french windows that gave on to the lawn. They were open now, and through them Nya heard the sounds of tennis being played nearby. It was a game she loved; the little of it she had played at St. Monica's had won her entire approval. You had to rely on physical fitness and a quick eye, and a suppleness of wrist which Nya felt she could easily possess one day. She always watched the tennis at "The Rising" when people came to play with Aunt Ethel and Uncle Nick, but although she was sometimes allowed to practise serving she was never invited to play. Even her practising didn't meet with much enthusiasm from Aunt Ethel who disliked her rackets being used by any one except herself. Aunt Ethel was a very good player. Nya usually watched her rather than the others, and admired her a good deal in secret.

"Perhaps", thought Nya, "the van der Hemm's will ask me to play tennis too next holidays. That would be fun. Daddy could come over with me and watch."

She stopped in her tour of inspection before the figure of a horseman made out of clay. It was a kind of pinky-white, and the horse was an odd shape, not quite like a real horse, and yet you could feel that it was just about to leap away as a real horse would when a man was trying to ride it for the first time. It was in a glass case, and she stood for some moments before it, discovering new things which pleased her at every glance. It had a most intelligent eye, wild and angry and rather terrified at the same time. And the muscles on the rider's arms, though you couldn't actually see them standing out, like you often could in bronze statues in parks and squares, yet they gave you a feeling of strength being exerted which the bronze statues never did.

Mrs. van der Hemm abruptly stopped talking to Aunt Ethel and came and stood behind Nya.

"Do you like it?" she asked.

"Yes, awfully."

"Then I shall tell you something about it." She put her arm through Nya's. "Not many people find their way straight to it, as you did," she said. "They like the pottery over there, or those inlaid daggers in the wall best. You've got excellent taste, my dear. This is far the best piece in the whole room. It's Chinese, very very old."

"I think it's lovely," said Nya.

She liked Mrs. van der Hemm, and enjoyed being arm in arm with her. It was like talking to an equal.

Aunt Ethel, feeling neglected, rose and joined them. But she couldn't honestly say she saw much in the Chinese figure; in her heart of hearts she agreed with the people who preferred the inlaid daggers. Their workmanship, so careful and detailed, was surely more laudable than that of the Chinese horse.

"Do you think Jinghiz Khan ever saw this horseman?" Nya asked.

("What on earth is the child talking about?" thought Aunt Ethel.)

"Yes, he might have," answered Mrs. van der Hemm. "Let me see, when did Jinghiz Khan live. Somewhere in the thirteenth century wasn't it? In that case he *could* have seen this figure—at least we'll imagine he did," she smiled at Nya. "It was certainly in existence then."

"You mustn't let Nya be a nuisance, Margot," said Aunt Ethel, feeling it was time she took part in the conversation again. "She asks too many questions."

"Quite right, too," answered Mrs. van der Hemm with an appraising nod at Nya. "How else is she to find out things?"

But though Nya was annoyed at Aunt Ethel's remark, Mrs. van der Hemm seemed to think it perfectly intelligent. At any rate she put her other arm through Aunt Ethel's and led both her guests towards the garden.

"Let's go and watch the tennis," she said. "I expect you're fond of tennis too, Nya, aren't you?"

"Yes. I think it's the best game in the world."

"You get that from your aunt, I'm sure."

Aunt Ethel was too taken aback to agree. It surprised her to know that Nya had any fondness for the game. Certainly she had never expressed it. If only she had, some of the difficulty of not knowing what to do with her during the last fortnight might have been solved. It would have been the simplest thing in the world to arrange an occasional game with some nice children who, like Nya, were just beginning to play. And the tedium of one or two afternoons might have been all the easier to while away if she had known that Nya would enjoy an hour's knock-up.

After a moment's pause she said: "To be quite frank, I didn't know Nya liked it. She's never said so to me."

Nya could find no polite answer to this, so she was silent.

"You must get Jessica to play with you, Nya," Mrs. van der Hemm said. "She's very good. She can beat her brother eight times out of ten."

"I'd love to play with her, if she'll teach me."

Aunt Ethel said no more for some minutes, and in her

silence Mrs. van der Hemm plainly read her embarrassment before Nya. Walking between them, with an arm through each of theirs, she could feel that they were both keyed up. They didn't seem at all able to relax, even during the rest of the afternoon, when she observed them closely.

"There's something wrong there," was her private comment. "I'll have to do something for that child. Ethel doesn't understand her in the slightest."

She said nothing to Aunt Ethel, however; nor did she intend to. But she set her brain to devise a means of getting Nya away from "The Rising" as much as possible next summer. She hoped Nya would like Jessica; it would be more than half the battle to have a young person as vital and kind-hearted as Jessica on her side.

She watched the two girls anxiously when they met. Jessica was hot and flushed from tennis, and was therefore not inclined to be ceremonious. She grasped Nya by the hand, and, as soon as she had introduced her to her brother, took her by the arm and walked a little away from the others.

It was the most natural action in the world. Even Nya thought so, for she smiled confidently and seemed to be enjoying herself. The two girls strolled up and down the tennis court, talking animatedly. Occasionally they would stop and lean against the wire-netting, or fiddle with the mechanism for tightening the net; then they would resume their walk, laughing and talking as if they had known each other for a year.

The assurance and intimacy of Jessica's conversation delighted Nya. She had no time to feel shy in her presence. Jessica quickly and firmly established a feeling of friendship between them by her frankness. Frankness was a quality which appealed to Nya above all others. Their talk passed from subject to subject. There seemed to be nothing one couldn't discuss with Jessica. Riding and swimming were interests that they had in common. Jessica had been to Switzerland but she knew nothing about Africa. She had been to London too, of course, and to theatres, concerts and museums there. She told Nya of a private collection belonging to a friend of her mother's, where you could see several Chinese horsemen even more beautiful than the one in her mother's drawing-room. And plates there were, with wonderful designs on them; drawings, jars, bronzes, all kinds of beautiful things. They were all works of art, Jessica said, like the horseman in the drawing-room. That was a work of art, too.

Owing to Mummy's love of music Nya's training in art had been chiefly musical and she had gradually confused the word "art" with "music". She said so, now, to Jessica. You could say things to her even if you felt they were wrong and rather stupid, and that you might afterwards regret having said them.

"I thought a work of art had to have something to do with music."

"Not necessarily," Jessica answered. "Poetry and painting, of course, and acting and playing the piano. and violin—they're all arts too. Do you play the piano?"

"Yes. I do. But I haven't played since I left Nyasaland. Aunt Ethel hasn't got a piano."

"What a shame! Do you like playing very much?"

"I love it. Mummy taught me and we used to play to each other; of course I'm not very good, especially now I'm out of practice, but I'd like to be."

"Won't they let you have lessons at school?"

"Not your first term. Next term I can. I'm rather

190

looking forward to it. It'll be lovely to be able to get away from the others sometimes and play."

"I know. That's what I used to like doing. Do you hate them all as much as I did? My first term I loathed the other girls."

"Yes. I did too."

"I got used to them later on. Now I've left, I quite like a lot of them, and there are one or two who are my friends. I never used to have friends before."

"You must have been like me."

"I expect I was. But you'll find it's much easier the older you are. How old are you by the way? Fifteen, sixteen?"

"Nothing like as much. I wish I was. I'm nearly fourteen, but not even quite that."

"Good Lord! I've never met any one as sensible as you that was only fourteen."

Nya smiled with pleasure. It was a compliment that flattered her more than Jessica realized.

"How old are you?"

"Sixteen."

"Oh! Aunt Ethel said you were about my age."

It was Jessica who smiled now. "Yes," she said, "she thinks I'm very young still."

Tea in the lovely drawing-room was a gay meal. Nya enjoyed herself even though Aunt Ethel was there. She also began to like Aunt Ethel, for here, among these lively, humorous people Aunt Ethel became quite a different person. She made jokes, and laughed quite a lot when other people made them. Half-way through tea Mr. van der Hemm came in. He was much older than his wife, with white hair and a moustache. He didn't actually make any jokes but he told stories in a quiet, dry way that was even funnier. He kept them all

191

in fits of laughter until Aunt Ethel said it was time to go. Then Jessica said:

"We'll meet you at the gate," and took Nya through the french windows and across the lawn towards the drive. In a moment Jessica's brother joined them. He was as full of conversation as Jessica and questioned Nya about Africa. He said he wanted to start a new kind of school and thought that somewhere in Africa would be the best place. He wanted to know all about Nyasaland, and when Nya told him all she knew, he thanked her politely and said:

"Oh well, that's evidently *not* the place for me. I expect it'll have to be Capetown or Durban after all. Thanks all the same."

When they reached the gate Jessica said:

"I'm sorry you've got to go back on Tuesday, but never mind, it's a short term. And next holidays you must come and stay with us for a week—will you?"

"Yes, please do," her brother said.

"I'd simply love to. Honestly I would. Only Daddy's coming home in May, and I expect he'll still be here for the holidays."

"Do you think he'd like to come too? I mean, what's he like? Would he like us?"

"Oh yes, he'd love you."

"Then you must bring him too."

"Really and truly?"

"Really and truly. I'll arrange it with Mother. You leave it to me."

"Thank you most awfully."

"And if we're still here we'll come and see you at your school at half-term."

"*Will* you?"

Her eyes sparkled with astonishment and incredulity. This was all impossible; people didn't load you with kindness like this except in dreams or fairy-tales. Breathlessly she got into the car as Aunt Ethel drove up.

Still breathless, she said good-bye to Mrs. van der Hemm, and then again to Jessica and her brother. And she was still intoxicated with the discovery of this wonderful family when she reached home.

In the evening Uncle Nick tried to teach her to play bridge. Aunt Ethel had confided to him her discovery that Nya was fond of tennis and suggested that bridge might appeal to her too. Tennis and bridge were inseparable in Aunt Ethel's mind. But though Nya did her best to pay attention she was unable to concentrate on Uncle Nick's explanations; there was too much to learn all at once, and in any case her thoughts were not on the game but on Simon's return. It was so near now. Scarcely twelve hours away. Uncle Nick soon saw that she was not profiting from his instruction and the game was abandoned.

Nya said good night and went to bed. But on the way up she sought out Emily in the kitchen and made her promise to knock on her door when she came down in the morning.

"I want to go for a walk before breakfast," she said. "You won't forget will you, Emily?"

"Even if it's raining?" asked Emily.

"Oh yes, that won't matter at all."

"All right, Miss, I won't forget. Though it's my belief you've got something up your sleeve."

"No I haven't, Emily, really."

But she could see that Emily wasn't convinced. So she laughed and said: "At least, nothing wrong. But you

193

won't let Aunt Ethel hear you call me, will you?"

"No, Miss, I'll just knock and slip into your room. Your aunt won't hear."

"Thanks awfully, you're an angel."

24

She was scrupulously tidy with her clothes as she undressed. It was just possible that Aunt Ethel would come in on her way to bed to see whether she was asleep. And Nya was determined that she should have nothing to scold her about, just as she had been determined, ever since Simon's last postcard came, that she would do nothing to provoke Aunt Ethel's disapproval until she had seen Simon.

It would be impossible to go to sleep at all to-night, she thought. How could you go to sleep when you were thinking so hard all the time—when you were imagining delightful scenes that might possibly come true the very next morning? Even reading didn't help when your thoughts were more exciting than a book.

She put out the light at once and lay in bed, staring wide-eyed at the stars through the window-panes. Those stars had been there the night Simon went away; how strange that she didn't notice them again until to-night, when he was back.

"Perhaps he's sailing in past the jetty at this very moment," she thought. "Or else he's at anchor already and is sitting on the cabin-top smoking his pipe. I wonder if he's thinking about me, and if he can feel me thinking about him. I wish you could go and see people in your thoughts, or in your dreams—really see them I mean, and touch them and talk to them. I'm sure I almost did it the night Simon went away. Daddy says he's heard of it being done, but he's never met any one who could do it. It would be like flying in a dream, I suppose, only you'd be able to fly where you wanted to instead of always being taken to places, like you are in a dream. Perhaps you could even go as far as Africa. I wonder where Daddy is at the moment? I do hope he'll like Simon. I hope he won't notice that I'm different when he comes back. I know I am, and I'm afraid he'll think I don't love him any more. But I do, almost as much as I love Simon, only not quite so much because somehow it seems different with Simon. Sometimes I feel shy with him which I never used to feel with Daddy. I wonder why it is. Mummy would have known. She would have liked Simon, I'm certain of that. What a shame, she can't even meet him now."

She began to think about Mummy and the memories of how she talked and laughed and sang, and played the piano, came back one upon the other so swiftly and tumultuously that she soon began to feel afraid. She knew it only made things worse to think too much about Mummy and John. Daddy had said so directly after the funeral, and she had since found that it was true. It made you feel unhappy, because you so nearly saw them or heard them talking to you, but you never could *quite*, and so you felt cheated, as if somebody was trying to baffle and disappoint you on purpose. The only thing to do was to say straight out—aloud if no one else was listening—"Mummy and John, I'm remembering you and I love you just the same. Please don't forget me." That way there was a chance that they might hear you

196

and understand that if you tried to put them out of your mind it was only because it made you unhappy to think about them and not because you were trying to forget them.

When she eventually fell asleep she dreamed—disturbed and broken bits of dreams, that didn't lead to any conclusion, and that she couldn't remember when she woke up. But oddly enough they had one thing in common; in all of them she seemed to be in a tearing hurry to get somewhere, and things kept happening to stop her; either people got in her way, or else huge hills rose up at her very feet, and once, as she thought she was about to reach her destination, whatever it was, a river suddenly came flowing past in front of her and she had to walk along beside it for a long time before she could find a boat. She tried to fly across but it was no good, she wasn't able to rise off the ground. Presently *Puffin* came sailing down the stream, and Simon was standing at the helm. He looked at her, but he didn't smile or wave, and he never even attempted to stop, but gradually passed out of sight again round the bend of the river. She was in despair by now, and plunged into the river to swim after him, but before she reached the water she awoke to find most of the bedclothes in a heap on the pillow and her head hanging over the edge of the bed.

She got up and remade her bed. Then she looked out of the window, but there was no sign of daylight yet. It wasn't worth keeping awake. In any case Emily could be relied upon. Sleepily she reiterated this to herself. Emily would wake her all right. There was no need to worry. She had said she would knock and slip into her room. So that would be all right. And she could see Simon in the morning.

She got into bed again and immediately fell asleep.

25

She awoke to find Emily shaking her by the shoulder.

"It's raining fit to break your heart, Miss," she whispered, "but if you still want to go for a walk it's six o'clock."

"What time did you say?" Nya opened one eye.

"Six o'clock, Miss. You told me to wake you."

"Oh yes, so I did. I wonder why."

She sat up, rubbing her eyes, too sleepy, for the moment, to remember anything.

"I'm sure I don't know, Miss, and you'll want to go to sleep again when you see how it's raining."

"Go to sleep again!" What an idea! Of course she couldn't go to sleep again. This was the day of days. She leaped out of her bed.

"Oh no, I can't do that," she said. "I must get up. It's most important, Emily. Thanks for calling me."

"It's all right, Miss."

At the door Emily stopped and said: "Maggie doesn't come till seven, Miss, so I'll make you a cup of tea in the kitchen if you'd like it."

It was six now, Simon had said seven-thirty. Yes there would be time.

"Thanks awfully, Emily. I'll be down in a minute."

She hardly waited for Emily to leave the room before she took her nightdress off. Then to the wash-basin; it would have to be cold water—it wasn't worth the risk of rushing to the bathroom to see if there was any warm left over from last night. Besides, it would take too long. She squeezed the sponge over the back of her neck. The shock of the cold water almost made her squeal. However, it was refreshing, and it certainly woke one up. Perhaps it would be a good thing to have a cold sponge all over. In the exhilaration of her mood the idea appealed to her. She put the basin on the floor, stood in the ice-cold water, and squeezed the sponge all down her body. Some of the water went on the floor. Some of it trickled down her spine and made her pant and gasp for breath. And then it trickled down her legs, which tickled.

By the time she had dried herself she felt wide awake and full of vitality. Her cheeks glowed and her eyes were bright and there was laughter in them, as if Simon was already there. He was so plainly before her eyes that she almost believed he stood beside her. It was just as well he wasn't really there, she thought, because she hadn't got a thing on. She threw her head back and laughed at the thought, and her curls tickled the back of her neck. Oh, it was lovely to be naked, and to have a cold bath —and to be going to see Simon again.

While they were having tea in the kitchen Emily said she oughtn't to be going out on a morning like this. But Nya's spirits were too high to be subdued.

"The rain'll stop in a minute—you'll see," she said, peering out of the window. "There's a long bit of blue sky there—between the laurel bushes."

"You ought to take your coat," said Emily doubtfully.

199

"All right I will—just to please you. Thanks for the tea."

She ran down the road as fast as she could. There weren't many people about yet—it was only a quarter to seven—and her mackintosh made a strange pattern of noise against the sound of her footsteps as it swished backwards and forwards. She hadn't bothered what she put on this time; her appearance seemed a very unimportant matter now that she was so sure that Simon would be pleased to see her.

She reached the jetty before the hour struck, and extremely dreary it looked. Not a soul was to be seen. She gazed out over the water which danced and glistened where the raindrops fell. There was no breath of wind, and scarcely any swell. Somewhere or other the sun must have been trying to shine because the clouds were getting higher all the time, and every now and then the water sparkled as if it were reflecting its rays. She looked up at the sky, screwing up her eyes to avoid the raindrops. Yes—in a short time—half an hour perhaps, the clouds would break. It might be quite a nice day after all.

She knew it was too early for Simon to be there, but she felt impatient with him just the same. If only he could have said seven o'clock; that would have given them more time together. She would have to go back for breakfast, there was no getting out of that, luckily breakfast was at nine o'clock on Sundays.

She peered through the rain, hoping to see some sign of activity on board *Puffin*, but it was all she could do to make out the shape of the yacht. She wasn't absolutely certain that it *was Puffin* but at least the hull and rigging were the same as *Puffin*'s, and she lay at anchor in nearly the same place. For ten minutes she didn't take her eyes off the yacht. It was getting lighter all the time, it might be possible to see more clearly in a few minutes. She walked to the other end of the jetty, partly out of restlessness, and partly because she thought she would see better if she went down the steps to the level of the water. But, though the mist lay less heavily on the water, she found she lost the vantage of the jetty's height, and impatiently climbed up again. As she turned at the top of the steps to continue her watch on the distant yacht her heart leaped into her mouth, for she could distinctly see a figure in a white sweater come up on to the deck, apparently to adjust something on the mainstay. Simon *had* a white sweater, she knew. She had seen it among the clothes on the fo'c'sle bunk. Then, as if by magic, a puff of wind cleared the mist a little and she saw that the burgee was being hoisted. Up it went, the little blue triangular flag, to the very top of the mast. She still couldn't make out what the man in the white sweater looked like, but she was certain now that it must be Simon. Oh yes—it must be Simon. It must be Simon, it must be Simon. Her heart was beating very fast; it told her plainly she was not mistaken.

She longed to shout aloud with joy; but she watched for a few moments longer before she could trust the judgment of her eyes. When she saw the man in the white jersey turn and gaze in her direction, shielding his eyes from the rain with his hand, she could resist it no longer. She shouted, at the top of her lusty young voice: "Si . . . mon."

He had been about to turn away again; no doubt he couldn't distinguish her light-coloured mackintosh against the white wall of the hotel. Now she saw him stop and look again. Then he suddenly disappeared into the cabin and, in an instant, was up on deck again, holding something to his eyes. Field-glasses! She waved and danced upon the jetty. If it wasn't Simon, no doubt he would think she was mad. She called again, but she was so excited that this time her call developed into a sort of screech. Evidently he spotted her then, for he waved too. One second longer he held the glasses up while she continued to wave, then he jumped into the dinghy and began to row towards her.

Half-way across he hailed her.

"Nya—is that you?"

"Yes, it's me, come quickly."

He had his back towards her as he rowed, so she couldn't see his face. She sang out his name every now and then to guide him in the right direction, and soon she found herself repeating it over and over again in an exultant sing-song. Just as the clock struck the quarter he reached the jetty. Without bothering to tie up he hung on to the piles and stood up, while Nya ran down the steps to the waterside.

"Oh, Simon, Simon, it's you, it's really you." She almost overbalanced into the water in her excitement. He dragged the dinghy round the steps, pulling himself from pile to pile towards her.

"I'm so glad to see you."

"Are you, Nya?"

"Yes, frightfully."

She seized the painter and tied it round a stanchion. Then he jumped out. She threw her arms round him and embraced him with all her might, and he hugged her to him, almost crushing her with the strength he exerted. Her curls fell all over her face and he laid his cheek against them until their sweet dampness was in his nostrils and her eager breath warm upon his face. Then, timidly, their yearning drew them together and for a fleeting second Nya felt the touch of Simon's lips. It was only the whisper of a kiss; it called up her love without arousing passion; creating for her a moment of sweet enchantment that fled before she knew that it was there. But as it fled it charmed away her doubts and all the longings of the past few days. For a moment they stood locked together, transported by an emotion which both could share, even if they were differently aware of it.

She had never known such absolute happiness as she now found in Simon's arms. She didn't think, she hardly even felt, she was content to be held, as it were between heaven and earth, inanimate and still.

He gazed at her with unseeing eyes, all his thoughts and all his feeling concentrated on the child he held against him. His every nerve tingled till the touch of any one but Nya would have been intolerable.

Nya stirred, and with a shudder he regained control over his errant senses.

"Dear beloved Simon," she said, "are you glad to be back?"

And, thinking of the sweet agony he had been through when he read her letters, and of the bewilderment of love into which they had plunged him, he replied:

"Little Nya, if you knew how much!"

"I've missed you, Simon, I've thought about you all day long."

He took her head in his hands, brushing the damp curls away from her face, and gazed into her eyes. "I'm glad," he said. Then he laughed. "And when I went away I pretended that I hoped you would forget me."

"Did you think I would?"

"I wanted to give you the chance, didn't I?"

"Is that what you meant when you said I'd change my mind?"

"Yes."

"Well, I haven't, you see. It's more made up than ever."

"Is it?"

She broke away from him, talking eagerly to convince him.

"Oh yes," she said. "It's quite made up. You needn't think I haven't thought about us, and wondered what I ought to do. You see, at first I thought that you'd forget *me*, and even when your postcards came, there wasn't much on them to go by, so you see——"

"I'm sorry, little one, I couldn't help that. I was afraid your aunt——"

"Oh, I know, I realized that very soon. It was just as well. But just at first I was a bit unhappy, and that made me imagine that I'd never see you again. So then I had to get used to the idea, and, though I tried awfully hard, I simply couldn't. Oh, I can't quite explain how I felt, because I'm not clever enough, but I didn't feel the same person any longer. I didn't feel like myself-before-I-met-you. I was myself-after-I-met-you; and it wasn't any good trying to change that. So I hoped you'd feel like that too, and that even if you thought you ought to forget all about me, you wouldn't be able to any more than I could, and one day you'd come back and say so."

"Well—I've come back to say so now."

She seized his hand and put it to her cheek.

"It's such a relief to see you again," she said. "I think I would have burst if you'd stayed away any longer."

"And it's the best feeling in the world to see *you* again," he said. "I was afraid you'd vanish away before I came back. I never thought you really existed, you know. You're like a sprite that dances along in front of

204

one and then suddenly disappears, and one can't be sure if one's really seen it or not. But", he pinched her arm gently, "you seem to be real all right, thank God."

She pinched him, too, and retorted:

"So do you!"

They laughed and passed at once from the emotional mood of their meeting into one of comradeship.

"Well," said Simon, "what shall we do? How long have you got?"

"Breakfast's at nine."

"Must you be in for that?"

"I ought to."

"Oh damn."

"Damn *and* blast."

"Never mind, we must make the most of our time together. I'll tell you what I'd thought. I was going to suggest our going back and cooking breakfast in *Puffin*. I've got everything we'll need. Would you like that?"

"I'd love it. Let's go."

They were so oblivious of their surroundings as they stood talking on the landing-stage, that they never heard the footsteps of a man on the jetty above. Suddenly there was a crash and an empty tin, and then the skeleton of a kipper fell on to the landing-stage beneath, narrowly missing Simon's head, and giving both him and Nya a tremendous fright. They had forgotten that time or other people existed, and imagined themselves alone on a deserted jetty in a kind of perpetual early morning when no one was ever astir.

Simon shouted indignantly, and an extremely surprised face looked suddenly down at them.

"Gor blimey, I didn't know there was any one there. Oh, it's you Mr. Byrne."

"Yes. Are you trying to bump me off or something?"

The seaman smiled to conciliate him. "It was an accident, sir. I kicked this here bucket by mistake."

"Damn nearly made me kick the bucket too."

"Awfully sorry, sir, didn't know you was down there."

"It's all right. Anything else coming down?"

"No, sir, that's all for the time being."

"Well, we're just off now. You'll be able to kick things about to your heart's content. Oh, by the way, Nya, do you know Dan?"

"Yes, we've met before."

"Why, so we have, Miss." The seaman touched his cap. "We're old friends, as you might say."

"She and I are old friends too, Dan."

"Any friend of yours, sir, is a friend of mine."

"Thank you," said Nya.

"He's a grand fellow," said Simon, as they rowed away. "Helped me out of many a fix in one way or another."

"He helped me out of one, too," said Nya, "in a way." She smiled.

"What have you been doing while I was away?"

"Oh, nothing interesting. I was just waiting for you to come back. Except yesterday," she added, suddenly remembering the van der Hemms. "I met some awfully nice people, it was tremendous fun."

"You mean to say that you actually *liked* some strange people?" he teased, remembering her half-humorous, half-angry descriptions of her aunt's efforts to find friends for her.

She chuckled. "Yes, I liked them all, even Mister. But I didn't talk to him much."

She told him about her visit of the day before, with a special description of Jessica, with whom, she said, she had made friends. There was no mistaking her enthusi-

asm. It was genuine and deep-seated, and seemed likely
to last. He noticed this with pleasure. These were evidently the kind of friends she needed. He led her on to
talk about them, and in the space of a few minutes he
had been given a lively description of the sort of person
that each of them was, of what they looked like, what
their house looked like, of the treasures in the drawing-
room, and finally of most of the things they had said.
Nya's chief delight was evidently in the conversation she
had had with Jessica about music. It surprised him to
find that Nya loved music so much. She had told him
that she played the piano but he had attached no special
meaning to that, since most girls of her age played it.
He realized suddenly that he knew very little about Nya
and she knew practically nothing about him. She had
told him a few facts—that her mother and brother were
dead, that her father was in Africa, that she lived with
her uncle and aunt. These were not the things about her
that interested him; he wanted to know how her mind
worked. He wondered what sort of things made her
happy or enthusiastic, what things she loved or hated
or feared, what she thought about, and what she longed
to do. Did she mean to be a great musician? Did she
want to get married, or hadn't she begun to think about
such things yet? There was a sweet fascination in exploring the recesses of her demure mind.

Did she ever wonder about him? She had never asked
him a single question and was totally incurious. She
seemed to accept him as he was, without a doubt or a
suspicion that he wasn't what he seemed. He knew he
could inspire confidence in people; at school, at the
office, sailing, he had become aware of this. But he had
always put it down to his theory that if you knew your
own mind in a crisis and acted accordingly, other people

would instinctively and thankfully follow your lead. This didn't apply to Nya, for there was no crisis, nor any need to follow his lead. In any case he didn't know his own mind very well, at the moment. He had a vague idea that Nya would somehow or other become his responsibility, for the question wasn't governed by ordinary standards any longer. He was Simon, and she was Nya, and he loved her and felt she belonged to him, and as long as she did, common sense and the ordinary standards, and even the office could go to hell. He wasn't going to stop seeing her as long as she wanted to see him, nor would he ever deceive himself again into thinking that it was wise to go away from her. She would be taken away from him quite often enough, by school and by her guardians. He would see so little of her—barely four months in every year, that he must make the most of what opportunity he had of being with her. So he thanked God that she loved and trusted him, even though she knew so little about him. His own mind was made up, his love for her was firm. Her confidence in him could do her no harm for he would never need to violate it.

"What are you going to be, Nya? Have you made up your mind yet?"

She shook her head.

"I don't know. I haven't really thought much about it. At the end of last term I began to get interested in all sorts of things, but then, when the holidays came, I forgot all about them. Since yesterday I've begun to get interested again, but I'm not quite sure in what?"

"Music, it seems."

"Oh yes, music. I'd love to be a famous pianist. But it isn't only music. You see, Simon, I get so muddled. There's such a lot to think about. Sometimes one thing seems more important than the other, but usually everything is equally important and huge and overwhelming and I feel as if I was standing all alone on the edge of a huge sea and wondering what I ought to do. Parts of the sea are called fame, and parts are music, and writing, and painting—I suppose they're called art—and parts are called"—she hesitated—"love." It was an awful effort to speak the word, which seemed to belong more to the domain of grown-up people, or to books and fairy-tales, than to this ordinary life. She wasn't quite sure what love was; whether it was something, like smoking or drinking, that you weren't allowed to have until you grew up properly. It would be all right for Simon of course, but possibly not for her. Yet it was connected with her in some way, she knew, if only because of Simon. She would ask him about it one day, when she knew him better and had more courage.

He was absorbed in her conversation, fearful to speak in case he should disturb her train of thought. But now she had grown suddenly shy, and seemed to be waiting for some sign from him.

"I understand," he said. He rested on his oars for a moment. They were getting near *Puffin* now, but he would rather have drifted about the harbour the whole morning than lose a word of what she was saying.

"And the question is," she concluded, "which part to plunge into?"

"But really it's all the same sea, isn't it?"

She thought for a moment before she answered.

"Yes; I suppose it is. In that case I think those things I said, art and fame and so on, must be islands, and it's a question which I want to swim to."

"I don't believe it matters," he said, "so long as you

209

plunge in and don't stand shivering on the brink like I've done."

"You?" she said, incredulously.

"Yes. I'm afraid so. I suppose I could have plunged in and swum towards one of your islands, I must often have had the chance. But I haven't taken it. That's why I'm in an advertising office now instead of being, say, an explorer, or a communist, or a parson—all of whom plunge in and swim out to some kind of island."

"Yes—I suppose they count too."

"Very much so." His tone was gently reproving. "If you're going to be an artist you mustn't make the mistake that a great many artists make of thinking that theirs is the only island in the sea."

"No, I didn't mean that, Simon. I only meant I hadn't thought about explorers and parsons being the same sort of people as painters and musicians."

"But they are in a way—provided that they have the courage to choose a job that they respect and to live entirely for their job—which you couldn't say about me, could you?"

He smiled, and by belittling himself removed the sting of his reproof and put her at her ease again.

The tide brought them slowly alongside the *Puffin* without a stroke of the oars. Nya patted the yacht's hull as they bumped against it.

"Darling old *Puffin*," she said. "I love you for bringing Simon safely back."

And Simon instead of giving her his hand to help her aboard, took her up in his arms and deposited her on the deck.

It was nice to be aboard *Puffin* again. It was like coming to a place you knew and where you felt at home. In fact it *was* home, in a way, because "The Rising" certainly wasn't, and presumably she would never see Nyasaland again.

"Oh, Simon, it's lovely to be back here. Can't I stay for ever, please? Nobody would know, would they? They'd never find me here. And I'd wash up and scrub the decks so that *Puffin* would look spotless when you came back from your advertising office. Couldn't I, please?"

"I wish you could."

"I wouldn't mind being alone, while you were away. But I'd like it better if you were here too."

For a second he ruffled the curls at the side of her head before he answered.

"I'm afraid it isn't feasible. I only wish it was."

"Oh damn."

There was a silence for a moment, but he could feel a tension in it.

"Tell me what made you think of a huge sea, and of love and fame in it?"

"I don't know. I seem to have heard of it somewhere before."

"Was it in a poem?"

"I don't remember."

"Was it this by any chance?

> " *then on the shore*
> *Of the wide world I stand alone, and think,*
> *Till Love and Fame to nothingness do sink.*"

"Oh yes, it's Keats. Of course that's what I was thinking of. That's 'cloudy symbols', isn't it?"

"That's what?"

"It's what Daddy and I used to call it," she explained. "He used to read it to me. And that's what I was trying to think of the other night—the night you went away—

when I was lying in bed looking at the stars—there's something about the stars in it too."

"The night I went away, did you say?"

"Yes."

"That's odd," he mused. "I was sitting at the helm, also looking at the stars, and thinking about you."

"I wanted you to come straight back. I hated you for going away."

He looked down at her mock-reproachful eyes, and the pout of her mouth. Once again he took her face in his hands and this time he kissed her full on the lips, gently and tenderly as her mother might have done. She didn't move back, nor take her lips from his, but he felt her draw a sudden breath, and at once relaxed his hold on her.

"I hate myself for having gone away," he said.

"It doesn't matter about that. You're back again now.

"I think I love you, Nya."

"Oh, Simon——"

She could have cried with happiness. At last, at last, he had said it. This was the most wonderful moment she had ever lived. To hear Simon say it at last, in that strange way which was so disturbing, which wasn't at all the same thing as when Mummy or Daddy said it, was even more entrancing than to be able to say it yourself.

"Nya! I've been imagining this moment for the last fortnight—ever since I was quite sure in my mind that it wouldn't be wrong for me to come back to you and say 'I love you'. And here I am, I've not only said it, but I'm actually talking to you about it, as if it hadn't been the most colossal ordeal."

"I don't understand, Simon, why was it an ordeal?"

"Let me boil a kettle and I'll tell you."

He disappeared like a rabbit down the fo'c'sle hatch and, as soon as he was out of sight, heaved a sigh of relief.

Outside in the cockpit Nya gazed at the scene around her with wide eyes. The world was the most beautiful place on this April morning. The mist had almost gone from the face of the water, and she could see right across the harbour, past Brownsea Castle, to the anchorage where all the steam yachts lay, and the big schooners and barquentines. Behind her the hills were gradually creeping out of the mist, their purple sides glistening where the sunlight fell. There was no breath of wind, and even the rain had stopped; and the water was like a sheet of glass, smooth and slippery. How funny! She hadn't noticed before that the rain had stopped. When could that have been? It was still raining when they left the jetty, or wasn't it? She couldn't remember. She heaved a sigh of deep contentment. She had never seen such a lovely morning: nothing in Nyasaland, even, when the rains had stopped and the orchids came out and made you think you were in fairyland; nothing she remembered could compare to the silver stillness of this scene.

People were beginning to stir on the other craft nearby. On one very smart steam-yacht, called *Queen of the Night*, a seaman was about to have his morning tub. He let down a bucket into the water, waited leisurely till it was filled, and then, as leisurely drew it up again. Then he took it in both hands, drew a deep breath—Nya could see him gaping like a goldfish—and sluiced the contents over him. He was naked to the waist, but even then a good deal of the water must have gone down inside his trousers. Nya shivered at the thought, remembering how cold and ticklish the same procedure had made her feel an hour ago. She was watching delightedly when Simon reappeared.

"Look," she said excitedly. "He's going to do it again."

They watched him. This time he was not so leisurely in his movement; probably the cold water had enlivened him. When he had poured the second bucket over his head Simon and Nya clapped and shouted, "Bravo!"

The sailor looked up and grinned cheerfully.

"Come on. It's your turn now," he shouted.

"I've had mine already," Nya answered.

The sailor gave himself a quick rub with a towel, then he pulled on his jersey, and, with a wave of the hand, disappeared into his quarters.

"Tea won't be long," said Simon.

"Good. Did you notice it had stopped raining, Simon?"

"By Jove, so it has. I'd forgotten all about the rain, somehow, and it was pelting when I rowed out to meet you. Come to think of it my sweater must be wet."

"Is it?" She ran her hand over it, and found it was quite damp. "Yes. It's frightfully wet, hadn't you better change it?"

"I don't know. I don't usually bother."

"Oh please, or you'll catch cold and die and then I shan't have any one at all."

"Silly child," he laughed. "It takes more than that to kill me. Still, I'll put a dry one on if you like."

"Here, lend a hand and pull."

He disappeared inside his sweater, and she pulled until he emerged again at the other end.

"It's like peeling a banana," she giggled.

She hadn't expected him to have nothing on underneath his sweater. For an instant she was embarrassed, but Simon evidently thought nothing of it, so she quickly recovered her unconcern. It was absurd of her, after all, to feel embarrassed, when they had both just seen a sailor at his morning tub. And yet, seeing a sailor stripped to the waist wasn't quite the same thing, somehow, as seeing Simon. What was it that made it different? Why was she always coming up against things of this kind that embarrassed her when she knew there was nothing to be embarrassed about—things that disturbed her and that she didn't understand? They all seemed to have something in common, but she didn't know what. When Simon had kissed her just now, though she had been pleased and not at all embarrassed, only a little startled perhaps, something had disturbed her in the same way as seeing him naked. What was at the root of it all?

"Simon." Her forehead took on its perplexed wrinkle.

"Yes, little Nya," came from inside the blue jersey as he pulled it on.

"It isn't wrong to love somebody, is it?"

"No, of course not, who's been telling you that?"

"Oh, no one. But it's puzzling."

"What is?"

"Loving someone. It makes one feel so strange, as if— I can't quite explain."

"Try."

"Well, as if it was something one oughtn't to talk about." It wasn't quite what she had meant to say, but he understood. He had at first thought that she was too young to feel love but it seemed he had been wrong. He came and sat beside her on the counter, and put his arm round her shoulders.

"Do you know what I think it is?" he said.

"What?"

"I think it's just a kind of shyness. It's difficult not

to be shy, when you fall in love for the first time. I'm shy, too, because I've never loved anybody like this before. It's a little strange, because you're so very young, but I don't see that it's any different, really, from falling in love with someone your own age. The only difference is in you; I'm afraid—or rather I was afraid—you mightn't know what you'd let yourself in for. But I believe you do now. You have a sort of idea, anyway. Of course you probably feel there's a whole lot you don't understand, but believe me, dearest little Nya, you don't need to. If you'll only trust me and let me help when things are too difficult for you to cope with; the rest will look after itself. If you really think you can trust me—I don't say love me, because that won't come for a long time yet, I expect—then nothing that happens to you can possibly hurt you or make you unhappy. I don't know whether you've thought about getting married, or anything like that——" he looked at her, for a second, and she thought he was waiting for an answer, but before she could collect her thoughts, he went on:

"You see, it's hard for me because I can't remember quite how one thinks at your age; I don't think marriage or anything connected with it ever entered my head. But I believe girls do think about it. And what I wanted to say was: don't let such problems perplex you for the moment. There'll be time enough for that when you're older. And then you'll be so much wiser that they won't perplex you any more. Do you see what I mean?"

She nodded. The tide was turning and *Puffin* swung slowly round on her anchor until she was pointing out to sea. *The Queen of the Night* was now behind them.

"It wasn't quite that that was worrying me," Nya said at last, "it was only that I didn't like feeling upset and—well, sort of guilty, just because I loved you."

"That's probably because you've read, or heard, people saying that it was wrong or wicked or unpleasant. Isn't that so?"

"Yes. I think it is. I didn't feel it was wrong myself."

"Well I need hardly tell you that those people, or the books you read, or whatever it is—are *all wrong*! That sort of thing is said by people who are jealous, or evil, or sometimes merely too stupid to know better. You won't let *them* spoil it for you, will you?"

"No, I should think not. Do you remember when I said I didn't want Aunt Ethel to meet you?"

"Yes."

"Well, that was what I meant, really. Of course she knows that there is a 'you' because of the postcard, but that's not the same thing. I don't care who knows about you now. I think I shall tell Aunt Ethel."

Simon looked at her in astonishment. "Do you really mean that?"

But she gave a short laugh and shook her head.

"No," she said. "I'd still rather not, if I can help it. But I do want to be able to be with you sometimes, Simon, I needn't always stay at school or with Aunt Ethel now, need I? I shan't be able to stick it if I don't see you for weeks and weeks. I'm going back on Tuesday, you know! That's the day after to-morrow."

"I know, little one, I don't know what it's going to be like without you for such a long time. *Puffin* and I will feel wretched."

"Oh damn, I wish I hadn't got to go back. And I can't even stay with you to-day because I've got to be in for breakfast, and then I expect we'll go to *church*."

"My God," he said springing up, "I'd forgotten about breakfast. I wonder what the time is."

To his horror the cabin clock said twenty past eight And Nya had to be back at nine o'clock.

"We'll have to hurry like the devil," he said, "if you're to be back by nine. The kettle's boiling, anyway."

"Simon!"

"Yes."

"Must I go to breakfast?"

"I wish you didn't have to."

"I don't think I will. After all it is my last day with you. Couldn't I stay a little longer?"

He came out of the cabin, with a frying-pan in one hand and an egg in the other.

"Oh, Nya. I don't know what to say. I'd rather not try and influence you. As long as you don't want me to go and talk to your aunt, I'm afraid the decision rests with you."

"Do you think it would be frightful not to go back?"

The complications that would ensue whatever he counselled! And the next few years would force many decisions of this kind upon him. Obviously he must make a firm decision in the first place and prepare the way for subsequent ones. But would she appreciate this?

"That depends", he said, "on what position you're going to take up about our being together. Whatever you decide on, I'll back you up, but I'd like you to make up your mind yourself. You see, your aunt and uncle won't like it if you see too much of me; and, as long as you live with them you ought to consider their feelings. Also, you have to go to school, and there's no getting away from that. The discipline is strict, you'll have to conform to the rules they make at school or else they'll probably kick you out. So you see, life isn't arranged to make things easy for us."

"But I'd rather be with you, Simon, than at school, or living with Aunt Ethel. If I have to choose I choose you. Do I still have to obey Aunt Ethel and the school rules if I would rather obey you?"

"Little girl, there's more in it than just that. If you were older, if you were of age, that is, and could legally make your own decisions it would be a bit easier. I'd take the risk then. But as it is I daren't. You belong to your father, and he and your aunt have complete control over you, however much we may want to belong to each other. To get away from them we should have to go very far indeed—probably to America or Australia or somewhere."

"I wouldn't care."

"Nor would I. But that needs money. And unfortunately I haven't got enough."

"Oh damn, I suppose you're right."

He glanced anxiously at the clock. It said half-past now. It was too late now to think of cooking breakfast.

"Nya," he began, "the time's getting on——"

"Yes, I know," she interrupted, "I'd either better go, or make up my mind to arrive back late. Would you think it mean of me, or unfair to Aunt Ethel, if I was just an hour late for breakfast? That would still give me time to go to church?"

She smiled a little forlornly.

"My darling child," he said, "you aren't capable of a mean action, or even a mean thought. No one could accuse you of that. I'm only being so hard-hearted because I want you to know what you are doing and to do it with your eyes open. I myself would give anything for you to stay here."

"Then I'll stay and go back late. I don't care what Aunt Ethel says, I'll make up some story."

"I'd try telling the truth. It might help."

"Yes, perhaps it might. I'll think about it."

26

So Nya stayed, and they breakfasted on board *Puffin* off scrambled eggs and bacon. It was the best breakfast she had ever had, even though the teapot had been rinsed in salt water and the frying-pan had last been used for cooking sardines and still retained a powerful impression of them. Half-way through the meal she announced suddenly:

"But if I can't bear it any longer I shall run away from school."

He looked up from his scrambled eggs.

"I shouldn't if I were you. It's never worth it in the end."

"I don't care. If I can't bear it without you I don't see what else I can do. Would you be very angry?"

He considered a moment. "I think I would. You see that might prevent our ever being together again."

"Not if they didn't know it was because of you."

"Where would you go? You wouldn't find your aunt sympathetic."

"Oh damn, I suppose you're right. You're always right. It's depressing."

"I'm sorry. I'm a brute, aren't I? It sounds as if I

tried to make things difficult. But you see, I'm supposed to be the older and wiser of us two, and it's up to me to give you good advice. I hate doing it because my instinct is to say 'to hell with everybody, let's not give them another thought.' In fact if I let myself go I'd be even more scatterbrained than you."

"Yes. But I'm the person who's got to put up with three months of girls, and lessons and discipline, without even a glimpse of you. It's all very well for you to talk."

"Don't be angry, Nya. I'm only trying to stop you from doing anything rash. Only for God's sake don't run away or do anything like that, unless you're absolutely desperate."

"All right."

"Because I shall feel responsible if you do. More bread?"

"No thanks. Oh—I feel lovely and full. I've had a huge breakfast."

There was silence in the cabin for a few minutes, broken only by the lapping of the water against the hull. The lamp above the table swayed gently to the yacht's motion. Nya lay down on the bunk, propped upon her elbow, her head on her hand. She watched Simon meditatively as he pulled out his pipe and began to fill it. He gave a short laugh.

"What is it?" Nya asked.

"I was just thinking of that time when I forgot my tobacco as I was sailing out past the jetty, do you remember, and I put in again to buy some more."

"It was the second time we met."

"The first time really. I don't count the time when you bumped into me. I didn't really notice you then—I was much too shy."

"You, shy?"

"Yes. Didn't I give you that impression?"

"I didn't notice. I was too shy myself."

They relapsed into silence again. Nya twisted round until she was lying on her stomach with her chin in her hands. From there it was just possible to see the funnel and bridge of the *Queen of the Night*. She thought of the sailor having his morning tub, and of Simon as she pulled off his sweater.

"I wish I was eighteen," she said suddenly.

"Why?"

"Because I'd know more about things then. I'd be more certain of myself. I can only imagine the things I want to say and do, but I don't seem to be able to say or do them."

He thought for a moment before he replied: "I wish you were eighteen too," he said. "I wouldn't be afraid, then."

"What of?"

"Losing you."

"Oh, Simon, keep me with you, don't lose me. I'm afraid too."

In one movement she got up from the bunk and went and knelt beside him on the floor, and buried her head in his lap. He put his arms round her shoulders in a sudden passionate embrace.

"Don't make me go away. If I once get back to school and have to behave like all the others, I shall never see you again. They'll make me think it's wrong. I know they will. They've got horrible ways of making you do things you don't believe in and hate doing. They'll tell me I'm not yet fourteen and I oughtn't to think about you. They'll say there's something wicked in it. But there isn't, is there? I know there isn't. I know it's not wicked. I want to be with you more than anything in the world. It can't be wicked to want that, can it?"

She was almost sobbing with the intensity of her emotion.

"Of course it isn't wicked."

"Oh, Simon, dear Simon, I don't understand what's happening to me. I feel that if I can't stay with you I shall die—and then I feel that if I don't go away quickly I shall burst. I don't know what's the matter with me."

He picked her up and held her in his arms. He hadn't realized before how very small she was; he could hold her whole body against his breast, could feel how the sobs racked her, how she buried her face on his shoulder. From her curly head to her bare knees seemed such a small extent—all contained in his embrace.

"Darling," he said, "don't cry. Don't cry, Nya. Oh dear, dearest Nya."

He rocked her in his arms as he would have rocked a baby. Her sobbing rent his heart. He could only hold her fast, murmuring comfort as best he could, hoping she would recover before she wore down his control. He knew so well what was tormenting her. It was a torment which he suffered too. It was this cursed question of their ages, the cruel barrier that time cast between them. If Nya had been four years older the barrier would never have been there—they could have met, as they ought to meet, with love and passion, without thought of care, as lovers, not in this impossible relationship of brother and sister. It was damnable for him to be always exercising self-control, never to let himself forget that she was not eighteen. It was cruel that she should have to fight so blindly against she knew not what. And it was wrong that she should know, unless he told her. And if he told her she could scarcely understand. She loved him almost passionately, no longer like a child. But still, she *was* a child. They were at time's mercy, and they could but wait in patience till she had grown up.

When her weeping had subsided he tried to speak. But for a long time the words wouldn't come.

"Little one," he said, at last. "I don't know how to comfort you. I can only tell you what I think. So listen, and try to understand me. You see, you and I, we've formed such a strange attachment. I never would have believed it possible, if it hadn't actually happened to me. We love each other, I think, as much as we can. There couldn't be any more perfect love than ours in its way. But it's also brought a great difficulty with it, one that nothing but time can remove. You're very young, you see, so young that I wonder, sometimes, how you can feel so intensely as you do. You have the capacity for love of somebody much older than yourself, but you aren't full-grown yet, and physically, you can't stand the strain of loving like that. It'll wear you out, and that isn't as it should be. We've got to put that right. And there's only one way, and that's for you and me not to be together too much until you're grown up. It's fairer that way for me, too. I'm older than you I know, and therefore in a way it's easier for me, because I have more control. But I can't help sometimes forgetting and longing for you to be older than you are. I can't help longing to love you, as I shall love you when you are grown up, but I mustn't love you now, because you aren't ready for it."

"When will I be ready?"

"Not for two or three years, anyway. Possibly not even then. And you may change so much in the meantime, that perhaps all this will mean very little to you by then and you'll want to wait for several years before you're certain of yourself."

225

"But I'm certain of myself now. I keep telling you I shan't change my mind."

"It's not your mind, my little angel, it's your body that will change."

She considered this for a moment before she spoke again.

"Simon."

"Yes, darling."

"Why will my body change?"

"Do you want me to tell you?"

"Yes, please."

"All right then, but you mustn't be frightened by anything I say, or let it worry you at all. Promise?"

"I promise."

"Well then. . . ."

She settled herself in his arms, and he moved to make her more comfortable. He was not in the least embarrassed, nor, evidently, was she. Her eyes looked up at him fearlessly, waiting to hear what he would say. He gazed straight before him as he spoke; and that gave her the chance to read his face without meeting his eyes.

"You've noticed, I expect," he said, "that since you were about eleven you have changed in various ways?"

"Yes."

"Well, you'll go on changing, that's only natural, not outwardly, perhaps—perhaps you won't even notice it much; but inwardly you'll be growing up into a woman, you'll be gradually preparing to marry and have children. Do you know how that happens?"

She nodded.

"Mummy told me you had them inside you. But I don't quite understand how. She said I would understand when the proper time came."

"She was very wise. It's no good bothering your head

226

about all that until it happens. But there's one thing you should know, because it applies to you and me. Nature's chief care in making men and women was that they should have children. And for this reason she made the most powerful of all the forces in them that of love, or attraction rather—because it's possible to love some one without being attracted by them, and to be attracted by them without loving them. This attraction makes men and women want to be together, close, close together, as close as possible, and ultimately leads to their having children. But long before that it begins to play the devil with their feelings. It makes them shy, self-conscious, unhappy or gay and carefree, as the case may be. I expect you've read about people who are 'lovesick'."

"Yes. Is that what it means?"

"More or less. And that, in a way, is what's happening to us. You see, since this force of attraction is primarily intended to make people want children, it never gives them any peace of mind until they have them. So it's usually better to go away from the attraction if you can, unless you want to have children. That's why I want you to go away now, so that you can grow up and get strong, and learn about people, and about the various other things that make up our life, like arithmetic, and English grammar and scripture, so that you can decide for yourself, when you know all that it implies, whether you want us to be together for ever or not."

"And to have children?"

"If you'd like to, by then."

She was quiet for a long time, lying still with her head in the crook of his arm. Then she sighed and sat upright.

"I think I feel better," she said with a grin, "it doesn't seem quite so awful as I used to think it was. It seems natural, and not at all worrying, as if somebody else had arranged it all and I didn't have to do anything about it."

"That's as it ought to be."

"I know. I can see that now. But I thought at first it was much more complicated."

"It's the simplest thing in the world, as long as you just let it all happen to you, and don't think or worry about it."

"I won't worry any more." She stood up and stretched her arms out. "Oh, Simon, I feel so much happier. Thank you for telling me all these things. I can even face going back to Aunt Ethel now. And goodness knows how late I'm going to be."

She hunched her shoulders and laughed to show him that she was prepared for anything.

"Perhaps we ought to go, then."

"Yes, I expect we'd better."

They embraced impulsively and clung together for a minute or two.

"Simon. When shall I see you again?"

"On the very first day of your holidays. Let me know when you come back. I shall be waiting for you."

"It seems an awful long time."

"We'll have to try and make it go quickly."

"Will you write to me?"

"Yes. And you?"

"As often as I can."

"God bless you, my little girl."

"Beloved Simon."

He kissed her gently on the cheek, then they went outside and got into the dinghy. They said no word on the way back. They were both contented now, even the prospect of parting did not disturb them unduly. They had founded a new relationship, in which each understood the other's reticence better than before they had understood each other's words.

On the quay she threw her arms round his neck.

"I love you, Simon. Good-bye."

"Good-bye, little love."

She walked quickly away with a smile on her lips. But the tears came into her eyes as soon as her back was turned. When she reached the corner tears came into his eyes, too, and blurred his last sight of her.

27

He wondered as he rowed back to *Puffin* whether it would be kinder to call on Nya's aunt and confess that he was to blame for keeping Nya out so long. It was five minutes to ten, Nya would be almost three-quarters of an hour late. Of course, it was possible that she would explain her absence in some way that satisfied her aunt. But he didn't think she would. He regretted now that he had advised her to tell the truth. He no longer knew whether it was good advice or not; it would have been wiser to let Nya form her own opinion. She would probably do that in any case. But either way might land her in difficulties with her aunt, and it was mean to be skulking out here on the water when quite possibly a word from him might put matters right.

It would probably be easier to talk to her father; she had hinted as much herself. But would her father understand? Would he be able to realize that a strange young man loved his daughter so much he was willing to wait for her, that he was willing to part with her while she went to school and even longer, while she gathered confidence in herself, but that all the time she belonged to him only, and that in the end, he must be allowed to marry her? No! Her father wasn't likely to understand that. He would say that Nya was so young that the whole business was quite absurd—if not unwholesome. He would call it baby-snatching. He would threaten him with the law unless he promised never to see Nya again. And he would twist and torture Nya in an effort to find out how far things had gone already. And she, not understanding, would feel shame and embarrassment and misery, and would, no doubt, ultimately be brought to believe that Simon was vile and hateful.

The more he thought of this, the worse the matter seemed. He wished he hadn't put any idea of telling the truth into Nya's head; it had been an idiotic thing to do. He was certain of that now. However stoutly she defended it, it would be sure to be misconstrued by her aunt and uncle. He must stop her at all costs. Perhaps there was still time.

He almost turned and began to row in the opposite direction, but he realized at once that his very presence at "The Rising" would lead to explanations and would defeat his purpose. He shrugged his shoulders, and continued on his way. But the subject wouldn't leave his thought and he found himself thinking of Nya and her aunt, and her father and himself as all embroiled in a stupid, unnecessary tangle together, which would never be satisfactorily straightened out.

Even when he had washed up the breakfast things and made everything ship-shape aboard the question still oppressed him; and during the day he thought more of it and of Nya's predicament than of his own sorrow that he wouldn't see her again for so long. He sat most of the afternoon on his bed at his rooms, staring at the sea over the Bournemouth roofs. It began to rain at tea-time. He watched the showers sweeping up the Channel and lashing the glistening slates of the houses by the sea. They came like grey veils of water, driven before the wind in waving curves that one moment enveloped everything in their path, and at the next had vanished into the atmosphere, leaving rainbows in their wake. When they had gone he walked along the front to stretch his legs, but he didn't stay out long for the thought of Nya soon drove him home to his rooms where he spent the evening writing a letter to her.

"I'm trying to imagine what you are doing and how you are. I see you sitting at dinner opposite your aunt with whom you have hardly been on speaking terms all day because of me. I hope you aren't too wretched. I am. It is all my fault that you are being made unhappy and the thought of that tortures me as much as the thought of you, of your lovely hair and your adorable impudent face, delights me. If I hadn't got to go to the office to-morrow I should spend the whole day outside your house. Perhaps your window looks on to the road, and I should see you moving about your room, pulling aside the curtains, brushing your hair, yawning perhaps, as you get up! I should rush inside and strangle your aunt if I found she had been cruel to you. I'd wait outside all night to see she didn't harm you, and take you to your school myself and tell the headmistress you were to be specially well cared for because you were my Nya, my very own Nya, and you were to be kept from all harm. I wish I could see you again—just once more —before you go back. I wish my stupid advertising didn't keep me from you. And I wish that no such people existed in the world as your aunt and uncle and even your father, if they are going to take you away from me. Because I love you, Nya. I love you now, but I shall love you more and more as time goes on, and one day perhaps, you will love me too, and we shall be allowed to be happy together. Don't forget me in the meantime; there'll be so much to drive me out of your mind, and if your aunt or anybody else finds out about me they will try to make our friendship seem something you should be ashamed of. Don't allow them to do that, will you, little Nya? Don't let them spoil and blacken a thing which we've created together out of nothing but joy and love. Don't believe them when they call it sin and wickedness. They can know nothing of love if they can call it that, so why should you believe them? But I hope you won't. I'm hoping you will tell them to go to hell. I'm even daring to hope you love me, or will love me one day, although it seems presumptious of me, my little goddess, my darling little girl."

28

Nya never spent a more miserable day in her life than that Sunday after she had said good-bye to Simon. She had parted from him with courage and a kind of gaiety arising out of their talk before she left, and of the new and wonderful prospect of friendship which it opened up to her. But her gaiety was shortlived. As soon as she was away from Simon, and from his comforting voice, her loneliness returned. Besides she was faced with the unpleasant task of explaining her absence to Aunt Ethel.

To her bewilderment Aunt Ethel didn't at first seem very angry that she was an hour late for breakfast. She had long ago finished her own meal and had begun to arrange her household affairs for the day; as it was Sunday, these were soon in order, and she returned to the dining-room to find Nya alone pretending to eat cold bacon and eggs.

"Where have you been, Nya?"

"I went for a walk, Aunt. I'm sorry I'm late."

"A walk?"

"Yes."

"Oh!"

Aunt Ethel seemed to deliberate for a moment, and then suddenly left the room. Nya wondered uneasily what was going to happen. Her courage was oozing fast and she hoped that whatever was to happen would happen soon. But she was left to finish her breakfast in peace; she could even have as much tea as she liked as there was no one to prevent her from pouring it out. But it was quite cold, and one cup was enough for her. She remembered vaguely that Simon had said cold tea could be good—"as good as beer"—if this was true it must be a different kind of tea. This tasted horrid.

Presently Aunt Ethel came back. "Emily says you told her to wake you when she got up, and that you went out at about half-past six. That means you've been out three and a half hours. Where have you been?"

There was a hard suspicion in Aunt Ethel's voice and an obvious determination to get at the truth, whatever it might cost her. Nya quailed to hear her speak. She crumbled a piece of toast and pretended to put the last scrapings of butter from her plate on to it, but she wasn't in the least hungry and she couldn't eat it. Aunt Ethel watched her for a moment, waiting for her to speak. When it became evident that Nya wasn't going to answer, she said:

"I'm waiting, Nya. I want to know where you've been."

There was another pause, during which Nya summed up all her courage. What was the best thing to do? To tell the truth after all, as Simon had suggested? But no, that would be bound in the long run to involve Simon, and it was better to avoid that except as a last resort. To tell a lie, then? But what lie? It must be extremely convincing this time, and must, above all, constitute an

235

excuse. Aunt Ethel's suspicions were aroused. On the whole, the best plan was to say nothing at all.

"I don't think I shall tell you!"

For a moment Aunt Ethel was nonplussed. She had hoped for the truth. She had half-expected a lie, but she was not at all prepared for such an emphatic negative.

"I don't understand," she said, after a pause, "perhaps you didn't hear me. I asked you where you'd been?"

"Yes, Aunt Ethel."

"Well, where have you been?"

Nya took a deep breath. If she could stick to her plan she was fairly safe—always providing Aunt Ethel didn't wear her down with questions. Even so, if you had admitted nothing at all, you were safer against repeated questions than if you said something that might be held up against you.

"I'm not going to tell you."

It was said quite firmly, without a trace of hesitation or doubt, apparently even without bravado. Aunt Ethel was uncertain what to do next. She realized she was powerless against a continued denial, even though it was practically a confession of guilt. Not really powerless of course. Although it might take time to extract a confession under these circumstances, there were several methods by which it could ultimately be obtained. But still it would be a nuisance to have to resort to them. For the time being it was better to assume that Nya was being silly and would soon be compelled to realize it.

"That's absurd, my dear child, I'm your aunt, and I'm asking you a question I expect to be answered."

Silence.

"Very well, I shall fetch your Uncle Nick."

But Aunt Ethel didn't move for a moment; it was a

ruse, the success of which she wished to observe. After a second or two she said:

"Am I to go and fetch him?"

"If you like!"

Now she lost her temper. The outrageous, impudent sangfroid of the child. She exerted all her self-control not to slap Nya's face, and the exertion made her tremble and grow pale and tight-lipped. Nya still avoided her gaze. She knew her last remark would move Aunt Ethel to fury, and she was afraid too that the spectacle might break down her own defences. She preferred not to watch. And she remained silent.

Aunt Ethel knew perfectly well that it would be worse than useless to call Nicholas in. He would probably only side with Nya, or at the very most dismiss the matter and return to his smoking-room as soon as she had asked a few questions.

"I give you one last chance to tell me before I call your uncle."

Still there was silence. There was no course left but to call him.

In the lonely interval that ensued Nya thought desperately of Simon and longed to be able to hold his hand and to ask his advice as to what she should do now. She was still determined not to give him away but it was getting increasingly hard to retain her detachment in face of Aunt Ethel's threat. Not that she was afraid of Uncle Nick, but obviously this was the prelude to more drastic measures.

"What's this I hear, Nya?" Uncle Nick said loudly as he came into the room. He had been goaded by his wife into assuming a lion-like rage from the very beginning.

"What have you been doing?"

"Nothing wrong, Uncle Nick."

237

"Nothing wrong! Oh well I'm glad to hear that. Do you hear, Ethel? Nothing wrong."

"Let me be the judge of that," returned his wife grimly. "I want to know exactly what it was."

"Now come, Nya, what was it?" he asked, this time in a gentler tone.

"Please, Uncle Nick, I'd rather not say. It isn't anything wrong, I promise, and it isn't anything to do with anybody else."

"Well, you can't say that, you know. It's very inconvenient for your Aunt Ethel your coming in late for breakfast like this."

"I know, and I'm terribly, terribly sorry I was late. I won't be late again."

"I'm sure you won't."

He turned to his wife like a triumphant bloodhound, as if to say, "There you are. I've done what you asked of me." But she was unimpressed.

"That's not the point, Nya," she said. "I want to know *why* you're late."

Somewhat crestfallen Uncle Nick returned to the attack.

"Yes, come now, won't you tell us why you're late?"

"I'd much rather not, Uncle Nick, I don't see what difference it can make."

"Why don't you want to tell us?" asked Aunt Ethel.

Nya had no answer ready so she was silent, till even Uncle Nick began to get impatient.

"Now look here, Nya," he blustered, "it really is very inconsiderate of you. Your aunt and I do our best to understand you, but sometimes it's extremely difficult. I confess I don't understand you now. If what you've been doing isn't anything to be ashamed of I fail to see why you can't tell us what it is."

238

Nya pondered for a moment before she answered. She got up from her chair, and facing Uncle Nick and Aunt Ethel for the first time said:

"I *could* tell you, Uncle Nick, but I'd much rather not, that's all. It's something private. You and Aunt Ethel often discuss things in private that you don't want *me* to know about. I don't see why *you* should want to know about this."

He couldn't help seeing Nya's point of view. She was only a child of course, and one didn't usually expect children to have secrets—not that sort of secret anyhow. Still, what she said was extremely sensible. It was what he would have said himself under the same circumstances. He confessed that he was beaten; with a shrug of his shoulders he turned to his wife:

"The kid's right, dammit. What's it got to do with us?"

But she was not so easily defeated. Once more she took the matter into her own hands.

"A great deal. But perhaps you'd better leave me to deal with this." She glared at him accusingly until he took the hint, and with a "What? Oh well, perhaps I'd better," departed to his newspaper in the smoking-room.

"Now, Nya."

There was an ominous formality about Aunt Ethel's words, as if she were saying, "It's your last chance." But Nya's courage had risen a good deal since Uncle Nick had admitted the soundness of her argument. She felt he had very nearly ensured her victory, for all she needed was encouragement and the support of some one more experienced than herself. To find that he agreed with her point of view was very gratifying; it gave her an added determination to stick to it. After all, what she said was perfectly true. It was her business entirely and didn't concern Aunt Ethel at all, except that she had been late for breakfast; and for that she had already apologized.

"Yes, Aunt Ethel?"

"Take that brazen look off your face and answer me respectfully."

"But I did, Aunt Ethel."

"And don't argue. Now are you or are you not going to tell me where you've been?"

"No."

"Very well, then. I shall have to find out. And I think I probably can. Emily tells me you said it was 'most important' when you asked her to wake you."

("How could Emily betray me like that, when I trusted her and she said she wouldn't say a word?")

"We waited breakfast for half an hour in the hope that you would condescend to come, but evidently your appointment was more important than Emily thought. I don't like my household arrangements to be put out by your mere caprice. I insist upon knowing what this all-important matter was or I'll have to punish you most severely."

Half-incredulously, half-anxiously, Nya blurted out: "What will you do to me?" and then instantly regretted having spoken. Idiot that she was; it was practically as bad as saying: "Please don't."

Aunt Ethel smiled in tight-lipped satisfaction.

"That depends," she answered. "I shall let you off lightly, even now, if you tell me the truth."

She waited a moment, hoping Nya would be induced to say something. It was Nya's secret she was after, not her chastisement, and she was still willing to exchange clemency for the knowledge she required. But Nya thought, "What's the point of telling her if she's going to punish me anyway?"

"Very well," Aunt Ethel continued, "since you're being so obstinate, I must do a little questioning on my own account. I suggest it was this Mr. Byrne you went to see."

It was the wildest shot in the dark—it only occurred to her on the spur of the moment, through a fortuitous chain of thought started in her mind by the memory of another breakfast questioning in this very room. Aunt Ethel hadn't thought of Nya's "beau", as Nicholas called him, since that morning, except to notice once or twice that she didn't appear to be getting any more postcards from him. Quite possibly the child had forgotten all about him. Her remark was intended to infuriate Nya, and to muddle her into admitting something else in her eagerness to deny this. It was made without any great conviction of success; and it succeeded cruelly well.

Nya's eyes blazed to hear the beloved name upon Aunt Ethel's lips. For a second she was too angry to reply. Her rage had been slowly mounting through the catechism and almost broke control when Aunt Ethel accused her of disrespect. Now it burst forth and she could do nothing to hold it back.

"I don't care if it was," she stormed, "it's nothing to do with you. You're mean and inquisitive, and you want to spoil the one thing that makes me happy. You must have been spying on me. I don't see how you could know if you hadn't."

"Nya!" Aunt Ethel's voice broke across her torrent of words like the crack of a whip.

"That's enough. I won't listen to your disgraceful language any more. Go up to your room."

And, because it was a refuge of a kind from Aunt Ethel and from this treacherous and unfriendly world, Nya went.

241

29

She locked the door the moment she got in. That was strictly forbidden but if you were in disgrace already it could make very little difference. She would unlock it again presently, but for the moment privacy was essential. She had to think; and to form some plan as to what she was going to do.

Aunt Ethel knew! Somehow or other, by fair means or foul, she had found out. It was no good wondering how she had found out, Aunt Ethel would never admit the truth. Could Emily have betrayed her, Nya wondered? But no, apart from telling Aunt Ethel that Nya had asked to be woken for a purpose, there was nothing she could know, unless she had followed Nya down to the harbour, and that was unlikely since she was far too busy in the early mornings to spare the time. Could it have been Dan, the seaman, then? He was surely above suspicion. Oh well, there was not much point in wondering how the truth had leaked out, since it *had* leaked out and there was nothing to be done about it. At least it had saved her telling a lie—if that *was* any saving. She didn't really believe so. A good lie well told at the right moment would have been a far better stroke of policy than her continued refusal to say anything, which had landed her in her present mess.

Her mind gradually ceased to work and her brain grew numb. It refused to think of anything, least of all an intelligent scheme of action. Aunt Ethel knew, and soon Daddy would know, no doubt even Miss Little-wood would be warned that she was a disobedient and dishonest child. Oh well, what did anybody at school matter? But Daddy! He did matter. He would be getting tired of hearing about her disobedience and "lack of respect". If only he would come home quickly so that she could tell him about it herself. He would understand and see her point of view. She hadn't been writing to him so much lately—at least, she had written just as often as before but she knew quite well that her letters were dull and self-conscious. Writing to Daddy had been a pleasure, often a necessity; now it had become a duty, not often a pleasure. The burning joy of writing to Simon had come instead. It had become a kind of religion in whose rites she indulged with passion and fervour. And she had grown so quickly accustomed to the change—it took place in the space of three weeks —that she now no longer even felt remorse because of it. It would be a relief to be able to have it all out with Daddy. Simon had not entirely ousted him from her affections; she rather blamed the great distance which separated them, and there was nothing to be done to diminish that, except for him to come home. She determined to write him a really good letter from St. Monica's begging him to hurry up. It might possibly make him catch an earlier boat.

She flung herself face-downwards on the bed and lay there in a kind of stupor, not thinking, not crying, not caring even, apathetically awaiting Aunt Ethel.

And Aunt Ethel, sitting downstairs at her writing-desk, wondering what to do with Nya, suddenly sprang up and went to the telephone. Whether by telepathy or by coincidence the thought of Miss Littlewood had entered her mind also, and with set features she took up the receiver and waited to be connected with St. Monica's. As soon as a voice answered Aunt Ethel smiled a little formally, as if she were already talking to Miss Littlewood. But the voice turned out to be not Miss Littlewood's but her secretary's. Yes, Miss Littlewood was there. But she was very busy preparing the lists for next term. Could she be given a message?

"I'm afraid it's rather important. I should like to speak to her myself," said Aunt Ethel.

When Miss Littlewood finally came to the telephone Aunt Ethel had grown impatient and bad-tempered. This state of suspended wrath was irritating to her nerves. She drummed with her fingers on the lacquer telephone-table till Nicholas emerged from his study saying he thought he had heard horses galloping down the road. Miss Littlewood's voice came just in time to prevent Aunt Ethel from throwing the telephone book at him.

The two women talked to each other for ten minutes at the end of which Aunt Ethel felt they understood each other completely. Then she hung up the receiver and went up to Nya's room.

But Miss Littlewood returned to her study with a furrowed brow.

"I've just been talking to a madwoman," she announced.

"You must be used to it by now," replied her secretary.

"Oh yes, I am. But most of the mad women I have to

deal with think their children are a sort of miniature archangel. This one practically told me hers was a devil."

"Who was it?"

"Do you remember Nya Russel? She was new last term."

"Yes, quite well. An attractive kid. A bit raw."

"Well—her aunt's the madwoman. She wants Nya to come back a day early—to-morrow in fact. She says she's been disobedient and she thinks it would be good for her."

"I haven't met her aunt, but I wouldn't mind betting it's six of one and half a dozen of the other."

"Possibly. I wouldn't have said Nya was *méchante*."

"What have we got to do with her?"

"Goodness knows. Of course, she can perfectly easily come back to-morrow if her aunt wants her to. There'll be the girls from France and Ireland here already. In a way I'm rather glad. I'd like to talk to the child."

Her secretary pushed over the engagement pad towards her.

"Look at that! You know quite well to-morrow's too full as it is."

"Oh, I shall find the time," said Miss Littlewood cheerfully. "Come on, let's do the sixth form now. Then we'll have finished the lists at any rate."

30

"Nya! Open the door at once."

"Oh damn," thought Nya, getting up from her bed. "I *would* forget to unlock the beastly thing—now of all times, too. That'll make her just about twice as angry."

She walked to the door as fast as she could, while Aunt Ethel, white with rage, stood trembling outside it.

"I'm for it," thought Nya, and turned the key. She withdrew to the corner between the wardrobe and the washstand. Might as well make Aunt Ethel stand with her back to the light. Her face would be less terrifying to watch if it was half in darkness.

"You know quite well I have forbidden you ever to lock your door," Aunt Ethel said, and there was no trace of kindness or even disappointment in her voice any more. It was as hard as iron. Nya merely nodded. It was no use trying to explain that she hadn't meant to lock her out.

"I don't propose to argue with you. I confess I'm sick and tired of your continual disobedience. It's easy to see you don't know there is such a thing as gratitude. Anybody would think you resented being here instead of appreciating our kindness in having you with us for the holidays. In view of your obvious dislike of us, and of everything here, I'm going to send you back to school as soon as possible. I've spoken to Miss Littlewood on the telephone, and she has agreed to take you back to-morrow. So you'd better start packing as soon as we get back from church."

Nya's heart went cold. She had scarcely given a thought to the punishment she would receive; she didn't believe Aunt Ethel capable of being ruthless. But this! To be sent back to school a day early, in ignominy, so that every one would know! She couldn't answer or make any sound. She could only stare at Aunt Ethel incredulously.

"But my main reason for sending you back is so that you shouldn't meet this Mr. Byrne again. It seems you see him chiefly in the mornings. Well, luckily you now have only one morning left. And I forbid you to go out of this house without my express approval not only to-morrow morning but from now until the moment you leave for St. Monica's. Do you understand? It is, of course, understood that you are never to see or communicate with this *person* again. You are to give me his address so that your uncle can write to him and tell him to go about his business. And I warn you that if he attempts to communicate with you he will be very severely dealt with. I shall consider it my duty to confiscate any letters you may receive from him, and I shall instruct Miss Littlewood to do the same."

Blow after blow! Nya couldn't stand it any more. She felt she would run at Aunt Ethel in a moment and hold her hand in front of her mouth to stop her saying these horrible things, or hit her till she turned and ran away. How could you go on for ever listening to such things and keeping a straight face? It wasn't possible. You simply couldn't. Nobody could.

Aunt Ethel derived great satisfaction from the change of Nya's expression, the relaxing of her muscles and her gradual loss of control. Unable to enjoy her triumph in silence she smiled grimly and said:

"I hope you have understood me and will remember what I've said. Now you'd better get ready for church. We'll be late as it is."

But Nya had reached the breaking point. Her self-control lasted only long enough to say, in a quivering voice:

"I'm not coming to church," and to await Aunt Ethel's supercilious, "Don't be so silly. Hurry up and get ready," and then every vestige of it left her. She burst into tears, and through her tears she shouted: "Shut up, shut up, shut up, shut up. I won't listen to you any more. I hate you, I hate you, I hate you."

Then she rushed at Aunt Ethel and started to hit her as hard as she could. For a few seconds Aunt Ethel imagined she would be able to ward off Nya's blows and possibly to administer some punishment herself. But she underrated Nya's despairing strength. Her tennis-player's arm was of little avail against Nya's wild but energetic blows. There was nothing to be done but to retire. She pushed Nya away as hard as she could, so that the child went stumbling across the room towards her bed still sobbing, "I hate you, I hate you," and slipped out of the room, forgetting even to take the key. As soon as she was gone Nya ran to the door and locked it. Then she bolted all the windows and flung herself on to her bed sobbing with all the strength of her wounded soul.

Emily, making the bed in Aunt Ethel's room across

the passage, stood transfixed, listening to the tumult. She saw Aunt Ethel come quickly out of Miss Nya's room and enter her own. Then she was curtly dismissed and told to come back later.

In half an hour's time, when Aunt Ethel had departed for church, Emily stole upstairs again and knocked timidly at Nya's room. Her conscience smote her because she had given Nya away in a moment of foolish anxiety arising purely out of affection for the child. She could still hear occasional stifled sobs within. But there was no answer to her knock, even though she made sure Nya must have heard it, so she stole quietly away again puzzled and unhappy.

31

An hour later Nya fell asleep, wretched and exhausted. She slept for twenty minutes and awoke feeling a little refreshed and better able to face the prospect of unhappiness that extended ahead as far as it was possible to see. There was nothing, no gleam of brightness, no consoling thought even, with which to comfort herself until Daddy's return. And that was still four or five weeks away. It was hopeless to think of Simon; probably she would never see him again now. Aunt Ethel knew all about him it seemed, except where he lived, and even that she would find out in the end by confiscating the letters he wrote. He had said he would write, and Nya believed he would keep his word. If only he would change his mind! It would be better never to hear from him again than to lose his friendship by so ignominious a means as Aunt Ethel had threatened to employ.

Oh God! It was wretched to be so young and helpless. Even Simon couldn't help her, because of her very youth. "If only you were of age," he had said, "I'd take the risk." But that was impossibly far off, seven years or more! Of course Daddy might understand that she wanted to be with Simon more than anything, but she didn't know if she could rely upon this.

She wasn't old enough to be married, she knew that. Daddy would no doubt say so. But she didn't think that was really anything to do with it. She wasn't quite sure what marriage involved, nor why she wasn't old enough to be married, but surely she and Simon could be together sometimes, as they had been this morning, for instance, without there being a tremendous fuss, and rows and punishment like this. To be sent back to school a day early!

"Oh well—who cares," she said aloud and began to pull her things out of the cupboard to pack them. Her trunk had been brought up already—Aunt Ethel liked to do things in good time, and had intended to "go through" her clothes with her this afternoon, she knew. No doubt that depressing function, which would now also be embarrassing, would take place just the same. The only thing to do was to have your clothes ready so that it would soon be over. But one thing must be done first, she suddenly remembered. She must write to Simon and warn him that his letters would never reach her, either here or at school. Perhaps he would think of a plan by which they could write to each other in spite of Aunt Ethel's intention to open his letters, but the main thing for the moment was to ensure that none of them fell into her hands. She would post the letter some time during the afternoon—there was a letter-box almost outside the gate—and he would get it first thing in the morning. That would be soon enough, he would hardly be likely to have written already.

She passed her hand across her forehead, as if the effort of scheming were proving too much for her harassed brain. She felt tired, and she had a headache, even though she had just been asleep. Thank goodness her eyes weren't swollen any longer. It would be embarrassing to know you looked as if you had been crying when you were trying to keep up appearances before Aunt Ethel.

She bathed her face in cold water, then took out her writing pad and sat down on her bed. She looked at her watch. There was still quarter of an hour before Aunt Ethel could possibly be back from church.

Dear beloved Simon,

The most terrible thing has happened, Aunt Ethel has discovered about you, God knows how, because I didn't tell her, and she was frightfully angry this morning before she went to church and said she would convescate your letters—I don't know how you spell it—and she says I'm to tell her your address so as Uncle Nick can write and be rude to you. But I shan't tell her, so don't worry, only I'm afraid if you write to me she'll find out, but if you wrote without any address on it she wouldn't know where you lived, would she? Oh dear Simon, I do want you to write to me so much, only somebody at school's going to be told to look out for my letters and keep back the ones that look suspicious, so I don't know what to say. You see what an old stinker my aunt is. Don't forget me, please Simon, I've been so unhappy since I left you this morning. I do love you so much, I hope you love me too. I wish I could see you again, but I don't expect I ever will again, they've all got suspicious now and I expect they'll be sending me to a convent soon. Anybody would think it was wicked to love you, instead of the most wonderful thing that ever happened. I want to go on and write pages even if I only say over and over again, "I love you", but I'd better post it before Aunt Ethelfreda comes back from church. Simon, I want to see you again please. I'd like best of all to be with you now this very minute, don't let

252

them take me away from you, tell me what to do and I'll do it. I love you so, much love from,

NYA.

PS. I'm being sent back to school a day early as a punishment. I think that's stinking, don't you?

Aunt Ethel returned in due course and the ordeal of packing for school began. They only had time to sort things out before lunch—which was a gloomy and uncomfortable meal—but after lunch they worked hard, checking Nya's clothes, looking to see if they needed mending, making a note of what she still needed, sewing on name-tapes, and finally packing the things into her trunk. Aunt Ethel made no attempt to find out Simon's address, rather to Nya's surprise. Possibly she was waiting for a more favourable moment.

At one point during the afternoon—just before teatime—Aunt Ethel's resolution almost faltered and she began to feel heartless and a trifle foolish at punishing Nya by a method involving the co-operation of other people. She very nearly decided to make some excuse and reverse her decision, but she remembered that the matter had been arranged with Miss Littlewood and the school authorities and she would look an even bigger fool if she suddenly changed her mind. But her conscience smote her nevertheless; and in a sudden access of remorse she went out of Nya's room on a pretext and told Emily to go to the restaurant down the road and buy a cake for tea.

"A specially nice one—a walnut cake if possible—they're the kind Miss Nya likes best."

When she returned to Nya there was a smile on her face which was quite out of keeping with her former sternness. Nya, ever anxious to be conciliating, was uncertain whether or not to smile back, but eventually decided against doing so, and tried to avoid meeting Aunt Ethel's eye. You never quite knew where you were with Aunt Ethel; it was better not to risk being rebuked too often.

By tea-time Uncle Nick had recovered his *bonhomie* and was nearly jocular; in a way this was more embarrassing than his silence at lunch, but Nya knew he was trying to be friendly, so she accepted his overtures as well as she could and their relations soon became fairly normal. Then Aunt Ethel thawed too, partly owing to the cake. Nya had taken it for granted she would not be allowed any. Aunt Ethel knew walnut was her favourite cake. Her puzzled and delighted, "May I?" when Aunt Ethel offered her a piece both satisfied her aunt's sense of decorum and gave additional zest to her gracious, "But of course, why shouldn't you? It's your favourite, isn't it?"

At one moment both Uncle Nick and Aunt Ethel toyed gingerly with the idea of suggesting a cinema in the evening but neither had the courage to plump out their suggestion without first consulting the other, which was impossible as long as Nya was in the room. When they eventually did discuss the matter after tea they decided against the cinema for a variety of reasons.

"After all," Aunt Ethel said, "we are supposed to be punishing the child. And I don't really approve of cinemas on Sunday."

There was silence between them. To Uncle Nick the whole matter was distasteful; he hated embarrassing and awkward relations with other people. If he had been alone he would have taken Nya out and forgotten the whole business. But Ethel had other ideas and after all she was in charge of the kid.

254

"What about that letter?" he asked uncomfortably. "Have I really got to write it?"

His very distaste provided the necessary goad to Ethel's melting zeal. She strongly disapproved of his lackadaisical attitude towards Nya's schooling.

"As soon as I have the address, yes," she answered firmly.

"I doubt whether you'll get it."

"Leave that to me."

"In any case, what am I to say? I don't know the fellow, we know nothing against him, we don't even know how well Nya knows him, whether he's simply a bumpkin she's struck up an acquaintance with—a waterman, say, or one of those sailors down at the jetty——"

"Sailors don't send little girls postcards of 'Yachting on the Orwell'."

"That's just it, they do. He might easily be a paid hand on somebody's yacht."

"And he might even more easily be a raffish good-for-nothing, who's pestering Nya with his attentions."

He removed his pipe from his mouth, and knocked it out on the fire-grate, before he spoke again. This perfectly unnecessary action was designed to conceal from his wife the fact that a smile played about the corners of his mouth and threatened to spread over his features. When he turned to her again it was to remonstrate with a serious face:

"My dear girl, aren't you painting things rather vividly? You can hardly accuse him of pestering her, when she obviously enjoys his company. And in any case, raffish young men don't *pester* girls of her age. If she were three or four years older. . . ."

He left the end of his sentence unfinished.

255

"Her development is extraordinarily advanced for a girl of her age. I've noticed it in several ways," Ethel began with some embarrassment. It was a subject about which she often thought but never liked to speak, even with Nicholas. "One never knows what liberties this man might not take. If he's honest and wants to see her, why doesn't he come and call?"

"Surely that proves my point. If he wanted to see her as badly as you seem to think he does, he *would* come and call. Or at least we would be bound to see something of him. Whereas Nya's only seen him once or twice to our knowledge, and he's sent her one postcard. I expect if anything he's a bit bored with the child and just humours her when he can find time. I wouldn't mind betting it means a lot more to her than it does to him."

But Ethel wasn't convinced. All through the sermon at church she had been embroidering her theory of a good-looking young seducer, and now she was too attached to it to part from it lightly.

"Do you think she writes to him?" she asked, more to formulate a doubt of hers than because she wanted Nicholas's opinion.

"How should I know?"

"I shall have to tell Miss Littlewood to keep an eye on the letters she writes."

"Good God, you don't mean to say you've told them at her school?"

She sensed the angry reproof in his voice. Put at once on her dignity she answered firmly:

"I've asked Miss Littlewood to help me to deal with this refractory child. She has more experience in these matters than I, or you for that matter. You must allow me to do what I think best."

"Oh, very well. It's not my business. But you'll regret it one day—if you really are fond of the child, which I begin to doubt. You'll forfeit every shred of confidence she ever had in you. I'd like to make it clear that I'm not with you in this. I disapprove most strongly."

Ethel smiled, the tired patient smile of a martyred saint. "I've known all along that I couldn't count on your support, Nicholas," she said with an ostentatious forbearance that conveyed a world of reproach; and she went out, softly shutting the door.

Upstairs, alone in her room, she knelt at her prayer-desk for several minutes. Then she went to help Nya with her packing.

32

Nya was woken next morning as usual by Emily; but it was a very different Emily. Instead of the cheerful, sparrow-like girl, with her optimistic remarks about the morning's weather, was a sad, and listless being who moved about her duties emptying the basin and drawing back the curtains, as though she had come from a funeral. Nya had woken suddenly, in her usual gay mood, and hadn't yet had time to remember the gloominess of the occasion, so she asked Emily what was the matter that she was so silent.

"Well, Miss," replied Emily with real distress, "I was thinking p'raps you was angry with me for giving you away to your aunt yesterday morning, and what with your goin' back to school a day early and all." She was ready to cry with remorse and sorrow.

"That doesn't matter, Emily. It's quite all right."

"I didn't mean to tell on you, Miss, honest I didn't, only I was so anxious because you 'adn't come 'ome, and your aunt was upset too."

"Yes, I understand."

"I never thought I might get you into trouble. Oh, Miss Nya, you won't remember it against me, will you?"

"No, of course not, Emily."

"Oh thank you, Miss. I'm ever so sorry."

"It's quite all right."

Emily departed, her conscience set at rest. But her sin had yet to be atoned for; and she made up her mind to watch for every opportunity of doing so.

To her delight a chance presented itself as soon as she went to collect the letters from the box in the front door. There was a letter for Miss Nya—a nice, clear handwriting too, a man's at a guess, perhaps it was the young man who was at the root of all the trouble. Enough conversation had filtered through Miss Nya's door yesterday when she was being scolded by her aunt to give her a good idea of what was being discussed. Evidently Miss Nya's aunt didn't approve of her getting letters from him, so there would be trouble again if this one was discovered. Miss Nya only ever got letters from her father, and this was certainly not from him. It was a different handwriting, besides it hadn't got those funny stamps. "Bournemouth", the postmark was! That must be Miss Nya's young man all right. She was terribly young to have a young man, even if she was so pretty, but still! . . .

The letter was smuggled up to Nya's room immediately, and when Emily had gone again, Nya locked the door and got back into bed to read her first letter from Simon. It was a delirious joy, which she never afterwards forgot—this eager scanning of his beloved handwriting, then the careful perusal of the letter; the dwelling on certain words to make sure she had read them right, the reading and re-reading of the passages which thrilled her most. It was a love-letter, she realized with tender joy, the first she had ever received. This was an experience, the beginning of something, the sign that at

259

last she was beginning to be grown up, even if she were only fourteen next birthday; it proved that she had every right to hold her own against Aunt Ethel because here was something that made her equal to Aunt Ethel, superior even in a delight which she was sure Aunt Ethel had never felt. Perhaps she would soon be a woman and not a little girl any longer. In her own eyes she was nearly one already. All that was needed was to make Aunt Ethel realize it. But for the moment this could not be achieved without betraying Simon, which was too big a price to pay. She would wait until next holidays, until she had had another term at school and found out exactly where and how she fitted in with all those extraordinary girls—if she did fit in with them!—until she had seen Simon again. He said he loved her, he had actually written it with his own hand. He must mean what he wrote; you could get carried away and *say* things you didn't mean, but surely nobody would *write* what they didn't mean.

She read the whole letter over again, and then again and yet a third time. She almost learnt it by heart; it would be comforting to say parts of it over to herself during the day, which was going to be one of the grimmest she had ever spent.

Aunt Ethel came out of her room to go to the bathroom. Nya hastily hid the letter underneath a pile of clothes, and, running to the door, silently unlocked it. Then she began to dress. When she was ready she folded the letter up and put it in her dress, envelope and all, right in the middle. It tickled there a bit, but it was much the safest place because her bodice held it tight. And it was better than her knickers; you couldn't very well put a letter from Simon in your knickers.

33

She was to arrive at St. Monica's at six o'clock and tea was ordered early. There was still some walnut cake left, even after they had all had some, so Aunt Ethel packed it in a box for Nya to take with her. While she was out of the room seeing to this, Uncle Nick gave Nya a ten-shilling note.

"Thought you might like this," he said rather sheepishly, "might come in useful, you know."

Nya thanked him with tears in her eyes; nobody had ever given her money since Daddy sent her home with two English pounds. Ten shillings was an awful lot, especially as it was almost impossible to spend it at school. But it might come in very useful in case of emergencies. With hardly a second's hesitation she decided not to give it to Miss Littlewood (which was the rule), but to keep it with her other treasure, Simon's letter. A safe place could no doubt be found somewhere or other.

Uncle Nick drove her to St. Monica's and luckily neither he nor Aunt Ethel tried to make jokes, nor to pretend that the occasion was anything but an uncomfortable and formal one. Miss Littlewood received them herself and told Nya to go and tidy herself, and put away her things in her new cubicle, and then come back and have some tea. Aunt Ethel said hurriedly, "Oh, she's had tea," but Miss Littlewood just smiled and said, "I expect she's ready for another cup."

So Nya said good-bye to Aunt Ethel who wanted to stay and talk to Miss Littlewood, and to Uncle Nick, who said he would wait for his wife in the car. Neither of them showed any emotion at parting from her. Aunt Ethel gave Nya a swift kiss with pursed lips and Uncle Nick shook hands.

At the door Nya turned and said: "Please, Aunt Ethel, will you arrange for me to have music lessons this term?"

It was a wish she had cherished ever since her conversation with Jessica van der Hemm. Jessica could do so many things she couldn't do, but, in music at least, Nya could hope to compete with her. And supposing they asked her to play when she went to stay with them next holidays?

"Music lessons?" Nya had never yet spoken about having music lessons. Could she be serious, or was this just a last taunt, flung out before she departed, for the amusement of seeing what the reply would be?

"Yes. Piano lessons, please."

Nya looked at Miss Littlewood, to see what she was thinking. But her face expressed nothing, except perhaps a slight amusement at Aunt Ethel's perplexity.

"But why didn't you say so before, during the holidays? We could have talked it over."

"I don't know, Aunt Ethel."

"Well—I must think about it first, Nya."

"I'm sure Daddy would approve. I always used to play when Mummy was alive—we used to play together." She turned to Miss Littlewood, for whose benefit she had said this. But Miss Littlewood only smiled and looked at Aunt Ethel. For a moment it seemed as if her request had no chance of being granted.

"You are the most extraordinary child, I must say." Aunt Ethel looked appealingly at Miss Littlewood, as if asking her to agree. "You've never said a single word about music or the piano as long as I've known you."

"But you haven't got a piano, Aunt Ethel."

"I don't see what difference that makes. But run along now. I must think it over."

"But please, Aunt Ethel——"

"Run along, Nya."

Her eyes filled with tears. Though she hated Aunt Ethel, this was an unfriendly way in which to part from her. She could see from the determined line of Aunt Ethel's lips that it was no use pleading. She looked once more at Miss Littlewood who seemed, this time, to smile in encouragement. Then she went out quickly in case her tears should overflow.

There was nobody about in the huge, cold classrooms, nor in the corridors and dormitories. It was just like the dream she always had about school: she had dreamt it again last night. Only there wasn't that green light over everything. Also these corridors, long and bare and draughty though they were, did come to an end sometime. Not like the corridors in her dreams that went on for ever or else ended in a blaze of light.

Alone in her new cubicle she unpacked her suitcase and then, after a furtive glance along the dormitory, shut the door and began to search for a hiding-place for Simon's letter and the ten-shilling note. It wasn't long before she found one. Between the cubicle partition and the wainscotting was a narrow slit, about four inches deep and three inches long which had evidently been

263

made by the joiner for some purpose he had afterwards abandoned. The envelope, with the letter and the note in it, fitted in quite safely, and was out of sight but easy of access. So far her secret was safe, thanks partly to Emily. She wondered why Aunt Ethel hadn't asked for Simon's address, as she had threatened to. It was unlike Aunt Ethel not to follow up a threat of that kind.

She couldn't guess that Aunt Ethel had only abandoned her resolution in order to be more certain of achieving it. It would have been useless to ask Nya for Simon's address, that was plain. Tight lips and obstinacy would have been her only answer. Much more practical, then, was the plan of leaving it all to Miss Littlewood. In time Mr. Byrne would write to Nya, his letter would be read by some one at the school, and its contents communicated to Aunt Ethel over the telephone.

She went back along the dormitory and the endless corridors, and through the empty classrooms where the inkwells stood ready filled, to Miss Littlewood's drawing-room; and knocked on the door.

"Come in."

Aunt Ethel and Uncle Nick had gone and there was nobody with Miss Littlewood but Miss Bowden-Smith. Nya advanced joyfully towards her with extended hand. In her gladness to see some one whom she felt she could trust a little and didn't need to fear, she forgot that she was a schoolgirl and Miss Bowden-Smith a mistress. Miss Littlewood noticed at once how differently Nya behaved when her aunt was not there and drew her own conclusions as to Mrs. Russel's relations with her niece. Besides, she had just had a quarter of an hour's talk with Mrs. Russel, in which she had understood even more of the real situation than Mrs. Russel intended.

Miss Bowden-Smith accepted Nya's hand with a surprised smile and asked a few polite questions about what she had done during the holidays. Nya, who hadn't expected her to be so distant, was a little hurt. In her imagination she was on the most friendly terms with Miss Bowden-Smith; it puzzled her that their relations should have grown so formal all at once. Miss Bowden-Smith then departed, saying she had a lot of work to get through, and Nya was left alone with Miss Littlewood.

Their conversation was general at first, but very soon Miss Littlewood said, with a frank smile:

"I gather you don't get on very well with your aunt."

Nya looked up startled, not knowing how to reply. There seemed to be no reproach in Miss Littlewood's voice, no disapproval even. Miss Littlewood read her perplexity in her face and added;

"Oh, it's all right, you needn't be afraid. I shan't scold you for it. I've just been hearing your aunt's view of the matter. Now I should like to hear yours."

"What did Aunt Ethel say?"

"A good deal. She seems chiefly worried about this young man of yours."

Nya blushed; and cursed herself for doing so. Miss Littlewood bending over her teacup and apparently examining its pattern, waited, to allow her to recover her self-possession.

"According to your aunt he is an undesirable person," she said then. "In fact she has instructed me to see that you receive no letters from him. But I shouldn't like to do that without at least knowing why. You're under my rule now, you see, not hers. You wouldn't like to tell me something about him?"

She spoke kindly. Nya glanced at her to see whether her eyes were kind too. They looked levelly into hers and seemed to demand her confidence.

"I'll try, Miss Littlewood," she began shyly. "Only there isn't much to tell. He's perfectly nice really, in fact I think he's awfully nice. I met him on the jetty, I bumped into him and broke his pipe. I'm sure Aunt Ethel would like him if she knew him."

"Why don't you introduce them to each other?"

"I suppose I ought to, really; Simon wanted me to but I refused. I'm afraid it's my fault."

"Why did you refuse?"

There was a pause before Nya answered. Miss Littlewood didn't seem a bit angry, or even particularly on Aunt Ethel's side.

"You'll think it rude if I tell you."

"I don't expect so."

"Well, I didn't want him to meet Aunt Ethel, or even to come to 'The Rising'—that's the name of my aunt's house—I wanted to keep being with him separate from all that. It was such fun. We used to go out in his yacht."

"Often?"

"No. Only about three times."

"But I gather he wrote to you often."

"No, honestly. Only some postcards. He went away on a holiday."

"I see. Do you expect him to write to you here?"

"I—I don't know. I hope not."

Miss Littlewood smiled as if she understood the whole matter. Nya watched her face anxiously, trying to guess her thoughts, wondering whether she had been a fool to tell Miss Littlewood so much. At length Miss Littlewood spoke.

"I'm afraid I'm more or less bound to observe your aunt's instructions," she said. "I only wish I needn't; though I'm not sure whether I think it's altogether a good thing to have young men writing you letters at your age. I shall have to stop any that come for you. But you needn't be afraid. I shan't read them. Nor will any one else."

"Oh thank you, Miss Littlewood."

"Don't thank me. The matter isn't closed yet. You'd better run along now. I've got an awful lot to do. We'll talk more about this if occasion arises. Good-bye."

She held out her hand. Nya took it, in a dazed way, uncertain whether she was being reprieved or merely having her punishment postponed.

"Oh, by the way," Miss Littlewood added, "I wasn't able to persuade your aunt about the music lessons, though I did my best. I think you should have them, myself. Your aunt says she's going to think about it. I expect it'll be all right, though."

"Do you think she'll let me?"

"I couldn't say for certain. I expect so."

34

Nobody asked Nya why she had come back early, so she was saved the necessity of inventing a plausible excuse. The other girls who arrived the same night took it for granted that there was good reason for Nya's presence there. Some of the girls Nya had seen last term; two of them had been in her form. Miss Bowden-Smith, who presided at supper, told them that they had been moved up.

"And what about me?" asked Nya.

"You've got another term with me, my child. And it's going to be a hard term too, I'm afraid. We've got a lot to get through."

"Oh bother," said a girl sitting beside Nya, "why do they always make us work hardest in the summer term?"

"It only seems hard because that's when you're laziest," said Miss Bowden-Smith.

"I don't care how hard the work is", said Nya seriously, "as long as it's interesting."

At which some of the girls giggled and made her feel uncomfortable. She relapsed into silence and said no more during the rest of the meal.

There was only one other girl in Nya's dormitory that night. They talked a little as they undressed, but without finding any subject of common interest, except speculations as to lists and forms and teams for the coming term. Nya's attention began to wander after a little of this. The other girl noticed and suddenly interrupted her flow of chatter to remark:

"You aren't frightfully talkative, are you?"

"No, I'm afraid not."

"What's the matter? Homesick?"

"No."

"I wouldn't let it worry you," said the girl, ignoring her denial, "you'll soon feel all right. It *is* a bit dreary when nobody's back and you're all alone in a huge dormitory."

After lights out Nya became even less responsive to the girl's questions and assertions. Conversation became increasingly difficult. Eventually the other girl gave up trying to talk.

"Stuffy," she said, and turning on her side, was soon asleep.

But Nya lay awake for a long time, till she heard two older girls going to bed in the room above and then the mistresses walking along the passage to their rooms, and till she saw the lights go out one by one in the wing across the courtyard, and heard the porter on his last round at twelve o'clock. As he shut the heavy courtyard gate and double-locked it and pushed the iron bar home she felt as if the door of a prison had clanged behind her and she was finally trapped. Gone were her dreams of happiness, the carefree, stolen hours with Simon on *Puffin*, the hope of eternally talking and laughing with him. Gone too was the gay, excited, little girl who had chatted to the officer on the boat-deck of a steamer, and who had bumped into a man on the jetty and made him break his pipe. In her place was a quiet, sad-eyed schoolgirl, dwelling already on the thought of black stockings and uniform and prayers and bells and uninteresting and uninterested schoolfellows.

The silence and loneliness in the black building gradually worked upon her nerves until her morale was quite broken. The tears came insistently to her eyes, and she soon made no more efforts to hold them back. Bitterly, bitterly she thought of the alternate ecstasy and misery of the last few days, and bitterly she sobbed with her face buried in her pillow, for Simon and comfort and love, until she fell asleep.

35

The morning, with the sunlight, breakfast and the prospect of several hours of absolute leisure, brought her morale back to its former strength. There was a feeling of frantic, impending activity in the air. Everybody else was busy, and that made you feel you wanted to be busy too. She asked Miss Bowden-Smith whether there was anything useful she could do. Miss Bowden-Smith, who sensed how lonely and ashamed Nya felt, compassionately gave her some lists to copy.

"Only they *must* be neat, *and* legible," she said. "They ought really to be done on the typewriter, but there isn't one to spare at the moment."

"I'll write very carefully, Miss Bowden-Smith."

"That's a good child. Run along, then. Do them in a classroom if you don't mind, we're a bit full up in here. Bring them back here when you've finished them."

She enjoyed her self-imposed task. It helped to pass the time. A girl who saw her writing asked what she was doing and commiserated with her.

"Jolly bad luck," she said. "I've got out of all that so far. I went for a walk. Why don't you go too?"

"I will when I've finished this."

"I can't make Bowy out. Sometimes she's decent to one and sometimes she's foul, all of a sudden, for no reason. To the girls she likes most, too. She was jolly decent to you last term. And now look what she's done to you."

"Oh, but I like doing this," Nya said incautiously.

"Do you really?"

"Yes, I asked if I could."

"Good Lord," said the girl, with a wealth of contempt and arrogance in her tone, and went out of the room.

Nya had the uncomfortable feeling she had experienced at supper the night before that she was being laughed at. Not only that but she felt anger too, at being laughed at for doing something which, outside St. Monica's, would have been an ordinary and reasonable action. It seemed one couldn't remain natural at school without instantly appearing unnatural and attracting attention to oneself. And Nya wished for nothing more passionately than to avoid attracting attention. She knew she was no good at behaving as the others did, and she simply couldn't bring herself to participate in their enthusiasms and codes of behaviour. She was sorry, because she didn't want to remain aloof from them, but they forced her to do so, or else to come entirely on to their side and be as they were. It hurt her that they should thus exclude her when she was willing to open her heart to them; and she in her turn antagonized them in her moments of impulse when she wished to be alone. So she grew cautious in her dealings with her school-fellows and they, when they were not in high enough spirits to tease her, treated her charily and not without respect. She was something of a puzzle to them. She seemed to have no enthusiasms, or none that she ever mentioned. And yet she was not apathetic in the manner

272

of some girls, who were content to do anything and be led anywhere by a stronger personality, but in a fierce resentful sort of way that made intercourse with her uncertain and unprofitable.

For the first few days of the term nobody noticed her much, and she did her best not to be noticed. This was simple to begin with, because she was among an entirely new set of girls, few of whom had known her well enough last term to think about her much now. But presently the harassment and novelty of the beginning of term passed off and the girls found they had more time for taking stock of each other. It was much the same as last term, Nya found, but a little more depressing, because of those few glorious moments of last holidays that had come between, and because school and England no longer even had the merit of being novel. The only comfort she had was to steal up to her room whenever she felt low-spirited and, taking Simon's letter from its hiding-place, to read it over to herself, although she knew it by heart now. There were such sweet things in it, things that moved her quite as much every time she read them. And above all there was hope in it. Even if Simon couldn't write to her, because of her aunt's cruel injunction, if she wasn't to see him again for at least three months, although he lived barely two miles away, still she could hope that they would meet again one day, and that a day might come when they would be together for good. He had said so, and he didn't lie. It was that part of the letter that she loved to read most, that and the sentence which referred to her "lovely hair", and her "adorable impudent face". Had she really got lovely hair? It would be exciting if she had. If only there were some means of making certain, if only somebody else would say the same thing. That would be something to go upon. But nobody had said it except Simon. And it wasn't likely that they would—at school. All you ever heard about your hair at St. Monica's was that it was untidy or needed washing or cutting or something. One or two other girls had hair like hers, but most of them had plain dark brown, or mouse-coloured hair, and a few had it quite black. On the whole she liked the chestnut and red-headed ones best, and the ones who called theirs "auburn". Auburn was a lovely word, but a little affected. Chestnut sounded so much nicer, and meant something, because it reminded you of the shiny rich chestnuts that fell from the trees.

Apart from Simon's letter the only ray of light in the gloom was Daddy's impending return. It couldn't be very far off now, although its exact date was still uncertain. Daddy's last letter had said "the middle of May". That meant about a fortnight hence, not so very long after all, when she thought of how long she had waited already. It would have been nicer to know the actual date of course, and the name of the boat. Uncle Nick said that all steamer sailings were in *The Times* and you only had to look them up if you wanted to know when to expect them. There was a *Times* in the library which the girls were allowed to look at, so it would be easy to find out.

It would be exciting and quite unbelievable when Daddy really came home at last. He had become almost a legendary figure. She hardly knew whether he really existed any longer. And she felt she had quite forgotten what he was like. Besides, there was Simon. What would Daddy say to him? There had never been anybody between them before, even when Mummy and John were still alive. And since they died Daddy and she had been greater friends than ever. Would he feel that she had changed? That he wasn't the only person she loved, not even the most important person? Would she have to tell him about Simon? Or would he perhaps guess in some inexplicable manner that she loved Simon best? Would he be angry if he did, or would he understand as he and Mummy always had understood her perplexities, and soothed and explained them away?

It was impossible to know. She must leave all that to take care of itself. Of one thing she was certain, however, and that was that she would try and bring Daddy and Simon together; that wouldn't be the same thing as letting Simon meet Aunt Ethel.

She was sitting on her bed, reading her beloved letter and pondering, in the interval after tea. At the very same moment Simon sat uncomfortably on a chair in Aunt Ethel's drawing-room, that very drawing-room which Nya had entered a hundred times.

It was Nya's letter, in which she jokingly said that she was to be punished, which had decided him to come and see Mrs. Russel. When he realized how his hands were tied, since he was allowed neither to see Nya nor to write to her, and when he had made certain in his mind, once more, that he would not hurt her by his action, and finally when, in the face of every counsel that his prudence gave him, he reiterated, "But I love her, I love her, I *must* be able at least to *write* to her," he saw that his only course was to speak to Nya's aunt. It would be idiotic and cruel to write to Nya in spite of everything when the letter was certain to be read and she would probably be punished. So he telephoned to Mrs. Russel.

"I'm a friend of Nya's," he said. "I expect she's told you about me."

She had told Aunt Ethel very little, as Simon well

knew, the greater was Aunt Ethel's desire to know more. After a perceptible hesitation she said:

"Won't you come to tea?"

It was agreed that he should call on her for a late tea after he left the office. Aunt Ethel had so arranged matters that her husband was out and they were alone. She expected a great deal from the interview.

But to her disappointment she got very little satisfaction from it. Mr. Byrne was taciturn and mostly spoke in monosyllables. Not only that, but he confined his conversation to one or two assertions which he repeated whenever occasion arose. For the rest he let Aunt Ethel talk, and only agreed politely, or disagreed still more politely when he saw the need. His contention was that it couldn't possibly harm Nya to "associate" with him, (it was Ethel's word), and that, even if it did, it was unkind to punish Nya for it.

"You misunderstand me, Mr. Byrne," said Ethel sweetly. "I wasn't punishing the child for that, but for refusing to answer my questions about you. I felt that she was becoming unmanageable. It was not the first time she had behaved so obstinately. There was once an incident about her dress, which I've no doubt was in some way connected with you."

This was an outrageous assumption, but as Simon didn't deny it—he wouldn't have bothered to deny it even if it had been false—she went on with a triumphant snap:

"That's what began it. And I considered that a stop ought to be put to her association with you, so I sent her back to school as soon as it was convenient. As to her punishment, no doubt that will come through her own remorse in time."

He understood now why Nya disliked her aunt and

276

refused even to speak of her. He had thought at first that it was simply a childish whim of Nya's, an affectation in which many children indulged at her age. But he saw now that there was an implacability about this woman, a fervent, almost a fanatic strength of will, wedded to an equally fanatical hypocrisy, that might well perplex and disconcert a child like Nya. He himself would have been demoralized by her if he lived for long in the same house. It would be no good to argue and reason with her; nor was it likely that he would touch her by opening his heart to her and telling her the truth. Once again he felt his hands were tied; his last hope of being freed, of gaining access to Nya fairly was gone. He knew it, and thought it waste of time to speak more words, and wisdom to be gone. Nya's father would be back soon. If he were really as she described him, perhaps there was some hope in him. He could do nothing but wait.

Mrs. Russel had evidently pursued a similar line of thought for she added suddenly:

"Thank goodness her father will be back very soon, and the whole matter will be out of my hands."

36

It was an intolerable situation. Nobody could expect him to wait patiently for three months without making a single sign to Nya, who was perhaps just as wretched as he at their inability to communicate with one another. It was necessary to do something to relieve the tension. Each day he waited made his blood boil hotter, until four days after he had called on Mrs. Russel, and six days after Nya had gone back to school, he could endure his enforced silence no longer. He *must* get in touch with Nya somehow or other. It would be best of all if he could see her, of course, even if it were only for two seconds, long enough to whisper, "Hang on! It'll be all right in the end." But this was almost impossible. For a time he entertained wild thoughts of calling on the headmistress and asking if he could see Nya. But the chances of his request being granted were so slender that he was forced to reject the plan. In any case, anything that involved ostentation, or violence, or even argument, would ruin his chance of ever seeing Nya again and possibly cause her much pain and embarrassment. There was no means left but to write to her after all, and to trust to luck that the letter would eventually reach her, even if its contents were read on the way.

As he wrote Nya was sitting in the library, during the letter-writing interval before bedtime, writing too. But not to Simon. Wretchedly and distractedly she had made up her mind that it would be too unwise to risk that. Like him she saw herself condemned to three months of tortured silence, of speculation and anxiety and gradual loss of hope. And her prospects of ever seeing Simon again almost vanished away, in spite of what he had said in his letter.

She could write with a fuller heart to Daddy now. Even if she didn't at first trust herself to say all she was thinking, her few sentences were so charged with meaning that they would have conveyed far more than she intended even to an obtuse man. And to her father they spoke volumes, when they eventually reached him. He had scarcely read the first six lines when he realized that Nya was not happy. There was a new fretfulness, an implicit despair in the way she wrote. This was quite unlike her last letters, which had been gay and friendly, but neither intimate nor communicative. They had puzzled him, those last letters; the insensibility they showed was a new trait of Nya's which he had never met before. Now, at last, miserable though she obviously was, she was her real self again. He had begun to fear that that dreaded gap, which always seems to open between a parent and his child at some time or another, and which he had dared to hope would never separate Nya from him, was in fact about to yawn between them. What had caused her temporary estrangement from him? One of a thousand things, probably, if one only realized how much more acutely than grown-ups children felt things. He considered every possibility; the conditions of life at "The Rising", the novelty of everything in England, the difficulties of school life. But none of these things seemed sufficient. There was mention in one letter of a certain Mr. Byrne, which he would hardly have noticed, except that she never put the names of people, only their descriptions; whereas in this case she had put no description but a name.

The first two pages of the letter were about school and the last few days of the holidays, including the rows and the fact that Aunt Ethel had sent her back to school a day early. She didn't complain about this; she merely mentioned it. She even added, in extenuation, that she *had* been very inconsiderate in coming back late to breakfast, and that she had afterwards been rude to Aunt Ethel who had tried to pry into her private affairs. As Daddy had always taught that this was an unforgivable sin, she expected he would understand why she had been rude.

"But", she added naïvely, "I don't think Aunt Ethel can think the same way because she often tries to find out what I've been doing and even sometimes what I'm thinking."

As all this was closely bound up with Simon, Nya soon found it impossible to continue writing about it without making some reference to him. And one reference would, of course, involve explanations, for up till then, as she well knew, she had said nothing to Daddy about Simon. So she put her pen down while she debated whether to tell him the whole story or not. Around her, in enforced silence, a hundred girls bent over writing-pads and scribbled, or gazed blankly in front of them in literary inarticulacy.

She had to think for a long time before she could make up her mind. There was no practical purpose to be served by telling Daddy now since he couldn't help her to see Simon from so far away. It would be time enough to seek his help when he arrived in England. But there was a kind of comfort to be had from setting it all down on paper in a letter to him; the only question was whether she would regret it once the letter was despatched. She was still deliberating when the bell went and a hum of conversation instantly burst out, and the girls began to clatter out of the room, carrying their letters, finished or half-begun, with them. Nya followed. It was no use thinking of writing in such a din; and in any case there was only ten minutes before she had to be in her dormitory. She would finish her letter next day sometime. By then she would know better whether to tell Daddy or not.

She felt particularly lonely that night as she got into bed. A week of school had somehow or other dragged itself out, and now it was Sunday again. She had always found Sunday a hateful day at St. Monica's. There wasn't so much to do and that meant that you had more time to think. And Sunday evening was the worst time of all, an empty, unsatisfactory sort of time, when you were supposed to feel rested and ready for the next week's work, but when really you felt tireder than usual, and not at all ready to face Monday.

Well, this evening in bed could be whiled away by trying to decide whether to tell Daddy about Simon or not. And if so, what was he to be told? Could you simply say, even to your own father, "I love him, please tell them all to allow him to write to me." What would that sound like to Daddy when he read it? Like an unreasonable and stupid request, probably.

"Well then, please let me leave school," she found herself saying. "I hate it, I don't fit in here."

Then even Daddy's patience would be at an end and he would tell her not to be so childish. But no! Daddy would never say that. Or would he? Thinking, wondering, arguing desperately, she found out soon that she didn't any longer know what Daddy would say, nor how she ought to put the matter to him. Daddy was a stranger to her now; even in her imagination she couldn't recall him properly, not the real Daddy, the one that lived and smiled and replied to your questions with surprising answers, or told you the names of the stars. She could only see a blurry outline which wasn't Daddy at all, but which "represented" Daddy, like one of those clichés, those things that Bernard Shaw never used. So what was the use of thinking about him, and wondering what to write in her letter? It would surely be better to wait until he came back, when she could see him and talk to him, and watch his face to see exactly what he thought.

37

It was grey and dismal when she woke next morning. There was a fine rain blowing in from the sea that made everything damp. And it drove against the window-panes. It was hard to have to get up so early. The water in the taps was cold.

"I might have known it," said Nya viciously, as she stood with chattering teeth by the basin, naked to the waist.

Her washing was perfunctory, and she dressed as quickly as she was able, in order to keep warm. As she was getting into her gym dress she knocked her hair-brush off her chest of drawers with her arm. It fell to the floor with a clatter.

"Don't make such a noise, Nya," said the senior girl.

To be openly reproved in front of the whole dormitory was a bad beginning to the day. But worse was to come. Feeling unaccountably depressed before she had been up ten minutes, Nya had a foreboding that the day would be an unpleasant one. So she went to the hiding-place and took out her talisman, read it over once again and kissed it before she put it back. It gave her a little comfort to do this, but not as much as she had hoped.

Much as she still loved the letter, she realized that its magic was beginning to wear thin. If there had been a successor to it, something to compare it with, and to lay beside it in the hiding-place, its effect might have lasted longer; but no successor had come as yet, and it was almost certain that none would.

She was tidying her hair just before going down to chapel when she heard a curious rustle coming from behind her chest of drawers, in the neighbourhood of the hiding-place. Swiftly she stooped down to see that her precious letter was safe and to her horror caught sight of it disappearing, in the grasp of a pair of fingers, to the other side of the wooden compartment. In a flash she realized that her hiding-place had not been so safe as she imagined. Evidently that gap left by a careless joiner gave access to the slot from both cubicles. And at this very moment the precious letter was in some one else's hands, its secret and most holy contents being devoured and defiled by another pair of eyes. She didn't stop to deliberate what she should do. She was out of her cubicle and into the next one—it was against the rules she knew—and fighting for her letter in an instant. Surprised and terrified, the other girl made little attempt to defend herself; and Nya's blows rained down upon her until she let go of the letter. It was torn in one corner, but it was unread. Without waiting to explain or expostulate Nya ran out of the dormitory and down to the library. There would be a fire there, where the letter, the precious, sacred letter could be burnt to save it from violation by the hundreds of eyes that would seize upon it and gloat and devour it as soon as the news became known. They would try to take it away from her, almost certainly. And that was likely to happen at any moment. Like a hunted animal she stopped to listen before she threw the letter in the flames. All seemed quiet but she could well imagine the scene up in the dormitory when the girl she had half-murdered appealed to the senior—and when the senior found out that Nya Russel had broken one of the strictest rules by entering another girl's cubicle.

She took the ten-shilling note out of the envelope, gave her letter one last despairing kiss, and threw it on to the flames. She watched it burn for a moment; then, when she was certain there was no trace of writing legible any longer, she turned away to the window, where she sat until the breakfast gong went, pretending to look at the *Illustrated London News*. Fortunately nobody came in, so she had ten minutes in which to collect herself and decide how best to face the storm that was to follow. Instinctively she clutched the ten-shilling note; it might prove a talisman of practical value.

The gong rang, and she went into breakfast, one of the first. There was nobody near her as she took her place; but in a moment a girl from her dormitory passed to go to her own table and slapping her on the back said:

"You're in for it. There's an awful shindy upstairs."

Her terror and misery increased and, when the other girls from her dormitory trooped in all eagerly discussing the very thing she least wanted them to think about, she longed for the earth to open and swallow her away from their eyes. Questions were rained on her, as fast as half-friendly, half-spiteful blows and nudges.

"What did you do it for? What did you do? What's the matter with Nya? Has she gone mad? You know Rosemary's frightfully badly hurt, she's had to go to matron." Taunts and idiotic, galling comments surrounded her on every side until the bell rang for silence and Miss Littlewood said grace.

During breakfast there was no other topic of conversation at Nya's table, and soon the adjoining tables got to hear of it and added their clamorous questions to the buzz. There was so much noise at that end of the room that Miss Bowden-Smith had to shout "Silence". Then the conversation became subdued in tone but far fiercer in intensity. Some girls, uncertain what the fuss was about, and exaggerating in their frivolity an already exaggerated account, confidently predicted that Nya would be asked to leave. Nya heard this and her hopes soared skywards, to be dragged immediately to earth again when she realized how improbable such an event was. Even if it came to pass, what would Daddy and Simon say? No! That was too terrible a prospect to bear facing. Much as she hated school she would beg and pray Miss Littlewood not to send her away.

She stared miserably at her plate, refusing to respond in any way to those who tried to speak to her. Miss Bowden-Smith sat at the head of Nya's table, looking on with a puzzled smile. Here was something she couldn't understand, something that concerned Nya Russel, who seemed to have committed some offence. It was out of the question for her to ask for information. But all the same it would have been interesting to know. More than that! She realized suddenly that her interest in Nya went far deeper. She could see the child sitting wretchedly, with downcast eyes, before a half-eaten bacon rasher. She had a momentary pang near her heart, which was an organ she didn't like to admit she possessed. It seemed to be complaining against having been ignored for so long.

"The silly kid has got into a tangle which three kind words from you would unravel."

Try as she would Miss Bowden-Smith couldn't bring

herself to regard the matter impartially as a mistress should. On her left sat Rosemary, the cause of all the trouble, as it seemed, blubbering and tearfully recounting a story of how Nya had kicked and bruised her all over. But *why*, she didn't say. Apparently Nya had simply come into her cubicle and attacked her. There was no mention of any valid cause. It looked as if she was suppressing something.

Towards the end of the meal, the maid who waited at Miss Littlewood's table came down the room and spoke to Nya.

"If you please, Miss Nya, Miss Littlewood says will you go and see her after breakfast."

Everybody around heard, of course. In fact, it seemed to Nya as if at that very moment a hush had descended over the room and every person in it was listening to what Polly said. One or two excited comments broke out, but as soon as Miss Littlewood, from her table on the dais, saw that Polly had delivered her message, she rang the bell for grace, and all conversation ceased instantly. Perhaps she knew the agony it is possible to endure when contemplating an interview with the head-mistress.

Nya's brain was nearly numb from fear as she trooped out of the room, jostled and buffeted unmercifully by whoever considered themselves, for the pleasure of the moment, a partisan of Rosemary's. Without any particular thought she made her way to Miss Littlewood's room. The senior girl would have told Miss Littlewood that Nya had gone into another girl's cubicle, but Rosemary would have suppressed the incident of the letter, and quite possibly nobody would believe Nya's story. So she would be punished—perhaps even asked to leave. She wondered what would happen if she did have to leave. Would Daddy and Simon refuse to have anything more to do with her? Aunt Ethel would, of course, that was certain. In that case she'd have nowhere to go, and would simply wander about until her ten shillings were spent and she starved to death. Perhaps they might let her in at Barnado's Homes. But they would be sure to ask her where she came from and when she told them she had been expelled from school they would refuse to let her in. Most probably she would have to go to a reformatory. That was what happened to people who were expelled from school. There had been one at St. Monica's once, so she had been told, who stole and was sent away to a place called Borstal. Perhaps she would have to go too, and there would be an end for ever of all the wonderful things she had been going to do with Simon and Daddy, and the van der Hemms.

She would have wandered up and down the passage outside Miss Littlewood's room for a quarter of an hour, so terrified was she of going in. But presently Miss Bowden-Smith came past, and, though Nya cowered into a dark corner with her back towards her, Miss Bowden-Smith saw her and spoke to her.

"Waiting to see Miss Littlewood?"

"Yes."

"Feeling wretched?"

"A bit."

"Cheer up. She won't eat you, whatever you've done."

Nya smiled wanly.

"I hope not."

"What have you been doing? Something you're ashamed of?"

"No, Miss Bowden-Smith." There was a slight hesitation before Nya's answer which aroused the mistress's suspicion.

"Honest?"

"Honest. At least—I only hit her because she took my letter."

"I see. Well, if that's the truth that seems to me perfectly fair."

"Do you think so?"

"Of course. What else?"

"Nothing else, Miss Bowden-Smith, honestly."

Miss Bowden-Smith patted her on the shoulder.

"Then if you've nothing to be ashamed of, don't for goodness sake go in looking ashamed, or you'll start at a disadvantage."

"I suppose you're right."

"Of course I'm right. Now then, buck up. Head high, shoulders back and a good loud knock."

Nya smiled in gratitude. "All right. And thanks awfully, Miss Bowden-Smith."

Miss Bowden-Smith disappeared into the common-room and Nya was left alone. Putting her instructions into practice as best she could, she knocked and entered Miss Littlewood's room.

Miss Littlewood was reading a letter and scarcely looked up.

"Ah, is that you, Nya? Sit down."

She returned to her reading of the letter. The suspense was agonizing, and yet there was something encouraging in Miss Littlewood's deliberation. If she were really angry she would hardly be likely to wait so long before she spoke.

Presently she laid her letter down. "I'm sorry to make you wait," she began with a smile, "but this letter is from your aunt. It's about your music lessons."

Hope surged up again in Nya's heart. Music lessons. If that was all that Miss Littlewood wanted to talk to her about, she was very happy. She would gladly give up the idea of having music lessons, if the fates would be placated thereby and overlook her iniquity of this morning. What did it matter after all whether she had the lessons or not, so long as she wasn't sent away from St. Monica's in disgrace, so long as she could see Simon again, hug him once more, once more hear him say, "Little Nya", or tease her about her impudent face?

"I'm afraid your aunt doesn't approve of your having them. She says she doesn't think you can seriously want them or you would have asked her before. In any case, she says, your father will be back soon and you'd better ask him."

Miss Littlewood picked up the letter and handed it to Nya. The tiny piece of paper with the tiny writing on it was only too familiar. Nya could hardly repress a shudder. But she read the letter and handed it back to Miss Littlewood without comment.

"I'm sorry," Miss Littlewood said. "I expect you'd have liked them."

"Yes. I hoped——" Nya hesitated.

"What?"

"I thought they might be a kind of escape."

"What from?"

"Well, from—from thinking about other things—and things like that."

It was a meaningless sentence, but the manner in which it was spoken conveyed a good deal to Miss Littlewood.

"I see," she said.

"If only you were allowed to practise, but you're not, unless you have lessons, are you?"

"Not as a rule. But I don't see why we shouldn't make an exception."

"Would it be possible?"

"It might. When's your father coming home?"

"I don't know. Sometime in May, he said. That's this month."

"Yes. Then we'd better wait till he comes before we decide about the lessons. In the meantime you can practise in the music-room whenever nobody else wants it."

"Oh, thanks most awfully, Miss Littlewood."

"That's settled then. Now for a more important matter."

Miss Littlewood turned back to her desk. Nya's heart sank. It was coming now, that was clear. Miss Littlewood had known all the time. She had simply been playing the cat and mouse game. How base and treacherous!

Oh well. It had to be gone through. The whole story of the letter would come out; she would be obliged to tell it in self-defence. She must claim some justification for breaking so strict a rule. She waited, unable to breathe for the choking in her throat, until Miss Littlewood should start the inquisition.

Miss Littlewood picked up two unopened letters off her desk.

"I'm sorry, my child," she said, "but we've got to discuss this business of your letters."

She was quite bewildered now. What letters? There was only one; the one that Rosemary had stolen out of its hiding-place. How could there be more than one, and what were these two envelopes in Miss Littlewood's hand?

Suddenly it dawned on her that Miss Littlewood still didn't know: she hadn't been playing with her after all.

This was quite another matter. It had nothing to do with Rosemary. It must be a letter from Simon that Miss Littlewood meant, from dear beloved Simon. He had written, after all, when she had quite made up her mind that she couldn't hear from him again until the holidays. He had written! But his letter was in Miss Littlewood's possession. Oh, if only it were still unopened. If only she could hold it in her hands and kiss it, she would gladly put it into the fire unread, so long as no one else read it. The mere fact that he had written was enough to buoy her up with hope for a long while. Her eyes blazed with joy to know that he had written.

Miss Littlewood saw the momentary gleam in Nya's eyes, and drew her own conclusions. For some reason, which she didn't understand till afterwards, she began to grow angry. It was an absurd situation to have to deal with, to intercept love-letters from a man to a girl of fourteen. It was distasteful, and she felt a sudden resentment against Nya and her aunt for placing her in this equivocal position. That a girl at St. Monica's should be receiving love-letters was bad enough; that she, the headmistress, should be called upon to intercept them and read or destroy them as she thought fit was intolerable.

"It's really most unpleasant for me to have to deal with this. I don't like having to interfere in other people's private affairs. However, your aunt has instructed me to, and so I must. Here are two letters which came for you this morning. One has a colonial stamp on it. I imagine it's from your father. But the other has a Bournemouth postmark. Do you recognize the handwriting?"

"Yes, Miss Littlewood."

"I'm afraid I must ask you who it's from."

Nya twisted uncomfortably in her chair under the torment of seeing Simon's letter before her and not being able to open it.

"It's from—from Simon."

It seemed sacrilege to pronounce his name under compulsion like this.

"I thought so. Well! What are we going to do about it?"

"I'd like to read it please, even if I'm not to be allowed to keep it."

"I'm afraid that's the one thing I can't allow."

"But, Miss Littlewood, the letter belongs to me——"

"My dear child, don't think it's any pleasure to me to keep it from you."

"Mayn't I even look at it?"

"I am afraid not."

"But I don't see how it concerns anybody else. What right have they got to stop me reading it?"

"Your aunt considered it's for your own good."

"Do you think so too?"

"Frankly, yes."

"But why? I don't understand."

"It's hard to explain. I don't of course know what's in the letter, I should have to read it first——"

"Oh no." Nya interrupted in agony.

"Don't be afraid. I gave you my word. But your very manner leads me to suspect that it's not an ordinary letter. And if, as I suspect, it's what's termed—a love letter, I consider it extremely bad for a girl of your age."

Nya hardly knew where to look; she was puzzled and upset by Miss Littlewood's tone. She turned her head from side to side, as if trying to see through an impenetrable forest. Miss Littlewood feared that at any moment she might burst into tears.

"You all say the same," Nya said in despair, "even Simon. Why am I too young? What has it got to do with my age?"

"I'm glad he realizes, at any rate. And if you don't realize why you are too young to have letters like that you must be stupider than I thought."

"But I don't, Miss Littlewood, honestly. If I love him, it can't make any——"

But Miss Littlewood's patience was suddenly exhausted. Nya's last phrase, coming from such young lips, shocked her beyond limit. The mere mention of the word "love" by a child of Nya's age. It was horrible.

"Now we'll have no more of this," she said, stern at last. "You can watch me destroy this letter here in this fire. The other letter you can have, I'm not concerned with it. And in order to wind up this unpleasant matter once and for all, you must sit down now and write to this man and tell him never to write to you again. Do you hear?"

Nya didn't answer. Her brain refused to believe the cruel information her ears conveyed. Was it possible that she was to write to Simon at Miss Littlewood's dictation? No. That she would never do. It would be wicked. Simon and Miss Littlewood were worlds apart, she could never bring them together like this. Oh, if only she had been able to keep Simon to herself in the first place. All this would never have happened. It was Aunt Ethel who had spoiled her friendship with him.

"Then we can consider the matter closed," Miss Littlewood's voice went on, but Nya scarcely understood what she was saying. In a dream she sat down at Miss Littlewood's desk, took a sheet of the grey notepaper with its black crest, in a dream she dipped Miss Littlewood's pen into the ink-pot, and waited, not knowing what to write, nor how to begin to think it out.

"Fortunately your friend called on your aunt and she made her disapproval quite clear to him."

Miss Littlewood came up behind her to the desk.

So Simon had met Aunt Ethel, and her last satisfaction was gone! Well, there was nothing left for it now, she supposed, but to make up her mind that she would never see him again. In view of this she might as well do all she could to make an end, even if it meant writing what Miss Littlewood commanded.

"What am I to write, Miss Littlewood?"

"I leave that to you. But I must see the letter."

"Very well."

So it was not to be dictated. She almost wished it were. She felt limp, unable to think or act, unable even to be angry or resent this shameful outrage. The sooner it was over the better; all that mattered now was to end it quickly. After a moment's thought, while Miss Littlewood stood behind her, she said in a listless voice:

"I don't know what to say."

"Do you want me to tell you?"

"Yes, please."

"Very well. What did you say his name was?"

"Simon."

" 'Dear Simon,' then. That's quite enough. 'I am writing at Miss Littlewood's instruction to say that you are not to write to me again. If you do, your letters will simply be burnt before they reach me.' That will do, I think."

"How am I to end up?"

For an instant Miss Littlewood hesitated while the warmer side of her nature struggled with her sense of decorum. Then she said:

"Put anything you like, and seal up the envelope."

And as if to give Nya confidence she crossed to the other side of the room. In frantic haste Nya added, in minute letters, that Simon might differentiate the postscript from the rest of the letter: "But I love you just the same—oh Simon——"

That was as far as she got when Miss Littlewood's voice broke in upon her secret message, and she hastily sealed up the envelope.

"Do you know his address?"

"Yes, Miss Littlewood, but I——"

"It's all right. I'm not interested in him. It's you we've got to look after."

"You aren't going to write to him?"

"No. I've nothing to say to him. But it means we needn't open his letter. I'll put it in the fire."

She threw it deliberately into the flames. Nya started up with a cry; but she stifled it immediately, and bit her lip to keep back her tears.

"Here's your father's letter. Now run along. It's nearly time for school."

She plunged headlong from the room. Once outside the door she wept without control and she was still sobbing as she took her place at her desk.

Miss Bowden-Smith noticed, and left her alone as much as possible throughout the lesson. Nya was grateful.

It wasn't until half-way through the lesson, when she gave up her unsuccessful attempt to attend to her work and miserably allowed her thoughts to wander over the events of the last two hours, that Nya remembered what she had expected Miss Littlewood to say to her. The senior girl couldn't have reported her. Possibly she didn't intend to and she would be spared the pain of another interview with Miss Littlewood. Not that it could be much worse than the first. Oh well! She was

296

past caring now. Let them do what they liked to her. Let them expel her if they wanted to. It couldn't matter very much now; except to Daddy. But even quarrelling with Daddy couldn't be so beastly as having to write that letter to Simon.

She remembered the letter from Daddy which Miss Littlewood had given her. She would read it in the next interval. Oh no! That wouldn't be time enough. She would ask to be excused at the beginning of the next lesson and read it in the lavatory. Daddy's letters always came when they were most needed. Surely there would be some comfort in this one.

But when she was finally able to read it, it contained nothing but disappointment of the bitterest kind. It was a short note, evidently written in haste.

This is not a letter, my darling Nya, but just a note to tell you not to expect me this month after all. I simply can't get away. I may be able to get to England by the end of June, but whatever happens you can count on my arriving in plenty of time for your holidays. No power on earth could keep me here after June. Forgive your wretched busy father and keep a look-out for him, and for a thumping good summer holidays with him.

Write to me here till the end of May. More by next mail.

Your affectionate

DADDY.

This was the ultimate calamity. Daddy wasn't coming home for at least two months. Two months more of school, of Rosemary and inquisitive girls and Miss Littlewood, without even the solace of a letter from Simon. It was more than any one could bear.

She began to sob again, unable to help herself, unable

to think of anything but the desolate prospect before her. She didn't know that Daddy had written the very day before Aunt Ethel's letter had arrived, containing its despairing appeal for him to come back to England as soon as possible. She couldn't know, either, that he had read between the lines of Aunt Ethel's letter and recalled many passages from Nya's letters, the cumulative effect of which had been to make him realize that all was not well at "The Rising", and that his little daughter was possibly unhappy. Nor that he had accordingly retracted a foolish promise to stay on an extra month and, saying that he had served his country and his service quite as well as any one could wish and that he was going to take his leave, which had been owing for a year, immediately, with or without official sanction, he had boarded the next boat for Southampton. As far as Nya was concerned all this might never have happened.

"Please God, let me die, let me die. I don't want to go on living."

Her sobs eventually exhausted themselves, but she was unable to face the thought of going back to the classroom. No, no. She would do anything rather than that. The question was, what could she do? She could throw herself out of the window. But that meant that she would never, under any circumstances, see Simon again. Whereas, as long as she was alive, there was still hope. What then? Was there no help to be found anywhere? Miss Bowden-Smith? Matron? Aunt Ethel? No, they were all in league against her, more or less. There *was* one person who would help. The only one who could, the only one she loved and wanted to see with all her heart. But at first she refused to think of him. As fast as his memory forced itself upon her she banished it by feverishly thinking of something else. At last, however, when she had tried all other plans that her despair presented to her, she had to admit that Simon was the only one who could help. And the moment she admitted this to herself her way was clear. Of course she must go to Simon, and as quickly as possible. Now was the time, while everybody else was in school.

38

She opened the door and ran down the passage without another thought but how to get out of the building unobserved. Luck was with her for she saw nobody until she passed the classroom corridor, when she had to dodge behind a door for a moment to let Betsy, the errand and odd-job woman, pass by. She little dreamt that Betsy was at that moment actually in search of her with an injunction that she should go and see Miss Littlewood again in the interval before lunch. Miss Littlewood had just learned of the affair of Rosemary from the senior. If Nya had known this she might have run at top-speed towards the gates. As it was, however, her fear was not so great as to rob her of caution, so she went through the emergency exit at the end of the classroom wing, climbed down the fire-ladder into the garden, and, dodging a gardener with a barrow who was coming down the path, made her way into the road.

As soon as she could she hailed a taxi and gave the driver Simon's address. So urgent was her manner that the driver never hesitated, nor doubted but that it was a matter of life and death. The ten-shilling note that, in her excitement, she brandished before his eyes, helped to convince him. Schoolgirls, he thought, don't get given ten-bob notes except in cases of urgency.

She made him stop at a post office on the way, where she bought a letter-card and wrote a hasty message to Simon. He would be out when she got to his room, she knew that, and in all probability the landlady wouldn't let her in. So the only thing to do was to leave a message and go to Sandbanks, trusting not to meet Aunt Ethel or Uncle Nick, and try to get aboard *Puffin*.

Her brain was working clearly now. The plan seemed simple as she evolved it in the speeding taxi. She would go to the jetty, where the dinghy would be waiting as usual, and she would row out to the yacht. If any one tried to stop her she would appeal to Dan.

She made the driver wait while she left the letter-card at Simon's flat. To her disappointment there was no answer to her ring, neither landlady nor servant opened the door. For an instant she wondered what to do. She didn't know where Simon's office was. This flat was the only place where she could reach him. Yet she must get a message to him; for it was only Monday and he might quite possibly not go aboard the *Puffin* for another five days. Trusting to luck she put the letter through the letter-box. She could have wished that she had written the address in a larger hand, so as to command attention. But if he looked in the letter-box he could hardly fail to find her message, and to recognize her writing at once.

She went down to the taxi and told the driver to take her to Sandbanks jetty.

But now he became suspicious. "It's a long way, Miss," he said.

"How much does it cost?"

"Well, it's not that so much, Miss, but I'm a Bournemouth cabbie, properly speaking."

He was simply making difficulties in order to find out what Nya's purpose was. If she were running away she might try to make him take her farther than she could afford. But her brain was working too fast to haggle over a question of mileage. So she told him to drive to the centre of the town.

"To where the buses for Sandbanks stop."

She didn't know where this was as she and Aunt Ethel had always done their shopping by car; but the driver knew. Shaking his head and sucking his teeth he started off in that direction.

She paid him off and stood in the road, waiting for the bus. She was running an enormous risk, she knew. It was true she looked like a girl from any other school, since she had escaped just as she was in her gym dress, without hat or blazer or distinguishing badge of any kind. But it was always possible that some one from St. Monica's might be in the town and recognize her. Then, too, she might meet some one she knew in the bus, or in Sandbanks. Uncle Nick might have come into town and be taking a bus home, as he often did. However, it was better to run the risk of being seen than to argue with a taxi-driver about how far it was to Sandbanks, and to raise his suspicions and cause him to tell the police or anybody else who might ask him questions. In any case, she no longer felt that she was connected with St. Monica's. She was Nya again, the Nya of the holidays, Simon's friend, the Nya who went out sailing sometimes in *Puffin*. She was on her way to *Puffin* now. There she would have to possess herself in patience until Simon turned up. It would be rather like that dream she once had, or was it only a scene she had invented? About swimming out to the yacht, and arriving cold and exhausted, and being found there by Simon? Only he had still been Mr. Byrne when she dreamed or invented that story. Now he was Simon, dear beloved Simon. Oh, how splendid it was to be free of that bad dream of a place, St. Monica's, and to be going to see Simon again.

The bus drew up, and she got into it with trepidation. Fortunately there were only four people in it, none of whom she knew. It took her in slow and uneventful stages to the jetty at Sandbanks and she saw no one at all. Sure enough the absurd little dinghy was tied up to its usual place on the pier-stanchion. It made her want to shout for joy. This wasn't at all how she had imagined running away would be. As a rule, in books at any rate, it was pitch dark or raining, or the town was full of spies or there was some other equally dreadful danger to be faced. But to-day everything had happened suddenly, swiftly and according to an impulsive but successful plan. Even the weather was helping; for though it had been raining when she got up, the rain had stopped, leaving nothing worse behind it than heavy black clouds. It might rain again later on, perhaps, but what did that matter? Once aboard *Puffin*——?

Dan happened to look over the rail as she was getting into the dinghy. "Hallo, hallo, hallo," he said. "What's going on down there?"

At first she was startled, but when she saw Dan's kindly face looking down at her with much the same expression of puzzled amusement as it had worn on the morning when he had upset the dustbin on to Simon's head, she heaved a sigh of relief and answered gaily. "It's only me, Dan. I'm going out to *Puffin*."

"And how's Mr. Byrne going to get out to her if you take away his boat?"

"He said he'd take a boat. He'll be down about seven, I think."

What a good liar she was becoming!

"Seven! Well, I'd better leave a boat out for him then."

"Yes, will you, please?"

"All right, Miss. Look out now. Mind that motor-launch."

He spoke just in time to warn her that she was heading straight for the oncoming launch. She thanked him, waved, and set about the business of rowing out to the yacht, which she found very difficult and exhausting. Fortunately the tide was making and she found that she got carried along by it, more or less in the right direction. *Puffin* lay at her moorings just as she had done last Sunday morning when Nya had been late for breakfast at "The Rising". After rowing for nearly a quarter of an hour the dinghy bumped alongside and Nya went aboard.

Now at last she had put all her fears, all her persecutions behind her, and was carefree and gay. St. Monica's and Miss Littlewood and Rosemary didn't seem worth thinking about any more. She dismissed them utterly from her mind, and looked forward with delight to seeing Simon again. In the meantime there was nothing to do but to sit and watch the seagulls, or to see the black clouds roll up like enormous puffs of smoke across the sky.

For nearly two hours she sat on the cabin top or walked up to the bows and peered into the water, delighted with her new domain, the confined deck-space of a tiny yacht where she felt far freer than within the massive masonry of St. Monica's.

Then she remembered that she had had no lunch, and foraged in the food locker, where she found some stale bread, and fresh butter and jam. There was also an egg, but she wasn't quite sure how to work the Primus so she decided not to risk setting the yacht on fire merely to cook it. After eating as much bread and jam as she wanted she lay on Simon's bunk and read a magazine she found among the charts. It was over a year old, but it was quite absorbing, and contained an improbable adventure story, a serial that looked very dull, and one or two shorter tales. One of them was about a girl's first kiss. It was a stupid story and she didn't understand it. Apparently a man who was already married kissed a girl of sixteen, and she thought that he wanted to marry her simply because he kissed her. Instinctively Nya compared herself with the girl in the story. She wondered whether Simon was married. But no, of course he wouldn't be. Then she read and re-read the description of the effect the kiss had on the girl, but it didn't seem to be at all the same as when Simon had kissed her. It kept on mentioning "flaming passion" and "hot blood", neither of which expressions conveyed anything to Nya. She suspected them of being clichés and tossed the magazine away, partly in disgust and partly because she was drowsy. She heard a clock strike a half-hour and saw by the cabin clock that it was half-past three. Then she settled herself pleasurably in Simon's bunk and went to sleep, lulled by the noise of the water lapping against the hull.

39

"Nya! Nya! For God's sake. Ahoy! Is there anybody there?"

The words seemed to be coming from Miss Littlewood who was chasing her down a long corridor trying to recapture her and make her sit down and write a letter. They were extraordinary words for Miss Littlewood to use, but they must have come from her because there was nobody else in sight, except the taxi-driver who was driving, only he was in front and she could see he hadn't spoken. But it was useless to wonder who had spoken; all that mattered was to escape from Miss Littlewood as quickly as possible. She leaned forward and knocked on the glass.

"Faster, faster," she said breathlessly.

But again that imperious cry, cutting through her dazed uncertainty as to where she was, piercing through the hood of the taxi-cab and echoing down the corridor.

"Nya!"

There was a bump and she was afraid that Miss Littlewood had caught her up. Terrified, she leaned her head out to look and then she suddenly lost all sense of where she was or what was happening to her, for she woke up.

It was pitch-dark. She could hear the bump of wood upon wood and a kind of lapping noise. Where on earth——"

"Nya?"

The voice was not imperious this time, questing rather, and a little querulous. "Nya?"

"Anybody down there?"

She got up quickly, bumping her head violently on the beam, but she hardly noticed the pain in her excitement. She yelled at the top of her voice:

"Simon."

"Nya, darling, my God, I thought you'd been drowned or something."

In an instant she was out in the cockpit and Simon had his arms round her.

"Simon, dear beloved Simon, is it really you?"

Safe at last. She was safe now from all the nightmares of the last week, clutched tight and close in Simon's arms.

"Oh, Nya!"

He rested his cheek on her hair. For a moment neither of them spoke, but they stood locked together while the bitterness of their week of separation slowly drained away and contentment stole back into them.

There was no need to speak, there was nothing to explain, nothing even to wonder at. They were close together again and it was right and natural that their longing should at last be satisfied. Later on, perhaps, there would be things to explain, but not now.

They stood silent in the darkness while the yacht swayed gently to the tide and the halyards tapped against the stays. Once or twice a block hit the mast with a smack. Otherwise there was no sound. *Puffin* shifted round on her moorings as the tide turned. Simon watched the stars wheeling into new positions, like an infinitesimal army performing evolutions in the sky. At last he heaved a happy sigh.

"Oh, Nya," he said softly, "what have you done?"

There was no reproach in his tone only a kind of amusement and happy wonder.

She looked up at him. "I couldn't stand them any more. I came back to you."

He laughed out loud. "I wouldn't have believed this was possible. I'd practically made up my mind that I should never see you again."

"So had I."

"I'm so glad to find I was wrong. Oh, Nya, I'm happy to see you again."

"You're not angry because I ran away?"

"Lord, no. I'm too glad to see you. I think if you hadn't, I'd have come and fetched you very soon."

"That would have been exciting. I'm sorry I didn't wait now."

"Oh, it's just as well. I don't know what I could have done. You were absolutely inaccessible. Much worse than if you'd been in prison. One's at least allowed to visit people in prison."

"It did feel like a prison. And not being allowed to write made it so much worse."

"Did you get the letter I wrote last night?"

"Yes. And that's how all the trouble started. At least that was one of the reasons. You see. . . ."

And she started breathlessly trying to relate the whole sequence of events which had led up to her escape.

"Here, wait a minute, this'll take a long time, I can see," he said. "Don't let's stand out here in the cold."

So they went into the cabin and lighted the lamp. He

made her sit on the bunk while he got out the Primus to cook some soup.

"Go on."

So she told him everything that had happened to her, every thought she had had, every longing since she left him a week ago. He listened without interrupting. It was a long tale, even longer than the story of her life which she had told him over coffee in the hotel one Monday morning a hundred years ago. By the time she finished the soup was hot, and he put a steaming bowl of it before her.

"If you left at twelve this morning you can't have had any lunch."

"Yes, I had lots of bread and jam when I got here."

"Still—you must be hungry. What do you say to some food?"

"I say 'Yes, please.' "

He ran his finger along the row of tins on the top of the food locker.

"There's only tinned, I'm afraid. Shall we have Macedoine of Vegetables, Sussex Lambkins, Steak and Kidney Pie, Baked Beans, Spaghetti, or New Potatoes?"

"Steak and kidney, I think."

"Right. And afterwards we'll have some loganberries and imagine the cream."

"Are you really going to let me stay and have dinner with you?"

"Did you think I was going to take you back to Miss Littlewood by the scruff of your neck?"

She laughed joyously to think he felt as impudent towards those bullying people as she did.

"Well," she said, "I thought perhaps you might think it was your duty to ring up Aunt Ethel."

"So it is. But fortunately there's no telephone on

309

board. I'd give a lot to see your aunt's face when she hears the news. You know I went and called on her?"

"Oh yes, Miss Littlewood told me. What happened, Simon?"

"Hardly anything, now I come to think of it. I might just as well not have gone, for all the use it was. I don't think I'm much good with aunts."

He told her all he could remember of the unsatisfactory nature of the interview. Then she took up the tale with an account of all she had forgotten to tell him before, of Miss Littlewood's manner when she was dictating the letter, of Daddy's letter, and of how she had to read it in the lavatory. They laughed a good deal and treated the whole affair as a huge joke. They talked themselves to a standstill, sitting opposite each other at the cabin table, Simon smoking, Nya drawing designs with a knife on the table. Their conversation gradually became less and less animated, their laughter less frequent. Presently there was a long silence, which Nya broke by leaning luxuriously back against the cushion and saying with a long-drawn sigh:

"Ah-h, I feel a lot better than I did this morning." She laughed and hunched her shoulders. "You know, I'm afraid I was a bit terrified of all those people, of Miss Littlewood and Aunt Ethel, and even the girls. I felt as if I'd fallen into their clutches and they could do anything they liked to me and I couldn't stop them. When Daddy's letter came I felt it was the end of everything. I felt I'd never get out of the prison alive. Wasn't that silly of me?"

"I understand how you felt."

"And now that's all over. I've woken up from the bad dream. Or else I've gone to sleep again; because being with you's so lovely that that must be the dream, and the rest the reality."

She looked him in the eyes and smiled. He smiled too, but vaguely, as if he were far away and not thinking of her at all. Yet his eyes never left her face, but watched her all the time, devouring every expression, every light or shadow that passed across her eyes, every dimple that came and went as she spoke. Slowly he shook his head.

"What?" she asked timidly, fearful all at once that he was reproving her.

"I was just thinking," he said, "what an improbable person you are—like some sort of a leprechaun that suddenly appears from nowhere, and sits impudently smiling up at one. Fancy being able to look impudent after all you've done to-day."

"I'm happy again, that's all. Oh, Simon, I won't have to go back, will I? Say I won't. Please."

She saw him hesitate and feared what he might be going to say. Would he try and persuade her to go back at once? That very night? Or suggest that he should take her back himself even? Instantly her mind conjured up a thousand phantoms of horror, all of which she would have to face if she went back. Miss Littlewood with a scowl like a thundercloud, Aunt Ethel pale with anger, Uncle Nick red-faced with expostulation, the police, perhaps, who had been asked to try and find her. She closed her eyes and shuddered. Simon could never be so cruel as to ask her to face them all this very night when she had scarcely been with him long enough to gather courage for the ordeal.

"Let's forget about the reality for a little longer, shall we?" he said. "And just dream!"

"Oh, thank God," she said in relief, when he had spoken. "I was afraid that. . . ."

The end of her sentence didn't bear thinking of. There was silence again. Across the water an outgoing tramp steamer gave a blast on its siren. Then again, and a few seconds later, once more. Their thoughts flew towards the sound, and they both imagined themselves aboard the tramp, making for the open sea, for freedom and unknown lands. Nya's eyes brightened, and she turned her head towards the open doorway. Then she closed her eyes and sank back on the cushions.

"Would you like to be aboard her?" asked Simon, after a pause. His eyes had not missed a single one of her movements.

"Yes. Oh-h yes."

Again there was silence. Then Nya got up suddenly and came round to where he sat and threw herself down on the bunk, her head in his lap, her arms round his waist. He drew in his breath sharply, as if she had hurt him. And indeed her presence so close to him was agony, a secret, intoxicating, intolerable agony. He closed his eyes for an instant. When he opened them the pain had gone from his face and he smiled down at her as she lay like a child in his arms. Neither spoke. It was a moment of magic, a delicious mingling of relief, joy, exhaustion, and longing, which words could never have expressed. For a long time they remained clasped together, truly close to each other now, closer even than when they had first embraced, two hours ago. To Nya, the moment was perfect, a consummation of all her longing, that sated even though it dissatisfied her. And Simon, looking sadly down at her, never permitted his longing to turn into desire, never by word or gesture allowed her to sense the sweet pain she caused him. Only his eyes fed all the time upon her, greedily. They seized upon the glint of her hair, the deep brown lenses of her eyes, the trembling beauty that lay in the tender curves of her body.

After a time he said:

"It's lucky nobody knows where you are, except Dan. He told me he'd seen you taking the dinghy and he'd got another boat for me. You'd better stay here to-night. Do you think you can manage by yourself?"

She looked up startled.

"You aren't going to leave me?"

"But, little one, I must."

"Why?"

He hesitated an instant. "Your aunt, and everybody else, would say terrible things. It'd be bad enough for you, but it would be worse for me."

"I don't understand, Simon."

"Darling, believe me, and don't ask me to explain more just now."

"Very well. But they needn't ever find out."

"Old Dan would know for one. He might let it out."

"I don't believe he would if you asked him not to."

"It's not a thing I like to ask of him."

"I wish I could understand why not."

A short pause.

"I'll tell you if you really want to know."

Something in his tone gave her an inkling of what she was asking to be told. Instinctively she shied away from the desire to know it.

"No, don't. I'd rather you didn't; not now, anyway. I believe what you say."

She raised herself and sat on the bunk beside him.

"Does that mean you'll have to go, then?"

"I'm afraid so."

She was silent for a moment. When she spoke she avoided his gaze.

"Simon."

"Yes, Nya."

"Will we never be able to be together? Properly, I mean. Will we always have to think of what other people will say?"

"Darling, what am I to say to that? You're so young. You're not even mistress of your own actions, your father or your aunt or somebody will have a right to determine what you do for several years yet."

"But if I make up my mind what I want to do, and just do it. Can they stop me?"

"They've always got the right to. By force if necessary."

"Isn't there any way for me to escape them? Must I always be in some kind of prison?"

There was nothing he could say to this. He put out his hand and stroked her hair. She rubbed her cheek against it.

"Nya?"

"Yes."

"Would you—do you think you could ever face the thought of——"

She looked at him impulsively, wondering why he hesitated.

"Of what?"

"Well—of marrying me?"

For an instant she didn't reply, but looked him in the eyes with great seriousness. Then as solemnly she nodded.

"You don't need to think that I'll hate you if you change your mind," he continued hastily. "In a way it would be only natural if you did. In fact I expect you

314

will. Only I hope, perhaps, you may change it back again, if only you can love me a little bit now."

"I won't ever change it."

"But don't think I'll hold you to it, will you? Or consider yourself bound at all by what you've said. It's just that I wanted to have something to justify our being together, if ever we are, if, for instance, I stayed here to-night. You see, if we got married, everything would be quite simple, neither your aunt nor your father could stop you doing anything then."

"Simon, couldn't we?"

"Well, actually, you're too young even for that, Nya darling. You'd have to get your father's consent and he'd never give it."

"I'd make him."

"I doubt it. You see it's all connected with—with the same problem that I wouldn't explain to you just now. It's a physical fact of nature, which there's no getting away from."

"But in Africa people much younger than me get married."

"I know. But it's different in England."

"I don't see why."

"No, Nya. It wouldn't work, honestly. But never mind, if you can bear it we'll wait until you're old enough by English standards. It's not *that* I'm worrying about; I could wait for ever—for you. It's the question of how to live during those three or four years, or however long it'll be."

"All that time?"

"I expect so. You won't find it too long, darling. You've still got your schooling and there are thousands of things that will happen to you between now and then which will make life wonderful and exciting. Don't be afraid. All this worrying doesn't matter, even Miss Littlewood and St. Monica's don't matter if you've something really true and right to look forward to and live for. It's only that I want to feel you believe in me, that you really think, now, this very minute, that you would like to marry me one day. That's why I'm talking to you like this. And if you say yes, I shall have a weapon with which to fight your aunt and your father if need be, and any one else who comes along."

She smiled confidently now, with pure happiness.

"Yes, Simon," she breathed. "Oh yes, yes, yes, yes, yes."

He took her in his arms again and held her. He hardly knew whether it was a child he held, or a woman, who might one day become his wife. But whether she was woman or girl, he was filled with love for her. After all, what did it matter *how* he loved her, since he did love her, with all his being, all his wisdom, his simplicity, his thoughts and all his longing. And now he found suddenly that this love for her didn't hurt him any more. He no longer felt two forces within him tearing him in opposite directions. All was quiet in his breast. It seemed as if, after groping through thickets of uncertainty, he had emerged into a still garden, where all was fair and spacious and calm. Why should he be surprised? Wasn't it only natural that he should stumble upon this pleasant garden? Hadn't he decided some time ago that love was of many kinds and not merely the short-lived physical business that most people made of it? Here, then, was another aspect of it, another delightful bower of its endless, fascinating labyrinth that was, for the moment, sufficient in itself, that offered its own especial pleasure and its own gratification.

He sighed and settled more comfortably into the

cushions, still holding the blissful, wide-eyed child in his arms.

Nya lay still, looking up at the cabin ceiling, at the vapour that danced in the lamp-chimney, and the strange, vague shadows that it threw on the skylight. But she scarcely noticed what she saw. Her mind was freed from her body; it seemed itself, like vapour, to be dancing fantastically through airy regions where it found no foothold, no facts, no thoughts—nothing it could seize upon or touch. And therefore nothing it met with had any meaning in relation to her body. It didn't seem to belong to her at all; it was like the ghost of somebody else, somebody like her, but not quite her. Somebody who was not quite real, or not created yet, perhaps. Yes, that was it! This vapour of her mind was not Nya as she was now, but as she would be one day, one blissful day, in three or four years' time, when she would marry Simon.

After many minutes her mind descended into her brain again. Gradually it became aware of Simon near by. How long would he be there? Would he stay until they could be married? Or would he break the happy spell and go away? Lazily she spoke—half-drunkenly it seemed, for her brain had very little control over her tongue, so drugged was she with happiness.

"Simon, are you going to stay?"

"Yes, Nya, if you like."

"All night?"

"All night."

END OF PART II

317

PART III: RESOLUTION

40

It was a magic word, once it was spoken, which unlocked the door to happiness. It meant, for one thing, that for the first time since they had met there was no hurry. Neither had to go away from the other, they need not fear intrusion. There was no need to think precisely and to say only the things that mattered most because time was short and Simon had to catch a bus or Nya had to run home for breakfast. There was time, now, for long silences, which were quite as full of meaning as strings of sentences; and for laughter, and story-telling, and invention; for shy confidences from Nya, and half-jocular admissions from Simon.

They talked till twelve o'clock; and then Simon said:
"I don't know about you, but I must get up early. We'd better turn in."

The mere thought that she would lose him in the morning frightened her. She realized that, however delightful it had been to forget Miss Littlewood and the world outside, and lose herself in the pleasure of Simon's company, the morning would bring her coldly face to face with her terrors again, and, since Simon had to go to his office, she would be left to deal with them alone.

It was a dreadful enough prospect now, in the snug security of *Puffin's* cabin at midnight. What would it be like in the morning when Simon went away?

She clung to him and wouldn't let him get up.

"No, no," she said, "don't go away from me even for a minute. Not until you've told me what to do about Miss Littlewood. There won't be time in the morning."

"My God," he said, sitting down again, "you're right. There won't. And I'd forgotten about the old monster."

"So had I."

Once again they sat silently opposite each other; but this time their silence was full of bewilderment. He knew that the responsibility of deciding what they should do rested with him. He felt that in some way he was to blame for the situation in which they now found themselves, that it was his fault that Nya had run away. Surely, then, he must tell her to go back; and the sooner the better. Not to-night, of course—but the first thing to-morrow. He must take her to St. Monica's himself before he went to the office.

He looked at her. She was watching him, waiting for him to speak, wondering what he would say. Her wide-open brown eyes, with their half-humorous, half-pathetic appeal, thawed his feeble resolution to deal with the problem before him. He gave up the attempt with a laugh that was half a sob.

"Come here," he said.

They clasped one another passionately. Now, for the first time, Nya didn't bury her face against his breast, but raised it confidently and laid it against his own. He could feel her cheek burning against his temple.

"And don't ever go away."

She stayed close to him for some minutes, until the beads of perspiration on his forehead moistened her cheek. Then, very gingerly, she lifted her hands and stroked his hair.

"Let me stay," she murmured. "Let me stay with you to-night, and to-morrow night, too. That'll give me all to-morrow to pull myself together in."

"I wish you could stay for ever and ever."

"I do, too. I'd like it more than anything in the world. We could sail away together in *Puffin* and never come back. We could go to Gibraltar."

"Yes," he said enthusiastically, "Gibraltar and the Mediterranean, and all the other places I long to take you to. And sailing by starlight on a fine night. In my imagination I've done that a hundred times with you already."

"Have you? Do *you* imagine things like that?"

"Since I met you I do."

"And do you imagine things about me, too?"

"Of course. That's the whole point."

"Oh, Simon. . . ."

She tried to receive this confession calmly, but her tone of voice betrayed the pleasure it gave her.

"And I imagine scenes with you in them. Once, before I even knew you properly, I imagined myself swimming out to *Puffin*, and waiting on board until you came."

"Which has more or less come true?"

"Yes. Except that I hadn't the courage to swim, and stole your dinghy instead."

"Very wise of you."

But all this was not to the point. She knew they were both trying to avoid the subject they should be discussing. With a sigh she brought the conversation back.

"But I know we mustn't run away to Gibraltar, or anywhere else. And I can sort of understand, now, why we mustn't, although I don't think I could explain it. It's something to do with the future, isn't it? It would be spoiling the future for the sake of being happy now?"

"I'm afraid so."

"Yes, I can see that it would. So I know I've got to go back to St. Monica's. Only I do want a little strength and a little happiness to give me courage. I expect they'll punish me like the very devil."

"Let them try!"

"Oh, yes they will. And there won't be anything *you* can do about it, Simon. So please let me stay. Let me be free just a little longer—all to-morrow, say. Then, the next morning, I'll go back to St. Monica's of my own accord."

"But supposing they find you before?"

"How can they?"

"Dan might tell them."

"Couldn't you ask him not to?"

"Yes, I don't see why I shouldn't. Did anybody else see you coming out here?"

"No."

"Sure?"

"There wasn't a soul about, except Dan."

"That's all right then. I'll talk to him. But you'll go on Wednesday morning, won't you, Nya darling? Otherwise this plan won't work. They're bound to look for you all over the country until they find you."

"Yes. I'll go. I promise."

There was such strength and calmness in the way she spoke; he wondered at it. Of a sudden she seemed to have grown older than he, to be wiser, in some unaccountable way, and entirely capable of managing her own affairs. It was just as well. After all, running away from school was her own affair; he couldn't very well help her to settle that. Still, he marvelled at her resolute tone, and felt, all at once, small and childlike in her presence.

He clasped her suddenly to him.

"Little Nya, I don't want you to go. I would like us to be together always, just like this. Even now, if you'd rather, I'll take you away with me somewhere, and we need never see all these wretched people again."

"No, Simon, it would be no good. You said so yourself." Her hand stroked his hair and then his cheek. "I'm not afraid to go back if you love me and won't forget me. You'll stick up for me, won't you, if it gets too awful?"

"Of course, my darling."

"And I'll know you're there, somewhere in the very same town, in those rooms near the sea, if I want you. That'll make me much less lonely."

She held his face in both her hands now, and caressed him as if he were indeed a child. It was absurd; but it was delicious. It was delicious for him to be at last the weaker, the adorer, and not only the adored.

"Dear, beautiful little girl, stay with me, stay with me, please."

She leaned back in his arms and looked at him, smiling.

"One day I'll be able to, won't I? You promised me I should; and I believe you. If I didn't, I should want to run away with you now."

"You said you would marry me, that's why," he explained, "but you may change your mind."

"No, I won't. Don't be afraid. When I've finished with school, and nobody can prevent me, we'll get married. Will that be too long to wait?"

"Not if you still want to marry me in the end."

"Oh, Simon, I love you so. I love you so, and that's why I can face going back to school. It's funny, isn't it? I'd be terrified otherwise."

She *must* go back he realized; of course, there was no other way.

He drew her to him gently. She knelt upright on the cushion beside him, and looked down at him. Her face, no longer puckered with doubt, but serene, with its large brown eyes, was framed in her chestnut curls. He drew her quite close, and laid his head upon her soft young breast.

41

"Which bunk would you like?"

"Whichever one you don't want."

"You can have either of these in here. I shall sleep in the fo'c'sle."

"Oh, I see."

There was a trace of disappointment in her tone. It had never occurred to her that he would sleep in the fo'c'sle.

"Oh, well," she said, "in that case I think I ought to sleep in the fo'c'sle. After all, I'm the one that oughtn't to be here."

"Nonsense. I'm the skipper, and the skipper always sleeps in the fo'c'sle."

"I don't believe you. Anyway, I'm sure the fo'c'sle bunk is much shorter than the others."

"No, it's about the same."

She measured it then, with a piece of rope from the well-locker—she was beginning to know her way about the yacht—and compared its length to that of the two berths in the cabin. Triumphantly she announced that the fo'c'sle bunk was shorter by quite a foot, as far as she could judge.

"Ah, but you can hang your feet out over the end," he observed.

"Perhaps. But it's better still if there's room for them in your bunk!"

"Anyway, there's a leak in the roof just where your head goes."

"It's not raining, so that won't make any difference."

"And I'm older than you, so I have a right to choose."

"You're taller than me, so I'm going to sleep in the fo'c'sle bunk."

"Mercilessly logical, aren't you?"

"Of course. You must always be logical when you're camping or yachting, or crossing deserts."

"What do you know about those things?"

"A great deal—all out of books."

He lighted the Primus to boil water for washing, while Nya began to arrange the blankets and cushions. She would have liked to make up both the beds in the cabin; it would have been lovely to sleep all night long only three or four feet away from Simon—like one of her wildest dreams come true. Still, she would be able to think about him and to listen to his breathing while Uncle Nick and Miss Littlewood were possibly searching everywhere. She felt a sudden pang of remorse at the trouble and anxiety she would be causing them. But it couldn't be helped. If you ran away, you ran away, and it was no use telephoning all the time to say you were all right. Of course, there might be some means of setting their *worst* fears at rest, and also it was probable, if she could let them know she was coming back on Wednesday, they might be content to wait until then, and not to try and recapture her before. Yes—there was a definite strategic value in that—so long as she didn't betray her whereabouts.

"Do you think I ought to let Aunt Ethel or somebody know that I'm all right?"

"Well—it might be kinder."

"I don't feel awfully like being kind, but still—— I could tell them I was coming back soon."

"How?"

"Telephone or something."

"No. Some one might see you if you went ashore."

"Well, then—I could send a wire."

"Yes, that's true—through me."

"They'd trace it eventually, of course, if they wanted to. But even then, they could hardly do anything before Wednesday morning. I'll send it to-morrow, on my way to the office."

When the water was boiling, Simon said:

"I'll go up on deck now, while you undress. You'll have to wash in that bucket, I'm afraid. That's all there is. There's a towel in the locker in the fo'c'sle. I haven't got any clean pyjamas for you, though."

"It's all right. I can sleep in my vest."

"Right, then. Give me a shout when you're in bed."

He went up on deck, shutting the cabin door behind him.

She washed her face and hands in some of the hot water, leaving the rest in the saucepan until he should need it. Then, without a thought, she undressed and got into the bunk in her vest. It was a short one and left most of her uncovered, so the blankets tickled and scratched a good deal until she got used to them. She wondered whether she dared use the lavatory, or whether Simon would hear her working the thing from up on deck. It was very complicated to use, though she had read the directions and thought she understood them. A moment's reflection convinced her that it

329

would be better to use it now, when Simon was on deck, than during the night.

Simon lighted his pipe and stood in the bows, with his arm round the forestay, looking at the lights of the harbour. He was not troubled by Nya's presence on board, nor even by the fact that she had run away from school and placed both herself and him in such a difficult position. He was inclined to thank the misery Nya had been made to endure, for driving her back to him for this sweet interlude. Of course, if one looked at it from a worldly point of view, the whole situation was bizarre and quite irregular. It might even happen that trouble would arise from it. But, after all, the irregularity of it simply depended upon a point of view, and if Nya's people would only understand her, they must admit that he was doing her no harm and that she was behaving quite logically. He was glad for her own sake that she had run away from school. She would be accepted as a person of character, and, though she would no doubt be kept strictly under discipline, she could hardly fail to command a greater respect from those who applied it. Of course, her escape would have done nothing to make her relationship with himself easier to pursue; on the contrary, he had made up his mind that it was out of the question, now, to communicate with her or to see her again until the end of the term. Not even then, perhaps, though as to this he was less pessimistic. All the more reason, therefore, to let her stay two nights aboard *Puffin*, whatever the result might be.

He heard Nya shout; and, knocking out his pipe, he went down to the cabin.

"Manage all right?"

"Yes, beautifully, thanks. And I left some water in the saucepan for you."

"Fine."

He took off his coat, and his collar and tie. Then he emptied the bucket overboard, refilled it with the warm water, and began to wash, while she watched him from her bunk. She noted with satisfaction that he didn't take his ablutions any more seriously than she had done—a soap and a rinse and that was all. Of course, she hadn't had a flannel or a toothbrush or anything else to wash with, except the corner of the towel. And he had all these things on board. He began to undress in the corner of the cabin where he was out of her sight. She was a little relieved by this; it saved her the necessity of looking away or pretending she couldn't see.

"What's the bunk like?" he asked suddenly.

"Simply marvellous."

"That's good. I hope you'll sleep all right. As a matter of fact, it is quite a comfortable one. It used to be mine when there were three of us on board."

"I'm glad."

"Why?"

"I shall like sleeping in it, if it was once yours."

For a second he didn't answer, and Nya, lying in the dark with her eyes focused on an invisible roof, wondered whether she had offended him. But he was only wondering how best to reply to her. Eventually he laughed and said:

"You're a funny child, aren't you?"

And she realized with relief that he was not annoyed.

A few moments later he asked her if she would like an apple.

"Much better for your teeth than cleaning them," he observed. "Or did you remember to bring your toothbrush with you?"

331

She giggled at this, but was unable to think of an equally absurd reply.

Then he stooped down and put his head in at the fo'c'sle door.

"Ready to go to sleep?" he asked.

"Yes, Simon."

"Good night, then, Nya darling."

"Come and kiss me."

He leaned over her bunk and, putting his arms under her shoulders, raised her up and hugged her. She whispered:

"Good night, darling, darling, Simon," and put her lithe young arms round him.

For a second she hung in mid-air, fervently clinging to him. Then he laid her down, kissed her on the forehead, and pulled up the blankets over her. Softly he stroked her hair away from her face, over which it had tumbled, waited while she held his hand to her cheek and then moved away. He got into his bunk, set the alarm clock, and put out the lamp.

"Good night, little girl."

"Good night, beloved Simon."

42

The alarm went off with a terrifying clamour at half-past seven. Simon put out an arm, groping for the screaming clockwork and finally stifled it.

"Good heavens! What a fright I got," said Nya, sitting up in her bunk.

"Yes, it's a damn sight too powerful for such a small cabin."

Two minutes later he got up, and came into the fo'c'sle to light the Primus. Remembering she had nothing on but her vest, she hastily got between the blankets again. Simon looked extremely tousled and sleepy, but he grinned at her and said:

"Are you sore?"

Nya considered a moment before she replied.

"No, not really. I woke up once feeling rather stiff because I couldn't curl my knees up under my chin. But I soon got used to it."

"No, it's one thing you can't do in a bunk. But it's very bad for you, anyway."

"Is it?"

"Yes. You should sleep with your shoulders back and your legs straight."

"Like a soldier on parade?"

"More or less. The Primus makes an awful din, doesn't it? Shall I open the hatch?"

"Oh, yes, please."

He removed the fo'c'sle hatch; and now Nya could lie in her bunk and look straight up at the sky. The shrouds, silhouetted against it, swayed slightly as the boat rocked. It was a bright May morning, full of sunshine; occasionally a gull flew across the square patch of blue.

Simon was dressing in the cabin. She wondered whether she ought to get up and dress, too. Presently he knocked on the door and said:

"Are you getting up?"

"No, I'm still in bed."

"Can I come in?"

"Yes."

The water in the saucepan was boiling.

"You're looking awfully stern this morning, Simon."

"Am I?" he laughed. "I'm rather hopeless in the mornings—besides, this morning is a particularly bad one."

"But it's not—it's simply heavenly. Look." She pointed through the hatch, and, as if in answer to her exclamation, the boat swung round so that the sun shone straight in upon her, lighting up her hair.

"Oh, the weather's all right," he agreed, as he saw her suddenly irradiated. "Thank God, too, because you'd have been wretched, out here, all alone in the rain. I was worrying about leaving you, that's all. Do you think you'll be all right?"

"Yes, of course I will. I'll have a heavenly time."

"I hope to God nobody comes out here and takes you away. What shall I do if I come back to-night and you're not here?"

"I'll be here all right, Simon. If I see any one coming, I'll batten down the hatches and stay inside."

"Will you? You'll be careful not to fall in, won't you?"

"I can swim."

"Still, there's sometimes a strong tide."

He picked her up in his arms as he had done last night. His hands encountered her bare back—her vest was half-way up her body—but he pretended not to notice this. He could feel her shoulder-blades move as she threw her arms round his neck.

She felt his hands lift her strongly up. How cold they were against her back! But they were kind, and their cool strength caressed her shoulder-blades so deliciously that she could have wished to hang for ever in his arms like this.

"Promise you'll still be here when I come back?"

"Yes, Simon."

He laid her down in bed again, carefully, so that she was still covered by the bedclothes. Casually he said:

"You know there isn't any need for you to get up till I've gone. Why don't you have breakfast in bed?"

"Oh, can I? Can I really, Simon?"

"Of course. It's much less trouble for us to have it in here than to go into the cabin."

He sat on the floor beside her bunk. Then he got the cups and opened a tin of milk, and put the frying-pan on the Primus.

"There are still two eggs left from Sunday, luckily. I vote we have them, with fried bread. What do you say?"

"I say, yes. I'm frightfully hungry."

"Oh, by the way, have you any money with you?"

"Yes. About four shillings."

"You'll need some food for lunch and tea. You can cook, can't you?"

"Yes."

"Well, there's a provision-launch that comes round to the ships in the harbour. Keep a look-out for it; you can buy practically everything you need from the fat woman who owns it. She's a foreigner of some sort, Belgian, I think. And it'll be safer than if you came ashore with me to get provisions."

"Yes, I suppose it would."

"Buy some green things if you can. Here's another half-crown. Too much tinned food isn't good for you at your age."

"I know. Green things stop you getting scurvy, don't they?"

"So I'm told."

"Magellan's men all had it because there weren't any vegetables on board."

She grinned at him, as he handed her a cold plate with a hot fried egg upon it.

They ate their breakfast in silence; but every now and then they caught each other's eye and smiled. She was completely happy; and even he, who could envisage the grim results their happiness might lead to, felt strangely at peace. It was as if they had known each other for a long, long time now; and it seemed the most natural thing in the world that they should be eating their breakfast together aboard *Puffin*.

Presently he glanced at the clock, and announced that it was time for him to go. His words made her uneasy, but she did her best not to betray this. And it was absurd of her to feel uneasy. It was such a lovely morning that even the presence of Miss Littlewood on board would have seemed a trivial matter.

"I'm afraid you'll have to wash up," he said. "Do you mind?"

336

"No. I'll have a grand time."

"I'm sorry about it. But I really ought to push off now. I must call at my rooms before I go to the office."

Suddenly she felt a pang of terror. She sat up, with one hand on her pillow; her plate slid off the bunk, and, if he hadn't caught it, would have broken on the floor.

"Oh, Simon, you will come back, won't you?"

"Yes, darling, of course I will."

"And I'll be safe here, won't I?"

"I think so. Don't show yourself too much when other boats are passing. It's just possible there may be some one on the look-out for you, since your aunt knows all about me and *Puffin*."

"When will you be back?"

"About six, or half-past. Look after yourself, little one."

"I'll be waiting for you."

She embraced him passionately, quite forgetting about the bedclothes and her vest; and he put his arms tenderly round her. He knew she was safer here than anywhere else, but he had a disturbing sensation, all of a sudden, that he was saying good-bye to her for the last time.

He kissed her gently, scarcely brushing her lips with his. Then he went out and got into the dinghy. She got up from her bunk and stood with her head out of the fo'c'sle hatch, watching him and waving to him until he was nearly out of sight. Then, with a sigh, she turned away. She was alone, now; alone on *Puffin*, mistress of the ship, of her own time, of her thoughts. It really was wonderful to feel free again. Not since she left Nyasaland had she been so happy.

43

She didn't bother to get dressed at first. It was lovely to wander about in your vest and know that nobody could possibly come in. The sun was shining, so it wasn't cold.

She washed the dishes as well as she was able to in sea-water, which she drew up in the bucket as she had seen the seaman do on the *Queen of the Night* at this very anchorage a week ago. Then she took a little fresh water —just a little, because it would never do to run out of drinking supplies—and put it on the Primus. The next thing to do was to light the beastly thing, which she had never done before, though she had watched Simon do it. She had to try three times before she succeeded, because at first she left the safety-valve open and the vapour escaped. She discovered this when a whistling noise drew her attention to it, and, at the third attempt the Primus began to function, much to her delight and astonishment.

Then she thought she would read until the water boiled, and she began to rummage among the books on the shelf, to see if there was one she liked. But it suddenly occurred to her that it would be rather absurd to

338

sit down and read, and above all to wash up, without any clothes on; so she put on her knickers and blouse. And by the time she had finished doing this, the small amount of water in the saucepan had boiled. She washed her face and hands first, and then she took the bucket—dishes and all—up on deck, where she washed up and dried the things in the sunlight. She hung the teacloth out to dry by knotting it to the shrouds; and then decided to swab down the decks. The thought of this manly operation reminded her of Simon's shorts and blue jersey, and she realized at once that she would arouse less suspicion from passers-by if she were dressed in them than if she had her gym dress on. Here, then, was the clothes problem solved at last.

It was tremendous fun swabbing down the decks. You dipped the end of the mop in the water, and then splashed it on the deck, where it made the most interesting patterns of wet on the dry boards. Another game was to try and wash down to the stern before the bows got dry again; but as the sun was gaining strength every minute this became very difficult to do. Eventually she managed to get the whole ship glistening wet at the same moment; so she stowed away the mop with satisfaction.

She decided to bathe. The idea had no sooner entered her head than she had taken off all her clothes and sat naked on the counter, dabbling her toes in the water. There were no boats in the anchorage, except the hulks nearly half a mile away, and Brownsea Island was deserted as everybody knew. Taking a deep breath, she dived in.

The water was simply freezing; and besides, it was the first time she had bathed since the ship left Suez on the way back from Nyasaland. She shrieked at first, and spluttered, and wished she had had the sense to stay in the warm sunshine on the cabin-top.

However she swam twice round the yacht, trying all her swimming strokes to make sure she could still do them. Then she did her best to clamber over the yacht's counter; but, try as she might, she hadn't the strength to draw herself on board. She began to grow frightened and imagined that her strength would gradually give out, and she would be compelled to drift down the harbour until somebody picked her up. And then, of course, the cat would be out of the bag. The people at school would get to hear of it and would think she had thrown herself into the sea.

But then she remembered the dinghy, and, laughing at her fears, swam round towards it, and, after one or two unsuccessful attempts, managed to clamber in without overturning it. There was still no one in sight. She darted like a dragon-fly for the shelter of the cabin, seized a towel and dried herself. Then she dragged some of the bunk cushions into the cockpit, and there, visible only to the gulls, she lay down in the hot sun.

It was the first time she had ever sunbathed naked. In Nyasaland the sun had always been too hot, so Mummy had never let them stay in it too long. Besides, it always made John feel ill. But here—sheltered from the world by the sides of the ship—it was just warm enough to be pleasant. She turned over from time to time, hoping to become as brown again as she used to be in Africa. She thought dreamily of Simon, and wondered what he would have said if he had suddenly come alongside, rowing so quietly, say, that she didn't hear him. Terrified for a moment that, if not Simon, somebody else might be sailing past, she raised herself on her knees and peered over the bulwarks.

There was no one to be seen, no cruiser, no motor-launch, no yacht even. She seemed to be alone in the harbour. Even the distant hulk showed no sign of life. She lay down again, reassured. Thinking dreamily of Simon, and of the delicious turn that life had taken in the last few days—decidedly, running away had been the wisest thing she had ever done—and giving neither Aunt Ethel nor Miss Littlewood a single thought—she presently fell asleep.

She awoke when the sun went behind a cloud, and a puff of wind found its way somehow into the cockpit. She shivered. Suddenly she heard the sound of a motor-boat not very far away. It might be the provision-boat —if indeed she hadn't slept too long and missed it altogether. She glanced anxiously at the clock, wondering how long she had been asleep. It said a quarter past ten.

She peered out of the cabin presently, and saw a white launch coming towards *Puffin*. There were three people in it, one man, at the tiller, and two women; and it was stacked breast-high with packages and crates and tins. Without doubt it was the provision-launch. She put on the shorts and Simon's blue jersey, though it was really much too big for her, and was waiting eagerly on the deck, with her money in her hand, when the launch drew alongside.

With great deliberation she chose some mushrooms, some tomatoes, half a dozen eggs, half a pound of bacon-rashers, three tins of condensed milk to supplement Simon's store, some macaroni, a pint of milk, and half a pound of sausages. Then she paid her money, and the launch proceeded on its way up the harbour. Simon had been right; the fat woman had an accent. She looked nice, though, and smiled in a friendly way when Nya

341

changed her mind about a pot of jam and bought the macaroni instead. The young man at the helm must have been a foreigner, too, for, though he smiled and nodded, he didn't speak, but only pointed at the things Nya asked for.

When they had gone, Nya sat in the sun and peeled the mushrooms. Then she thought she would read until it was time to cook her lunch. So she fetched a book from the cabin—*Cruising and Ocean Racing*, a huge and fascinating volume, full of diagrams—and stretched herself out on her stomach on the cabin-top, her chin in her hands.

44

Neither Miss Littlewood nor Miss Bowden-Smith was very surprised when, at the end of morning school, it was ascertained that Nya was not to be found even in the lavatory.

Miss Bowden-Smith agreed with the headmistress that Nya's "young man" was probably at the root of the trouble.

Miss Littlewood telephoned Aunt Ethel at tea-time, and told her that her niece had run away from school. Aunt Ethel was both frightened and shocked. She asked Miss Littlewood pathetically if there was to be no limit to Nya's wickedness. Never in her life before, she said, had she met with such a wilful, disobedient child. Almost in tears, she asked Miss Littlewood's advice as to what she should do. Miss Littlewood replied by assuring her that she had dealt with much more formidable cases of disobedience than this and that it would be better to do nothing till night had fallen and Nya had failed to appear either at the school or at "The Rising".

"But she may be run over."

"In that case," Miss Littlewood replied, "we should

certainly have heard about it. There is just a chance that this young man may know where she is. I think we should try to get in touch with him."

"Oh yes, yes, of course. That's very clever of you, Miss Littlewood. Do you know how to get hold of him?"

"No; but I was hoping you might."

"I can tell you his name, but I don't know much more about him."

"I would rather leave it to you and Captain Russel."

"But, Miss Littlewood——"

"Believe me, I'm as distressed as you are, but in a matter of this kind I would rather you took what action you thought best."

"Do you think we should inform the police?"

"If she isn't back by ten o'clock to-night, yes."

Ethel turned away from the telephone with blank despair written on her face. So worried and hurt was she by Nya's action that she forgot to control her features before Emily, who was at that moment passing through the hall with the tea-things.

"Lor', Ma'am. 'As something 'appened? You do look pale."

"No, no, Emily. Nothing at all. It's quite all right. At least—yes, there is something. Miss Nya's run away from school."

" 'As she, Ma'am? What a thing for her to do."

Emily was not disposed to view the matter tragically, for she realized that Nya could perfectly well look after herself.

"But there, don't you worry about her, Ma'am. We'll 'ave her back 'ere this evening, looking downright ashamed, before dinner-time."

"Do you think so, Emily?"

With a drawn face Ethel sat down before the tea-things; but she was unable to perform even so habitual an action as pouring out the tea until Nicholas—whom Emily had gloatingly enlightened—came striding into the drawing-room.

"Oh, Nicholas, whatever shall we do?"

He had already formed a plan of action, during his swift passage through the hall.

"We must get hold of this young man, first of all."

"That's what Miss Littlewood says. But how?"

"What was his name? Byrne, wasn't it? Did he leave a card when he came to call?"

"Yes, I think so."

"Where is it?"

"In the hall, I suppose. In the pewter plate."

Nicholas returned from the hall dissatisfied.

"It's got no address on it."

"I don't know where he lives, either."

"We'll soon find that out." He went out again, to return in a moment with the telephone book. Her brain was quite numb and incapable of action; his was evidently working at a furious rate. She hadn't seen him angry for many a long year, and it thrilled her now to watch ten years of apathy drop from him, and to see him as he was when she first married him.

The telephone book proved of no use—there were no Byrnes in it at all. Even the people at the Enquiry Office could tell him nothing.

"That's no good," he said, sitting down at last and drinking his cold tea. "We must try something else. Hadn't that fellow got a yacht, didn't you tell me, down in the harbour somewhere?"

"Yes, yes, he has. Off Sandbanks, I imagine, because that's where Nya used to go when she went sailing with him."

"H'm. That doesn't necessarily mean he keeps the yacht there. Still—it's worth trying. I'll go down to the harbour and see what I can find out."

He put on his mackintosh and went out. Ethel sat on for a while in the drawing-room, until Emily came in to clear away the tea-things. Then, rather than endure the girl's chatter, she got up abruptly and went into the garden. She was wondering what she could do to help, but her brain was still incapable of constructive thinking, and the only plan she could formulate was to ring up Miss Littlewood and see if there was any news of Nya; only she knew that this would be pointless, since Miss Littlewood's final assurance had been that she would telephone again as soon as she had anything to say.

So she gave up all attempts at action, and abandoned herself to the mixture of grief and disappointment and remorse which had taken possession of her. It really was wicked and ungrateful of Nya to behave like this. What could possibly have happened at St. Monica's to justify her in running away? Miss Littlewood was kind, and there was at least one other mistress whom Nya liked— she had said so—and the girls could not very well *all* be barbarians! No, it was a thoughtless and selfish action of the child's; and, though she regretted her own inability to understand Nya, she was certain that she had every right to be angry and offended at her behaviour.

45

Nicholas found the jetty almost deserted. There were one or two loafers leaning on the rail, spitting into the water, and an ancient official of the boat service who became exceptionally obtuse when he was questioned, and seemed to be interested in nothing except shutting up his office. The last boat was almost due, and it would probably be empty. This sort of weather kept people indoors, he said. Nicholas asked him whether he had seen Nya, or knew anything of Mr. Byrne; but he only nodded his head sagely and said:

"There's many people with strange names hereabouts. And strange clothes, too," he added, having formed a bizarre impression of what Nya must have been wearing from Nicholas's description. And the loafers, who looked as if they had stood there all day long, had seen no one of Nya's description.

Nicholas put a few questions to the ferrymen, but without eliciting a satisfactory answer. They had seen one or two little girls in gym dresses, but they were accompanied by mothers or nursemaids, as far as they could remember. In any case, not one of them remembered having seen a girl with reddish hair.

He wandered disconsolately home. He had achieved nothing at all, except the certainty that Nya hadn't been on the ferry boat. He would have liked to talk to the fat seaman who usually stood on the jetty. He would be almost certain to know Mr. Byrne, and possibly even where his rooms were. But there was no sign of him, nor could anybody tell him where he was to be found. He could be questioned in the morning, of course; but it was hard to wait as long as that; anything might happen to Nya in the meantime. And it was harder still to go home and admit to Ethel that he was none the wiser than when he set out.

When he got back to "The Rising", it had been dark for an hour. Miss Littlewood had telephoned to say that there was no news of Nya yet, and to ask if she had by any chance been seen or heard of in Sandbanks.

"I'm still quite convinced she can look after herself," she said, "so I'm very reluctant to inform the police, unless you particularly want me to."

"But where do you think she'll spend the night?" asked Aunt Ethel in an agonized voice.

"I imagine she has some friends near here," said Miss Littlewood.

"She's never told me about them. Except, of course, about this young man. You don't think she might spend the night in his rooms?"

"I think it's possible."

"But that would be dreadful!"

"Not so dreadful as you imagine, I think. What would be dreadful would be to call in the police before we have to, and create a scandal, and possibly ruin both Nya's life and the young man's."

"Do you suggest that we should show him any consideration?"

"No, no. I only suggest that we should be cautious. But of course it is for you to say what you want done."

"I see. Well—I'll talk it over with my husband, and let you know what we decide."

To Ethel's surprise her husband agreed with Miss Littlewood's point of view, with the one reservation that, if necessary, they should ask the police to help them to *find* Mr. Byrne.

"Once we've found out where he lives, I can deal with him better than the police. The more I think about it the surer I am that she's with him. That business of the letter this morning, that Miss Littlewood told you of, points to it. Especially as Nya wasn't allowed to read it. If only Miss Littlewood had followed your instructions and opened the letter, we should at least know what the blighter's address was."

"Yes. Or if she'd only read his address from the letter she dictated to Nya."

Nicholas strode up and down his study, with his hands in his pockets, while Ethel sat in his favourite arm-chair, occasionally darning a little, but more often laying down her work to listen or advise or expostulate.

"I know it seems to you to be waiting much too long, old girl. Perhaps you think it's even a bit heartless. But I'm sure I can find out where the fellow lives in the morning, and honestly I'd rather deal with him myself than set the police on his tracks. Goodness knows what harm it mightn't do to Nya."

"You seem very sure she's with him."

"So I am. And I believe she's fond of him, and he of her, if it comes to that. Otherwise, he'd never have come to call on you. Wish to God I'd been here when he did. I'd have formed some sort of idea of his character."

"As I told you, he seemed a perfectly honest young
349

man, but I don't think it's very good for Nya to go about with him. He's ten years older than her to begin with."

"I can't help thinking that if we'd been willing to be on friendly terms with him, all this might never have happened."

"Are you blaming me, Nicholas?"

He was instantly repentant.

"Of course not, my dear. Nothing was further from my thoughts. I don't even know why I said that. At any rate it wasn't to the point. The point is whether we should tell the police to-night or not. I think not, myself."

"But supposing she's come to grief somehow, or been kidnapped by a—by a—you know, one of those Argentine people."

"Argentines? Who on earth——? Oh, you mean White Slavers?"

"Yes."

She hastily took up her darning. For a second he was nonplussed. Then he burst into a guffaw of laughter.

"That sort of thing only happens in magazines," he laughed.

"Not only. And she's an attractive child, you must admit."

"I do admit it. I always have." He rubbed his chin perplexedly. "Oh well," he said, "I suppose it *is* possible, but——"

"And if something of the sort has happened," Ethel eagerly followed up the doubt in his voice, "every second is of value, isn't it?"

"Yes—— But the *police*. No, really. I'd rather risk it. I'm perfectly certain it's this Byrne chap we want to get hold of."

She saw that he had made up his mind, and she knew from long experience that on the rare occasions when he did so, it was useless to argue with him. She was secretly relieved at not calling in the police, especially since Nicholas was responsible for the decision and she was exonerated from blame. So she asked him to telephone Miss Littlewood, which he did at nine o'clock.

Miss Littlewood agreed that he was right to wait until the morning; and he drew comfort from her approval, and from the kind, level voice in which she expressed her conviction that Nya had not met with a disaster but was perfectly happy, if a little frightened.

"I still think she may decide to come back again to-night."

"Let's hope she does."

"Yes. Good night, Captain Russel."

"Good night, Miss Littlewood."

46

But in the morning there was still no news of Nya, although Nicholas telephoned St. Monica's at eight o'clock to find out. Miss Littlewood was not down yet, they told him; she would no doubt telephone him as soon as possible. Miss Russel had not come back to the school.

Nicholas hurriedly swallowed a cup of tea, kissed his wife, and went out with a determined air. He didn't say where he was going, but Ethel gathered he was bound for the harbour. He took his field-glasses with him.

"And whatever Miss Littlewood says when she telephones," he admonished, as he left, "don't let her get hold of the police until I've spoken to her. Tell her I'll give her a ring in about an hour."

Three-quarters of an hour later, however, there was a ring and a double knock at the door of "The Rising" and a messenger handed a telegram in at the front door. Emily took it with quivering fingers, and her heart missed a beat as she considered the possibility of bad news. She hardly dared to take it to her mistress at first, but as soon as it occurred to her that the telegram might require action, which ought not to be delayed, she cast an anxious glance at the waiting messenger, shut the door in his face, and went upstairs to find her mistress.

Ethel opened the telegram with such haste that she fumbled and took twice as long over it as if she had gone about it in a normal manner. Emily was unable to leave the room.

Coming back Wednesday morning. Don't worry.
                                    Love, Nya.

And to-day was Tuesday!

At first Aunt Ethel accepted the news with relief and whole-hearted faith. She was so pleased that she even showed the telegram to Emily, since Nicholas was out, and there was nobody else with whom she could discuss it. But of a sudden it occurred to her that this might be a hoax; perhaps on Nicholas's part, to comfort her. She calculated rapidly whether he could have sent the telegram since breakfast—yes! there *was* just time. But no! It was handed in at Bournemouth. It couldn't possibly be Nicholas. Was it—she closed her eyes in horror at the thought—had it been sent by one of those dreadful people who kidnap little girls, in order to put Nya's relations off the scent until it should be too late, and Nya should be safely aboard a steamer bound for Buenos Aires?

She began to be full of misgivings, and any relief she may have felt at the good news was quite overweighed by her increasing certainty that the telegram was a hoax. Emily, watching the play of emotion on her mistress's features, didn't know what to think. Surely this was no occasion for bewilderment; the telegram contained good news, glad news, so why was Mrs. Russel so upset?

"Will there be any answer, Ma'am?" Emily asked,

353

more in order to attract her attention than because she desired to know.

"Oh, no, no. Of course not. There's no answer."

What was the best thing to do? As Nicholas was out, she must ask Miss Littlewood.

But Miss Littlewood, whom she disturbed in the middle of her breakfast, didn't share her gloomy view of the telegram's origin, and expressed nothing but satisfaction.

"I suspected something of the sort," she said. "But I didn't think she'd last until to-morrow. It makes me more than ever sure that this young man is aiding and abetting her."

"And you don't think we ought to do something about it?" Ethel asked in a pained voice.

"What is there we can do now, except call in the police?"

"Oh no. My husband said we mustn't do that on any account."

"I must say I share his opinion."

There was silence on the wire. Miss Littlewood thought of her coffee, which was slowly getting cold. Ethel thought, not very coherently, that she oughtn't to let the matter rest there. At last she spoke.

"You don't think I'd better come over and see you?"

"If you think it's necessary. I'm rather busy to-day, and I don't think there's much we can do."

"We could talk things over."

At the other end of the wire, Miss Littlewood smiled broadly.

"Do you mind if we leave it till to-morrow? I'm quite sure Nya will come back."

"Very well, if you think so."

Ethel hung up the receiver in frank disappointment, and Miss Littlewood with gloomy foreboding that Mrs. Russel would nevertheless find a pretext, one way or the other, for "talking things over".

47

When he turned the corner of the road by the bus stop Nicholas caught sight of Dan leaning in his habitual manner against the jetty rail. He could hardly contain himself to walk at a normal pace, so great was his impatience to reach him. He strode swiftly along the jetty and touched Dan on the shoulder.

"Excuse me."

The two men had a nodding acquaintance. This was Captain Russel, the young lady's uncle, about whom Mr. Byrne had told him. It behoved Dan to be on his guard against the questions the Captain would ask.

"Excuse me, but I'm in a bit of a hole, and I think you may be able to help me."

"Yes, sir. Anything to oblige."

"It's this. My small niece, aged about fourteen, in a gym dress—you know, a dark blue affair like all small girls wear—I'm looking for her. I think she may have come down here either yesterday or this morning. Have you seen her, by any chance?"

"What was she like, sir?"

Nicholas told him, as well as he was able. At the end of a halting and not very accurate description of her, he added:

"I'm keen to find her. The fact is—she's run away from school, and I'm afraid something may have happened to her."

The Captain's anxiety was so evident that Dan felt tempted to assure him, mysteriously and omnisciently, that the little girl was all right. But that, of course, was too dangerous.

"No, sir. Haven't seen anybody answerin' to your description here."

"Not yesterday, even?"

" 'Fraid not, sir."

"Oh."

Nicholas was silent for a moment. Then he tried another course.

"Do you by any chance know a Mr. Byrne who has a yacht here in the harbour?"

"No, sir, can't say I do."

"Are you sure?"

"Yes, sir."

"That's very strange, because I imagine he's kept his yacht here for some time."

Nicholas's eye wandered towards a group of men who were standing by the landing-stage. One of them, Dan knew, would admit to knowing a Mr. Byrne who kept his yacht in the harbour. He might even point the yacht out to the Captain, and then the fat would be in the fire. And that would never do, for Mr. Byrne would be mightily angry.

"If any one—her uncle, or some one—comes nosing around, put them off with some story, or a lie, or anything you like," Mr. Byrne had said. "Just till this evening, till I come back. She's a good kid. I shouldn't like to let her down."

Those had been Mr. Byrne's words, but they hadn't

been spoken in the hearing of the other watermen. And now there was a danger of Mr. Byrne's secret being betrayed if the Captain should take it into his head to question that lout Larry, over there. The best thing to do, obviously, was to question him oneself.

"Hi! Larry! Come over 'ere a minute."

Larry turned and regarded him benevolently.

"Who, me?"

"Yes, you."

"Want a boat?" Larry asked, when he had spat the tobacco from his mouth.

"No. Just a few facts."

"Huh! Then I'm not your man. I don't know any."

"Stow it and come over here."

Larry came, slowly, almost reluctant, it seemed, to leave the convivial party near the landing-stage. He nodded a curt "good morning" to Nicholas, and stood awaiting developments.

Dan manoeuvred himself into a position behind Nicholas, and put his horny finger to his lip, winking at Larry at the same time. Then he asked, with another broad wink and a shake of the head:

"You don't know a Mr. Byrne, who keeps a yacht 'ere in the 'arbour, do you, Larry?"

Larry grinned amusedly at Dan's cryptic signs, and soon caught the drift of his meaning. In the ordinary course of events he would have backed Dan up, but it was a grand May morning, and, though he hadn't so much as a shilling in his pocket, he was feeling fit, and independent. Besides, any one could see with half an eye that the gentleman in the plus-fours with the long face would pay much better for good news than for bad. Under these circumstances, it would be wicked to tell a lie.

So he shook his head and looked blank and stupid, and forced Dan to repeat his question.

"Yes, sir. 'Course I do. And a very nice young gentleman he is, too."

"I'm delighted to hear that," Nicholas said. And his face bore out the truth of this statement; to Larry's amused eye it seemed to grow shorter by a couple of inches. "I wonder if you can tell me where he lives."

"Why no, sir. That I can't. But I can tell you which is his yacht."

"Which is it?"

"That one, sir, over there, at anchor just this side of the island. The yawl."

"White, and green on the water-line?" Nicholas brought his field-glasses out of their case and examined every detail of *Puffin's* structure through them. In spite of himself Dan, too, cast an anxious glance in her direction—his storm-hardened eyes had no need of field-glasses—and was secretly relieved that there was apparently no sign of life on board.

For the time being, Nicholas was satisfied. He tipped Larry half a crown and Dan a shilling, which Dan refused disgustedly, and retired to the top of the cement wall that ran along the shore, from which vantage point he watched the yacht through his glasses, absorbed and motionless.

He had scarcely left the jetty before the air was filled with curses as Dan gave the traitorous Larry a piece of his mind. The muffled venom of their argument made its way to Nicholas's ear, and set him wondering at the richness of their vocabulary. When they had exhausted their stock of obscenities, the argument subsided, and they fixed their eyes on the Captain, fascinated by his strange behaviour, Dan watching him the more anxiously because he knew the reason for it.

At the end of ten minutes, during which the Captain never took the glasses from his eyes, Larry observed, with his customary good humour:

"Seems to be mighty interested in Mr. Byrne's yawl. Think he wants to pinch 'er?"

And Dan, thinking of Nya rather than of the yacht, answered:

"That's just about it."

However, the Captain presently lowered his field-glasses, and even at that distance they could tell he was disappointed. His whole body had a dejected air. He cast a last glance towards the yacht, and began to walk slowly away towards the road. Dan muttered a thankful imprecation, but too soon: for before he turned the corner the Captain lifted his glasses once more, and he had scarcely put them to his eyes before the two men heard a startled "Oh"—or thought they heard it, for they could see his lips move. Dan swore beneath his breath:

"Why the hell couldn't the kid have kept out of sight two minutes longer?"

The Captain had evidently seen what he was waiting for. He dropped the glasses, letting them hang by their strap round his neck, and strode back towards the jetty. He spoke directly to Larry this time.

"Can you get me a boat? I want to go round the harbour."

"Yes, sir. What kind of a boat?"

"A motor-boat."

"Certainly, sir. If you'll wait here, it'll be along in about ten minutes."

"Be as quick as you can."

48

Now that he had made certain Nya was aboard the yacht, he was all impatience to recapture her. As far as he could make out there was no one else aboard, which was a good thing. The less other people were mixed up in this business, the better it would be. Thank God, at any rate, that Nya was found. There could be no mistaking that curly head, even though she was wearing shorts and a blue jersey. He smiled to think that she should so whole-heartedly have taken to the nautical life in her few hours on board. That was just like Nya. His heart went out to her of a sudden—relief and affection taking the place of his former anger and anxiety. He imagined himself already seated in the motor-boat approaching the yacht and hailing her. He wondered with amusement what Nya's face would look like when she recognized him. Secretly he was glad that his wife was not with him, for the occasion could be treated lightly and passed off more or less as a joke. As far as it was possible to understand the workings of Nya's mind, he had confidence in them. She usually turned out to have a reason for what she did. No doubt she had a pretty good reason for having run away from school.

He looked again through the field-glasses. Yes, there

she was, lying on the cabin-top and reading—quite collectedly and, as far as he could judge, without a care in the world. The brat! She little knew the worrying sort of night he and her aunt had spent.

The noise of a motor-boat rounding the buoy from the yacht yard brought his glasses into his hands again. Yes, it was the waterman. He waited impatiently till the boat drew up at the landing-steps, and seated himself in it with satisfaction. Dan noticed this, and wondered grimly what sort of a time the Captain's niece was going to have during the next few hours.

As he opened the throttle and the boat sped away, Larry pulled a face at him and Dan was compelled to watch impotently while his colleague vanished across the sparkling water to carry out an action Mr. Byrne had particularly asked him to prevent.

"If only I could've taken 'im myself," he grumbled, "I'd at least 'ave seen 'e didn't treat 'er too bad. Damn the Boat Service for keeping me standing 'ere like a dummy all day long."

He went into his shelter and brought out an old telescope, through which he watched the scene of Nya's recapture until the boat arrived from Poole and he had to clip and issue tickets. He wondered afterwards if he had issued any wrong ones, for his mind was only half on his work, and he kept at least one eye on the distant yacht, hoping to make out something of what was happening on it. His heart and all his thoughts were in Mr. Byrne's yacht. He felt suddenly caught up, after seven years of inactivity on the Sandbanks jetty, in the lives of a group of other people whom he hardly knew, but for whom he unaccountably felt a deep attachment. There was Mr. Byrne; as nice a young gentleman and as good a yachtsman as you could find on the whole South

362

Coast. And if he was acting strangely in keeping Miss Russel on his yacht, he no doubt had a very good reason for it. She had run away from school and didn't want to go back for a day or two—that was reason enough. And Miss Russel; she was a plucky kid to behave like that. He liked her, too, with her straightforward eyes and her gingery hair. Nothing mean about her. And her uncle! Well, he was quite a decent man after all; he was only doing his duty in taking her back. He seemed a kind sort of gentleman, as if he could understand a kid running away from school.

"I dare say he's not so bad. Probably been up 'alf the night looking for 'er. Hope 'e doesn't meet Mr. Byrne before 'e's had time to cool off."

Nya had found *Cruising and Ocean Racing* dull in its first chapters, because they contained a minute account of how to build a boat, which didn't interest her at all. Her enthusiasm, as far as boats were concerned, was only for the finished craft afloat upon the water. So when she had looked at all the photographs and tried to decide wherein a yawl differed from a ketch, and a schooner from a cutter, she turned up the chapter on knots, and, with a length of line from the rope-locker, spent a fascinating half-hour practising bowlines, clove-hitches, and sheepshanks with the help of the diagrams. She was absorbed in this amusement, sitting cross-legged on the cabin-top, when she heard a motor-boat coming towards her and, looking up, saw with horror that Uncle Nicholas was standing up in it, waving and shouting to her. For an instant she sat spellbound, not knowing what to do, scarcely able to believe that she was really looking at Uncle Nicholas. It seemed so impossible; he didn't fit in a bit out here in the harbour, on Simon's yacht. But her eyes convinced her that there could be no mistake, and that she must at once make up her mind what she was going to do if she didn't want to be ignominiously recaptured. The rope dropped from her hand on to the book; she scarcely noticed it. Her attention was riveted to the swiftly nearing motor-launch, and she sat like a statue, her mouth open, her eyes wide with fear.

It was no good bolting into the cabin, for he had obviously seen her, and he would only come aboard and take her away by force. If only she could manage the yacht single-handed, could hoist sail and weigh anchor and be away half-way down the harbour, before Uncle Nick came alongside. How could he have found her out? How? How? How? Was it Dan who had told him? Well, the point was, he *had* found her, and was rapidly approaching the *Puffin* in a horrible little motor-boat, driven by that horrible, long-legged seaman from Sandbanks pier. Nya cast a swift glance at the water and then at Brownsea Island, and wondered whether she could swim ashore before she was caught. She might be safe on Brownsea Island—for a time, at any rate. She could take refuge in one of the empty houses, or simply hide in the woods—if she only had ten minutes' start she knew she could easily outlast Uncle Nick and the seaman. But even as she considered this plan she knew it was a futile one. The motor-boat would simply change its course and cut off her escape to the island. The only thing to do then was to stay on board and face things out. But oh! if only Simon could be here!

"Nya! That is you, isn't it?" Uncle Nick once more brought up his field-glasses, searching her face to convince himself that his eyes were not deceiving him. She wondered what she must look like through field-glasses, all magnified and distorted like an absurd bug. If she

364

made a face at him, would he see her? Or was he still too far away? The temptation was almost irresistible, but she overcame it. It would be too stupid to indulge it. Uncle Nick was hardly likely to be in the best of moods, and to anger him still further would be bad policy. Though she hardly realized as yet that she was finally recaptured her instinct warned her that she might need to ask Uncle Nick for favours before very long. So she sat still upon the cabin-top, waiting for the launch to come up. Even when Uncle Nick repeated his question, she only nodded in answer. Her face grew sullen, her eyes half-closed, and she protruded her lower lip.

But Uncle Nick was too glad at seeing her to notice these things. He forgot even to be stern as he put his hand on *Puffin's* bulwark and jumped aboard. The motor-boat swayed and splashed alongside from the recoil, and Larry switched off the engine and leaned back luxuriously on the gunwale to watch the ensuing comedy. Nya saw him out of the corner of her eye, and the scarcely perceptible dislike she had felt for him that day on the jetty when he had pulled her leg, telling her about Mr. Byrne and the girl he took on his yacht, flared now suddenly into hatred.

"Well, you young brat, so here you are." Uncle Nick had come aboard and was standing beside her. But she didn't get up. She remained cross-legged on the cabin roof, the book with the rope coiled in a half-finished sheepshank on it on her lap.

"We've had no end of a worry about you. Didn't know where you could have got to. But you seem to be safe and sound, thank God."

Nya didn't answer. She only sat and frowned. Determined that she shouldn't feel he was angry or reproach-

365

ful, he made up his mind to humour her a little further, although he was feeling acutely uncomfortable, partly because that wretched waterman was looking on. He would have liked to send him away for ten minutes, but that was hardly practicable, and yet——! Suddenly he thought of an expedient, and, turning to Larry, who was lighting his pipe in anticipation of a lazy quarter of an hour, he said:

"Go back to the jetty, will you, and put through a telephone call to Sandbanks 991, and tell Mrs. Russel that her niece is safe. Then come back here."

Larry stopped filling his pipe and looked at him with good-natured contempt.

"Can't do that, sir. Not my job. My job's looking after this motor-boat."

"I know that. I'm not suggesting you should leave it behind."

"Of course not, sir. I only meant—I don't understand the telephone."

"You can get some one else to do it for you. I don't mind."

But Larry was determined not to miss the fun if he could help it, and, totally misjudging the Captain, he showed himself one degree too obstinate.

"I couldn't very well do that, sir," he said.

"Very well," Uncle Nick retorted furiously. He was suddenly very angry. Nya, who was watching him intently, knew the signs. She had seen him like this once before.

"In that case, I shall pay you off now."

Uncle Nick put his hand into his pocket with so determined a gesture that Larry put away his pipe and looked at him with renewed interest. He swiftly considered the additional cost to his customer of a return journey to

366

Sandbanks, and, deciding that an extra five shillings was of more value than the pleasure he would lose by earning it, answered with a conciliatory grin:

"Ah, now, don't you do that, sir. I'll get some one to telephone for me, if I lose my reputation to do it."

And he cranked up the engine and pushed off from the *Puffin's* side before the Captain should change his mind.

When he had gone, Uncle Nick turned to Nya and smiled. And this time she allowed herself to be cajoled into returning his smile. At first she tried not to; but she found it increasingly difficult to maintain her sullen frown, and after a few seconds she gave in. He had completely won her heart by sending Larry away, so what was the use in pretending she hated him?

"That's better," he said. "Friends again, eh?"

She smiled, but still said nothing. It was hard to know how to begin this conversation. She waited for him to make a move; and he, at first, waited for some overture from her. When none was forthcoming, he continued:

"Not that we were ever enemies; but I was afraid you might dislike me for performing my unpleasant duty as your uncle and guardian." He laughed self-consciously, and was silent.

For a few seconds she looked at him, suddenly resentful again of his presence on Simon's yacht. All round her were the yachts, the islands and the water which she loved and to which she felt she belonged. The sun glanced up into her face off the ripples, familiarly, as if to remind her that she belonged to him too, and that it was his right to dazzle her and make her blink. Above, the gulls cried out to her, wailing "Stay, stay."

But Uncle Nick was standing in front of her, and his eyes said plainly, "I've come to take you back."

Her holiday was over, that was clear; and all these—the harbour, the sea, the gulls—were things of the past.

"What are you going to do?" she asked.

"Take you home with me."

"Why?"

"Do you really want me to explain?"

"I don't see why you should take me if I don't want to go."

"Unfortunately I'm responsible for you. So I must."

"Why are you responsible? I ran away all of my own accord."

"I know. And I sympathize too, old girl; you needn't think I don't. Only, you see, your father wouldn't think much of me if I let you go off into the blue, and he never saw you again."

"I'd have come back. I was coming back to-morrow anyway."

"Were you?"

"Yes, honestly."

A suspicion flashed through his mind that she was lying; but he was ashamed of it the moment he looked her in the eyes. There was anger there, and a kind of proud unhappiness, but no deceit.

"I'm sorry," he said, "but I had no means of knowing."

"I sent a telegram—at least Simon did."

"As far as I know it didn't arrive."

She realized at once that to reproach Simon in her heart or to explain to Uncle Nick why the telegram hadn't yet arrived would be waste of time. She would wait and see whether it was there when she got back to "The Rising". For she realized she would have to go. It was no good struggling; there was nothing she could do. Even Simon couldn't help her now. Only, it was hard to have to *acknowledge* her defeat, and that was why she argued.

"In any case," he added, "I would rather take you back myself than let the police do it."

"The police?"

"Well—when you didn't turn up at home last night, we naturally got a bit worried. We thought something might have happened to you."

"I see. I hadn't thought of that."

"We didn't expect you to." He smiled, anxious still to keep the discussion friendly. It wasn't so difficult as he had feared it would be. As far as he could read her mind, she seemed resigned to coming back with him, and all this talk was simply to put off the evil moment. Well—let her talk. The great thing was not to rush her, not to let her feel she was being forced into returning, but to try and get her to come back as she said she had run away—"all of her own accord". That, surely, was the way to treat her. It was what Tom would have done if he had been here.

She looked up at him, now, as he stood on the deck beside her. That was at least the third time he had smiled, so he couldn't be very angry. This was the moment at which to make a friendly gesture.

She got up, and putting her arm in his, she spoke without meeting his eyes.

"Have I really got to go back, Uncle Nick?"

"I'm afraid so, old girl."

"Oh, damn. And I was just beginning to enjoy myself."

He gave her an affectionate cuff on the head.

"Were you, indeed, you young brat? Let me tell you that your aunt and I spent an entirely sleepless night."

Even now he wasn't angry, only a little reproachful;

369

she could see a smile beginning to flicker round his lips. So she looked up at him and said, with a grin:

"I'm sorry, Uncle Nick."

"I don't believe you are, a bit," he retorted. "Now, go and get those nautical togs off, there's a good kid. I expect that villainous waterman will be back soon with the motor-boat."

"All right, Uncle Nick."

There was not the least constraint between them now. They were on the same affectionate terms as they had been that night when they went to see "Desire". She was not afraid any longer that there would be trouble at "The Rising" when she got back. Even if Aunt Ethel was angry and hurt, Uncle Nick was on her side. Without another thought she went down to the cabin to change.

Once away from Uncle Nick her mind began to work swiftly again. It was all very well to think of herself all the time but what about Simon? What would he think when he came back this evening and found *Puffin* deserted? She must write him a note and leave it on the cabin table. But supposing he didn't come? Supposing something terrible had happened to him? Uncle Nick had mentioned the police; they might even now be on Simon's tracks, trying to find out where he had hidden her. Or perhaps they, or Uncle Nick, had lain in wait for him as he went ashore at half-past eight, and that was how they had found out that she was aboard *Puffin*. In that case they had probably taken him prisoner—he had said dreadful things *might* happen to him because of her—and that was why he hadn't been able to send the telegram.

The more she thought of this possibility the likelier it seemed, until she became quite convinced that Simon was even now in prison, and all because of her. Finally, she could bear the dreadful thought no longer and, half-dressed as she was, she put her head out of the cabin door and spoke anxiously to her uncle. She had a vague feeling that, as long as she was on board *Puffin* she was still in a position to demand favours by threatening not to leave unless they were granted.

"Uncle Nick, how did you know I was here?"

He had been gazing at the shore through his binoculars, trying to follow Larry's movements. The motor-boat seemed to be away a long time. He turned to Nya now, and seeing her half-dressed, with a worried frown on her face, he grinned cheerfully and waved his binoculars at her.

"I took a squint through these, and saw you lying on your tummy here." He pointed to the cabin-top.

"Yes, but—how did you know where to look?"

"That waterman-fellow told me."

"The beast!"

"Not at all! I was grateful to him."

Even now she hadn't found out what she wanted to know, only it was so difficult to ask outright.

"But—didn't you see Simon?"

"No."

"Honestly, Uncle Nick?"

"Honestly."

"And you don't think the police will have done anything to him, do you?"

"Good gracious, no. We never called them in."

"Oh—thank goodness."

She disappeared into the cabin again, like a frightened animal into its hole; but it was relief she felt, and not terror. Simon was safe! Even if she had been recaptured, he was still free!

371

She tore a piece of writing paper off the pad that was kept in the table drawer, and with a blunt pencil wrote Simon a letter, hastily, for she was afraid that at any moment Uncle Nick would get tired of waiting and come in.

Darling Simon,

Uncle Nick has found out where I am and so I've got to go home. He's out on the deck now, so I have to hurry. I wish I didn't have to go. I'm sorry I shan't be here when you come to-night, only I can't help it. I hope you are all right. If you're all right I don't mind so much having to go back. Thank you for letting me stay, dear darling Simon. Good-bye,

love from
NYA.

She put Simon's jersey and shorts on his bunk in the fo'c'sle and cast a glance round the cabin to see that it was ship-shape. Even with Uncle Nick waiting outside, she wasn't going to leave it untidy for Simon. She wondered whether the letter would be safe on the cabin table, and, as she looked about for a better place, she thought suddenly of adding a postscript. She sat down again and wrote swiftly and almost illegibly.

"I love you, so please don't forget about me. I'm sure they'll try to stop me from seeing you. Oh, Simon, don't let them. I must see you again. I can't wait until I'm twenty-one. Good-bye."

She folded up the letter and left it on the table where he couldn't fail to see it. Then she went out, shutting the cabin doors behind her.

"Ready?" said Uncle Nick.

"Yes."

She didn't trust herself to say more. There were tears

in her eyes, and in a minute, she feared, they would come into her voice.

"The motor-boat *has* started back. I was afraid the fellow was going to leave us in the lurch. You look better in your own clothes, I must say."

She gave a little laugh, so that she shouldn't have to speak. Then she went and stood on the counter, looking out across the harbour. She could see the motor-boat returning, and wished it would make haste to end this awkward period of waiting. She wondered what Uncle Nick was thinking, but she didn't dare to look at him for fear he should see she was crying.

He realized this. He could still remember the sickening helplessness that one felt when tears insisted on coming. It was no use, he knew, trying to speak or even to move; that only made them come the faster. He watched Nya's back. It was motionless; there were no sobs yet. He began to whistle, and took a step or two away from her to try and seem concerned with something else. He looked towards the hills and said:

"By Jove! I've never seen those hills looking quite so lovely. You know, we really ought to go for a picnic there next holidays."

Then, lest she should think she was supposed to answer, he hurriedly began whistling again. In a minute or two, as a result of his clumsy and well-meaning non-chalance, she had recovered herself enough to ask him a question. She remembered, suddenly, that the dinghy was no use to Simon out here, and that he would want it this evening when he came back from the office.

"Uncle Nick."

"Yes, old girl."

"Please could we take the dinghy back with us to the jetty? That's where it belongs."

She still hadn't the courage to meet his gaze, but spoke with her eyes on the distant shore. He came towards her and put his hand on her shoulder.

"Yes, Nya, of course. It's Simon's dinghy, I suppose."

She nodded. Then the sobs refused to be stifled any longer, and burst through, softly at first, then with increasing strength until she was crying desperately. Uncle Nick's hand on her shoulder, and Simon's name —his sacred Christian name—had finally unnerved her.

Uncle Nick put his arm round her, and patted her on the cheek.

"Now, now, don't you cry, old girl; it's going to be all right. We'll take the dinghy with us."

But now that she had broken down she had no control left over herself at all. She cried, quietly and hopelessly, until the motor-boat was near enough for her to hear its engine. Uncle Nick said:

"Don't you worry, Nya. I'm not an ogre, you know. I know perfectly well what it's like, running away from school. I did it myself once—for an hour or two."

"Did you, Uncle Nick?" She smiled through her tears.

"Yes. Rather. So you see, I understand. And there's nothing to be unhappy about."

"It wasn't that so much, Uncle Nick. It was——" She stopped.

"What?"

But she shook her head, and didn't answer.

"If it's Simon you're worrying about," he said, "we could go and call on him one day. I'd like so much to meet him, you know."

"Oh *would* you, Uncle Nick?" She looked suddenly up at him, gay, in spite of her red eyes. His suggestion held out hope for the future. They would like Simon, and he would try to like them, they would become friends, and

374

she would be allowed to see him. She forgot, in her happiness, how she had sworn to herself that she would never let him meet Aunt Ethel—she forgot even that he already *had* met Aunt Ethel—she didn't care any longer whether he discovered that she was "just like other little girls"; she wanted only, at any cost, to see him again.

"You'd like him, Uncle Nick."

"I'm sure I should."

She was quite consoled now, and by the time Larry drew alongside in the motor-boat she was feeling almost happy.

"Did you put that call through?" Uncle Nick asked.

"Yes, sir."

"Thanks."

"And Mrs. Russel said there was a telegram for you, and would you come back as soon as possible."

"I see."

Nya and Uncle Nick looked at each other, and in that look they cemented their friendship anew. From now onwards Nya felt complete confidence in him, and she could sense that he believed in her and tried to understand. She remembered how disappointed she had been when she first met him to find that, although he looked so much like Daddy, he didn't behave in at all the same way. She thought again of those rather uncomfortable afternoons when Uncle Nick was tinkering with the car and she had tried to get him to talk to her. She supposed now that he must have been shy, and not bored with her, as she had thought.

They didn't speak on the way back; Larry's presence embarrassed them both. When they had made the dinghy fast to the motor-boat they sat silent until they reached the jetty. Larry cast a quick glance at Nya and noticed that she had been crying.

375

49

They took a taxi from the jetty, to Nya's great surprise. It was such a little way that this seemed awfully extravagant. Worse than that, it meant that they would arrive all the sooner at "The Rising", and she was still not quite prepared to meet Aunt Ethel. Uncle Nick said nothing at first. She was afraid he was angry again, so, half to test him and half to placate him, she made conversation.

"I don't like the man who brought the motor-boat, do you, Uncle Nick?"

"What's that?" He was wondering whether it would be best to take Nya back to school at once, or to wait until to-morrow. "No, he's an out-and-out villain. Tried to charge me a fortune for telephoning to your aunt."

"The one I like is the fat, grey-haired man. He's called Dan."

"Oh, he's a friend of yours, is he?"

"Yes."

"So that's why he refused to tell me where you were."

"Did he? That was nice of him!"

"I suppose it was—from your point of view."

As they drew up at "The Rising" Nya quailed. Uncle

Nick's eyes had suddenly gone stern, and he alighted and paid off the driver with the quick jerky movements of an angry man. She followed him into the hall, and there, at the foot of the stairs, stood Aunt Ethel. Nya didn't know whether to smile at her or not. After an instant's reflection, she decided to smile. There was no point in putting oneself in the wrong. The thing to do, as Simon had once said, was to "crack yourself up"; then people believed what you said and admired you. Not that Aunt Ethel was ever likely to admire, but she might by this means be made to respect. The thing to remember was that she had run away from school because of the business about Simon's letter, and because Daddy, who could have put things right, wasn't coming back for so long. And that she had been *right* to run away. And that she wasn't ashamed.

The telephone message had given Ethel time to collect herself, or she probably would have gathered Nya to her arms and wept for sheer joy that she was safe, then have regretted her rash overture of friendship later, when she wanted to scold the child. By now she was already beginning to feel more angry than relieved. So she came forward, kissed Nya frigidly on the cheek, and said:

"So there you are. Well, I expect we should be thankful to have you back safe and sound."

Her tone was not cordial, but Nya was beginning to be able to distinguish what people said from what people meant, and she had a suspicion that Aunt Ethel wasn't as angry as she would like to be. The fact that she had kissed her showed this, even if it had been a rather distant peck.

Encouraged by this, she determined to show a bold front, and met Aunt Ethel's frigid caress with a smile.

"We'd better go into my room, I think," said Uncle Nick, and Nya could see that he had dropped his friendly manner and was looking very fierce. With a sick heart she wondered whether she had misjudged his kindness, whether he had never been sincere at all, but had simply lured her into returning without making a fuss. He became an ogre to her now.

Uncle Nick led the way, Aunt Ethel followed him, and Nya automatically followed her. She was thinking hard. She knew that she must have some plan of action, some comforting thought to give her strength with which to argue, for she was certain now that there would be a long and gruelling catechism in Uncle Nick's study, followed by a desperate argument. And you couldn't argue if you didn't believe in the thing you were arguing about, you couldn't "crack yourself up" to other people.

Aunt Ethel sat down in Uncle Nick's arm-chair, and Nya was told to sit by his desk. Uncle Nick shut the door, and came and stood by the fireplace. There was a short pause while Nya thought, absurdly enough, that Aunt Ethel was about to have her fill of "talking things over".

Then the inquisition began.

"Now, Nya, I want you to answer my questions, because there are several points your aunt and I would like cleared up."

He paused for a moment, cleared his throat, and looked at Aunt Ethel. She nodded almost imperceptibly.

"First of all," he said, "we'd like to know if you've seen your friend Mr. Byrne—Simon."

Something inside her went tight, and refused to let her answer his question. He had to repeat it.

"Now, come on, Nya," he said. "You've given us an

extremely difficult twenty-four hours" ("It's nothing like as much as that," Nya calculated quickly), "so don't add to our difficulties by refusing to answer my questions. I want to know whether you've seen Simon at all in the last two days."

"What difference does it make?"

"A great deal to us."

"And to you also," Aunt Ethel added. "We shall know what to do with you according to your answer."

"She's trying to frighten me," thought Nya. "I must show her I'm not afraid or ashamed."

"Yes, both yesterday and to-day."

There was a smile on her lips, a little smile of triumph. Why shouldn't she be proud of it?

"To-day? You must mean this morning, early this morning!"

Uncle Nick's eyebrows drew together.

"Yes. First thing on getting up," she affirmed, taking a sudden delight in telling the whole truth now that she was committed to it, "and last thing before going to bed."

"Do you mean," Uncle Nick hesitated as if he were reluctant to speak the words, and when he spoke his tone implied his incredulity, "do you mean he spent the night on board the yacht with you?"

"Yes, Uncle Nick. It was the greatest fun."

Uncle Nick's eyebrows now drew hurriedly apart, and went up in search of the wrinkles on his forehead. Aunt Ethel opened her eyes wide, and Nya wondered for an awful instant whether she was going to cry. But the moment she caught her husband's eye she looked away, and Nya was unable to see whether or not her eyes filled with tears. There was silence for several seconds, a grim silence, Nya realized suddenly, not the usual sort of silence that occurs every now and then in a conversation but a silence charged with meaning and growing more oppressive the longer it persisted. What was it all about? Why was there this silence, so profound that she could hear a bus passing at the end of the road, and the ticking of the wooden clock that Uncle Nick had carved himself seemed like the panting of a huge steam-engine? Why did Uncle Nick look embarrassed and Aunt Ethel as if she were going to cry?

The silence grew longer still. It was becoming unendurable. What *could* be the reason for it? She ran over in her mind everything she had said since she came into the room—no, there was nothing that could have upset her aunt and uncle.

When all three had stared at the floor in perplexed discomfort for some seconds—which seemed whole minutes—the silence was mercifully broken by Aunt Ethel (she wasn't crying apparently), who said:

"Are you quite sure, Nya? I mean—it's a very serious accusation to make, you know."

"But, Aunt Ethel, I'm not accusing any one. What do you mean?" She turned perplexedly to her uncle, certain now that some strange thing had happened of which she was entirely unaware. "Uncle Nick, what's it all about? I don't understand."

"No, no, my dear," he replied, "of course you don't. But never mind; that's all we wanted to know."

He was certain from her perfectly genuine bewilderment that she didn't know what they were hinting at, and his simple mind was satisfied with this as an assurance of Nya's innocence. Unfortunately for Nya, his wife was not so sure. Unable now to resist the longing to make quite certain, she took over the role of inquisitor from Uncle Nick, who dropped into the other chair, apparently exhausted.

"Tell me, Nya," she began, as it were fingering her words before she placed them in Nya's ears, so that they arrived with Aunt Ethel's unmistakable taint upon them, and were all the more hateful. "Tell me just what happened on board the yacht last night. Was Mr. Byrne there all the time?"

"Yes."

"Did he sleep in the same cabin as you?"

"Well, it's really all one cabin, only there *is* a door between."

"I see. Was the door shut between you?"

"No, of course not."

A horrible premonition which now entered Nya's mind grew rapidly into a certainty in the next few minutes. Simon had said once that people would think unpleasant things of them for being together, would ask difficult and unanswerable questions and would do their best to try and make their love appear unnatural and wicked. This was what was happening now. The realization made her shudder, and it hurt and angered her all the more that Aunt Ethel and Uncle Nick should be the ones to ask these questions, when they ought to have been the very ones who trusted her, and to whom she could turn for protection. She had thought hardly of them sometimes, she admitted, but she had never considered them capable of this.

Remorselessly Aunt Ethel continued:

"Did he come into your part of the cabin during the night, or did you go into his?"

"No," said Nya. This wasn't true, she knew. He had come to say good night to her. And then, of course, he had come in first thing in the morning to light the Primus.

"Are you sure?"

"Yes."

381

But somehow, because it was a lie, even though such a little one, Nya found it impossible to meet Aunt Ethel's eye properly, which, as she knew, was essential if you wanted your lie to be believed. Her eyes kept straying to a point somewhere on Aunt Ethel's bosom, chiefly to the tie-pin she was wearing about half-way down on her blue silk tie. Or they would wander up again and examine the pattern on the collar of her blouse. She was quite close to Aunt Ethel—only about four feet away.

"Did nothing at all happen between you during the night?"

"I say, Ethel, steady on, you know."

But Aunt Ethel was, as she thought, hot on the scent of whatever she was hunting, and it would have needed much more than her husband's remonstrance to call her off.

"Nonsense, Nicholas, we've got to find out once and for all. Now, Nya, tell me exactly what did happen."

When she thought swiftly of what *had* happened during the night, Nya was seized with the desire to laugh.

"Well, Aunt Ethel, it was like this you see. I undressed and got into bed. I didn't wash frightfully well because there wasn't much water except sea-water, which isn't any good. Then, after a time, I went to sleep. I dreamed about something, but I can't remember what—I expect it was about Miss Littlewood. Then I woke up because the tide turned, and, as the wind was against us, it got quite choppy for a bit. Then I thought how lovely it was not to be at St. Monica's, and how funny it was sleeping without any sheets. And then I went to sleep again, and I can't remember what happened until the alarm went."

She searched their faces eagerly at the end of this narrative, to see whether there was a smile to be extracted from either of them. Oh, if only there were! It would take away the pompous earnestness of this discussion and make it into a friendly affair. It was so much easier to answer questions when you were on friendly terms. She longed now for one little word of kindness or even of chaff to break the depressing tension and to make them all friends again. If they were angry with her for running away from school she would make up for it somehow. Only, let them not be angry all the time. Let them be friends for a little before she had to go back again.

Uncle Nick got up and went to the window. Aunt Ethel looked at the floor. Then, after another silence which promised to be as agonizing as the first, she spoke.

"Very well, Nya, that will do. Go up to your room now, and I shall be up presently with Doctor Newnes."

Nya's jaw dropped and her eyes grew wide.

"Doctor Newnes? But why? There's nothing the matter with me."

"We'll leave it to him to find out, shall we? Run along."

"But, Aunt Ethel——"

Suddenly Aunt Ethel rose out of the chair to her full height—and she was a tall woman—and said in a voice of steel:

"Don't argue with me. Go up to your room at once."

There was nothing for it but to go.

50

When Nya was gone Nicholas turned furiously to his wife.

"Good God, Ethel, you aren't really going to send for Newnes?"

"Naturally."

"But for the Lord's sake, don't you realize what you're doing to the child?"

"I only realize that we've got to have definite knowledge and this is the only way to get it."

"Nonsense. It's perfectly clear to me that there's nothing whatever wrong with Nya, and even if there were, it's the young man you've got to get hold of, not her."

"I hardly think we should get much satisfaction out of him. And besides, Nya wasn't telling the truth. I could see that."

Something snapped inside Nicholas. Her apparent determination to make the whole business much more serious than it really was and her refusal to look at it from the child's point of view incensed him to such a degree that he forsook that patience with which he had treated his wife for fifteen years, and started actually to dislike her. At any rate, he realized with shame afterwards, for these few minutes he disliked her. Suddenly, with disconcerting clarity, he saw her as she was and wondered however he had managed to live amicably with her for so long.

"Very well, then," he said, "we will get no satisfaction out of him. We aren't even going to try. We're going to leave the whole damned thing alone, do you hear? I believe myself that if there is any satisfaction to be given he will give it of his own accord. And if he doesn't, we can't possibly make him. But whatever happens, I'm not going to let Nya be made to suffer for it. Any one would think she was a kind of animal from the way you're suggesting we should treat her. Whereas her only offence is that she's run away from school, and you know perfectly well that any child with a certain amount of initiative will and does do that. It's the obvious answer to the school authorities if you don't consider they're treating you justly. I did it myself. Why on earth, if you must punish the child, can't you stick to what she *has* done, instead of inventing monstrous punishments for what she hasn't done?"

After a second she shrugged her shoulders and, without meeting his eye, went into the garden. She had nothing to say. She was not merely upset that he should have spoken so rudely to her, she was utterly astonished. Once again, his eye had blazed, and he had reminded her of the days of their youth when he had been so masterful. She had loved him then, he was so overwhelming he simply hadn't allowed her not to. And now he had expressed himself just as vigorously again, and about something far less important—anybody would have thought Nya was his own child from the way he behaved—so again there was nothing for it but to obey.

Only by now she was so accustomed to making him do what she wanted that it cost her an effort to adjust herself to the new conditions; which was why she went into the garden. She must keep some vestige of authority in his eyes because of this business of Nya. Whatever Nicholas might think about calling in Dr. Newnes, the child would have to be punished for the breach of etiquette she had committed: Miss Littlewood would expect it.

"And yet," Ethel thought, tying up the leaves of the dead daffodils, "isn't it perhaps more Miss Littlewood's business than mine? After all, it isn't me that Nya ran away from."

And gradually she began to change her mind about the whole affair, until she felt quite kindly towards Nya again, and actually caught herself looking for an excuse to keep her at "The Rising" a little longer, and so postpone the fateful interview the child would have to have with her headmistress.

Nicholas stared after her for a moment, wondering whether he should follow her or not. But the garden was an unsatisfactory place in which to continue a discussion; the gardener would be certain to overhear, and besides, Ethel evidently didn't want to listen to what he had to say. He walked up and down his study for a little and then tried to settle down to read a book. But his mind refused to be interested by the printed word, and continually returned to the subject of Nya. He wondered what the child was thinking, a prisoner up there in her room. He wondered whether his wife would go and talk to her and make matters worse. He decided to go out for a walk, but then it occurred to him that Ethel might telephone Dr. Newnes while he was gone. Besides, it was getting on for lunch-time—well, no, not exactly. Without any set purpose he wandered up to his room, where he fiddled about with a box of studs, throwing away the useless bone ones that came back from the laundry in his shirts. He moved about the room, now looking out of the window, now gazing at the photographs of school and rowing groups on the walls, whistling "Yip-I-addy-I-ay". Then, acting on an impulse, he went and knocked at the door of Nya's room.

Nya was moving about her room like an animal in a cage. It was just as she had left it, a week ago, but it looked a little tidier, a little more impersonal. Her blue and white counterpane had been changed for a more imposing one of shot silk, for this room was a guest-room while Nya was at school. Not that she had ever heard of anybody using it; as far as she knew no one ever came to stay at "The Rising".

She opened the bottom drawer of her chest of drawers. Yes; there were all her things, the clothes she couldn't take to school, her books, and, best of all, Mummy's watch. That, of course, was much too precious to be taken to St. Monica's. It was lovely to see it again. It reminded her of Mummy and Daddy and John. Oh, why, why couldn't Daddy come home quickly? She began to wind up the watch.

She shut the drawer quickly when she heard the knock.

"Come in," she said.

It was Uncle Nick who came in, and there was no sign either of Aunt Ethel or of Dr. Newnes. That was a relief; Uncle Nick was much easier to deal with, especially alone. He grinned at her, closed the door, and came and sat on her bed. She was still standing by the chest of drawers.

"Do you mind my sitting here?"

387

"No, of course not, Uncle Nick. Anyway, it's not really my bed now, is it?"

"Why not?"

"Well, not at the moment, I mean."

"Nonsense. It remains yours whatever happens. As long as you like to think of it as yours, that is."

"I do think of it as mine. I've rather wanted to come back to it all this week. I hate my cubicle at school. It's like a rabbit-hutch."

He nodded sympathetically, and there was silence for a few seconds; then he said:

"Tell me what the trouble was, old girl."

It was a strange habit that Uncle Nick had got into since this morning, of calling her "old girl". It made her want to giggle, only she knew he meant it affectionately and she didn't want to hurt his feelings.

"Why I ran away, d'you mean?"

"Yes."

She told him, as well as she was able, about Rosemary and Simon's letter. Uncle Nick himself had suggested that he should take her to see Simon, so she no longer felt shy of speaking about him. She told him, also, about the letter that had come from Daddy, and how disappointed and lonely it had made her feel. And Uncle Nick wasn't at all angry. He seemed to understand everything, even that the only way of coping with such an overwhelming situation was to run away from it for a while.

"And I was going back to-morrow morning, Uncle, honestly I was."

"Yes," he said, "I believe you." Then he added, as an afterthought: "The telegram came; I saw it on the hall table as we came in."

There was another short pause, until Nya asked:

"Will I have to go back at once, Uncle Nick?"

He smiled at her.

"How are you feeling?"

"All right."

"Well, we'll see. I must ask your aunt. Would you rather go at once?"

"In a way—yes." With any luck, she would get away before the doctor came.

Uncle Nick grinned at her.

"Want to get it over, eh?"

"Yes."

He got up and held out his hand to her.

"Come on, then; we'll go and find your aunt."

For an instant she hesitated, just long enough for him to notice.

"What's the matter?"

"Aunt Ethel said——" she began.

But he cut her short.

"Don't worry about that now; there's really no need for you to stay cooped up here, or you'll soon be thinking this room's like a rabbit-hutch, too."

She smiled at that, and took his hand, and together they went down into the garden.

Aunt Ethel was talking to the gardener about the gooseberry bushes. Out of the corner of her eye, she saw her husband approaching with Nya. They waited, hand in hand, until she had finished talking. When she turned to them she was smiling and self-possessed. Nicholas was relieved, for he had expected a dark frown.

"Nya says she'd like to go back straight away and get it over," he said.

But now Aunt Ethel's face clouded over.

"What a strange child you are."

"Why, Aunt Ethel?"

"I was certain that was the last thing you'd want. In fact"—she picked an imaginary caterpillar off a gooseberry leaf—"I'd rather hoped you'd like to stay until to-morrow morning."

Coming from Aunt Ethel, this was an astonishing suggestion. Nya hadn't even considered the possibility of staying, it seemed so remote.

"Still, it's just as you prefer."

The imaginary caterpillar was dropped on to the path and delicately trodden out of the existence it had never known.

Friendly gestures from Aunt Ethel were not so frequent that they could be regarded lightly. "I might as well take full advantage of this one," Nya thought. She was beginning to know the signs now. Aunt Ethel was a shy person, who detested saying things outright—except unpleasant things, which sometimes came out very roundly when she was angry. And even when she said nice things she was apt to say them rather as if she meant them to be nasty. The only thing to do, then, was to overlook her manner and to accept the immense concession which she was making.

"Oh, but of course, Aunt Ethel," she replied, a little breathlessly, "I'd *love* to stay until to-morrow."

"Would you?"

It gave her pleasure to see Nya's eyes light up.

"Yes, please. And can I really sleep the night here, in my own bed?"

"Yes, of course."

"Oh thank you, Aunt Ethel, thank you!"

"That's settled then. Now let's go and see whether Maggie's got enough for lunch."

"I don't want anything, Aunt, honestly; a piece of bread or something will do."

390

She was terribly anxious not to be a nuisance. But she was very hungry and even more anxious not to be taken at her word.

"That's splendid, then," said Aunt Ethel, "there is a crust left over from yesterday's loaf. Will that do?" She smiled a little sheepishly, conscious that it was her husband's prerogative to be facetious. And Nya, smiling also sheepishly, uncertain for an instant whether Aunt Ethel could have made a joke or not, answered:

"Yes, of course."

With that Uncle Nick laughed, and pulled the lobe of her ear, and said:

"Ha, ha, she believed you, Ethel. For a moment I declare she really believed you."

Nya pinched him amicably, then she put one hand in his and the other in Aunt Ethel's and together they went into the house.

As it turned out, there was cold beef for lunch, with pickles—not chutney, but real sour pickles, and a salad, with a dressing that Aunt Ethel was trying out of a book, she said. It was made simply of cream and celery salt, and tasted awfully good. Nya and Uncle Nick commented with relish upon it, and even Aunt Ethel admitted modestly that it was good.

51

Uncle Nick telephoned to tell Miss Littlewood that Nya was found, and that she would be returning to St. Monica's after breakfast the next morning. After this, the matter was not referred to again in front of Nya, except when she asked if she could go out for a walk after tea. She wanted to meet Simon on the jetty before he went out to *Puffin*. But Aunt Ethel categorically forbade her to go out, on the grounds that she was supposed to be at school and people might ask questions if they saw her about the village. It was a poor reason, but Nya realized it was probably not the true one. No doubt Aunt Ethel guessed something of her intentions.

So Nya spent the afternoon in the garden. Just before tea she happened to be looking through the garden fence when she saw the Grasshopper passing by. She called him in an undertone—Aunt Ethel was not far off —and held a long whispered conversation with him. He bore her no malice for their broken friendship; on the contrary, he seemed as pleased to see her as she was to see him, and when she told him she had run away from school, which she was unable to resist, he grew more pop-eyed than ever with admiration.

392

"And how about you?" she asked. "Why aren't you at school? Have you run away, too?"

"No such luck," he groaned, "I'm in quarantine for chicken-pox. My brother's got it."

"Rotten luck."

"Oh, well, it's not so bad really. It means you get an extra three weeks' hols. But there's no one to go about with, and even if there were, the quarantine'd spoil our fun."

Aunt Ethel began to approach down the path, and Nya hurriedly wished the Grasshopper good-bye.

"I'm supposed to be in disgrace, you see," she explained, so as not to hurt his feelings.

She soon put him out of her mind, and when she remembered him again later in the day, it was only with amusement. She felt a little ashamed at this; but she couldn't bring herself to regret the loss of their company.

"After all, I'm older than the lot of them put together —not in years, of course, but in other ways. And then, there's Simon."

She managed to think quite detachedly about Simon, with a kind of fatalistic acceptance of the state of affairs which had been forced upon them both. He would go down to the quay, she didn't doubt; Dan would tell him the truth, would show him the dinghy. Simon would find the letter in *Puffin*, he would read it, and, like her, he would be compelled to accept the situation. St. Monica's was an impregnable fortress; he couldn't get into touch with her there; "The Rising" was equally inaccessible, since it was guarded by Aunt Ethel and Uncle Nick. She wouldn't see him again until the end of the term, that seemed certain. The one comfort she had—a new comfort, which she had never felt before—

393

was that in the end, in the long, long run, things would come right and they would be able to be together. Since last night she was confident of this; she knew now that Simon wanted it as much as she did. He had said so. He had asked her to marry him, and, though she quite realized she was too young to do so immediately, she intended to as soon as it was possible. She was not very sure what it depended upon; not so much upon herself, she thought—*her* mind was quite made up—but upon other things, like her age, and her education, and Simon's job—oh, yes, and, she supposed, upon Daddy. What would he say when she told him? For of course she would tell him as soon as he came home. He would understand, and he would make it easier instead of harder for her to see Simon. And then all this idiotic deception would be unnecessary and she wouldn't have to run away from school when she wanted to talk to him. Uncle Nick, too, had promised to take her to see Simon—though, of course, it wouldn't be quite the same thing with him— and she was inclined now to believe that he meant it. Yes! On the whole the prospect was not too dismal.

And yet! There was Aunt Ethel, walking slowly down the path towards her, picking dead leaves and withered flowers off the plants as she went. She could never quite trust Aunt Ethel, her kindnesses and her strange, sudden forgivenesses. Aunt Ethel might still spoil everything if she got in first with Daddy and if he, by some unfortunate chance, believed her.

"It's true she's being nice to me at the moment, but that may be for a particular reason. Something to do with the doctor, perhaps," she thought suddenly. "He hasn't turned up yet, but that doesn't mean to say he won't. Doctors don't usually come till the evening, anyway, unless it's for something urgent. Perhaps that's why

394

she wouldn't let me go back to St. Monica's till to-morrow!"

And, concerned with these gloomy thoughts, she began to wander back towards the house. Ethel noticed her serious expression, and let her pass without molesting her. It occurred to her that Nya was probably wondering what she would do when she got back to St. Monica's.

"And that's a problem the dear child must deal with by herself."

52

After tea Nya sat in the drawing-room, looking at the
Illustrated London News. Uncle Nick was in his smoking-
room, and Aunt Ethel had gone out to shut up the hens
as it was getting dark. It was a lovely evening, but the
shadows seemed to fall very quickly and it soon became
impossible to read, even perched upon the window seat,
and practically leaning out of the window. She put on
the tall reading-lamp that stood in the corner near the
french windows, and sat in an arm-chair. Then she
changed her mind and went over to the fireplace, lighted
the other lamp and sat on the sofa. There was no fire in
the grate, but it was cosier over here than by the window. For some unaccountable reason she was feeling
depressed and a little frightened. She supposed it was
because night was falling.

Then the front door bell rang.

She raised her head and looked anxiously towards the
hall. Her instinctive fear was that it would be Miss
Littlewood, or somebody from St. Monica's, in which
case they would be shown into the drawing-room and
she would be imprisoned with them. It might even be
the doctor. She got up and tiptoed towards the door,

but just as she was about to open it she heard Emily crossing the hall to the front door. Then she heard a man's voice, rather indistinct, and Emily repeated:

"Captain Russel? Yes, sir. What name shall I say?"

She couldn't hear what the voice replied, but Emily said:

"Very well, sir. If you'll just wait a moment I'll give it to him."

"That's his card," thought Nya.

With any luck, the stranger would be shown straight into Uncle Nick's room, and she would be safe to stay where she was. It was evidently nobody from St. Monica's.

She wondered whether it would be possible to open the drawing-room door the tiniest bit, and have a peep at the man in the hall without betraying her position. He would no doubt be standing by the chest, looking frightfully sheepish. People always did, when they were waiting rather nervously in strange houses. She turned the handle, but the catch creaked and she thought it better to desist. She went back to the cold fireplace and took up her paper.

After a moment she heard Uncle Nick stride out into the hall and say loudly:

"How d'you do? I'm extremely glad to get to know you."

There was a mumbled response from the stranger, but Nya couldn't hear what he said.

"He must be jolly nervous," she thought.

"Let's go into my room," Uncle Nick said, from the hall. "I've just lighted the fire in there. I find the evenings are still cold, don't you?"

There was a monosyllabic grunt from the stranger, which sounded oddly familiar to Nya.

397

"Stupid, to think you recognize a grunt," she thought. But though she ran through in her mind all the men who were likely to call on Uncle Nick at this hour, she couldn't place the grunt. Eventually she decided— because the matter had to be decided one way or the other—that it was somebody who wanted to play golf with Uncle Nick next day. The door of Uncle Nick's study closed. She imagined the two men settling down beside the fire.

"Lucky dogs—with a fire," she said aloud; and kicked the empty grate before her.

In the smoking-room Simon was uncomfortably wondering how to explain to Captain Russel why he had come to see him. To his relief Captain Russel didn't leave him long in perplexity.

"I expect you've come to see Nya," he observed amicably.

"Well, yes. But I expect she's gone back already, hasn't she?"

"No, as a matter of fact she's still here."

"Oh, thank God."

There was a quiet fervour in the way he spoke. Nicholas looked at him with added interest during the pause that followed, observing his features, trying to read his mind. His face showed unmistakably that he was honest and kind. Energetic, too. There was nothing weak, no lazy acceptance of other men's opinions in that frank, weather-beaten forehead. And he was not at all bad-looking; Nicholas's hesitating eye was quick to admit this. Ah no! Here was nothing to fear for Nya. Why should there be? It was simply one of those friendships that children have for all sorts of strange people, such as bargees, ship's stewards, and every kind of man who possesses the unaffected simplicity which appeals to children. Why not, then, this friendship between Nya and the young man before him?

"Look here, Byrne, you'd like to talk to the child, I know; and so you shall. But I'd awfully like to ask you a question or two first, if you don't mind. Of course, you needn't answer if you don't want to, but it'll make my job considerably easier if you do. I don't like playing the heavy uncle, you know." He finished with a self-conscious laugh.

"No, no, of course, I quite understand." Simon leaned forward earnestly. "To tell the truth, sir, I'd have been glad to have a talk with you before this. I did call the other day, but unfortunately you were out."

"Yes, my wife told me."

Simon looked up wryly. "Did she? Yes, I suppose she must have. It wasn't a very satisfactory interview, I'm afraid. I'm not good at talking to women—except Nya. Somehow I seem to be able to get along with her."

He caught a quizzical look from Captain Russel. "Does that surprise you?", he asked.

"No, no, not at all." The Captain's reply was a little too hasty to be convincing.

"Oh, I understand. You're surprised that I should refer to Nya as a woman, I expect."

"Well, it seemed strange, just for a moment."

"Yes, I suppose it did."

There was a pause. Simon stretched his hands out towards the fire, embarrassed. After a moment he spoke again.

"It seemed strange to me, too, when I first thought of her like that. But I came to the conclusion before I'd known her very long that it was no good regarding her as a child simply because her age happens to be fourteen."

"H'm, well, I confess I don't quite follow you there. However, I'm not concerned with that aspect of the matter. What I am concerned with—as Nya's guardian, you will understand—is something quite different. Only I don't quite know how to put it into words."

Simon looked at him sharply; and, from his red face and uncomfortable stance before the gas fire, he guessed at once what it was he was trying to say.

"Oh, as to that," he said, with slight scorn in his voice, "I daresay I can guess what it is. I need hardly say that nothing in the world would induce me to harm Nya in any way whatever—I mean, literally, in any way whatever."

He caught the older man's eye and forced him to meet his gaze. "And as for her spending the night on my yacht—I gather you must have fetched her from it this morning—it was her wish; and I only consented to it, very much against my will, because I could think of no alternative that wouldn't have made her unhappy. Naturally, I behaved as if it were the most usual thing in the world."

It was exactly what Nicholas, in his embarrassment, was longing for. He beamed with satisfaction, and clapped Simon on the shoulder.

"That's all right, then, I'm very glad to hear it. I may say I knew all along that this was what I should hear from you."

Simon rose, embarrassed by the Captain's sudden effusiveness.

"My wife'll be glad to know it—to know you're here, I mean," said the Captain in some confusion. "She's down seeing to her chickens at the moment. Perhaps you'd like to see Nya in the meantime."

"Please."

Nicholas led the way into the hall and shouted for Nya. She answered from the drawing-room. He pointed the door out to Simon, and himself went through the front door to find his wife.

Simon opened the drawing-room door and came face to face with her.

"Nya?"

He spoke calmly, without a trace of the excitement she showed when she recognized him, an instant later, in the semi-darkness.

"Oh, Simon, it's you. Darling, darling Simon."

"Can I talk to you somewhere where we won't be disturbed?" He still spoke quietly, rather as if he were on enemy ground.

"In here," she whispered, and pulled him into the drawing-room. "Then, if they come, we'll be able to hear them in the hall." She closed the door. "Simon! How did you get here? Did you find my letter? Was that you at the front door just now? And I thought it was a friend of Uncle Nick's."

Her arms were round his neck and her face was close to his.

"Listen, darling," he said, disengaging himself and sitting on the arm of the sofa. "We haven't much time, and I've got a lot to say. First of all, have your uncle and aunt been bullying your life out of you because you ran away?"

"No, Simon. It was rather horrid this morning, but they've been sweet all the afternoon."

"What happened this morning?"

"Oh, nothing really. Aunt Ethel lost her temper with me because she said she was going to send for the doctor and I said I wasn't ill."

"The doctor?"

"Yes. He'll probably come this evening, I suppose."

"And *is* there anything the matter with you?"

"Of course not."

"But—they can't mean it seriously."

"Well, they've said no more about it since this morning."

He considered a moment. This was something that he hadn't expected. No! Surely there had been nothing in Captain Russel's inarticulate remarks that would lead one to suspect. . . .

He seized Nya by the shoulders and made her look into his eyes.

"Little Nya!"

"Yes, Simon?"

"I'm going to ask you a difficult question. It may even seem a stupid one to you. If it does, you must say so."

"What is it?"

"You must think what you're saying. I know it's hard for you, but if you trust me it will make all the difference in the world. I want to know; do you trust me?"

"Yes, Simon."

"You have thought about it a little, haven't you?"

"Yes, ever since—ever since you first took me out in *Puffin*."

"And you think you know what it implies?"

"I only know that I love you. And I trust you."

He drew her to him and kissed her hair. For an instant he held her; then they heard footsteps in the porch, and Aunt Ethel kicking off her Wellingtons.

He went and stood by the window. Nya sat down on the sofa. In the pause before Aunt Ethel came in Nya whispered:

"Simon."

"Yes, darling."

"It will be all right, won't it?"
"Of course it will."
Then the door opened.

53

For an instant Aunt Ethel and Simon looked at one another. He said "Good evening", and she nodded frigidly in return. Then she sat down beside Nya on the sofa.

"Nya, I think you had better go into the study," she said.

"Why!"

"Because I tell you to."

Nya seethed inwardly. What objection could Aunt Ethel have to her staying, when it was she whom Simon had come to see, when the whole conversation was to be about her? She was about to retort indignantly when Simon said:

"I am afraid I must ask you to let her stay. I think she should hear everything you or I have to say about her."

"Yes, I think that's only fair, Ethel," said Uncle Nick.

Aunt Ethel shrugged her shoulders.

"As you please." She tapped with her foot on the carpet. "Just out of time with the clock," thought Nya.

After a moment Aunt Ethel continued. "My husband tells me that you have behaved as I confess I didn't expect that you would behave, Mr. Byrne. At least he seems satisfied that that is the case. If it is true, I can only say that I am glad. And now I want this whole disgraceful business to end. It has gone on long enough. Perhaps I ought to apologize for the way that Nya has pestered you; I don't know whether or not it has been her fault, I'm sure. At any rate I can promise you that she won't do so again."

"Oh, I haven't pestered him." Nya broke in, furiously; but Simon silenced her with a gesture.

"I imagine your implication is rather that I have pestered her," he said. "I can see it must seem so to you. But I would rather not waste time discussing that now. There is only one thing that I want to say. I am fond of Nya—more than that: I love her."

Aunt Ethel closed her eyes for a moment in evident pain.

"I can see that you think that a disgraceful thing. But I don't think of it like that. When the time comes, when she is old enough—and always providing that she hasn't changed her mind by then—I am going to marry her. Nya has said she agrees to this, and, though I know that she doesn't realize fully yet what a promise of marriage implies, still it does give me some sort of right to talk like this."

He spoke calmly, as if he had thought out every word beforehand. Even Aunt Ethel was a little impressed. She had hoped to treat the matter lightly, to dismiss it in a few words and send Mr. Byrne home feeling like a naughty schoolboy. But his gravity and obvious sincerity made this impossible.

Nicholas came to her rescue by interposing heartily:

"That's very honourable of you, Byrne. Of course, we quite understand your feelings. But I don't think there need be any talk of marriage yet; that's a matter which doesn't really concern us. You had better discuss it with Nya's father when he comes home."

"I intend to, of course. Only I felt I ought to give you and Mrs. Russel an explanation."

"I never heard anything so absurd," said Aunt Ethel vehemently. "Nya is fourteen, and you are—whatever it is—twelve years older; you've barely known her for a month and you say you are going to marry her."

"You misunderstand me," Simon said patiently. "I didn't say I intended to marry her immediately, as you seem to imply. It is possible that I may never marry her, if she should change her mind when she is older."

"Or you yours."

"No." Simon's voice was even and low, making Aunt Ethel's scornful interjections seem the more strident. "No, there is no chance of that. I am old enough to know what I am doing."

"But she isn't, Byrne, you must admit that."

"Yes, sir, I do admit it. But we aren't here to make an irrevocable treaty about this matter; you asked me what my intentions were towards Nya, and I am doing my best to explain to you why I consider that I have a right to interfere in her affairs."

"It is disgusting," said Aunt Ethel.

"It seems you are doing your best to make it so for Nya."

"Why on earth is it disgusting, Aunt Ethel?" Nya inquired hotly. "I *want* to marry him. And I shall as soon as ever I can."

"My dear child, you don't know what you're talking about."

There was a pause; almost as long and as tense as that dreadful pause during the morning's conversation. There seemed nothing to say, or at least she could think of nothing. She felt tired, and her brain refused to work. She must leave it to Simon. He would know how to deal with Aunt Ethel.

"Please don't make things worse for Nya than they already are, Mrs. Russel," Simon said at last. "None of this is her fault. If it can be said to be anybody's fault, it's mine. But there's really no need to discuss that. All that matters for the moment is to simplify things for Nya. Since she's got to go back to school to-morrow, I want her to go with a certain amount of self-confidence. She must be able to feel that we shall come to a happy solution of this problem. Won't you please give her some assurance of that?"

He turned to the Captain, whom he felt to be the kinder of the two.

"I don't know what there is I can say." Uncle Nick shifted uncomfortably in his chair. "Except that my brother will be home soon now. He's an understanding sort of fellow; much more broad-minded that any one else I know. In fact," Uncle Nick smiled, "he's almost too broad-minded for my wife and me. Perhaps you think us a little old-fashioned. I honestly believe you would do best to talk to him."

"But I must be allowed to see Nya again. As I said before, I think I have some right to ask that."

"Yes, perhaps you have," Uncle Nick replied. "Though I confess I shouldn't have admitted it a week ago, or even yesterday."

"There is no need whatever for you to see Nya again before her father comes home. When he comes, the matter will rest entirely with him."

Simon smiled wryly and turned to Nya. That, it seemed, was the best that could be done for the moment. It wasn't very comforting, but there was strength

407

and comfort in his voice when he spoke to her.

"Don't you worry, little girl. We'll arrange things between ourselves. I want you to go back to school trusting in me to put things right. Will you do that for me?"

He was speaking to her now as he had spoken last night in *Puffin's* cabin—as if they were alone. Uncle Nick and Aunt Ethel ceased to exist for a moment. And she answered him with all the courage he had given her last night:

"Yes, Simon. I feel quite happy now I've seen you."

Aunt Ethel sensed the triumph in Nya's voice and saw the sweet devotion with which she looked at him; and she grew suddenly angry.

"That'll do, Nya. Say good-bye to Mr. Byrne now and run upstairs. There's been quite enough of this preposterous conversation."

Once again Simon intervened. "I would like to say good-bye to her alone."

Ethel's first impulse was to forbid this; but when she looked into Simon's level grey eyes—and he forced her to do so—she changed her mind. There was an unspoken command in them which her weaker nature respected. And worse than that; against her will she was beginning to like him.

Nicholas watched in amusement, wondering what her answer would be.

"Very well," she said. "I give you permission for that. But I shall return in five minutes. Come, Nicholas."

"Don't worry, old girl. I'll put things right with your father if I can."

"Thank you, Uncle Nick."

For an instant Nya and Simon were silent. Their last moments together were so precious that neither wished to speak; words so often had a way of getting twisted, and then time had to be wasted in straightening them out. Nya's eyes were large, and Simon thought he could see tears in them.

He took her hand and pulled her towards him. So they stood for a few seconds, her head on his breast, as it had been that day when she met him on the jetty.

"Oh, Simon."

It was something between a sigh and a sob that came from her. It reminded him disquietingly of how he had held her in his arms in *Puffin*'s cabin and talked to her intimately for the first time, and of how he had sworn to himself that he would wait for her for ten years if need be.

"Must I say good-bye to you?" she whispered.

"For a little time, Nya."

"Not for ever?"

"Lord no. Of course not."

She put her arms round his neck.

"Then I really will see you again?"

"As soon as your father comes home and I've had a chance to talk to him."

"That's not really very long is it? July, at the latest." She chuckled, and he looked down at her in surprise.

"What is it?"

"I was thinking that yesterday, when I got Daddy's letter, July seemed a terribly long way off; much too long to wait for. And now—I don't know——"

Her sentence ended with a sigh as she laid her cheek against his coat.

"And now what?"

"Now I don't mind so much. I think it's going to be all right—our being together, I mean. It is, isn't it?"

"Of course, my darling."

"Yes." She nodded sagely. "I've got a feeling inside me, like I always used to have when something was going to come right. You said it was an instinct, do you remember?"

"Did I?"

"Yes. I haven't had any instincts for such a long time."

He laughed, and took her face between his hands.

"I must go, little girl, before your aunt comes back. Or we shall have to say good-bye all over again, in front of her."

"That would be frightful."

"Don't lose courage, darling. We'll meet again the very first day your term is over. Can you hold out till then?"

"I think so, Simon."

"There'll be no writing, remember, nothing but your faith that I love you. You won't forget?"

"No."

"Good-bye, then, Nya."

"Please, Simon, kiss me good-bye."

He kissed her on the mouth. For an instant she drew away: he wondered anxiously whether he had hurt her. But she sought his lips again, gropingly, as if feeling her way in the dark, and let her mouth rest for an instant on his—two kisses so pure, so sweet, that he remembered them to the end of his life.

He embraced her and went. She heard the door shut behind him, and then the front door. For a moment she stood still, in a trance, her hand clasped to her side. It seemed she had a pain there; or perhaps it wasn't a pain, no, a feeling of excitement rather. As if her heart had filled up suddenly and was overflowing. It must be love, she decided. Yes, that was it. Because she did love

Simon. She might be only fourteen but she knew now what love was, that books and poems talked about.

She ran to the window to catch a glimpse of him, but he was gone.

54

Next morning she realized that she had changed once more. Whether this was because of her decision to run away from school, or because of the long hours of thinking on board *Puffin*, or because of the kiss which Simon had given her the night before, it was difficult to say. Anyhow, she was quite self-confident, not only before Aunt Ethel but before Miss Littlewood with whom she had half an hour's gruelling conversation. And she noticed now that Simon had been right; if you felt confident inside, nobody could possibly do anything to hurt you. Only, of course, in order to feel confident you had to feel happy, and without the knowledge that Simon loved her this would have been impossible.

So the prospect of not seeing him again until the holidays, of not hearing from him even, no longer made her wretched. There had been such assurance in his voice when he spoke of their being together one day, she no longer doubted that it would be possible. And with this assurance she could face any punishment.

The punishment was not as unpleasant as she expected. It consisted firstly of a long lecture by Miss Littlewood (Aunt Ethel refrained from saying anything at all), and secondly of enduring the girls' gibes. Entering another girl's cubicle under provocation was no great crime in comparison with running away from school; and running away from school was such a crime that it was difficult to punish. So Nya was sent to bed early for a week which, in fact, brought her more relief than discomfort; and that was all.

Miss Littlewood managed to suppress all mention of Simon, so Nya was spared the pain of mockery on his account. But, for some days, there continued to be repercussions of her escapade, the chief of which resulted in a wave of sympathy in her favour. None of the girls liked Rosemary very much, and they all secretly admired Nya for having the pluck to run away; so that one day she actually had to interfere between Rosemary and two girls who were tormenting her, after which Rosemary became her devoted slave.

But Nya was still reserved in her dealings with the girls. She was too modest to presume upon her popularity, always feeling, in her detachment from the others, that it was something undeserved and odd. The exaggerated affection they now showed her disgusted her occasionally as much as their former dislike. So she locked her thoughts away in her mind and allowed the life of the school to lead her where it wished.

Three weeks after Nya's return came a letter from Daddy. She received it from old Betsy with equanimity, as if to convince herself that she was now able to deal with whatever news it might contain. She read it on a seat in the garden. It was a hazy May morning; raindrops from the night before still hung on the bushes. She smiled to think of the conditions under which she had read his last letter, and before she opened this one she went over again in her mind the dreadful hours she

413

had spent that Monday morning. "But all that must have happened to somebody else. I don't feel as if it had any connection with me. It happened to the other Nya, the one who was shy and frightened and who didn't know whether she would ever see Simon again, whereas now. . . ."

Like the last one, Daddy's letter was quite short.

My darling Nya,

Your aunt writes that you are unhappy. Bear up for a little longer. I'll be with you on 25th of June. It's meant moving heaven and earth, but I've managed it. Come and meet me at Southampton. I'll write to your aunt to arrange it.

Your loving
DADDY.

Well! That was exciting. Another four weeks and Daddy would be here. Another eight weeks and then the holidays, Daddy and Simon. It seemed quite natural now to think of bringing them together; and only three weeks ago she had wondered and wondered whether or not it would be possible. There wasn't much point in writing to Daddy; he would hardly be likely to get the letter. And she couldn't write to Simon. There was nothing to do but to wait for everything to come right.

A week later she was called to Miss Littlewood's room. Miss Littlewood was standing by the fire, with an envelope in her hand. For an instant Nya's eyes grew large; could it be a letter from Simon?

She found herself hoping it was not from Simon. He was so securely locked in her heart that she didn't need news of him, unless it was urgent, serious news. Oh, pray God, the letter wasn't from Simon.

"Nya, there's a letter for you here. It's got a local postmark."

"From Bournemouth?"

"No, not Bournemouth. Langton Matravers."

"I don't know any one who lives there, Miss Littlewood."

"So I supposed. But it's comparatively near here, which made me think that this letter might be from Mr. Byrne."

"Oh!"

Miss Littlewood held it out to her.

"It's not his writing, Miss Littlewood."

"Even then it might still be from him."

"Can I read it, please?"

"I'd like to say 'yes'. But I imagine the rule about your letters still holds. At least, your aunt hasn't said anything to the contrary."

"Oh, I see."

It seemed that the whole business was going to start again.

"I'll just open it and look at the signature, shall I?"

"I'd rather look at it myself."

"Of course you would, my dear child; don't imagine I don't realize that. But these are unusual circumstances."

"Simon *said* he wouldn't write to me again."

"Then we'll hope this letter is from some one else. Well—what do you say? Am I to open it?"

"All right, Miss Littlewood."

She opened it with the ivory cutter from her desk, Nya standing as close as she dared.

"The signature is 'Jessica'."

"Oh yes! I know now. They're some friends of Aunt Ethel's."

"Nothing to do with Mr. Byrne, eh? I'm sorry, my

dear child! I seem to have made a mistake." There was a wry smile on Miss Littlewood's face. "Take it away and don't let me see it, or you, again."

"I'm dreadfully sorry . . ." Nya began.

"It's all right. Run along."

Jessica wanted to know when half-term was, and whether Nya would be allowed to come and stay a night with them at Langton Matravers. This would mean asking Miss Littlewood's permission first, and then Aunt Ethel's. Probably Aunt Ethel's wouldn't be so difficult to obtain; Jessica had said that she would see to that. But Miss Littlewood's? And after the embarrassing interview just now?

She carried the letter about with her most of the day, waiting for an opportunity to ask Miss Littlewood's permission. As it was her second term she was allowed to go home for a night at half-term; but it was conceivable that Miss Littlewood might object because she had run away. By dinner-time she had plucked up enough courage to knock at Miss Littlewood's door.

"I know you said you never wanted to see me again, but please may I ask you something?"

"I can't very well say 'no', can I?" Her voice was kind. "What is it?"

Nya showed her the letter which she had desired not to see again. When Miss Littlewood had made certain that the van der Hemms were friends of Aunt Ethel's she gave Nya permission to go, subject to Aunt Ethel's approval.

Two days later Aunt Ethel's letter came, saying Nya might go. And next Saturday morning Jessica came to fetch Nya in an old red car.

"They won't let me drive the big car," she explained. "And I'm not really old enough to drive this one. But luckily everybody else is busy, so they had to let me come."

They set off in good spirits. Jessica drove cautiously and hooted at every corner.

"I have to be jolly careful not to get into a crash or anything, or there'd be the hell to pay. I'm going to swear that I'm seventeen if anything happens. And you'll have to back me up and say you know it's true."

"All right."

"You can say you were there when I was born, or something."

Nya laughed. A few moments later she asked:

"Do you think that would be allowed?"

"What?"

"To be there when some one was born."

"I should think so. Lots of people have to be."

"I mean ordinary people, like you or me."

"We're a bit young. And I shouldn't think it's very pleasant."

"Why not? I'd like to know what it was like."

"Oh, that's a different thing. I know more or less what it's *like*. Mother told me. Shall we take the ferry or go the long way round? We've got heaps of time."

"Let's go the long way round."

"Good. That means I can drive farther. Also we go past Corfe Castle."

"I went there once, with Aunt Ethel and Uncle Nick."

"We sometimes go there for picnics."

It was a fine, windy day, more like April than June. The sun painted the buttercup fields gold and drew flashes of colour from the yellowhammers which started up on every side. There were wild orchis and cuckoo-pint in the marshes at Lytchett and a dark blue flower on the

417

heaths beyond Wareham that Jessica said was a form of gentian.

A rain cloud blew up from the sea as they were nearing Corfe, and they saw the sunlit ruins silhouetted against a purple sky for a few moments. Then the rain passed, leaving the village pavements glistening.

"It would be a good day for sailing," said Nya.

"We've got a dinghy which we take down to the sea sometimes. We'll go out in it next holidays. Are you going to come and stay with us?"

"If I'm allowed to. I'd love it."

"Everything's opening, opening, opening." Nya's heart sang within her. "It's going to be all right about Simon. It's going to be all right about Daddy. Even at St. Monica's I don't feel shut in any longer. And here, it's all wild and windy and free."

"Oh, look! The sea!" She caught sight of the sun sparkling on Swanage Bay.

"Jessica, do you ever feel sort of imprisoned?"

"Sometimes; chiefly by ideas, when it's something that frightens me, or that I don't understand."

"I know."

"For instance, I used to worry frightfully about babies. I felt I'd never get to know about them. Sometimes I even felt I'd rather *not* know. And when I did know I felt so relieved it was like being let out of prison. It was silly, really; there's simply nothing to worry about once you know the facts."

"I s'pose there isn't."

"Of course not. One day, when I'm feeling like it, I'll tell you. And then you'll see."

Mrs. van der Hemm received her as if it were the most natural thing in the world that a small girl should come to stay. She was still very large, and she still had the yellow beads, but she wasn't wearing the purple dress. At first Nya had to get used to this. She remembered her only in the purple dress, just as she remembered the Chinese Horseman as Jinghiz Khan's, and the inlaid daggers as inferior workmanship.

There was lunch at an enormous table which would have seated twenty people; the three places laid at one end made it look absurdly huge. Mrs. van der Hemm asked her about Aunt Ethel, odd questions which it was impossible to answer without betraying the fact that Aunt Ethel was rather difficult to get on with. Mrs. van der Hemm didn't seem to mind, whatever her answers were. Jessica didn't join in this conversation. Then they talked about music and piano lessons; and Nya realized that she had forgotten to take advantage of Miss Littlewood's permission to practise.

"You see I had so much to think about," she said and blushed.

In the afternoon Jessica made her play tennis, and, though she wasn't very good, she enjoyed herself. After an hour of this they walked up and down the court, talking, as they had done at their first meeting, until tea-time.

Jessica's brother came in to tea. He was very polite and handed Nya cakes and bread and butter as if she were somebody of importance. He still hadn't made up his mind where to start his school but he said he had some good ideas for it.

He had spectacles which he fiddled with when he spoke. And whenever he said something serious you wanted to laugh, because he spoke in the same dry way as his father did. He insisted on making Nya play snooker after tea.

At dinner she met Mr. van der Hemm—there were

five of them this time at the long table. He was just as she remembered him, and kept her in fits of laughter with stories that weren't funny at all when you came to think them out afterwards. There were wonderful things to eat, most of which Nya had never tasted before. Mrs. van der Hemm insisted on her having everything, so that she ate too much, but felt extremely happy.

Mr. and Mrs. van der Hemm went out after dinner, and Roger disappeared somewhere, saying he had to work. Jessica took her into the library, which was a huge room filled with bookcases, with a gallery at one end and a fireplace that you could sit in at the other.

"We built it when we came here. It's rather frightful, but it is at least comfortable."

"I think it's lovely," Nya said, and lay back on a vast sofa.

"If you like, I'll play to you."

She played for nearly an hour and Nya listened avidly, her eyes wide open, staring at the ceiling. Sometimes she recognized the music, more often it was strange to her; but she drank it in, with all her five senses. Her thoughts soared, as they had done when she watched the vapour dancing over the lamp in *Puffin*'s cabin; and she remembered, one after another, confusedly, all the things that had happened during the last few weeks. They seemed to have no connection with one another; they were like the pieces of a jig-saw puzzle, all spread out before her on the ceiling. If she had wished to, she could have placed them together to make a picture. What sort of a picture would it be? A jumbled portrait of Simon and herself, swimming in a sea of fame, to some island near Gibraltar! But she was too happy and too lazy to take trouble, and the picture remained a fascinating jumble of bits.

"I expect you've had enough."

"No! I haven't heard any music since Mummy died. Don't stop!"

"You come and play for a little."

"I haven't practised for months."

"Start now."

"I'd rather not. I'd only do it badly and spoil the effect of your playing. I'll start again on Monday at St. Monica's. You've made me long to, now."

They talked after that, animatedly at first, and then as people do who sit by a dying fire, with fewer words and lower tones of voice. Presently Roger came in. He told her about the farm, which he intended to show her next day, and confessed that he was extremely doubtful in his mind whether to become a farmer or a schoolmaster.

"You see, either's quite a good job to be doing; either way you're breeding things. Only I suppose it's really better to breed people than cows."

Nya laughed so much that he offered her a whisky and soda to calm her down. Then Jessica intervened. "I think I shall take you to bed, Nya, before he depraves you entirely."

"Well, I'll have to go sooner or later."

Her room was opposite Jessica's, and they talked across the passage.

"Do *you* go to bed so early too?"

"Usually. I don't like staying up late in the country."

There was a fire in the grate, a hot-water bottle in the bed, a glass of milk on a tray, some books, and scented soap. And the bathroom was next door. What a wonderful house this was!

When she had finished her bath Jessica came to say good night to her. She was wearing a white dressing-gown of heavy silk—"marocain" she said it was—which suited her black hair.

"You look lovely, Jessica."

"I'm not as lovely as you're going to be one day."

"Do you really think I will? Honestly?"

"Certainly I do."

"Sometimes I long to be, so that——" She stopped, realizing suddenly that, even to Jessica, she couldn't tell the story of Simon.

"So that what?"

"I—I'm afraid I can't tell you."

"All right."

"You don't mind, do you?"

"Lord no, why should I?"

"I mean, I didn't want you to be offended. I'd like to tell you one day—only not just yet."

"I know. . . . Have you got all you want?"

"Yes, thanks."

"Then I'll say good night."

"Good night, Jessica."

"It's nice having you to stay."

"I love it."

It was a marvellously comfortable bed.

"Shall I really be beautiful one day? If what Jessica says is true, Simon will be pleased. Beloved Simon, I wonder what you're doing. It's Saturday, so I expect you're somewhere out there in *Puffin*. I wish I was with you. Good night, darling Simon. I hope you're safe because I love you so."

It had been her prayer every night for some weeks.

55

Simon was at that moment at *Puffin's* helm running into Yarmouth where he intended to anchor for the night. The lights of the town winked to welcome him; beyond them the dark cliffs of the Isle of Wight promised shelter from the stiff south-easterly wind.

He felt restless and disturbed. He had intended to sail all night, but a tiring week had led to a late start, and had robbed him of his customary enterprise. For a fortnight he had managed to banish Nya from all except his most insistent thoughts but lately she had obtruded herself continually, even in his dreams. At first this gave him pleasure. Then he began to lie awake for hours thinking of her until his yearning grew into a passionate desire to see her again and to hear her voice. "It wouldn't be so hard if I had something to *do*—rounding up bullocks, or stoking a ship. It's sitting in that damned office, within a twopenny bus-ride of her that's so demoralizing."

He went to bed late because he couldn't sleep; and he got up early for the same reason. When he was not working he spent his time in his beloved yacht because everything on board reminded him of Nya. He slept most nights on board, and, because he had to have some outlet for his energy and some pastime for the small hours, he repaired the canvas and refitted sheets and did the thousand and one repairs which a yacht continually needs.

At the end of a fortnight he was irritable and hollow-eyed, but his yacht was in excellent trim.

"Ready to sail to Gibraltar," he muttered.

And because the very idea offered an ultimate escape from his unhappy restlessness he accepted it in his mind as if it had been a serious resolution.

"Her father'll be back in a week or two now; I'll wait and see him. After that—well, it's obvious I'd better keep out of her way for a bit."

Without knowing why—without even thinking much about it—he began to study his charts and sailing directions, first of the routes to Gibraltar, and then of places to which he had never dreamed of sailing. He wondered whether Madeira was worth visiting, and how much of an undertaking it would be to sail *Puffin* there single-handed. Then he thought of the Atlantic, of New York, whose skyline he had often seen in dreams from *Puffin*'s fo'c'sle, and of the opportunity he had once been offered of earning a living among its skyscrapers. He had refused it, because it meant leaving his beloved ship: but supposing he should sail *Puffin* over there? No! That was too absurd to be worth contemplating. Even if he got there he would have to stay to earn money with which to return. And that meant leaving Nya for at least a year. Was that what he desired to do?

He put away his charts after that, and gave up whipping rope-ends and greasing running gear. The result was to hurl Nya up against his thoughts in grotesquely magnified proportions, as a railway train is hurled towards an audience on a screen. Two days of this was as much as he could stand. He sought refuge in his charts once more, and by obsessing himself with soundings and tide-tables and sailing directions, succeeded in ousting his obsession with Nya. He took *Puffin* to the yacht yard to be scraped and overhauled. An additional water-tank holding twelve gallons was fitted under the boards in the cockpit, and she was provided with a new flax mainsail and a spare jib.

"If the worst comes to the worst," he thought, "she'll be ready."

56

"Gracious, you do sleep soundly. I've been trying to wake you for about ten minutes."

"I dreamt I was in a sailing boat on a frightfully rough sea."

"Nonsense; it was me, shaking you!"

"I did honestly. It was dark; there were some lights from a town, and behind it some huge, dark hills."

"Well, what I was going to say was, there's a huge, dark wood up the hill, full of foxgloves, which is heavenly in the early morning. Would you like to come and see it?"

"Now?"

"Yes. Or would you rather sleep a bit longer?"

"No, I'd like to come."

She was about to get out of bed when there was a knock at the door. It was the maid, bringing early tea.

"Will you have yours in here too, Miss Jessica?"

"Yes, please."

So Jessica curled up under the eiderdown at the other end of Nya's bed. They began to talk, and the foxgloves were forgotten.

"I wanted to stay and talk last night, but I thought you'd better go to sleep."

"It wouldn't have mattered!"

"Well, it wasn't only that. Somehow, at night, one gets rather sentimental. Haven't you noticed? One doesn't say things one really means, only things that one feels at the moment—and regrets afterwards."

("Then she was joking when she said I'd grow up to be beautiful!") Oh, well—it would be dreadfully vain to be upset. Nya smiled at her, to convince her that she agreed about the unreliability of the things one said at night.

"Whereas I can talk about anything in the early morning, without feeling silly."

"I think it's the other way round with me," Nya said. "Last night there was something I wanted to ask you. But I don't know whether I can now."

"Try! I love answering questions. It makes me feel I know such a lot."

"You won't laugh at me?"

"Of course not."

"Well—you know when I said I couldn't tell you why I wanted to grow up to be beautiful?"

"Yes."

"It was because—because I'm going to marry somebody I know—only not yet of course, because I'm too young."

"I should think you are!" Jessica smiled; but it was a kind smile, and the twinkle in her eyes was not mockery; so that, instead of being hurt by her amusement, Nya felt impelled to confide in her still further.

"Only what I wanted to ask was, *why* am I too young? Just because it's not the custom for a girl of fourteen to get married?"

"Yes. But all customs have a reason. And the reason

427

for this one is that at fourteen we're not physically developed enough to be married—not in England, anyhow. It's different in hot countries."

"Well, I've lived all my life in a hot country."

"Yes, so you have. I hadn't thought of that. It makes no difference to what people in England would think, of course, but I suppose it makes a terrific difference to you."

"Well, it makes everything so difficult. Simon says he ought to go away and not see me again for ages."

"How old is he?"

"Twenty-six."

"Oh, God!"

"Why?"

"I'm sorry. I thought at first he would be about my age. That makes it far more complicated."

"I wish I could understand why."

"Well—perhaps I'd better tell you."

She rearranged the eiderdown over her legs, and sat up against the end of the bed. Nya was looking at the leaves in her teacup, too worried and too shy to meet her eyes. There was a pause. Jessica was not embarrassed as a rule, but now, looking at Nya, she felt suddenly constrained.

"Shall I?" she asked, trying to see into Nya's face. But Nya didn't raise her eyes. She continued to push the leaves round in her cup with the teaspoon. After a tiny hesitation, she nodded. But she said no word.

("Somebody's got to tell the poor kid, and I can't imagine her aunt doing it. Of course there's Mother; she'd do it better than me, but I doubt if Nya'd ever be friendly enough with her.")

Still, she hesitated. To have discussed such a thing with her own mother was natural; but to tell it to Nya

428

—a comparative stranger—demanded the conquest of her instinctive shyness, and, above all, a conviction that she was not doing Nya more harm than good.

She looked at the window as if to gather this conviction from the sunshine and the creatures that teemed and quivered outside, demanding to live and to love and to know. A blackbird sang in the ivy underneath the sill. He shouted to her that life was exciting and full of passion and beauty and mystery, as she well knew, and that Nya must be told all.

So it was in that gay room at Langton Matravers, with the sun patterning the window-pane on the blue carpet, and the blackbird whistling under the sill, that Nya learned the true nature of her love for Simon, and of his for her; of the delight and sweet agony that love could be; of the ecstasy of birth and marriage, the magic of a kiss, and the fire of passion that it could arouse.

57

"Gracious, it's nine o'clock. We must hurry or Roger'll have first go at the devilled kidneys and he's frightfully greedy."

From that moment until Nya left for St. Monica's, Jessica was full of laughter and bright spirits, and not at all the serious, sensible person, of whom you could ask even the most awkward questions. It was fun, in a way, because it made the rest of the day one of the most amusing Nya had ever spent. Everything became a joke, breakfast, the farm, the walk to the foxgloves, lunch and an absurd game called "Pokerface" which they played after lunch.

It really was splendid, knowing Jessica. Everything seemed so natural to her. And she spoke all the time of what they would do together in the future, so that you didn't have to feel this was the last time you'd ever see her. Best of all, she continually asked about Daddy, and whether it would be possible to get him to come on picnics, or even to stay at Langton Matravers.

They sent her back in the big limousine, alone, because they were going out to dinner. She found it hard to wrench herself away; she already felt at home in this vast, friendly mansion, where it wasn't necessary to be on your best behaviour all the time.

58

A fortnight passed away without incident. There were lessons, and games, and prayers; bells rang and gongs sounded, as if tolling away the days until Daddy should arrive. That was the most exciting thing at the moment, even more exciting than the prospect of seeing Simon at the end of the term. Because, somehow, the thought of seeing Simon again was not altogether happy; it was complicated by too many other feelings. The success of their next meeting would depend so much on what Daddy thought of him. She had an uncomfortable fear that Daddy might not approve. Simon had said he might not; and now that she had not seen Daddy for so long she couldn't be certain how he would feel. It's true it was only five months since she had last seen him, but five such extraordinary and eventful months!

Aunt Ethel wrote to ask permission for Nya to accompany them to Southampton; they were taking the car, she said, so there would be room. They would call for her if Miss Littlewood agreed, at eleven o'clock. Nya said she had nothing to wear. Miss Littlewood told her not to be foolish, she could perfectly well go as she was.

"But I can't go and meet Daddy in a gym dress."

"I fail to see why not. However, you'd better talk to

your aunt about it. I haven't time to argue with you about that sort of thing."

So Aunt Ethel was called to the telephone and Nya was allowed to speak to her from Miss Littlewood's room.

"Please, Aunt Ethel, would you bring my grey costume when you come to fetch me? I can't meet Daddy in a gym dress."

"My dear child, what absolute nonsense. Of course you can go in a gym dress."

"I'd much rather not, Aunt Ethel."

"And I'd much rather you did. We shall waste so much time if we wait for you to change."

"Couldn't you send it to me by post?"

There was a pause before Aunt Ethel replied.

("She can't think of an answer to that!")

"It's quite unnecessary to do that. I can't think what you can have against your gym dress."

"It's only that I want to look nice for Daddy. You see he bought me my grey costume."

"I'll have to think it over."

"Please send it, Aunt Ethel. I'd rather not go at all if you don't."

Miss Littlewood, who was standing by the fire reading a paper called *The Spectator*, looked up sharply when she said this, and Nya thought there was a gleam of anger in her eye. However, that couldn't be helped; she must have the grey costume at all costs. It was Daddy's, just as the yellow dress was Simon's. Each had its own particular associations. Whereas the gym dress was the badge of her slavery to school authorities, the sign that she was still a little girl.

"You're an obstinate child, aren't you?" Miss Littlewood said, when Nya left the telephone.

432

"I'm sorry, Miss Littlewood. Only you see, I've got a special reason."

"Trust you! Well, thank goodness I don't have to cope with you at home. You're quite enough of a handful here. Now go away."

She rolled up her *Spectator* and tapped Nya on the shoulder with it.

"I don't think she could be really angry, or she would never have done that," was Nya's comment as she shut the door. "I like her. Ever since she said I could practise, I've liked her more and more. Even when I ran away she wasn't too bad."

Practising the piano had helped, more than anything, to make the time pass quickly. There wasn't much opportunity for it, but it was a tremendous pleasure to feel your fingers getting supple again, and to do arpeggios without looking at the notes.

Next morning the grey costume came. Aunt Ethel had been secretly afraid that Nya might carry out her threat if she were not allowed to wear it; which would have upset her father and led to unhappiness at "The Rising" from the start.

"As it is, I'm not quite sure how we shall get on with him," she confided anxiously to Nicholas. "It was all right before; Mabel was here to smooth him down, and Nya wasn't the bone of contention I'm afraid she may be now."

"What on earth do you mean?"

"Well, as regards education; you know Tom's ideas really won't do for England. I disapprove most strongly of the way he wants Nya brought up—without religion, I mean, and now this obstinacy about a dress. I wish you would tell him so."

"Why don't you?"

433

"It's much easier for you."

"I don't feel strongly about it as you do."

"I wish I could get you to take an interest *sometimes*, Nicholas."

"Oh come, Ethel, I say——"

But she was gone, through the french windows, before he could think of an answer. It was her invariable stratagem when she foresaw defeat.

59

Nya awoke to find the sun shining through the tiny window of her cubicle into her eyes. She dressed in a state of suppressed excitement and hurried so much that she knocked the hair-brush off the chest of drawers.

"Don't make such a noise, Nya," said the senior girl.

"This has happened before," Nya thought, "I must have dreamed it, or else——"

In a flash she remembered another morning which had started exactly like this. She had dropped her hair-brush; in the very same words the senior girl had told her to be quiet; and then had started the wretched sequence of events which finally led to her running away.

"Anyhow, to-day it won't be like that!"

There was a French lesson at nine, and history at ten. In history Miss Bowden-Smith taught them about Jeremy Bentham, a favourite character of Nya's, who always asked, "What is the use of it?" and about a man called John Stuart Mill who said that women ought to be allowed to vote in all elections. Miss Bowden-Smith thoroughly approved of him. As he was somehow connected with Jeremy Bentham, Nya approved of him also, and enjoyed that particular history lesson very much. It was the first time since she had come to St. Monica's that she had met one of those legendary figures about whom Daddy used to tell her. Perhaps, later on, she would encounter the others. At any rate this made one feel that, whatever knowledge one were trying to acquire, it was all the same knowledge, whether one learned it from Daddy or Miss Bowden-Smith, and that one day, all the different bits of it that you got doled out to you in lessons would be seen to fit together.

She was allowed out five minutes before the class ended, which gave her time to change and to be waiting on the steps as the car drove up at eleven o'clock. Uncle Nick and Aunt Ethel seemed pleased to see her, and asked whether she was happy now at St. Monica's. She answered without much enthusiasm; the subject bored her at the moment. Her thoughts were full of Daddy. What would he look like? Would he remember her? But of course he would; wasn't he coming home specially to see her? And she hadn't changed as much as all that. You grew up, and therefore you obviously couldn't remain exactly the same. Daddy would understand that; he would understand that she was still the Nya who had said good-bye to him on board the ship at Beira, in spite of all that had happened to her since.

It was a wonderful day—the same sort of day as when Jessica had fetched her in the old red car. The drive to Southampton took them past woods full of bluebells. Aunt Ethel and Uncle Nick talked to each other, mostly about their friends, and about which of them they should introduce to Daddy. Nya, sitting silent in the back of the car, found herself disagreeing with every choice they made, thinking, "Daddy won't like *them*: they're so pompous," or "They'll think Daddy's extraordinary because they're frightfully ordinary."

436

There was no point in saying anything to Daddy because he would judge for himself. She decided to introduce him to the van der Hemms. He would be sure to like them, anyway.

Daddy's ship wasn't in when they arrived at the dockside, but they could see her steaming slowly towards them. "She's pretty punctual," said Uncle Nick.

There seemed to be hundreds of people on board, all waving hats or handkerchiefs.

"They can't possibly see who they're waving to yet," thought Nya.

It took almost half an hour for the boat to dock, during which Nya's eyes searched excitedly for her father among the people on deck. Aunt Ethel thought she saw him once but it turned out that she was wrong. Nya was secretly relieved. She wanted to be the first to see him.

"He's not there. I can't see him anywhere. Oh, Uncle Nick, do you think he's had to take another boat?"

"No, no, he's on this all right; we had a radiogram from him this morning."

At last, just as the gangway was lowered for the passengers to descend, a man appeared on the very top deck of all, near the lifeboats. He was waving a green silk handkerchief and he had a tussore coat on, so you couldn't help noticing him. And he had a lean, brown face, awfully like Uncle Nick's. He smiled straight at her.

"Look, look! There he is. It's Daddy. It's Daddy."

"Nya!"

His voice called down to them, strong and clear above the babel of sounds. Daddy's voice!

"How are you, Daddy?"

Her squeaky treble barely reached his ears. But he waved again and shouted.

"I'm coming down!"

"Better wait here," said Uncle Nick. "Might miss him if we go on board."

Presently he appeared at the top of the gangway and looked down. She could see him quite clearly now. He was just the same. He handed something to a man in uniform, then he came down the gangway. A steward carried his luggage and his coat. This left both his arms free, and Nya was in them almost before he had left the gangway."

"Darling, darling Daddy."

"How's my little girl? Hullo, Nick. Hullo, Ethel. It's nice to see you."

People were coming down the gangway all the time, and they were asked to move aside. Nya clung to him, so that he almost had to carry her. It was some time before he could disengage himself enough to shake hands with Nick and Ethel.

"Let's get the Customs over, then we can go home and talk."

He didn't say much on the way to the Customs, nor while he was waiting for the luggage, of which there was an awful lot, to be loaded on to the trolley and taken to the car. He just looked at her and smiled once or twice, and once he pulled the lobe of her ear. She clung to his arm whenever he didn't need it. Aunt Ethel did most of the talking, and Daddy answered yes or no whenever it became necessary.

It was long past lunch-time when they eventually got into the car. Aunt Ethel had brought a picnic lunch, so they drove a little way and ate it by the riverside, where they could watch yachts and rowing boats and listen to the sirens from the docks.

Nya wished with all her heart she had been able to meet Daddy by herself. If she had, they would have been friends from the first moment as in the old days. Now, with Aunt Ethel and Uncle Nick there, it was difficult to know what to say. For the first time in her life she felt shy with him, and she could see that he felt so too. So half-way through lunch she gave up imagining that all was as it used to be in Nyasaland and reconciled herself to the dismal fact that she was meeting Daddy under English conditions. For the time being she had to behave as Aunt Ethel's niece. Later on, when they were alone, she would show Daddy that she was still his daughter. She kept her eyes fixed on him, to assure him that it would all come right; she scarcely looked at what she ate, nor minded how she ate it. Ethel noticed how Nya's eyes devoured him.

"Really, the child has no self-control," she thought, with a twinge of annoyance. "She does everything to extremes."

Daddy sat beside her on the way back, and she was able to put her head on his lap and to hold his hand. Then it didn't matter not being able to talk to him. He spoke a little to Aunt Ethel and Uncle Nick, but even they realized, after a time, that he was not in the mood for conversation. Every now and then Nya would look up at him and he would smile. Once or twice he blinked, and Nya felt a curious choke in her throat. She could tell what he was feeling, as she used to be able to do sometimes in Nyasaland. After Mummy died he used to come and sit on her bed before he said good night to her, smoking his pipe and saying nothing. Nya would wait, silent, for a few minutes. Then she would get out of bed and curl up in his arms, and for a long, long time they would stay like that, not speaking, but conscious of each other's thoughts.

When they reached the road which led up to St.

Mica's she looked at him with a frightened eye.

"We've nearly got there! To my school, I mean."

It would be dreadful to separate just as they were getting to know each other. Daddy must have felt so, too. He asked Uncle Nick to stop the car.

"We'll go for a bit of a walk before I take her back. I can catch a bus out to Sandbanks."

The car departed, Daddy's luggage on the grid bouncing as it went over a bump in the road. When it was out of sight Daddy said:

"What's a nice place to walk to?"

"Don't I have to go back?"

"Not till we've talked for at least an hour. And not even then perhaps. I can see I've got to get to know my little girl all over again."

"Well, there's a sort of common near here."

"That'll do."

They set off, hand in hand.

"It's funny, your saying that, Daddy, because I felt *I* should have to get to know *you* all over again. I thought you'd have changed."

"Why?"

"I don't quite know; perhaps because I have."

"Yes; you're different in some ways. A little more grown-up, I think."

"I want to be."

"What on earth for? I like you better young."

"Well, I don't want people to think I'm a silly little girl."

"Has anybody said you are?"

"No, not really."

"Then what's the danger?"

"I can't quite explain; only——"

"Only there's something you'd *like* to explain, is that it?"

He noticed her hesitation.

"Perhaps I shouldn't have asked."

"Well, you see, Daddy, it's rather difficult. I didn't know whether to tell you or not, at first. But I'd much rather tell you, really. Only I don't know whether to tell you now, or later."

"Why not now?"

"Because I've only just met you, and there are lots of other things I want to talk about."

"Any more important?"

"Yes—in a way."

"Are any of those other things worrying you?"

"No."

"Whereas this thing, that you're not sure whether to tell me or not—it *is* worrying you, I gather."

She didn't answer for a moment. Had he said too much? Had he intruded upon her? Had he given her the impression that he was inquisitive, and forfeited her confidence in him before he had properly acquired it again? It was what he had been in terror of doing, what he had schooled himself, all the way back in the ship, to avoid at all costs. Had he failed so soon? He watched her face anxiously. Suddenly she smiled up at him:

"Well, a little," she admitted.

"You wouldn't like to tell me? Or another time, perhaps," he added, hastily, afraid of appearing importunate.

"No. I'd rather tell you now."

Where should she begin? And how much should she tell him? All there was to tell, of course, or would that make things difficult for Simon? If she only told him a little, he would guess there must be more, he would want to be told all. And if he was to help, surely the more he knew the better.

441

"It's about Simon."

"Who's Simon?"

"He's a friend of mine. I met him down on the jetty. You remember I wrote to you about him? Aunt Ethel and Uncle Nick don't like him—at least, Uncle Nick likes him a little, I think. But *you've* got to like him, because it all depends on you."

"I'm sure I shall like him. Tell me more about him."

She told him. Walking across the heath, round it, back and across again, she told Daddy the whole story. It took a long time. When she had finished, their shadows were leaning away from them like long paper men in the orange sunlight, and they both felt that they had walked for miles. They sat down on a seat to rest.

"But you see, it's all perfectly all right, because I want to marry him." She ended with a sigh of relief.

He had listened at first with a forbearance calculated to inspire her confidence; probably she would tell him of some mild distress which her innocence had turned into a nightmare. But she had scarcely spoken for two minutes before he realized he must entirely discard this preconception. Here was no tale of distress or disappointment; indeed she seemed to have the situation well in hand. And what an extraordinary situation! Of course Nya was exaggerating. Her inexperience made her attach absurd importance to her relationship with this fellow, made her use words like marriage and love when she didn't know their implications. Still, the matter was evidently of vital importance to her; in a remarkably short time she had allowed this fellow to grow roots in her affections, had even, so she said, grown roots in his. He cursed silently as he listened. Every now and then he looked at her. She had taken off her hat, and walked, swinging it in her left hand, grasping his hand with her right. Her head was like a copper flower in the sunlight.

("Even now she's lovely. What will she be like in six years' time?")

She was too absorbed in her narrative to notice his eyes upon her, so he observed her for a while. He saw her forehead puckered with the intensity of her thought; it reminded him of the worried frown she had worn for a week after she knew she had to leave him and go back to England. He watched her walking by his side with the firm grace of a young animal—"the little leopard" they called her out there. She had walked beside him to the cemetery; and at the grave she had held his hand like this.

Why did he suddenly remember that—now that it was past and done with? Well, it was not so very long ago after all. Of the six intervening months he had been unconscious for five. He had forced himself not to think; he had forced himself to work all night; he had been fool enough to think he could go without his leave. He had ceased to be able to feel.

And now this little copper-headed witch was forcing him to feel again. He struggled no longer, as he had done ever since that ghastly funeral, with the persistent surges of emotion in him. He found his desire to repress them defeated by the sweet young girl beside him, by the innocent wisdom of her mind, and the feel of the lithe hand that so trustfully gripped his. And, as he recognized the power she exerted over him, and admitted it to himself, the conflict of the last months was resolved and peace began to return into his mind.

When they dropped exhausted on to the seat he found himself gazing at her with affectionate admiration, eager to catch the words from her lips, fascinated by the plot of the eventful story she had told.

"How does it go on?" he longed to say. But before he could decide to ask the question in all seriousness, she added one more statement, and that the most astonishing of all.

"But you see, it's perfectly all right, because I want to marry him."

There was a long pause, during which his eyes never left her face. Nya returned gradually out of her trance of enthusiasm to the reality of Daddy sitting beside her on the seat, and of his questioning eyes.

("Is he going to laugh at me? Or will he be angry?")

Suddenly her confidence left her, and she wondered anxiously whether she had been a fool to tell him.

But he didn't laugh. He wasn't angry. He didn't even agree patronizingly, as he might have done to a child, "Oh; so you intend to marry him, do you?" and then dismiss the whole thing as unimportant. He looked at her steadily for several seconds. Then he smiled, but rather as if his thoughts were far away, and put out his hand towards her and took her chin, and looked into her eyes.

"You little witch," he said. "You little witch."

For half an hour longer they sat there, while the sun shone into their faces, lighting them up with a strange, yellow glow, as if they had been gazing at a fire. Presently it set behind hills that turned first purple and then black.

It was Daddy's turn to talk now. He asked questions, one after the other, and Nya answered them without hesitation. The answers were so clear in her mind. It was easy to talk to him; it had been easy from the first moment they were alone, she reflected. He seemed to believe that you meant what you said, and to consider your remarks just as carefully as if they had been made by some one of importance.

But one of his questions was not easy to answer.

"Tell me," he said, "do you like Simon well enough to kiss him?"

For the first time she hesitated and looked away. The answer was "yes", that was simple enough. But a kiss was not simply a peck on the cheek, as Jessica had told her. It was a caress, a promise that had to be fulfilled; it aroused passion. Daddy would know that. If she said "yes", he would think that Simon had kissed her in that way, and he would be angry, even though it was not true. Yet if she said "no", Daddy would think she didn't love Simon and he might not be so anxious to help her. Perhaps the best thing would be to admit it, and to trust to Daddy's good sense to understand what she really meant.

"Goodness yes, I've kissed him lots of times."

Daddy smiled and said, "Oh", in an odd way.

"You see, I love him."

"Do you know what love is?"

"Yes. I found out the last time I saw him."

"What!"

"It's a kind of pain in one's side—here, isn't it? Or else, perhaps, more there—in one's tummy." She put her hand on the correct spot as she remembered it.

Daddy laughed.

"Well—sometimes."

They were silent for some time after that. For the first time in her life she had not told Daddy the absolute truth; it was a tiny lie—scarcely a lie at all, really. But yet it was not the truth. Loving Simon seemed to complicate life terribly; although it was the most wonderful

445

thing in the world it seemed to lead you into what Aunt Ethel called "prevarications". She remembered that dreadful event during her first term, which she had been unable to tell Daddy about; and, linking it up with what Jessica had told her, she realized that the whole trouble had begun then. And yet "trouble" wasn't quite the right word; there had been a certain amount of trouble, of course, but that was only to be expected since the circumstances were unusual. If you looked at it in the way Jessica did, it was simply an exciting adventure, the adventure of "coming alive".

The sky was a vast lake of marble-coloured fire, with copper islands floating in it; it was rather like the sea of fame as she imagined it. Somewhere behind them, a motor-boat panted up the Stour and made everything else in the yellow evening seem silent by comparison.

"You've got to help me, Daddy," she said at last. "You see I told Simon you would. He said you mightn't understand and that you'd think him wicked, but I can't see why. Anyhow, you won't think so when you see him."

"He evidently realizes he's up against a difficult problem."

"What kind of a problem?"

"One that can't be solved till you're at least three or four years older."

"But, Daddy, I'm not quite the same as other girls."

"No, I can see that!"

"I want to be with Simon always. I want to marry him. But even if you don't agree to that, couldn't I at least see him every day—and all day if I want to?"

"It could be managed, I suppose. I'm wondering whether that would be the best thing—for either of you."

"Oh well, you know best, Daddy. Can I leave it to you, please?"

"Of course, darling."

Again they were silent for a moment, each pursuing their own thoughts, watching a breeze chase the copper islets from the sky. A clock across the valley struck seven.

"When can I see you again, Daddy?"

"Sunday?"

"I don't expect they'd let me. But Sunday week."

"All right then. And we might go and call on Simon together. What do you say?"

"Oh, *yes*!"

60

She went into the dining-hall five minutes late for dinner, but exultant and bright-eyed. Talking to Daddy had transported her into another world from whose exhilarating atmosphere she had drawn the strength to walk carelessly through this one. She must remember to let Simon know that they were coming to see him or he would be away for the week-end in *Puffin*. Perhaps they would let her write to him now that Daddy was back. If not, she could always telephone Daddy at Aunt Ethel's. It was a relief to have him within speaking distance at last. He didn't seem to have changed in the least. He was still Daddy, silent and friendly when you didn't particularly need him, and ready to answer questions when you did.

It was the custom to report oneself to the mistress in charge who, to-night, was Miss Bowden-Smith.

"I've been out with my father."

"All right, Nya."

It would not have been etiquette for Miss Bowden-Smith to ask questions or she would have done so. She sought every opportunity of watching Nya's mind working. It fascinated her to observe the child's attitude

448

towards the problems which school life continually presented; Nya was so quick to grasp their true significance, so oblivious, once she had grasped it, of anything that might distract her from dealing with them. One often forgot that she was only fourteen, especially in class. She had only to understand the ultimate significance of a fact to remember it for good; in history she was less interested in battles and coronations than in their results. She did not learn with the woolly goodwill of the adolescent but with a discrimination (misguided, sometimes) which made her an intelligent pupil. She distinguished herself from the other girls by an unusual singleness of purpose. Miss Bowden-Smith's hopes that she would grow up to be a true specimen of the New Woman seemed likely to be realized.

"She's uncompromising, which is the great thing. She has a little too much heart, perhaps, but that doesn't matter for the time being. Later on she'll keep it in control."

Nya lay awake for some time that night, thinking of her walk with Daddy on the common, and of the things she had told him. It hadn't been so difficult, really, once she had begun. In the end she waded deeper into the matter than she had intended. And, as it turned out, it had been the right thing to do.

She yawned contentedly and turned over on to her right side; you could go to sleep better on that side, one of the girls had told her, because it left your heart more room to function properly. But her brain was still active; she was too excited by seeing Daddy to be able to sleep.

She heard the seniors going to bed, chatting and laughing along the corridors until they reached their rooms. Outside a bird sang somewhere, drowsily.

449

"He can't know how late it is," she thought. "It must be half-past ten."

When she raised herself on her elbow she could see out of the window. It was almost dark outside. There were stars in the sky, the stars she had seen that night when she dreamt that Simon was close to her, in her room. That had been a strange dream; and the other night, at the van der Hemm's, she had had a similar one, where she was in *Puffin* in a rough sea. Simon was there, too; he was sitting in the cockpit, reading the compass and she was sleeping in his bunk. Outside were twinkling lights and dark hills. It was what you called an uncanny dream; but of course it wouldn't have been possible to tell Jessica about it.

She heard a car come in at the big gate, which was slammed after it. She remembered hearing that gate slam with quite a different sound on the first night of this term. She had been wretchedly unhappy that night. She had been parted from Simon—for ever as it seemed —after hours of quarrelling with Aunt Ethel; she had been forbidden piano lessons; she had been sent back to school a day early. She had lain awake until the porter locked the gates at twelve o'clock, and then cried herself to sleep. That was eight weeks ago.

And to-night? To-night she had only the happiest thoughts. To-night she was so excited that it seemed she would again be awake until twelve o'clock. Daddy had come home. He was going to take her to see Simon. He had promised to put everything right. Life was opening, opening, opening. She was finding out how to live in England, a country which at first had seemed entirely made for grown-up people. She could play tennis almost every day; she could swim. She was popular with the other girls, though this did mean not being friendly with any of them. Still—there was Jessica. She sensed that life in England would one day be full of pleasures of a kind which she could never have known in Nyasaland. Next holidays she would go and stay with the van der Hemms, and so would Daddy. Perhaps Simon might be asked too. It would be exciting to be in the same house with him—like being married. Or wouldn't that be allowed? Daddy had looked oddly at her when she spoke of marrying Simon.

61

The moment she woke up she wanted to see Daddy again. There were hundreds of things she had forgotten to tell him yesterday, and hundreds of things she had wanted to ask—about Nyasaland, and her pony, and about the ship he had come on, and where on earth he had got that frightful green handkerchief. Perhaps some one had given it to him as a parting present. She must write to him and find out.

But there was so much to be done all day long—in the summer term it was possible to spend every spare moment out of doors—that the letter never got written.

"What's the use anyway? You can never say what you mean in a letter, and I shall be seeing him in a few days."

Now that he lived so near it was no longer necessary to write. He evidently found the same, for he only sent her funny postcards with two or three words on them. The other girls grew to expect them as eagerly as she did because of their idiotic jokes. After a week he telephoned. Betsy came to fetch her in the middle of a class. She felt vaguely guilty as she went to Miss Littlewood's room; telephone calls were usually about urgent or unpleasant things.

"I told them to tell you the headmistress wanted you. Were you scared?" he teased.

"*No*, I can deal with *her!*"

There wasn't any news, except that he wanted to know how she was. She chatted for a few minutes, then he said:

"I'd better not keep you, if you're in the middle of a class."

"I like talking to you though."

"Yes, it's fun; but a telephone's rather unsatisfactory. I can't see what you look like."

"Just as well; I might be making a face at you!"

"If you are, I'll take it out on you when we meet— next Sunday, eh?"

"Good. Oh, and Daddy; are we going to see Simon?"

"Would you like to?"

"Yes, *please.*"

There was a short pause before he answered. Was he, by any dreadful chance, going to say it was impossible?

"All right."

"Could you please tell him we're coming? Otherwise he'll be out sailing."

"What's his address?"

Instinctively she lowered her voice as she gave it. Not long ago, in this very room she had struggled against having to write it on an envelope. But that time, Miss Littlewood had been watching her; now it was only old Betsy.

"Right. I'll fix it with him."

62

On Sunday Daddy met her after church.

"Have you been in church too, Daddy?"

"Yes."

"Goodness. I didn't think you liked going to church."

"I don't, as a rule. But I rather enjoyed it this time. I watched you."

"I never saw you."

"I was a bit to one side."

"Oh. We had some good hymns, didn't we?"

"Not bad. You certainly sang them loud enough."

"Oh well, that's all you can do with them. They're not frightfully good music, are they? That's why I like the shouting ones best. Let's go for a walk."

"I don't know if there's much time for that. We're supposed to be lunching at 'The Rising'."

"Oh damn."

"Don't you want to?"

"Yes—quite. Only I wanted to have you to myself."

"I'm sorry. I might have thought of that. Only it seemed rude to your aunt not to go. She asked us, you know."

"Oh well, it can't be helped."

454

They set off in the direction of the bus stop, and presently found themselves among a crowd of people waiting for the bus to Sandbanks, just where she had waited on the day she ran away from school. Daddy must have read her thoughts, for he said:

"Tell me about when you ran away. I've been hearing some of the story from Aunt Ethel. I'd like to hear more from you."

"Aren't you angry with me?"

"Not if you had a reason."

"Well, some of the reasons I told you the other day. You see it's all to do with Simon."

"Tell me more."

So she whiled away the bus journey by telling him, in a low voice so that the people round them shouldn't hear. He looked out of the window most of the time; she wondered whether he was smiling and didn't want her to see, or whether he was angry, or whether he had simply noticed something interesting outside. Unlike last time, she felt self-conscious with him; chiefly because she found continually that she had to tell him about Aunt Ethel, and she was afraid he would notice that she didn't like her. And Aunt Ethel was, after all, his sister-in-law, and they were going back to "The Rising" for lunch.

"I can see you don't get on very well with your aunt."

"I'm sorry, Daddy. I expect it's because I'm still young. I'll improve, honestly I will."

"Don't worry about improving. Just try and understand how your Aunt Ethel's mind works. She was quite differently brought up from you, you see. And she's been accustomed to meeting only people of her own kind, so she's perhaps a little narrow-minded. But she's actually rather fond of you. I've talked to her a lot and I'm quite sure of that."

"It's only when she treats me like a baby that I get angry with her."

"I know. Well, I'm not suggesting you should reform too much. After all, you've got to grow up into somebody fifty times as grand as she is. Only there are one or two things you can learn from her; and when you disagree, just keep your mouth shut and remember it's harder for her to alter her opinions than for you to conceal yours."

"All right, Daddy, I will."

"I dare say you'll find her narrow-mindedness is curable; having to deal with you will be enough to cure it. I tell you what. We'll reform her, shall we? We'll spend next holidays doing it."

"Shall we be staying at 'The Rising'?"

"Yes. So we'll have plenty of opportunity."

"It'll be fun as long as you're there."

"We've got to think of when I am not."

"No, don't let's think of that!"

"Well—prepare for it then."

The extraordinary thing was that, from that moment, she began to like Aunt Ethel better. For one thing, when Daddy was there, Aunt Ethel wasn't so full of commands and prohibitions; she left it to Daddy to order her about, and Nya enjoyed that. A year or two later she realized that Aunt Ethel only ordered her about out of a sense of duty. It was not, as Nya had at first imagined, out of a desire to thwart her and impose her will upon her.

She thoroughly enjoyed that lunch at "The Rising". Uncle Nick was in the best of spirits, just like that night when they had gone to see Marlene Dietrich together. It was the greatest fun comparing him to Daddy: it was rather unfair, of course, because Daddy was so far superior, but still, they *were* rather alike. Aunt Ethel had a pink face and a smile that she kept trying to suppress, but which broke out every time Daddy or Uncle Nick said something amusing. At the end of lunch Uncle Nick proposed toasts to Daddy because he had come back safely, to Nya, because she had run away "from the yoke of authority", as he said, to the villainous boatman who had helped him to recapture her and even to Miss Littlewood because Nya had said she was "not such a bad old thing really". Nya and Aunt Ethel drank the toasts in cider, and Daddy and Uncle Nick in beer.

Then a rather embarrassing thing happened. Suddenly, after all the toasts had been drunk Uncle Nick said: "By Jove, there's one chap we've forgotten. Nya's young man. Must drink a toast to him."

Nya blushed violently and felt a fool for having done so. She saw Aunt Ethel frown at Uncle Nick, but Uncle Nick pretended not to notice, and Daddy helped to smooth the whole thing over by saying:

"Here's to Simon. Let's hope we'll all be friends with him soon."

He looked at Nya, as much as to say, "But we won't tell *them* we're going to see him."

At about three o'clock Daddy said:

"Nya and I are going for a stroll. Don't wait tea for us. We may have it in the town."

The moment they were outside the gate she asked: "You didn't tell them where we were going, did you?"

He looked down at her solemnly, wondering whether to tease her, but there was so anxious a petition in her eyes that he had not the heart.

"What d'you take me for?"

She squeezed his hand in relief.

They walked for some time without saying anything. She was wondering what the ensuing meeting with Simon would be like; firstly there was Daddy, but apart from that, she herself hadn't seen him for weeks.

"Daddy!"

"Yes, my girl?"

"I do hope you'll like Simon."

"I do like him."

"Have you seen him then?"

"No, but he wrote me a letter. I think we shall get on famously."

"Oh, thank God!"

He smiled to himself at the fervency in her voice.

"Were you afraid we'd come to blows?"

She replied quite seriously. "No-o. But I was afraid you'd make me promise not to see him again or something like that."

As they climbed the stairs to Simon's rooms she remembered absurdly enough one of the questions she had meant to ask.

"You know that green hanky you were waving on the ship?"

"A green hanky? Oh yes, I remember."

"Did somebody give it to you as a parting gift? You didn't have it in Nyasaland."

"No. I borrowed it from the steward. I wanted something gay so that you should see it."

"Oh, I see."

"What made you ask?"

"I don't quite know really. All sorts of things go round in my head; things about you and Simon and, even about Mummy. They all seem to be connected. It's an awful muddle sometimes."

She brushed the back of her hand across her forehead,

as if to wipe away the thought of that awful muddle. He noticed the strange gesture—a gesture that a tired, harassed adult might have made:

"Here, steady on," he said. "There's no hurry. Rushing up the stairs like that!"

"Sorry. I was so keen to get to the top."

She smiled, bright-eyed; she didn't look tired or harassed. He must have been mistaken. And yet. . . .

She rang the bell. He watched her closely. But even her puzzled frown had disappeared in her eager expectation of seeing Simon.

63

For the last quarter of an hour Simon had been walking from one room into the other, waiting for the bell to ring. Now that it had rung he stood still, trying to collect himself for what he felt would be a difficult half-hour. He yearned to see Nya again; ever since her father's letter had come and he could be certain that he would see her he had thought of nothing else. What would it be like, talking to Nya with her father there? Would it be as uncomfortable as that dark evening at her aunt's house? And had she changed since then? Would she still be the Nya he had been imagining for the past two months, the Nya to whom, in his deepest soul, he had bound himself for ever? Or had he formed the wrong conception of her nature, deluded himself into believing she could love him? Was it wrong of him to think of her with such yearning, to be able to see so clearly, when he closed his eyes, how the curls fell round the nape of her neck and how, when she looked at him, shy and confident at once, her nose tilted so mischievously up? He loved her so well—this miraculous creature of his imagination. She could not change. But the real Nya?

460

She was standing on the other side of the door, and he was almost afraid to open it.

"He *must* be in, Daddy."

It was her voice. Its puzzled whisper stole into his ears as he stood deliberating. It woke his longing for her, and brought him back to a realization of the present moment. The image in his mind faded; outside, on the landing, stood the reality.

He opened the door.

"Simon!"

For an instant he stood wondering. Should he—could he bring himself merely to shake hands with her; or should he pick her up in his arms and kiss her as he longed to do? Her father stood beside her, watching, smiling. Nya solved the difficulty for him. Without any thought of the embarrassment it might cause him, without even an inkling that he *could* be embarrassed, she threw her arms round his neck.

"Oh, Simon, I'm so glad to see you again!"

"Are you, Nya?"

She was as lovely as her image, but far more full of life.

"Aren't you glad to see me?"

"Yes, of course, Nya."

His voice was cool and controlled; out of the corner of his eye he watched her father.

"I don't believe you are one little bit."

"Oh, my darling, don't say that!"

The gentle reproach, the tiny pain in her voice melted him at once. He picked her up in his arms, hugged her, and set her down again. From that moment all embarrassment left him and he behaved as naturally as if they had been alone.

"Look! I've brought Daddy to see you. He's going to help us!"

Over her head Simon looked at him and put out his hand.

"I'm very glad you've come, sir."

They went inside, and Simon closed the door.

It was exciting to be in Simon's rooms. There were two of them, one with a large window which looked towards the sea—that was the sitting-room. The other one was presumably his bedroom. And there was a tiny kitchen and a bathroom.

They had tea from a brown teapot, in yellow cups with flowers in them. Simon said he bought everything at Woolworths.

"You see, sir," he explained to Daddy, "I hardly feel I live here properly. My yacht's my real home."

On the walls were drawings and prints of yachts, and photographs of two men. Nya asked who they were.

"They're the two fellows I shared *Puffin* with."

"Where are they now?"

"In India, damn them. They decided to go and dispense justice out there!"

"That's my job, too," said Daddy.

Daddy and Simon talked about everything under the sun, politely and at last (thought Nya), boringly. It seemed they had no intention of discussing questions of importance. They were simply wasting time; presently it would be half-past five, she would have to go back to St. Monica's, and the problem which they were here to solve would never even have been mentioned.

She controlled her impatience until after tea; then she burst out suddenly with a remark which astonished them both from their self-possession.

"Daddy, please will it be all right for me to marry Simon?"

Daddy looked at Simon out of the corner of his eye;

then he looked at her. Simon stopped in the act of putting aside a teacup; she could see his anxious glance directed at Daddy.

("Why doesn't Daddy answer?")

He was wondering what to say. To listen to her talking glibly of marriage when they were alone was one thing; to discuss it seriously in front of Simon was quite another.

"Daddy, why do you look so surprised?"

"Well, darling, it's rather a surprising question."

"Oughtn't I to say that?"

"I suppose so—as far as I'm concerned. It's Byrne I was thinking of."

She looked at Simon. He seemed ill at ease; but his eyes met hers levelly and there was encouragement in them.

"Oh, Simon knows all about it!"

"Then perhaps I'd better let him tell me."

Simon hesitated for a moment; then he put the teacup aside and began to speak in a determined voice that soothed away her anxiety.

"It's rather difficult, sir, with Nya here, because I must naturally explain things differently to you, and that may make her think that in the past I've said things which I don't mean."

Daddy nodded encouragingly. She settled back in the arm-chair to listen to what Simon was going to say. All this that was happening was of tremendous importance; it was experience, part of life, something that made St. Monica's and temporary evils of that sort fade into insignificance. The light came from the window behind her on to Simon's face; she could see every expression of his, every cloud that came into his eyes, and also a sort of fire that flickered in them every now and then.

"I suppose it's an absurd situation, really, from most points of view; I thought so at first, but I don't any longer, and I would like to convince you that I'm in dead earnest, that I—I love Nya, even though she's so young, that I'd like to marry her one day, and that I'll wait as long as you think necessary. That part of it doesn't trouble me. What does trouble me a little is, firstly, the thought that she may be too young yet to know her own mind. She may entirely change, I mean. Though, if she should, it will be I who suffer and not her; and, of course, I must take that risk. And the second difficulty is to know what to do about the three or four years which must elapse before we can get married—provided you approve, that is. If you don't approve, of course, we shall have to wait for seven years, until she's of age."

"You've got to approve, Daddy. Seven years is a dreadfully long time."

"What do you know about it, child, you've only been alive fourteen!"

"Well, anyhow, it's longer than I can possibly imagine."

He was silent for a moment, and she wondered anxiously what he was deliberating. For the first time she began to doubt. Would he make it easy as she had expected? Or was he going to disapprove as Simon had feared? She looked at Simon, hoping to get encouragement from his glance; but he was looking steadfastly at Daddy, almost as if he were daring him to disapprove.

"You take it for granted, I see," Daddy said, "that I shall ultimately give you my blessing. It hasn't occurred to you that I might put a stop to the whole thing, once and for all?"

Black clouds formed in Simon's eyes.

464

"I don't see why you should want to do that. I *did* consider the possibility, of course, but now that I've met you I don't think you would. I'm perfectly sincere; I'm willing to do anything to prove it."

"I'm sure you're sincere, my dear fellow. But unfortunately that doesn't solve the problem. Obviously the next three or four years are going to be difficult for Nya and the fact that you live practically in the same town, and that she'll have all these thoughts of marriage and what not, that a girl of her age ought not to have to worry about—— Well, I can't help feeling life will be impossible for her. My instinct tells me I ought to try and protect her from all that, for her own sake."

"I'm the last person to want to make things harder for her."

"Well then, you must see that——"

"That I must go away? Yes, I quite see that!"

The conversation came to an abrupt stop. They looked at each other, Daddy surprised and Simon defiant.

What had Simon said? He couldn't leave her to face St. Monica's and Aunt Ethel by herself. And for such a long time! What were they talking about? What was the meaning of phrases like "difficult years", and "life being impossible for her". As long as Simon was near, nothing was impossible or even difficult.

"Simon, I don't understand. What are you talking about?"

He heaved a deep sigh, and looked at her. She had never seen him so sad as he was then. He spoke to her now, to her only, as if they had been alone on board *Puffin*.

"Oh, Nya darling, I wish it hadn't had to come out like this. But it had to be said, I suppose, and there didn't seem an earthly chance of ever seeing you alone

465

again. I've been thinking about you all day and most of the night since I last saw you. You've been in my mind; I'm not ashamed to admit it. I realized all the things your father says, and more. If I stay here, if we can meet just occasionally—go sailing together perhaps in the holidays, and if at the end of every meeting I've got to deliver you up again into some one else's care, if your friendship with me makes your relations with other people difficult—which it's bound to do—and if that should start to prey on your mind, as my love for you preys upon my mind now—well then, it seems to me I'd better go away in order to come back one day when you're grown up and marry you, than stay here and be forbidden ever to see you again."

"Oh, Simon!"

"Little girl, what else can I do?"

She was silent for a long time, her eyes turned away. He watched her dumbly, knowing he had hurt her, unable to soothe away the pain. He longed to put his arms round her, to talk to her softly.

A tiny sob escaped her; it was scarcely more than a catch of the breath, but it tore his heart. He looked at her father, who was watching her almost as wretchedly as he himself. Each of them sensed the cruelty of looking on at her unhappiness, but each thought the other had the better claim to comfort her. She began to cry.

"Darling! Don't, little girl."

She heard the pain in his voice and instantly her self-control left her. She forgot Daddy, she forgot herself, she knew only that she loved Simon, that she longed to be close to him, in his arms. She flung herself on to the floor beside him and buried her head in his lap, and her sobs, unrestrained now, seemed to break and flow over him like a warm sea.

466

"Oh, darling, darling Simon, I do love you so!"

He too forgot that they were not alone in the sweet pain of comforting her unhappiness. He clasped her to him with one hand, and with the other he stroked her hair, "It's all right, my darling, hush now!"

Her father stood it for a few moments. Then, on the verge of breaking down himself, he got up and walked to the window.

"Look here, Byrne, I feel rather in the way. I think I'll go out for ten minutes. Fix it up as you think best. Perhaps on the whole it would be better if you went away; but after all you live here and you've got your work. There can be no harm in your seeing her every now and then."

He hesitated a moment, then added, "Anyhow I trust you absolutely," and went out of the flat.

64

Nya wept with less restraint once Daddy had gone. The relief of being close to Simon, and the comfort of feeling his arm protectively round her had undermined her self-control in the first place, and now the delight of being alone with him chased away what vestiges of it remained. If Daddy said it was impossible for her to be happy with Simon for several years, she could at least be miserable with him now for a few moments, so she abandoned herself to that pleasure.

As soon as they were alone Simon picked her up in his arms, as he had done once in *Puffin*'s cabin, and laid his cheek against her head. The silky caress of her hair drove away for the moment the despair he felt because he had to go; and he rocked her to and fro like a child, contented and relieved that at last they were close together again.

He knew that his pleasure must be short-lived. Before her father returned he would have to explain to her why his half-formed resolve to go away had developed into an iron resolution. He would have to persuade her that he was doing the right, the kindest thing, and not the cruel thing she would feel it to be. He ached to postpone as long as possible the pain he would give her and to continue rocking her in his arms like this, as if she were his child, his sister, his lover; but he wanted, too, to put the misery behind them, that they might have time, before they were interrupted, to strike up a new friendship, a new love that should last them until he returned.

He looked over her head towards the sea that would, in a few days' time, be carrying him away from her. It was deep blue to-day, and flecked with white-capped waves, as it had been the first time he ever took her sailing.

("Might as well go to New York as anywhere else; the farther the better, if I'm to go away.")

He pictured the lonely voyage across the Atlantic, its possible privations, and his chances of successfully reaching the other side. It was possible alone, of course; it had been done. But it would be far easier with a companion. Yet who was there who would undertake such an enterprise with him, who, even if he had the courage and the inclination, would have the time? He had no friends, he realized sorrowfully, unless he counted the man with whom he had cruised on the Essex coast—a mere yacht-club acquaintance. It was really rather dreadful to be so unsociable; it was almost abnormal. What sort of a husband would he make for Nya when the time came, if he went on living as he had done up till now, in the office by day, and on board *Puffin* at night. Well—New York would do him a world of good.

Her weeping died away; she sighed and lay still. After some time she said:

"I wish I could always stay in your arms like this."

"If only you could."

"Simon!"

"Yes, little one?"

"Are you really going away?"

"Darling, I think it's the only thing for me to do."

"For how long?"

"Well—until you're seventeen, I suppose."

"But that's three years!"

"I know."

"I can't go on living by myself for three years."

"It'll be hard, perhaps—anyhow at first. But, my sweetheart, I've got to think what the alternative would be. I suppose it's selfish of me, but I don't think I could stand it if I had to live in the same town as you. It's been such hell, the last few weeks."

"And I was just beginning to be happy. I was beginning to enjoy everything and all because I thought I should see you again soon, and Daddy would arrange it so that we could be together."

"I think you'll find that life gets more exciting from now on. You're such an adorable child, every one will do their best to make you happy. Even your Aunt Ethel I dare say. Make the most of it, darling. It'll be a wonderful carefree time."

"But I don't mind about all that. I want to be grown up and spend my life with you."

"That will come in good time, little love."

"Yes—*in three years*!"

He smiled at the emphasis she put on the words, and clasped her to him in a sudden access of love.

"Pray God you'll still love me then."

Now, for the first time, he allowed himself to look her in the eyes; they were close to his, for her head lay on his arm. She felt a perturbing fire enter into her from him, so that every point of contact her body had with his began to glow with heat, to be sensitive to his touch even through the clothes they had on. She shuddered, but not with horror. It was a kind of ecstasy that came over her now, like the throb she had felt that morning on board *Puffin* when his hands touched her naked shoulder-blades.

Then deliberately, moved by some power of which she knew nothing but yet was conscious, so that it seemed she was obeying a command received centuries ago in some half-remembered dream, she put up her arms and drew his head close to hers. Her lips parted. Her eyes glowed, for there was a haze before them, a hot, vibrating haze, that wrapped Simon in a cloud of fire.

"Simon, I feel—so strange. I think . . . I would like you to kiss me, Simon."

"No, darling."

His voice was low, almost a whisper, hoarse. She nestled close to him, and closer still to the fire she felt burning in him, the fire that came from inside herself. He drew his breath sharply, and his eyes closed, as if he were in pain.

And strangely, frighteningly, she realized that she felt, not sorry, but exultant.

It was because of her that he was in pain! It was because he loved her! Love could be pain sometimes. And Simon had said that love made people want to be close, close together, like this. No wonder! It was such delight to feel the warmth of this hot stream running in every vein. But it was disturbing, too. It ran so violently, it seemed it would burst and overflow at every point. If only he would kiss her! Her lips tingled most of all, and longed to settle upon his.

"No, darling."

Suddenly he turned his head away. The spell upon her lips was broken. She could no longer see his eyes.

The fire began to die. Presently it flickered out, but it left a peaceful warmth behind. She took her arms from round his neck, and he began to breathe more freely. Then she stood up, but she was afraid to break the contact between them, so she kept hold of his hand and laid it to her cheek.

"Little one, you're burning hot."

She nodded, as if to say, "Yes, it's because of the fire," and smiled to herself. For an instant she had glanced down through the window of some high tower that was her prison, into a splendid garden which she had not known was there. And, though the glimpse of it was gone now, she knew the garden would remain. She would walk in it one day, when she escaped!

He watched her, enjoying hungrily the last pleasure he would have at seeing her; her graceful boyish walk and every quick unconscious movement that she made. She swept her hair back with her hands, as if it lay too heavy on her temples, and moved towards the window like an animal disturbed. He let his eyes rest upon each separate part of her body, caressing her in secret, unknown even to herself, kissing adoringly her arms, her shoulders, her bright head that was set upon her neck so proudly, and her tender breasts.

"I think I understand now why you've got to go, Simon. But I don't know what I shall do without you."

There was silence. She stared out of the window at the white-capped sea, her back to Simon and the darkening room. She supposed she would have to say good-bye to him now; or would they allow her to see him once more before he went? But no; it was better to say good-bye at once, or that disturbing fire might flare up again.

It was getting late. Daddy would be back at any

moment. It had been wonderful of him to go out and leave them alone.

"Oh God, it's damnable hell!"

He whispered it; but the agony in his voice cut deep into her heart. She turned at once. He sat looking away from her in the shadow at the back of the room. His head was on one arm on the back of the chair; his hand hung down at his side, its fingers clenched.

She watched him, uncertain whether to go to him or not, helplessly conscious that her nearness might cause him pain. But she heard a sob—it was scarcely a sound, so quickly did he stifle it—and she felt her heart, her stomach, her whole body, being drawn to him as though shackled to a chain that he was slowly hauling in. She had not the strength to resist for long.

She crossed to him in a single swift rush.

"Don't be unhappy. Oh, Simon, it's more than I can bear."

She put her arms round him. And now it was she who was comforting him, it was she who held him to her breast while the dry sobs racked him. It was she who was older now, stronger and wiser than he.

They clung together, silent, miserable, but exalted in their new relationship. At last she could feel his weakness when before she had only admired his strength. At last he could feel her vigour, her power to comfort him, her patience to wait for his return. From now onwards they would meet as man and woman, as man and wife, even, in their thoughts.

Therefore, neither people nor time nor distance could part them any longer.

65

A fortnight later—it was the first day of the holidays —Nya stood on a cliff of Studland Bay, watching a white sail fast vanishing out of sight. She presented a forlorn figure against the skyline, her whole being concentrated on the dwindling sail, her hand up to her eyes, though there was no sun this mournful day. The wind swept her hair across her face and flattened her dress along her bare legs—the very wind which was driving Simon out of her reach.

Puffin drew abreast of the foreland, heeling down to the easterly wind and shouldering the scud from the cream-topped waves. That was Simon at the helm; every now and then the motion of the boat showed his white jersey against the water. On the cabin top, his bulky form outlined against the new mainsail, stood Dan, snatching the scattered foam into his lungs, exultant to be once again at sea.

As *Puffin* cleared the headland and began to pitch in the chop of the up-Channel tide Simon turned her about. For one frantic minute Nya held her breath, daring to hope he would return. Then she saw the ensign dipped, and remembered he had said, as he embraced her for

474

the last time, that he would do this as a final greeting. Soon—far too soon—*Puffin* completed the wide circle and heeled down again to that cruel wind. One moment longer she remained, loath to sever the last tie which bound her to the tiny figure on the cliff. Then she slid behind the headland and was gone.

A gull wailed overhead.

And because of its melancholy cry, Nya could not longer keep back the tears that came.